TWIN-BRED

(Revised Edition)

Karen A. Wyle

ISBN 978-0-9905641-0-2
Printed in the United States of America
Oblique Angles Press

Cover design by David Leek

Cover art by Livali Wyle (with minor
modifications by Karen A. Wyle)

Author photo by Alissa Lise Wyle

To my family.

And to the Office of Letters and Light.

A Note re Character Names

There are quite a few characters in this book (though fewer than in the original edition), and many of their names are unfamiliar ones. I have included an Appendix at the end of the book listing the names of major characters and some recurring secondary characters. The descriptions are intentionally cryptic, to reduce spoilers.

These characters are listed in related groups where appropriate, and otherwise alphabetically.

PROLOGUE

THE LITTLE GIRL gazed in awe at her birthday present. It was a picture book — a real book with pages.
"What's it called, Mommy?"
"The Journey."
"Play it, Mommy!"
"You don't play this kind of book, honey. You read it. Like this."

Many years ago, before you were born, there was no one like you on this whole planet. There was no one with two arms instead of four. There was no one who could smile. There was no one with a twinkle in her eye.

The people like you all lived far, far away. They lived on a planet called Earth. And there were oh, so many of them!

There were so many people, the sky was always full of planes, and the streets were always full of cars, and there was no room for empty places. There was no room for cows to graze in the fields, or horses to run in the meadows —

"Oooh, look at the cows!"

"We might have cows when you're older. The Council says we might. After all, we have chickens now."
The little girl's mother read on.

So some people on Earth decided to look for other places to go.

They looked through huge, enormous telescopes.

They sent out little robots on little ships that could travel very fast, and travel very far, and take pictures of all the new places they found —

"Did the robots find our planet, Mommy?"
"Remember, honey, it isn't just our planet. The Tofa live here too. They were here before we were."
"Did they mind when we came to Tofarn? Did they want us to go away?"
"No, honey. They didn't seem to mind at all. We couldn't exactly talk to them, not even as much as we can now, but they — sort of pointed to places, and said we could live there."
The little girl wrinkled up her forehead. "If we couldn't 'zackly talk to them, how do we know that's what they said?"

Part One

Chapter 1

Colony Year (C.Y.) 49

ELIZABETH CADELL liked to knit. Her daughter Mara, age four, liked to draw. So they sat together at the kitchen table, Elizabeth knitting a sweater for Mara, Mara holding a Child's First Tablet. A warm breeze came through the open window. Seeds floated past under a pale green sky, seeds resembling those of the dandelions that no one on Tofarn had ever seen.

Elizabeth counted her stitches, then glanced up at Mara. Mara wasn't looking at her tablet. Her eyes were closed, her lips moving slightly.

"Mara? . . Mara!"

Mara jumped. She looked wary for a moment, then donned the innocent gaze of untroubled childhood. "Yes, Mommy? I was drawing."

"Oh?"

Elizabeth looked Mara in the eye and waited. Mara visibly weighed her chances of outlasting her mother, and surrendered. She laid the tablet carefully on the table. "Well, I wasn't drawing just at that moment. I was — well, I was —"

"You were pretending again. About Levi. Pretending to talk to him."

Mara wriggled in her chair. "It doesn't feel like other pretending. Not exactly."

Elizabeth put down her knitting and clasped her hands together. "If something isn't real, it's pretend. Is Levi still alive? Do you really have a twin?"

Mara looked away. Quite abruptly, she started to cry, to sob. Elizabeth jumped up and lifted Mara from her chair, carried her to the window seat, held her and cuddled her. She kissed the dark head. "Mara, sweetheart. Let's look out at what's real. Look, darling. See the river. See all the little creeks coming from the river. Count them with me."

Mara sniffed and swallowed and wiped her nose on her sleeve. "One. Two. Three. Four." She pointed. "See, Mommy? The tree-seeds are blowing. They're blowing across the river. And some of them are landing on the river."

"Yes, honey. They're going on a journey, down the river. If — if you want to pretend something, why don't you pretend you're following the seeds, to see where they go."

Mara sniffed again and nodded. She leaned against her mother and gazed out the window. Whatever she was thinking she kept to herself.

C.Y. 55

The children of Campbell City's largest elementary school trooped down to the clearing, chattering, glad for the break from routine. Their teachers smiled indulgently or frowned impatiently, according to their natures. The older children kept the younger from wading in any of the adjacent streams. The warm weather made the prospect tempting.

Soon the children were all in place, mostly quiet, waiting for the show. The flimsy wooden facsimile of a spaceship stood to one side. The older children had spent the last two weeks constructing it.

The history teacher nudged the math teacher. "No real Tofa today?"

"No. We couldn't get any to show up. Which rather undercuts the point of Landing Day, wouldn't you say?"

"I don't know about that. Real Tofa might scare the children. And the janitor makes a good substitute. He's almost tall enough."

As if on cue, the janitor strode forth, wearing a light brown costume approximating Tofa body coloration. The principal and the music teacher, self-conscious in their antiquated dress, stepped from behind the wooden ship and marched side by side to meet him.

The janitor spread his arms. He spoke a short phrase in what the language teacher claimed was Tofa. Then he spoke again, in Terran. "Welcome, strangers."

The principal held out a plate on which lay a necklace of colored glass beads. Watching from the sidelines, the history teacher almost choked with suppressed laughter. How many more Landing Days would go by before the principal got the joke? Oh, well, he was close to retirement, anyway.

C.Y. 61

The tall thin figures passed by in a long thin line. Most were carrying large cases with sturdy handles, using their two lower hands, leaving the upper hands free. Some held their cases in their right set of hands, leaving the left arms free to carry small children.

The crowd of humans stood and watched. A few of them, those who had spent more time with their alien neighbors, might have noticed that the characteristic odor of charred toast had been largely replaced by a smell closer to rotting fruit.

A high-pitched young voice rose above the buzz of muttered conversation. "Where are they going? Why are the Tofa leaving town?" The child's father, holding the child on his shoulders, did not answer.

Mara stood a bit apart from the other teenagers. She made one quick sketch after another on her tablet as the Tofa filed past. One of the Tofa children turned and looked at her. She stared back, mesmerized by the alien eyes, with their swirls of white and brown and green.

"What's your answer, Mara? Why are they leaving?"

Mara no longer needed to close her eyes or move her lips. "I don't know, Levi. Things just kept going wrong. We don't understand them, and who knows what they understand? I guess they thought it would be simpler, living away from us."

"Simpler. But less interesting. For us at least. This town is going to be serene, and peaceful, and dull."

The front end of the column of Tofa, now distant, was a blur of light brown against the muted yellow and beige of the landscape. For a moment, Mara thought she saw that one of the distant figures had five arms instead of four.

"Someday, Levi, we'll go away to school, and we'll live where there are Tofa again. In Varley, or Campbell City, or somewhere. And we'll learn about them. We'll find a way to learn more than anyone ever has."

"You'll have to do the learning, Mara mia. But I'll listen in. I'll keep you on your toes."

The Tofa were gone. The crowd dispersed. Mara walked home, imagining her future.

C.Y. 63

"Sir? Sir, we have a problem."

The mayor of Varley looked up from his monitor. "A problem with whom, or with what?"

His assistant considered whether to offer an opinion on whether the Tofa were Who or What, and decided against it. "It's another complaint from the Tofa, sir. They say that humans are shaking hands."

"People are trying to shake hands with Tofa? Which hand, I wonder."

"No, sir. With each other. The Tofa are upset that humans are shaking hands with each other in public. Quite upset."

"How can you tell? Oh, I know, they vibrate, or smell different, or something. If a job dealing with Tofa has done anything for me, it's made me appreciate faces, proper ones that tell you what's behind them. . . ."

C.Y. 67

The Campbell City police chief slammed her hand against the file cabinet. "We had an agreement! After last time, we talked to them, and we worked this out! They knew when we were holding our elections, and they knew where people would be gathering and when. We even told people not to wear blue this time! Damned if I know why, but no blue, whether your candidate wants you to or not. So why the hell are they blocking the streets?!!"

The deputy showed little emotion. He had already taken a tranquilizer. "We've tried to reach our Tofa counterparts, if that's what they are. And all our snitches, plus the nearest Tofa equivalent. Nobody can explain it — at least, nobody that'll talk to us can explain it, and whoever might be able to, won't talk to us."

The chief reached for a medicine patch — not, the deputy noticed with alarm, a tranquilizer, but an energy and reflex enhancer. "That is IT. We are through tiptoeing around those damned troublemakers. Get every uniform here in fifteen minutes. We are going to clear the streets, and we are going to have our elections, and we are going to do it any way we have to."

The deputy's phone buzzed. He answered it and listened, first confused and then relieved. "Chief, we've just heard from the local Tofa spokesman. They'll be gone in two hours. No explanation, but — we can keep the polls open a little longer. We don't want our people getting hurt, if we can just wait it out."

The chief hesitated, then balled the patch up in her fist and tossed it across the room. "No, we don't want our people hurt. I wouldn't give one good goddamn whether we hurt some of *them*. Sooner or later, we'll have to, and I won't lose any sleep. And I won't need any of your tranquilizers."

C.Y. 70

Mara paced back and forth in the small apartment. Every time she approached the window, she could see the looming buildings of the university. The apartment complex had few amenities and no architectural charm, but it had been convenient for a graduate student. And it was cheap. With her second doctorate in hand, Mara might have prospects that would support a more comfortable lifestyle. She had other priorities.

"It's late, Mara. Shouldn't you be sleeping? Big day tomorrow. The great Dr. Cadell tells the politicians how she's going to solve their problems."

"I can't sleep, Levi. Maybe I should practice the pitch again. Or rewrite it. I'm not sure about the beginning."

"How's this? *'Humans and Tofa drive each other crazy. Which is a recipe for disaster. As in lots of screaming, bloody death.'* "

"That'd go over splendidly. I don't think you've mastered the idiom of bureaucrats. . . . But I still don't know how to start."

"Then skip that part for now and move on. And remember not to sound like me."

"All right, here's why they should trust me with a huge amount of money and large chunks of the lifetimes of many people. Imagine you're a politician, and tell me if this might just persuade you to take a chance."

Mara forced herself to stand still, as she would have to stand when speaking to the Council.

"None of the blended human and Tofa communities is doing well. Those that haven't formally disbanded are on the verge of falling apart. There are too many misunderstandings and communication failures, and they always go on too long before they're recognized as such. And even when we recognize these failures, we then fail to resolve them. Neither our slowly improving knowledge of the Tofa language nor the Tofa's somewhat greater

mastery of rudimentary Terran has overcome a deeper, more basic lack of comprehension.

"It seems that we cannot live in harmony together. And yet, we cannot simply resolve to live apart. We can buy some time that way — time which we must use as fruitfully as possible — but ultimately, as our human communities continue to expand, separation will become less practical. Nor can we be sure the Tofa will consistently cooperate with maintaining such separation."

"Ah, expansion. What's that German word?"

"Lebensraum. Hush."

"Say lebensraum. It'll impress them."

"It'll annoy them. Which, as you might point out, is your style and a bad idea."

"When do we get to how you're going to save the day?"

"Patience, Levi. I need to set it up. Now where was I?"

"After seventy years of the old approaches, we need something else: a whole new way to learn about each other."

Mara paused. "Snack break. I can't think with low blood sugar."

"Eating, now. I don't get eating. Of course, I understand that you don't have our initial fuel delivery system, but it does seem incredibly cumbersome, and unnecessarily complicated."

Mara opened the bakery box sitting on her kitchen counter. The small cakes were only slightly stale. "I am truly sorry that you'll never understand about chocolate. Take my word for it, food is satisfying on multiple levels, and chocolate is what Prometheus really brought down from the gods to improve the lives of men."

"Especially women, I gather."

"OK, brother, tell me to get back to work."

"Back to work, sis! Consider the whip cracked."

Mara stretched and yawned.

"I've distributed abstracts of several studies about the interactions of twins in utero. The full studies have been provided to your staff.

"We have observed extensive interaction between fetal twins. This interaction has been shown to be purposeful. Twins in utero touch each other. I've distributed an ultrasound image of one twin kissing the other's cheek."

"Carefully put. We don't want them recoiling from the idea of intra-uterine makeout sessions."

"Shut up! Don't talk like that!"

"I'm sorry. You know I don't really get sex, either."

"Even more significant, the movements of twins in utero are highly synchronized. We can posit that something is going on that could be classified as communication. Then we have the extensive anecdotal evidence that twins — and not only identical, but fraternal twins — can sometimes sense important events that happen to each other, despite geographical distance.

"And twins separated from each other experience significant stress. The ultimate separation — the death of one twin, even if it occurs before or shortly after birth, results — results — results in a significant and prolonged sense of loss —"

"Hey. Hey. Don't do that."

Mara gripped the window sill and stared at the white knuckles on her hands as she fought for control.

"Come on, now. This is old news. You can cope. I'm how you cope. You can keep me around for as long as you need me. Or longer — just for the pleasure of my company.

"I'm sorry, Mara. I wish I could hold you."

"So do I. So very, very much. . . . OK. Going on now. You know, maybe I should drop that last part."

"That might be prudent."

Mara took a deep breath, then another.

"While much more work remains to be done, it appears from our preliminary research that with sufficient medical support, a human woman could carry a Tofa fetus to term. Similarly, a human woman could carry twin fetuses — one human, one Tofa. It is possible an adult Tofa could do the same."

"Why bring twins into it? Aside from our personal reasons for leaning that way. Why not just see what happens between human host-mother and Tofa fetus?"

"We could try that too. But we don't have evidence of the same kind of synchrony between mother and fetus, other than what the fetus' movements force on the mother. And the bond between mother and child has evolutionary and hormonal explanations that don't apply to explain what happens between twins."

"Male or female human fetuses? And does that question apply to the Tofa?"

"I don't know, to both questions. If there's a reason for one or the other to be better suited, we don't know it yet. Why, do you have an opinion?"

"How could I? You know a lot more about males than I do, under the circumstances, to say nothing of females."

Mara started pacing again.

"It is therefore possible that human and Tofa fetuses carried in a human uterus, or the Tofa equivalent, as twins would have some type of communication or understanding that has so far eluded our two species. And which might hold the key to our jointly surviving and flourishing on this planet.

"Of course, this is uncertain and speculative. But the importance of the goal, in my view, justifies at least exploring, at least beginning, the attempt."

"What are you calling this project? Prenatal Politics? Natal Native Negotiations?"

"Cute. I'm thinking of the Long-Term Emissary Viviparous Initiative."

"L.E.V.I. Thank you. Though it may not be smart. Which reminds me, someone's going to ask you how you came up with this idea."

"I've always been fascinated by twins. Twins run in my family. I had two sets of twin cousins."

"That gets a little too close to the truth. They can't find out about us. They'd write you off as unbalanced, at best. The lady pushing new types of twins who turned her own lost twin into an imaginary friend."

Mara looked out the window into the night. The brief evening rain was over, but the streets still glistened under the street lamps. Two students were leaving the laboratory wing. They were too far away for her to hear their conversation, but she could see the sweeping gestures with which they shared the excitement of their discoveries.

"No, Levi. I didn't imagine you." She turned away from the window. "I imagine what you became."

Chapter 2

THE FAMILIES gathered in the small meadow, surrounded by what they, if not the Tofa, called trees. Sleepy-eyed children snuggled against the legs of their parents. Adults quietly greeted each other. All wore their warmer clothes, to wait comfortably in the chill air before dawn.

The light grew stronger. The crowd was still, the silence broken only by the sound of the water in the nearby creek and river, and an occasional murmured question from one of the children.

The first ray of sunlight — as they called it — hit the first tree. Murmurs rose to exclamations as the light filled the meadow. With the light came a change more dramatic than the light, as every leaf of ground cover, every frond or scale of every tree, turned from a muted yellow or beige or tan to some shade, any of a dozen shades of purple — violet or lilac or mulberry or mauve or those for which no name had been needed on Earth.

The change swept over and around the meadow, and the children, now fully awake, jumped up and down and clapped and yelled, and some of their parents joined them.

The children's energy had begun to flag for want of nourishment. Yawning, a mother unpacked her family's picnic basket. A friend came up and spread her own family's blanket nearby.

"I hear the mayor asked the Tofa again," confided the latter. "Invited them to be here. They gave her the brush-off, as usual. You'd think they'd want to celebrate. And it's not as if they go off and do it on their own. They never seem to go anywhere on Change Day. Just hole up in those buildings of theirs."

The first mother unfolded a napkin. "Do they even see in color? Does anyone know?"

Her friend had no time to answer before the children descended on them, shouting for food. The muffins and hot chocolate were gone in minutes.

After a suitable amount of discussion, dithering and what Levi called posterior protection, the Council voted to endorse — and far more important, to fund — the project. Some members hoped the twins, to be called the Twin-Bred, would become effective mediators. Others dreamed of human Twin-Bred ruling both human and Tofa communities. A few anticipated more modest results, an increase in knowledge about their enigmatic neighbors.

All expected grave difficulties in winning the Tofa's cooperation. The Council set its staff to writing up possible objections and responses thereto. Experts on human-Tofa communication, or what passed for experts, conducted role-playing exercises. Artists prepared storyboards: stick figures of humans and Tofa; the same figures, each now carrying in its outlined abdomen an human and a Tofa fetus; the figures stick-thin once again, each with a tiny human and Tofa by its side; and finally, a crowd of humans and Tofa, not quite as tall as the first, mingled together. An initial drawing showing clusters of humans and Tofa shaking their fists at each other was vetoed as possibly inflammatory. The artists could only hope the symbology that seemed obvious to humans would not be meaningless scribbles to alien minds.

The preparations dragged on until Mara asserted her authority as Director and called a halt. Sick with dread, tempted by hope, she sent the contact team on its way and waited for the next unforeseen challenge.

But in the event, the Tofa proved cooperative. It wasn't clear whether they understood the project's purpose, or how they weighed its chances for success. They agreed to provide the required number of Tofa embryos, as well as Tofa host mothers, if such were desired. They refused, or at least failed, to answer questions about how the embryos would be obtained. The researchers tried to explain the need for typical, healthy Tofa embryos. No one could say if they got through.

The Tofa's only condition, if the humans understood correctly, was that they be allowed a veto over the human women who would serve as host mothers. But first, the women must be found.

Mara lay back in the recliner, stretched mightily, and heaved a great groaning sigh.

"Long day at the office?"

"More like long three months at the office. Interminable months. Oh, Levi. How did I get myself into this? When have I ever been any good as an administrator?"

"As I recall, until now you've avoided any such obligation, so your abilities in that area have been, shall we say, untested."

Mara reached over toward the lamp, then let her arm fall again. "I'd forgotten what it felt like, to be so unsure. It's been years since I was — incompetent at anything."

"Let's not jump to conclusions. Or labels. So the interviews have been exhausting, as well as exhaustive. That doesn't make them unproductive."

"Oh, we're finding good candidates. It's surprising, in a way, how many women we've found who are ready to put their lives on hold and more or less disappear. Either we have a rather public-spirited generation of young women, or a restless and dissatisfied one. . . . Even a few of the applicants with political connections are promising. But some of them! That last one today — Veda something, Councilman Channing's daughter. She's one of those people who never seem to *mean* anything." Mara glanced at the cartoon she had drawn after Veda's interview: an unnaturally slim figure with clasped hands, eyes uplifted toward heaven, and price tags hanging from her clothing. "She rattles along about the joy of selflessness and devotion to public service, and I doubt she even hears herself. And I can't remotely picture her as nurturing."

"Don't write Veda off, Mara. I think there's something there. Beneath the admittedly disquieting surface. As a subterranean creature myself, I may have a feeling for people with unsuspected depths."

The short cool season was over. The shades of purple were once again yielding to shades of yellow and ivory and brown. With the return of warmer weather, the parks were becoming more crowded.

The picnic area at First Landing Park was occupied. Children at the playground smelled cooking and wondered if the food would be, at some point, unguarded and accessible. The young men playing soccer were distracted by the crowd of young women, all notably healthy and many of them attractive. There was no banner or sign to indicate what had brought them together. It could have been a reunion of some kind, but few of the women seemed to know each other. The small groups shuffled and reshuffled, and the prevailing mood seemed to be one of uncertainty, almost embarrassment.

Laura Hanson fetched herself a beer and stood watching one of the more animated groups. One woman, petite and well-toned, with expensive hair, seemed to be the center. She was asking questions, drawing people out, and occasionally nodding to herself as though collecting information that gave her satisfaction. The high clear voice was familiar — and the last voice Laura had expected to hear. She put down her beer and came closer.

"Veda? Veda Seeling?"

The woman turned and was raising an inquiring eyebrow when she saw Laura. Her eyes went wide, and the expression of amused control fell away for a moment.

Laura rushed forward and held out her arms. "Veda, I'm so glad to see you again!"

Veda looked around at the crowd, now full of smiles and clearly expecting a touching scene. She walked quickly into Laura's hug and as quickly led the way to a more isolated spot. "Let's sit here and catch up." She sat on a stone bench and patted the spot next to her. Laura obeyed.

"Dear Laura. It's been so long. What *have* you been doing? The last I heard, you were getting another degree in something."

"I was. Sociology. Terran Literature is all very well, but I wasn't sure how I would use it. And then I heard about the Project, and I thought, this is a way that I can *do* something that matters, instead of just learning about it. And what about you? I remember! You got married! Congratulations! His name's Brian, isn't it?"

Veda preened. "Yes, we've been married a year now. He's in the Bureau of Financial Relations. It's all very difficult and complicated, finding ways to trade with the Tofa. It'd be so much easier if they could *understand* each other better. And whenever things get — nasty, well, you can guess what that does to the markets . . . . So he's *very* interested in the Project. And Daddy too, of course. Even more so. What about your father? Did he — well, was he hoping you'd get involved?"

Laura looked down. "Well, he's not so sure about it. He'd like to be hopeful, and he certainly thinks something needs to be done, but he's a little concerned about trying something so — experimental. But if it's going to happen, he wants to know all about it."

"I might have known you'd be here. You were always so — so *interested* in our Tofa neighbors."

Veda had a way of saying things — a hint of mockery or threat, hovering behind the words. Or so it was now, with this older and harder Veda. Was her friend still there somewhere, stifled and helpless? She wanted to call her forth, to lure her out.

She started to say, "Remember —" and stopped herself. She was sure that Veda remembered. That was the trouble.

Laura bounced on her toes as the copter touched down. Her mother held her hand to keep her in place until the motors shut off and the door opened. Released, she ran forward and grabbed her friend by the hand.

"Veda, Veda! I'm eight today! Did they tell you? It's my birthday! I'm eight!"

Veda sniffed a bit. "I'll be eight in a month. Everyone's eight, sooner or later." She relented. "But happy birthday." She gave Laura a kiss on the cheek, forgiving her for being first.

"And I've got another surprise." Laura pulled Veda away from where the grownups were standing and chatting. "By the creek behind the house. Come and look with me. I don't know if he'll be there, but he might be."

Veda followed her, patting her curls and fluffing her dress. "A boy? What's so surprising about a boy? Where I live, in the city, there are lots of boys, all over."

"Not like *this* boy." Laura led Veda around the house and down the hill to the creek. As they approached it, she looked around anxiously, then relaxed, smiled and pointed. "There he is! Lat-ran! Over here! Come meet my friend!"

A young Tofa was approaching the creek on the other side. Veda gave a little shriek, then glanced quickly at Laura. Laura pretended she hadn't noticed, waving to the Tofa and urging him on.

Veda stood rigid as a statue as the Tofa reached the creek and crossed it in one long stride. Laura hoped she had not miscalculated. Veda had always seemed ready to handle anything. Laura patted her friend on the shoulder. "Don't be scared. Lat-ran is my friend. Lat-ran, this is my human friend, Veda."

Veda stared at Lat-ran. Lat-ran may have stared back. It was difficult to be sure when eyes were the only feature in what passed for a face.

Veda leaned over and whispered, "How do you *know* his name?"

"He told me, silly. At least, he said it and pointed to himself. With all his hands."

"How did he *talk*? He's got no mouth!"

"Daddy says there's something like a mouth that we can't see, behind a — a mem-brane, I think he called it. Now stop whispering — it's rude."

Reminded of manners, Veda turned toward the Tofa. "Nice to meet you, Lat-ran." She bobbed a little curtsey.

Lat-ran tilted his upper body to one side. Whatever it meant, Veda seemed to view it as a bow or other respectful gesture. She smiled regally. "I think he *is* nice."

Now Lat-ran was gesturing, pointing across the creek. Laura tugged on Veda's sleeve. "Come on. He wants us to go to *his* side. We can make it if we run and jump."

Veda hesitated. "Are we allowed?" She sidled closer to Laura and -- despite Laura's previous remonstrance -- whispered, "Is it safe?"

It was strange to be the one taking charge. "Oh, sure! As long as we stay in sight of the house, it's all right. I do it all the time. Well, since I met Lat-ran, the week before last."

Without further ado, Laura took a few paces back, ran at the creek and jumped across. She landed with a dusty thump, almost toppling, but managing to stay upright. "Come on!"

Not to be outdone, Veda retreated a substantial distance, ran full steam at the creek, leaped across, and fell forward on her hands and knees. She sprang up and inspected herself. Neither skin nor clothing was damaged, to Laura's as well as Veda's relief. Veda beamed proudly and announced, "That was fun!"

Lat-ran stepped across to follow them, and promptly stepped back again to where the girls had started. Laura giggled and made another running jump across. Veda did the same, calibrating her run more carefully this time and landing upright. That seemed to be enough for her: she waited, tapping her foot, while Laura and Lat-ran crossed the creek three more times.

Not wanting to annoy her guest, Laura called a halt, pointing firmly at her side of the creek when Lat-ran moved to cross to his side yet again. She picked up a handful of pebbles and offered them to Lat-ran, who took them with his nearest hand. Veda jumped just a bit at the reach of the long thin arm.

"Just see what Lat-ran can do!" Laura swept an arm in Lat-ran's direction. In response, Lat-ran began tossing the pebbles, one by one. They landed in a neatly curving line, which soon became a circle.

Veda found some pebbles of her own and tried to imitate this feat, without notable success. She scowled.

Laura hoped Veda wasn't going to be a spoilsport. "I can't do it either. But see? It's a face! He'll probably give it pig-tails, like mine. It's a picture of me!"

And indeed, one side of the circle had sprouted a line that could with generosity be deemed a pigtail. But as the girls watched, the other side of the circle sprouted a circle of its own, and then another. Lat-ran pointed to Veda.

"Oooh, how clever!" Laura clapped her hands. "He's made it half pig-tailed and half curly! It's a picture of both of us!"

Mollified, Veda smiled at Lat-ran and joined in Laura's clapping. Lat-ran used two free hands to imitate them.

They were interrupted by the ringing of a bell. Laura tapped Veda on the shoulder. "That's the lunch bell! Lat-ran, we've got to go. Thank you for the picture! We'll see you later!" She grabbed Veda's hand and tugged her toward the house. As they reached the top of the hill, Laura turned back toward the creek for a moment. Lat-ran was looking after them. Then he dropped the rest of his pebbles and stepped back across the creek.

For the rest of the day, the girls were busy with family events and their own games. There were a couple of times that Veda seemed about to say something, and then changed her mind. Did she want to go see Lat-ran again? Laura wasn't sure. She didn't want to spoil things by pressing the matter. And there were plenty of other things to do.

Next day, however, after breakfast, Veda took the initiative. "Do you think Lat-ran would be around this morning? Let's go and see, before I have to leave."

The girls trotted eagerly toward the creek. As they approached, they saw that Lat-ran was indeed visible, standing not far from the creek. He was not alone. An adult Tofa loomed behind him. Laura had thought of Lat-ran as tall; the adult's height was truly intimidating.

The girls came to a halt, at a similar distance from the creek on their side. Veda whispered to Laura. "What do we do now?"

Laura hesitated and then stepped forward. "Hello, Lat-ran! It's nice to see you again. Is that your, uh, your father?" She hoped she'd guessed right, or that the Tofa weren't easily offended in matters of gender.

Veda stepped up beside her and curtsied. "Good morning, Mr. Tofa."

The adult made a barely visible gesture in Lat-ran's direction. Lat-ran stood very still. The adult gestured again. Slowly, as if reluctant, Lat-ran bent sideways and picked up some pebbles. He straightened up again, raised his long arm, and threw a pebble hard in the girls' direction. It landed between them. Lat-ran threw another. It landed just to Veda's right. And another, just to Laura's left.

Laura and Veda turned to each other in consternation. The pebbles kept falling, always close but never quite reaching them. The girls backed away, staring. The pebbles followed their retreat. One just touched the edge of Veda's shoe. The girls turned and ran, Veda crying openly, Laura fighting back her tears.

Veda packed up her overnight things with brisk angry gestures. Laura sat on her bed, trying to think of something to say.

"You know how well he throws. He could have hit us if he wanted to. He *didn't* want to. The other Tofa made him do it — and he still didn't hit us."

Veda slammed her suitcase shut. "I don't know what he wanted, and I don't care. They're great big horrible creatures, and I never want to see another one as long as I live."

"But Veda — they're *around*. Aren't there more of them in the city?"

Veda tossed her head. "We don't live *near* them, the way *you* do. And if they started to, we can move. Daddy would do it, for me."

Laura knew a lost battle. Timidly she approached Veda and touched her hand. "Veda, I'm so sorry. I wanted you to have such a good time. Will you ever visit me again?"

Veda's lip trembled. "I *want* to. It was a lot of fun — until the last part. But maybe you should visit me, next time." She drew herself up proudly. "*I'll* keep you safe."

Laura pulled her thoughts back to the present. "Veda?" She would make an attempt to get through, after all. "Are you — at all afraid?"

Veda looked startled at the question. "Well, I don't know. Of course it's all very different. No one has done anything like it before. But there will be doctors watching all the time. If anything bad even *starts* to happen, they'll put an end to it. And if they don't, well, Daddy and the others will make them."

"It's just that — after what happened when we were children, I thought you didn't want anything to do with Tofa. And even if Brian and your father have their reasons, I know you wouldn't let them force you. Nobody could."

Veda laughed. For a moment, she was the friend Laura remembered. "You do know me at that!" Then the mask again. "But really, Laura, I wouldn't let childish fears come between me and such an important *mission*. And besides — " and now Laura could hear sincerity — "these Tofa will be *different*. That's what it's all about. Making Tofa we can live with. And they'll be just children, little children, for years and years. I won't *need* to be afraid."

It made sense — Veda-style sense. Veda had never liked to be defeated. It must have rankled, retreating in tears from the field of battle. Now was her chance to remake the past. She would personally reshape the feared alien into something else. And for years and years, she would be the adult. The tall one, even.

The Tofa rejected ten of the recruited human host mothers. No one on the team could come up with any plausible hypothesis as to why those particular women were rejected. Veda and Laura survived the cut. They would carry Twin-Bred.

Officially, it was the Long-Term Emissary Viviparous Initiative. But everyone called it The Project.

Chapter 3

MARA DRUMMED on her desk, then stopped: she must not show anything but firm and unshakeable confidence. "Mr. Chairman, it will not be feasible for me to report frequently in person. My duties will be extremely demanding in terms of time and energy. I am confident we can establish adequately secure channels for off-site communication."

The Chairman's expression remained mulish. "The Committee on Tofa Relations will insist on the closest involvement in every stage of this project. The members would find it highly inconvenient for you to limit communications in the manner you suggest. The Committee will need the frequent opportunity to ask questions, to have detailed exchanges —"

It was time to bluff. "Mr. Chairman. You have already committed quite substantial resources to the Project. You have exerted yourself admirably, and within the Council you have identified yourself with the Project to an extent which would make it quite embarrassing to change course. I do hope you will not put us both in a position of having to abandon this investment. I cannot be at the constant beck and call of roomfuls of politicians while engaging in an unprecedented and all-consuming scientific project.

"Mr. Chairman, if we are to proceed, then it is quite simple. You must give me the autonomy I require to do what you require. I will pay you due deference in all recorded communications. But on this Project, Mr. Chairman, I will call the shots."

Councilman Alan Kimball sat listening to the silence that followed the intercepted call, stroking his chin. Then he buzzed his confidential assistant.

"Siri, my dear, please send me all resumes on file in the areas of biogenetics, educational psychology, and — no, just come in here. You can fill in the gaps, once I tell you what I have in mind."

Siri came into his office, tablet at the ready, and closed the door. She perched in a chair near his desk as Kimball turned on the scramble field. Kimball reclined in his own chair, upholstered in well-worn leather, and tapped his toes in slow rhythm.

"The Council appears to be holding Dr. Cadell on a rather loose rein, Siri. Please investigate whether this policy includes the hiring process for her little project. I rather think it will."

Siri tapped out notes on her tablet. Kimball continued to tap his toes.

"Long ago, Siri, a Terran philosopher of war advised his readers to know their enemies. We have been rather hampered in that regard, have we not? Dr. Cadell may enable us to rectify that situation.

"The good doctor's project will be hiring. She will need specialists in a number of areas. You'll be able to ascertain what those are. Please match up the vacancies with the people we know who could fill them. Don't stop with the resumes — go through my contact files. I want a list — names, specialties, contact information, circumstances of previous contact — by the end of the day."

Siri stood up and turned toward the door. Kimball sat up and cleared his throat to recall her attention.

"And of course — maximum discretion, my dear." Siri barely raised one eyebrow. Kimball pressed his palms together in apology. "I know, I insult you by mentioning it. Forgive me." She smiled, nodded slightly, and left.

Kimball reclined his chair again, closed his eyes, and made plans.

* CONFIDENTIAL *
CLEARANCE CLASS 3 AND ABOVE

LEVI Status Report, 11-15-70
Executive Summary

<u>Staff Issues</u>

Interviews are continuing to fill the remaining vacancies for scientific and technical staff (human). While preference continues to be given to sets of fraternal twins, this rather small pool of applicants may have been exhausted.

Planning continues for recruitment of Tofa staff. The difficulties with assessing applicant qualifications and motivations have not been fully resolved.

<u>Test Subjects</u>

To date, 20 human host mothers have been selected and briefed. A total of approximately 40 host mothers will be required. A surplus of embryos will be required in case preliminary examination requires that any be discarded.

Human embryos from sources of approved quality have been obtained and are in storage. Tofa embryos have not yet arrived. The preliminary schedule calls for staggered initiation of ten pregnancies at a time at six-week intervals. Discussion continues as to whether to use chemical means to compensate for the slight difference in human and Tofa normal gestation periods. The advantages are likely to outweigh the relatively slight risk factors involved in the introduction of additional substances.

While the scientific and technical staff await the decision as to use of Tofa host mothers, they are continuing preparations therefor.

* CONFIDENTIAL *
CLEARANCE CLASS 3 AND ABOVE

LEVI Status Report, 12-30-70
Executive Summary

<u>Test Subjects</u>

For reasons not yet determined, the Tofa have delivered 55 rather than 40 Tofa embryos. When questioned about appropriate methods of storing the embryos, the Tofa representative indicated that only short-term storage would be feasible. While the Tofa may be underestimating the technological capabilities of Project staff in this regard, their objection to any long-term storage attempt was sufficiently definite that such an attempt has been deemed inadvisable, as has any disposal of the additional Tofa embryos. The staff is seeking approval of an expansion of the initial stage of the project, and preparing to recruit additional human host mothers. Additional human embryos can be procured as needed. . . .

Mara closed the door of her apartment behind her and hesitated, wondering whether to check her messages or simply collapse.

"So, Mara mia, how was your date?"

"Awkward. Uncomfortable. He wanted to talk about how he overcame his difficult childhood. Difficult because he disliked his siblings."

"I can see why that failed to appeal. I'm sorry, Mara."

Mara wiped her eyes. "I would have been distracted anyway, because the damned Project is all I can think about."

"Such language about my namesake! My godchild, even."

"I may swear off dating for the duration. Since I can't talk about the Project to people."

"Whoa, there. The duration of a project that starts with a gradually produced series of babies and follows them for decades? Consider the possibility that your coworkers, to whom you can talk, include some actual people. Or at least your future coworkers. Check out the applicants as date material. Or recruit someone dateable."

"I'm waiting for you to ask how the Project is going."

"Why wait? Just talk."

"It's going crazy, is how it's going. Or what I'm going. The mothers are driving me crazy. You know we have to expand the Project in a frantic hurry or see it all fall apart. Which is what it's doing anyway, because while we try to recruit more host mothers, the ones we had are slipping away from us . . . ."

Cheryl woke up screaming again, and waited for the neighbors to start pounding on the walls. Silence, somehow shocking after the screams. She was in luck, it seemed — the neighbors must have left for work early.

This time, it was conjoined twins. Or more like a scrambled assortment of human and Tofa limbs and features, crawling out of her and lying on the floor and writhing and shrieking.

It didn't happen, she told herself over and over. It was just a dream. It didn't happen.

It wouldn't happen.

Cheryl lay on the tangled, soaked sheets until she felt strong enough to get up. Then she called her mother. Her mother knew nothing about the Project. She would never have allowed Cheryl to apply. Once

Cheryl told her mother, the nightmares would end
and the nightmare would be over.

Emily gazed up at Rob, afraid to believe. "But Rob
— you said you could never settle down and give me
the future I deserved. You said you were giving me up
for my own sake."

"I wish I were that noble. I was just petrified of
what it would mean to make a promise and have to
keep it. But I've found out the hole in my life with you
gone is a whole lot worse than the fear."

"But you sounded so sure. I believed you. I've
made plans. I've commited to the Project."

"I'm begging you to make a different
commitment."

Julia looked at the strip for a third time. It hadn't
changed.

How? When??

She'd always assumed that if she couldn't
remember the night before, nothing worth
remembering had happened. So much for that notion.

So much for free room and board, free health
care, lots of attention from people who thought she
was doing something brave and important.

And it wouldn't help to get rid of it. The rule was
no pregnancies, even aborted ones, within the
previous two years.

Shit!

The Honorable Council Vice Chair, Pomerand
Dur, counted to ten. His daughter tapped her foot
impatiently in a dissonant rhythm.

"Uria, you have had every advantage you could
conceivably derive from my position. You had five
years of entertainment and frivolity while you

pursued what we laughingly called your education. You have every form of transport known to mankind — not to mention that Tofa river raft you somehow acquired. Neither your mother nor I nor your government nor your community have ever asked anything of you except the slightest degree of discretion in your frequently lawless activities.

"It's your turn, Uria. The bill is due. And this obligation is also a stupendous opportunity. This planet has no natural ruling class. We are going to create one. With your strength of will, your eye for your own advantage, imagine what you could do as the mother of one of the first generation suited to govern all the inhabitants of Tofarn.

"And if you don't care what you'd be gaining, think about what you risk losing. Three other Council family members have already volunteered. What chance do I have of increasing influence, of even retaining my position, without that competitive advantage?"

Uria appeared to deliberate as to her best response. Finally, satisfied, she spat copiously in the direction of her father's shoe.

"This is the most perverted and disgusting and revolting idea that even you have ever come up with. You don't just want me to get *pregnant*, now, at my age — and with *two* brats — you want me to spend who knows *how* long living in some *lab*oratory, and with *Tofa* everywhere I look! When you won't even spend two hours in the same room with one unless you're tranked to your nonexistent hairline first! There is nothing that could ever make me consider it for the tiniest fraction of an instant!"

Vice Chair Dur decided that his daughter needed more time to consider the idea.

The planners lowered their heretofore rigorous standards, and lowered them again. They could give no more ground without what was deemed unacceptable risk. Still they lacked sufficient human host mothers for all the embryo pairs.

In the end, the recruitment difficulties decided the issue. Ten of the Tofa embryos would be implanted, along with human embryos, in Tofa hosts.

Chapter 4

MARA APPROACHED the small building that she thought of, privately, as Dr. Shrink's office. She climbed the familiar stairs, knocked on the familiar door, received the familiar greeting.

"Hello, doctor. It's good to see you. It's strange to think that after this session, we'll be meeting by video call instead."

Dr. Tanner waved her toward the armchair. "I look forward to discovering how we'll work together at a distance. It may be easier for you to open up with that sort of protection."

"I have to make sure I can set up a good enough privacy screen. These sessions have been important to me, but I will not risk the Project or my place in it."

Dr. Tanner set his rocking chair gently in motion. "You still feel that no one else can know about Levi without seriously compromising you."

"What would you think, if your coworker, or your boss, said that she chatted with her dead twin every day?"

"I assume you are not asking what I, with my training and experience, would conclude in such a situation. You are postulating a coworker or subordinate who would think as you sometimes do. That you are mentally unbalanced, a multiple personality perhaps, or suffering from hallucinations. I would be flattered —" with the usual half-smile — "if you, at least, were eventually to accept my assurance on this point."

"I really don't think that any more." Mara looked down at her hands, restless fingers twisting and twining. "I don't think I think it."

"In my profession, I have the opportunity to see and delight in the many creative ways human beings find to deal with pain that could otherwise hijack their lives. These solutions often pose challenges of their own. As in your case . . . ."

"In my case, having a secret — and having comforting company always available — keeps me isolated. Levi thinks I should date more."

"If and when you come to accept that desire, I'm sure you will find a way to pace the movement toward intimacy, in a manner that lets you assess whether you have found someone you can sufficiently trust." Dr. Tanner opened a drawer, pulled out a box of aroma sticks, selected pipe tobacco. He extended the box toward her. When, as usual, she declined to reach for it, he went on.

"How do you currently experience Levi's presence?"

"The same as always. We talk. It's more immediate than, say, hearing music in your head — but it's not like someone's in the room."

"Have the contents of your dreams changed?"

"The details change, but it's still the same theme. I'm expecting him. Usually it's something pleasant — we're going to go out for dinner, or it's our birthday and I made a surprise party. . . ."

Dr. Tanner passed Mara a handkerchief. "Take your time. And when it isn't pleasant?"

Mara sat shivering on the bank. The dissonant music played faintly from nowhere. She could see the search and rescue team throwing and hauling the net, over and over. Now they had stopped. They were hauling something in. The net was heavy.

The boat came closer and closer. The net and its contents were hidden in the bottom. One of the men called out something she couldn't hear.

Dread filling her and twisting her stomach, Mara stood and approached the bank. The boat was almost at the dock. The men's faces were sober, apprehensive about her reaction. In a moment she would be able to see —

Mara woke to Levi's voice. "Mara! Wake up! It's a dream, baby, just wake up. Come on! Snap out of it!"

"And you never see his face?"

"Or any part of him. When I'm awake, I sometimes wonder what he'd look like — like my father, maybe — but I never see him, awake or asleep."

"And you never draw him."

"No."

"Why is that, do you think?"

"I'm not sure. But I think — it's something I can't have, that's all. I know it. Even in my dreams."

Dr. Tanner brought his chair to a stop. "Mara, I'd like to change the subject at this point. There is a topic you've been reluctant to discuss. You've told me just enough to keep me from regarding it as an emergency. But I believe this is the time to explore it further. The thoughts of suicide you have had from time to time."

Mara closed her eyes for a moment and opened them again. "All right. If we don't talk about it today, I doubt I'd do it on the phone. But there isn't that much to say."

"When was the first time you remember thinking about killing yourself?"

Mara flinched slightly at his wording. "The first time I remember, I think I was about fourteen, give or take a year. But I don't think that was the first time I thought about it."

"The memory is not of contemplating it for the first time."

"No."

Dr. Tanner's chair started rocking again. "And after that?"

"It became a — a bit of a preoccupation, for a while. When I was feeling sorry for myself, or lonelier than usual, or when my hormones were getting the best of me. I sometimes thought of it as a way to follow Levi. But one day that thought led to another, and that's when I more or less snapped out of it."

"And that thought was?"

Mara smiled a little. "I'm sure you've guessed it. I realized that, in light of the — the existence I'd given Levi, killing myself would be killing him as well."

"And that was the end of the thoughts of suicide?"

"Not the end of them, exactly. But the end of my indulging them."

It was Dr. Tanner's turn to smile. "Another form of self-indulgence you rejected." He looked serious again. "An indulgence you couldn't afford." Rock, rock. "Do the thoughts still recur from time to time?"

"I guess so. But they just sort of flit through my mind, and get whisked away again."

Rock, rock. "So you chose not only life, but your way of living, your approach to life, over flirtations with death. If we may call your, hmm, your relationship with Levi a fantasy —"

Mara blinked back tears. "Yes."

"Then you chose the more healthful fantasy, the fantasy that helps you cope with your problems, over the fantasy of escaping them. A good job, that."

Mara sniffed and smiled again. "So I escape reality in an admirable way. I can live with that."

"Precisely."

Dr. Tanner opened the box of aroma sticks once more. "Our time is almost up. Let us part with a reminder that indulging yourself is not always too emotionally expensive. This time, Mara — as we say a kind of goodbye — take one."

Mara stood up, walked slowly over to him, bent over; gently kissed the bald spot on top of his head, and selected a stick of cottage rose.

Councilman Kimball paused in his run-through of the week's schedule. "By the way, Siri, before I forget — good work on our little project. Our project within the Project, so to speak. Excellent work. Now we await developments. Please make sure — but of course, you know this — that any communications from our contacts are received under maximum security conditions."

Siri nodded. "Do you have any other standing instructions on this subject? Before we return to your schedule?"

Kimball stroked the leather arm rest on his chair. "Nothing you wouldn't expect. If I'm not available, establish a time as soon as possible for next contact. Note the caller and time of call in a secure file."

He paused, then sat forward and held up a finger. "And report to me at once if any of our contacts gives any indication of knowing that there are others, or their identities." He picked up a figurine of a knight in armor from his desk, turned it this way and that. "There are complexities in managing multiple agents. But we have no way of knowing in what area our best opportunity will arise. And there is the value of redundancy. If I may indulge in an appropriate analogy — in early Terran fertility treatments, it was customary to implant multiple embryos, whether or not the mother actually sought multiple births. It increased the chances of at least one successful outcome."

He leaned back in his chair. "And now to the rest of my schedule."

Chapter 5

IT WAS TIME to finish packing. Mara was not fond of packing. She sat surrounded by chaos, fighting a headache.

She was weary of deciding what was worth taking. For respite, she turned to the things she was sure she wanted with her. She wrapped the framed holos in her favorite soft towels. Here was her five-year-old self with her parents on Change Day. Here was her class visit to the chicken farm. And here —

She sat back, remembering.

The tree house was remarkably stable, considering. Her parents had been skeptical, not to say nervous, about a seven-year-old undertaking such a project. Now they were saying she must have engineering ability. She supposed she did, not that she cared that much. Science was so much more exciting.

She had been careful to face the open side away from the house. Facing the river, and up so high, she could be unobserved. No need to watch her expressions, to pretend some other activity. Although she kept a sketch pad there, in a waterproof case, and could truthfully tell her parents that she liked to draw the view. Today she was bundled up against the chill. From time to time she put down her purple pencil and blew on her hands to warm them.

"Mara Cadell. Princess of all you survey."

"Make fun if you like. I love it up here."

"What's that, across the river? What you're drawing?"

"It's a combine harvester. For grain. I'd like to climb up on one -- they're so big and mechanical."

"And what was that, splashing, right under the tree?"

"A beetle-biter. They swim just under the water, and when the water-beetles touch down — snack time."

"And you sit up here, watching the mayhem."

"Well, beetle-biters need to eat, too."

"Long may they lunch."

Mara shook herself and wrapped up the holo. Placing it in the box, she looked for something to fill the remaining space.

The diplomas would do. They were piled in the boxes she had brought from her office. She grabbed another armful of towels. The glass was dusty. She wiped the dust away and saw the light glint on the gold lettering. "This is to certify that MARA CADELL . . ."

"So my last name is Thomas. Not that I need one. But why?"

"Well, when Mommy and Daddy got married, they had different last names. Naturally. And their boys were going to get his name, and their girls were going to get her name. So I'm Mara Cadell. But there wasn't — well, your name should be Thomas. Daddy gets left out, otherwise."

"Sentimental Mara. All right, then. Levi Thomas it is."

Unpacking was easier. For one thing, it was not essential to complete it. If her belongings stayed largely in boxes, it was no one's concern. And she was spending most of her time in her office, anyway.

Mara jumped when the phone signaled. The long and incomprehensible budget document had put her to sleep at her desk. Rubbing her forehead to dispel her disorientation, she pushed the receive button. The friendly face on the monitor looked familiar, but she could not immediately place it.

"Dr. Cadell? I don't know if you remember me. I'm Laura, Laura Hanson. I'm one of the host mothers. You gave me my final interview."

Of course. That was one of the few interviews Mara could still recall. She remembered Laura's obviously genuine desire to bridge the gap between human and Tofa, and her gift for putting people at ease. Even a scientist who dreaded sitting across a desk from strangers, and had somehow doomed herself to an unending series of such encounters.

"Yes, I do remember you, and it's very nice to hear from you. What can I do for you? Are you feeling all right? Is there anything you need?"

Laura looked down for a moment and then back up, apparently overcoming some diffidence. "Actually, I was hoping we could get together, for lunch or just for coffee. I know you must be terribly busy, but I would so much like to hear more about how you came to conceive the LEVI Project. And I was hoping you might have some thoughts about how I could make myself useful — areas I could research, or skills I could try to acquire."

Mara blinked. "That's a wonderful suggestion. Let me do a little thinking and try to come up with some ideas. And dig myself out from under a bit. I'll get back to you as soon as I can."

"Now what do I do?"

"Eat lunch, Mara mia. Drink coffee. Make a friend."

"She would make that easier than I usually find it. If it weren't that her curiosity is in a rather dangerous direction. However did I come to conceive the Project? . . . And she's so open and direct. I don't think this friendship of yours could get started if I were hedging and obfuscating."

"By all means, concede defeat before the attempt. It's so much more efficient."

"And I really do have work to do."

"Much of which is actually worth doing, and even interesting. But not inevitably all-consuming."

"Maybe. Maybe I'll give it a try."

Mara took a swig of her coffee and sighed happily. The dining facilities were still in the shakedown stage, with limited selection and uneven quality, but she had exerted herself to ensure that the coffee would be strong and plentiful.

Laura sighed, less happily. "I'll be glad when I can have coffee again. The tea they're allowing us isn't much of a substitute. I'm making do with hot water."

"How are you feeling?"

"Not bad, considering. It's hard to say whether I've got morning sickness as such. They're giving us drugs to prevent it, if we ask, but we're taking so many other concoctions that most of us end up nauseated anyway from time to time. Today I'm all right. I can smell food without, uh, difficulties." She smiled. "Even this food. Oh — I'm sorry, I wasn't thinking . . . ."

"Please don't apologize. I'm well aware of our commissary limitations, and I should be the one to apologize for them. I'm working on it. In fact, you've given me an idea. Maybe I can get some quicker action if I say the food is aggravating the mothers' symptoms and making it harder for them to stay nourished."

"I'll be glad to provide a testimonial. . . . Speaking of ideas: have you thought of anything I should be doing in these next few months? Besides lobbying for more tempting lunch menus?"

Mara played with her soup. "You're already doing a fair amount. Boning up on colony history, on the early human-Tofa contacts; reading the summaries of research on increasing empathy in children; making sure you have the templates for the reports you'll be doing. That is, I assume you're actually doing these things. I'm not sure all the mothers are."

Laura laughed. "Don't ask me. I'm not going to snitch."

Mara did a double-take. "Now you've given me an idea. Something you could do, that'd be useful beyond any reading list. It's too soon, really, to guess what you'll need to know as things unfold. But what we, the other administrators and I, need to know, right now, is what the mothers are thinking and feeling. Things they might not tell us, or even their doctors. Whether they're having second thoughts. What sort of emotional reactions they're having. Whether they've got their own bright ideas about things they should learn, or about what their future role should be."

Laura looked as if the food odors might be affecting her after all. "Dr. Cadell. I really don't see myself —"

"You don't have to name names. It's the information we want, not the sources. You could tell them what you're doing, or not, depending on what seemed right at the time. But you'd be doing them, and the Project, a real service."

Laura looked down at her neglected sandwich. "I could do a little poking around and see what comes up. And then I could decide if I felt right about sharing it. That's the best I can do."

"And that's all I could ask. Thank you. For wanting to help, and for considering my suggestion. I hope I haven't spoiled your appetite — any more than the food has."

Laura picked up her sandwich and took a tentative bite. When it was safely down, she changed the subject. "You were going to tell me about how you came up with the idea. The Project."

Mara ran through her available tactics and decided on flight. She took a last spoonful of soup and pushed back her chair. "I'm sorry, but I won't have time today. I've got to get back to work. Thanks so much for this little respite!"

She hurried through the goodbyes.

"So you've recruited a spy. Well, that's much better than making a friend."

"I've probably managed to do neither. She was clearly uncomfortable about my request. But she did offer to help. And she can help a lot more by providing information than by consuming it, at this stage."

"That may be. Although the more important the information, the more likely you are to hear about it. Eventually. Though perhaps too dramatically."

Nurses and technicians heard the clatter and crash, and came running. In the exam room, they found a wild-eyed patient, a rapidly retreating ultrasound technician, and on the floor the remains of the ultrasound machine. The woman's hospital gown was askew, which seemed to be the least of her concerns. She was twisting from side to side as if in search of the next object to attack. Those who had rushed in first halted in the doorway; the others piled into them and thrust them inside despite their efforts. The scrum in the doorway drew the patient's attention. She pointed at them, at the ultrasound technician, at the machine, and then simply waved her arms around.

"THERE'S A *THING* INSIDE ME! GET IT OUT! GET IT OUT!"

The nurse who had been pushed farthest into the room decided she might as well be brave. "Ms. — please, honey, tell me your name. We'll take care of you. We'll make it all right. What's your name, hon?"

The patient looked blankly at her as if the question were too unexpected and irrelevant to cope with.

"Please, honey. Your name. To start with. Then we'll talk about the rest of it."

The patient seemed less agitated now. She took a deep breath. "Nancy. Nancy Fowler."

"Good. That's very good. Nancy. Now, Nancy, why don't we sit down. You sit right there, on the exam table —"

This was a miscalculation. The patient's eyes grew wild again. "No! Not *there*! That's where — there's a THING inside me! I saw it!!"

"Shhhh, Nancy, Nancy, it's OK. You're going to be fine. Here, let me take you somewhere else. Somewhere safe." The nurse gestured frantically behind her for the crowd to clear the doorway. When they had managed to do so, she led the patient to a waiting room and then to a deep and comfortable armchair — one from which it would take her some seconds to arise.

The nurse sat on an unobstructed bench nearby and took her hand. "It's all right, Nancy. Here we are. Now let's talk about it. You're here because you were willing to — to carry babies. Do you remember that?"

The patient nodded. She whispered, "Babies. I was going to carry babies."

"Yes, that's right. And you knew they would be special babies, didn't you? One would be a human baby, and —"

The patient started to push herself out of the chair. The nurse got up and crouched next to her, trying to hold her in place without alarming her further. "Nancy! It's all right! Take a deep breath. Yes, that's right. Now let's go on. Let me see your armband. OK. You're in the second group. You're at nineteen weeks. You came in for a checkup. And you were feeling all right?"

"I was sick." Her voice grew louder. "It made me sick! I wasn't getting better! I should have been better!"

"Nancy, shhh now. Different people get over morning sickness at different times. Even with, uh, regular pregnancies. But I'm sorry you've been feeling sick. It's no fun, I know. I've had two children myself. I remember what it's like. But you get over it, sooner or later."

The patient sat rigidly upright. "*You've* never had a THING inside you! You don't know what's going to happen! Nobody knows!"

That was a stumper. The nurse ignored it and moved on. "You were having your checkup. And the technician asked you if you wanted to see the babies. Is that right?"

The patient's eyes filled with tears. "I wanted to see the babies. To see babies. And I saw the one little baby. It was so little. And then — right there next to my baby, there was the THING!" She struggled against the nurse's hand.

The nurse decided it was time to punt. "Nancy, I'm going to take you somewhere where you can rest. And then I'm going to find the people who can help you. We'll make it better. Would you like to rest now?"

The tears were falling now. "I haven't been able to sleep. And I keep being sick. And I'm so tired."

"We'll help you sleep. And then we'll figure out how to help you. We'll help you."

* CONFIDENTIAL *
CLEARANCE CLASS 3 AND ABOVE

LEVI Status Report, 6-15-71

. . . Two of the human hosts have developed psychological abnormalities. Use of psychotropic drugs is contraindicated given the pregnancies. These mothers are being monitored and termination of the pregnancies, or attempted transfer of the fetuses to other host mothers, is a possibility. A mild tranquilizer is being administered to the other hosts as a prophylactic measure. The ultrasound technicians will no longer suggest that host mothers view their ultrasounds . . . .

Mara put down the status report and answered the call. "Laura! It's good to hear from you. I have to admit, I hope I know why you're calling. You heard about Ms. Fowler and Ms. Tennant?"

"Nancy and Linnea. Yes. And it would have been better, wouldn't it, if they'd gotten help earlier. . . . I'd like to come and talk to you. About a few other things I've noticed lately."

"That'd be wonderful." Mara smiled. "I'll make the hot water."

She hung up and allowed herself a moment of satisfaction. "See, Levi? My idea is bearing fruit."

"Of a sort, sister mine. Though not, perhaps, as nourishing as it might have been."

Chapter 6

MANY PROJECT personnel reveled in their opportunities to observe Tofa at close quarters. While other humans might be repulsed to see the Tofa ingesting food through an orifice under the chin, they were simply intrigued.

Chief Nurse Harriet Gaho, who had done her early training in obstetrics, particularly admired the Tofa solution to multiple pregnancies. She was always pleased to see a Tofa host mother sweep by, carrying her twins one above the other on her tall frame.

Until that sight became far less common.

* SECRET *
CLEARANCE CLASS 2 AND ABOVE*

LEVI Status Report, 8-1-71
Executive Summary

<u>Gestational Schedule Status</u>

Human host pregnancies (successful): First Group are at 32 weeks gestation; Second Group at 26 weeks; Third Group at 20 weeks; Fourth Group at 14 weeks.

<u>Unsuccessful and Otherwise Problematic Outcomes to Date</u>

Human Host Pregnancies

The percentage of unsuccessful human host pregnancies has dropped with each successive group, as the technical teams examine previous results and refine their techniques accordingly.

To date, there have been four spontaneous abortions of human embryos/fetuses and six spontaneous abortions of Tofa embryos/fetuses in human host pregnancies. In two of these cases, both twins were aborted. This leaves, to date, four human singletons and two Tofa singletons total in these three groups. These subjects, together with those surviving the events described in the next section, will potentially be subject to some unpredictable variant(s) of "lost twin" syndrome.

Some psychological impact on host mothers with unsuccessful pregnancies was expected, particularly for any host mothers who bore and lost a genetically related embryo/fetus. However, those human host mothers who lost a Tofa embryo or fetus appear to have suffered more distress than anticipated, given the lack of genetic relationship and the disparity of species. Treatment efforts are ongoing.

Tofa Host Pregnancies

At the request of the Tofa, these pregnancies were begun simultaneously and are now at 25 weeks gestation.

One Tofa host mother suffered what appeared to be a variant of toxic shock at Week 3 of her pregnancy. The Project team attempted medical intervention to save the embryos, but was prevented by other Tofa host mothers present at the scene. Neither the mother nor the embryos survived.

Within the last week, all but two of the remaining Tofa host mothers have spontaneously aborted the Tofa fetuses. The human fetuses are gestating within expected parameters. . . .

"What have I done, Levi? What the hell have I done! All those children. . . ."

"What you've done is tried to save this planet from generations of conflict, or climactic catastrophe. During which twins would lose twins, and children would lose parents, and parents would lose children."

"And these babies now are the tools, and tools get broken, and that's just how it goes. I can't stand this."

"You can, Mara. You will. You'd better. Unless you think that those children — all of them — would be better without you here, and caring."

Dr. Tanner's secretary took the call, and quickly put it through.

"Mara, I was concerned to get your call between our scheduled sessions. Is something going on that you find particularly difficult?"

"Yes. Very difficult."

"Take your time. You're pacing. Please sit down. As if you were in my office. That's better. Please go on."

"The problem is that I can't talk about it. I mean, what happened is confidential. But it's something I should have foreseen. Or at least, I should have known it might happen. I of all people."

Dr. Tanner stroked downward with his hand, his usual way of telling her to slow down and to breathe. "Then let me do some deducing. Some detecting. You needn't tell me if I get it right. Just tell me if I get it significantly wrong."

Mara slumped down in her chair, suddenly exhausted. Dr. Tanner went on. "This project — you're passionate about it. You care enough to uproot yourself, to commit yourself for a period of years, to attenuate what few human contacts you have managed to build. It seems likely there is some connection to the central trauma in your life."

Mara waited, clenching her hands together, trying to make herself breathe more slowly.

"So this project either literally involves twins, or some other bond that speaks to you in a similar way. I would guess that its aims include healing, or the prevention of traumatic loss. And yet, on the way to that goal, there was a risk — a risk, I gather, that has been realized — of causing more loss, more trauma. So that now you say you should have focused on that initial risk, as well as on the goal.

"Mara?"

"You aren't in your rocking chair."

"What's that?"

"Your rocking chair. I guess it isn't near your phone screen. I miss the sound of it. And your aroma sticks. I have quite a good sense of smell. I could smell them from where I sat. I liked your pipe tobacco."

"I know."

"Oh."

"You miss me."

"Yes."

Dr. Tanner leaned back in his office chair, making the springs creak. "Mara, did you ever tell your father about Levi? About how you kept him real to you, made him part of your life?"

"No. And not just that — we never talked about him at all. About my having had a twin. Not the way I did with my mother, a couple of times."

"As I recall, you and your father did share some interests, and activities related to them."

"He was a biochemist. He would come home and tell me about things he'd learned, things he was working on. His excitement made them exciting. When I was old enough, he'd take me to his lab, give me little projects to do, ask me what I thought about problems. I doubt I'd have become a scientist without him. And he was proud of me."

"Did you confide in him about more personal things? About friendships, social conflicts, romantic interests?" Dr. Tanner chuckled a little at Mara's expression. "Not the last, I see."

"Particularly not the last . . . but not much about any of it. I didn't volunteer, and he didn't ask."

"Would you agree that it's no accident you chose a male therapist of your father's generation — and one who's chosen to retain that appearance?"

"I didn't do it consciously. But I guess not. No accident. But why are we talking about this now?"

"Now you're asking for my trade secrets. But I will say, sometimes we all work by instinct. I'm following mine. And you seem less distressed than when you called."

"Yes. Doctor — the way you described my problem. The one you 'detected.' You seemed to be saying — you were reminding me. About the goal, that I had a goal, that I was trying to help, to make things better."

"That you were?"

Mara took a long, deep breath, and then another. "That I am. I am."

Chapter 7

* CONFIDENTIAL *
CLEARANCE CLASS 3 AND ABOVE

LEVI Status Report, 9-15-71
Executive Summary

Tofa Names

The Tofa have supplied recordings of a number of individual designations (names) to be used for the Tofa twin subjects. It is not known whether these designations are common in Tofa society.

Living Quarters

The majority of the human host mothers are currently housed in dormitories within the main facility. Several, however, are housed in cottages nearby.

Due to the difficulties in maintaining information security should many host mothers return to their places of origin following delivery, more commodious dormitories and additional separate dwellings are under construction.

Housing assignments have depended on various factors, including the marital status of the host mother and the wishes of certain parties related to some participants. . .
.

Veda Seeling, daughter of Councilman Channing, offered her visitor tea. Nikki Roberts, daughter of Councilman Simpson, simpered and declined.

"I know they say it's all right — it *is* the bin-tan leaf, isn't it? — but I want to be *so* careful."

And I didn't even poison it, bitch, thought Veda. "How was your check-up?"

"Oh, just marvelous. I *insisted* they show me the twins. One of them — the Tofa — was touching the other's cheek! I teared up, I really did."

"Oh, I know, isn't it splendid? I thought I saw mine kissing last week, but the nurse wasn't sure. *I'm* sure."

"And is the human twin a boy or a girl?"

"I told them not to tell me. I want to keep the mystery. I'm just an old-fashioned girl, I guess."

Nikki didn't quite hide her smirk. "It's so nice that you can hold onto your old-fashioned values, even while you're doing something so — un*us*ual. But when so many people *know* — not just the tech, but all those medical people, and the people who write the reports, and the people who *read* the reports —"

Veda sniffed. "I do not concern myself with those people. Of course I'm doing this to serve the community, and for the advancement of science — but I will not be distracted from my maternal experience by all those buzzing little officials and whatnot."

Nikki donned her most serious expression. "I consider it my duty to in*volve* myself in the Project as *much* as I can. One never knows when one may be able to offer some helpful *in*sights. . . . Doesn't Brian want to know?" She glanced around at the elaborate vases, some glass, some metal, adorning the room. Most were empty; a few contained flowers, a bit past their prime. "You *do* at least *talk* to him regularly?"

"Of course! Even though he's so busy, we talk every night at *least*. He wishes so much that he could be here. And he's going to be here when they arrive, no matter how much the Bureau needs him. I do miss him so. . . ."

"I can *see* that, darling," cooed Nikki, nodding at the steamy cover of the romance novel Veda had not sufficiently hidden. Veda blushed, then forced herself to think of glaciers. And knives.

"At least you don't *have* that problem, Nikki, with Nolan out of the picture. I'm sorry. There are so few chances for you to meet someone, out here. The staff are so busy — and they do tend to be stuffy, don't they, about any personal entanglements? . . . but maybe when you're — looking yourself again, it'll be easier. . . ."

The light glinted off the varnished hair sculpture as Nikki tossed her head. "I haven't the time to worry about such things *now*, Veda. This is too im*por*tant. I've been meditating, you know. I sit in the half-lotus position and com*mune* with my babies. I picture them out there in the world, leading the way, bringing humans and Tofa together. I just *flood* them with positive energy. They're going to know how *proud* I am of them, from the *mo*ment they're born."

From the moment they're born, Veda said to herself, she'll have them out of her door and in a dormitory before I could spit. And a good thing for them. Not like me. I'm going to have mine right here, where I can make sure they learn what's important. What, and who.

The comfortable sofa and armchairs, the yellow and white checked curtains at the windows, the braided area rugs, were meant to be cozy, but Councilman Petter appeared immune to their effect. He sat rigidly upright on the sofa. "I thought we were clear on this. Of course you'll report to me regularly. Do you think I care what agreements you've signed? Why do you think I let you do this?"

Laura sipped her hot water and let him wind down. "You always see what you want to see, Daddy. I never said I'd be your 'inside man' — or woman. I would have done this no matter who you were. I've seen how little you and the others can do about the conflicts. Don't growl, I'm not blaming any of you! I think it was wise and foresighted of you to realize the limits of what you could achieve with the usual diplomatic tools. Dr. Cadell has given you a chance, an opportunity, to keep us safe, and you'll have a place in history for having the courage to try it."

Her father harrumphed. "That's very kind, child. I wish we could trust everyone to take that view of it. The secrecy is an administrative strain. And I suppose it would be a bit awkward, sending me reports. Wouldn't do to have you caught breaking the rules."

"We'll talk when you visit me, of course. You will visit? And get to know the twins? Judy is really your grandchild, you know. Biologically. They used my ovum."

Councilman Petter's eyes glistened. "You're naming her after your mother. It's a lovely thought. But — sweetheart, you'll have to keep her human. As human as you can. I couldn't bear it if . . . with your mother's name . . . ."

Laura came to him and gave him a hug. "I'll wait a bit, until we see that the human babies are — well, that they're all right. But you know, I can feel it. Don't worry — she'll be a human girl, a wonderful girl, one you can be proud of."

Petter wiped his eyes. "Like her mother." He straightened up and visibly donned his Councilman persona again. "Yes, I'll visit. Regularly. I want to know all the important things as they happen. No surprises."

He turned to don his coat and then turned back. "The Tofa baby. Do you have a name for it as well?"

Laura took a deep breath. "I'd thought: La-ren."

"La-ren." Petter cleared his throat. "Hmm. That's rather like — yes." He looked away. "Of course. As you think best."

"I do."

Mara left the staff meeting and considered heading straight to her quarters. A long day would only get longer if she went by her office, where who knows what problems might be waiting to ensnare her. She sighed. Yes, and those problems might grow more tentacles if she left them overnight. She trudged back to her office, sank into her chair and called up her messages.

She rather expected to see one from Laura Hanson. Laura had been reporting in about once a week, either with some news from the host mother front lines, or with the welcome word that nothing needed discussing. Finding neither, Mara searched back and saw that it had been almost two weeks since Laura had made contact. She quickly scanned her other messages, forwarding a few to other staff for action or review; made a few notes on the most problematic items, and then called Laura. The recorded response sent her hurrying to the hospital wing.

The charge nurse was reassuring. Some spotting, some cramps, other symptoms, all made bed rest a necessity, at least for a while, but everything was under control. Yes, the patient could have visitors. Yes, she had been awake a few minutes ago. By all means, go on in, Dr. Cadell.

Mara knocked softly on the open door. Laura looked up and beamed. The warmth caught Mara by surprise. "Dr. Cadell! How nice of you! Please come in. I hope you haven't been worried."

"I was. But they tell me you're doing fine. How are you feeling?"

"Bored. Relaxing is all very well, and I usually enjoy it, but this is ridiculous! And it's quite a come-down from playing detective."

"You're handling it better than I would. I find relaxing difficult, and bed rest would drive me to distraction in short order. Can I bring you anything to help pass the time?"

"That's very kind of you, but I have my tablet, and even some real books." Laura gestured to a small pile at the bedside. "What I'd like — if it isn't too much trouble, and please feel free to tell me it if is — is just a chance to sit and chat."

Mara could hardly refuse. She pulled up a chair. "Was there anything you would have reported this week, if you'd been able?"

"Not really. A few of the mothers are still planning how they and their children will be running things in a few years' time. Running the government, that is, not the Project — so I don't think you need to worry about it just now. . . . There is something I'd like to hear about, rather than tell. Except I've asked before, and I have the impression that you don't really want to talk about it."

Mara suppressed the urge to wriggle in her chair. "You mean, how I came to propose the Project in the first place. May I ask why you find the question so interesting?"

Laura looked surprised. "I think anyone would. Especially anyone who's a part of it." She looked around the hospital room. "Anyone whose life is going to be different because of it."

Mara was struck with sudden shame. This young woman had offered her body and months or years of her life to fulfill Mara's vision. Wasn't she entitled to know more? But what could Mara tell her?

"It's true that I find it hard to talk about. You see, it's more personal than you may have supposed. I had my own reasons to research the development and bonding of twins."

Mara paused. She half hoped and half feared that Laura would fill in the next step.

"You're a twin? But I've never, none of us has heard about a brother or sister. . . . Oh!" Laura stopped, wide-eyed. "Dr. Cadell — did you have a twin who —"

"He died. Yes." Mara swallowed hard. "Quite a long time ago."

"I'm so sorry. You were very close?"

"We were — very young. It's hard to say." Hard to say without saying far too much.

Laura looked distressed. "I'm sorry I pressed you. I didn't know I was prying into something so private. And I'm guessing you wouldn't want anyone talking about it."

"Indeed not." Mara hoped Laura would not be offended at the emphatic reply, but she could hardly say less.

"Oh, I won't say a word. To anyone. And if I hear anyone speculating, I'll try to steer them in some other direction."

"You don't need to go to any trouble. Just — I would appreciate it if you wouldn't mention it to anyone."

Laura reached out tentatively as if to take Mara's hand, and then pulled back. "Thank you for confiding in me. For trusting me."

Mara would have liked to demur. She knew she had really done neither.

"It's going to be strange, seeing her again. She thinks I've opened up to her, when I haven't. It feels dishonest."

"That's one way to look at it. The other is to look at it as Step One. A baby step, at least. Of course, that would leave open the possibility of making a friend. So by all means go with the first option."

"Is friendship always so exhausting? Because if it is, Levi, I really can't afford it."

Laura lay back in bed and listened to the rain, trying to rest, but her mind wasn't ready. She kept replaying parts of Dr. Cadell's visit. Maybe she'd imagined it, but Dr. Cadell had seemed more uncomfortable than ever as she left. Probably she was regretting having shared a secret with someone she barely knew.

Laura would have liked to get to know her better — possibly even to become her friend. But she had the feeling it would take quite a lot of effort. Dr. Cadell was not easy to know. She probably had other priorities than befriending someone who was, after all, a test subject. And Laura would have other demands on her energy.

But she had let herself become too isolated. Laura resolved to make more time, once she was mobile again, for getting to know the other host mothers. And of course, there was one she already knew. Veda had been a friend once. The Project might be their chance to be friends again. And perhaps, now that Veda was no longer immersed in the world of political power and intrigue, Laura could help her find other interests. She shrank from the presumptuous thought, but it was there — perhaps she could be a wholesome influence, and do her old friend some good.

Chapter 8

AS LAURA MADE her way through the cafeteria line, she looked around for possible lunch companions. She was pleased to see Veda and several other mothers sitting at a large table with some vacant seats. It might be easier to approach Veda with neutral parties present.

As she carried her tray closer, she began to wonder. The conversation was no idle lunchtime chatter. This might not be the best moment for a casual restoration of contact. On the other hand, maybe something was going on that Dr. Cadell would want to know about.

She reached the table and hovered for a moment. One of the mothers whom Laura knew slightly was holding forth with some vehemence. She looked up for a moment and gestured toward a chair. As Laura sat down, the woman resumed her tirade.

"I couldn't believe it! I just asked for any tips about breastfeeding, and the nurse clams up and calls the doctor in, and the doctor pulls out his tablet and punches up some 'directive.' Some scientist who's probably never even *touched* a baby has decided that we can't nurse the human twins, because the Tofa twins can't nurse from human mothers and treating the twins differently would 'introduce an unnecessary variable.' I told the doctor that anyone who thought nursing my baby was 'unnecessary' had another think coming."

Several of the other mothers nodded vigorously or muttered agreement. Laura was intrigued to see that Veda was one of the most indignant. She would not have picked

Veda as likely to nurse a baby. And indeed, Veda's comments soon showed a different basis for her concern.

"It's clear these people have no idea who they're dealing with." (Or whom, Laura refrained from interjecting.) "Do they really expect us to let them dictate every aspect of our maternal experience, as if we were some desperate recruits they'd picked up for the sake of a roof over our heads? Don't they realize that we include people of *influence*?"

Tilda, a shy woman whom Laura had seldom heard speak, visibly gathered her courage to interject. "But they *are* scientists. We're all here because of science. They must know what they're doing."

Veda snorted. "My dear Tildie, there are scientists and scientists. I myself have a fairly extensive scientific background." Laura looked sharply at her, startled. This was not information that had come her way. "I assure you that this rule of theirs is meddling and bureaucracy. And I would be *delighted* to tell them so."

Laura cleared her throat. "If you really feel that way, Veda, I think I can make it happen. And you won't have to bother with some underling," she added shrewdly. "You can go straight to the top."

Mara took Laura's call with some foreboding. She had not heard from Laura in some time. Despite the potential value of Laura's information, she had been just as glad. It was easier not to think about her awkward and incomplete revelations at Laura's bedside.

With Laura was another host mother whom Mara vaguely remembered as disagreeable and politically connected. The two were enormously and impressively pregnant. Mara suppressed the urge to ask them to sit before their standing precipitated labor.

"Dr. Cadell?" Laura's manner was that of someone overcoming an awkwardness of her own. "I believe you've met Veda Seeling. She wants to tell you about, um, a situation."

Veda took over. "A situation that must be redressed, and promptly too."

Mara listened impassively to Veda's crisp summary of the diktat concerning breastfeeding of human infants. She realized with chagrin that the policy must have been mentioned, without catching her attention, in one of the innumerable reports she had scanned in recent weeks.

"It's obvious that the staff here expect us to *genuflect* at the word 'science', rather than to examine their claims." Veda paused to catch her breath and steadied herself against a nearby desk. "So tell me, Dr. Cadell. Is the Project tasked with studying mother-infant bonding? Or comparing the responses of Tofa and human infants to nutritional formulas? Is there any pertinent question — let alone a question important enough to justify the funding this Project has received, and the political risks my father and the other Council members are taking — is there any such question that would be in *any* degree scientifically compromised by letting mothers nurse their babies!" She stopped and panted again. Mara caught Laura's eye in alarm. Laura left Mara's field of vision and returned with a chair, toward which she gently steered Veda. Veda gave a brisk nod of thanks and returned to the attack.

"Well, Doctor?"

Mara frowned in thought. "There could be — nursing is a powerful bonding mechanism. If the host mother bonds in this way with only one twin, there is potential for some attenuation of the twin bond. Creation and preservation of which *is* crucial to the Project's mission. And you're right — that isn't a scientific objection, but then the Project is more than a scientific research opportunity. As I'm sure your father and his fellows would agree."

Veda pursed her lips. "Well, then, at least we've agreed on one thing. That this business of 'unnecessary variables' can be dispensed with." She turned to Laura. "You've spent some time talking to the other mothers. How many of them would you expect to feel strongly about nursing? That is, to insist on it?"

"It isn't something I've thought about, or talked to them about. But if you want a wild guess, I'd say maybe a third of them."

Veda nodded, vindicated. "I'd bet money it's less than half, in any event. *Which* sets up a perfect little science experiment, if anyone wants one. And by the way, *I'm* not planning to nurse the human twin." Veda shuddered theatrically at the thought.

Mara raised both eyebrows. "You're not? Then why did you put yourself forward this way?"

Veda gave her the look a professor might direct at an inattentive student. "My dear Dr. Cadell, it is *not* in my interest to sit idly by while the mothers are intimidated and bullied. We are not a set of experimental rodents. Talk of necessity — *we* are necessary. We are indispensable. And we will be treated as such."

The matter had been tentatively resolved. The mothers would be surveyed. Depending on their numbers, those who felt strongly about nursing their human infants would probably be allowed to do so. Laura and Veda headed to the mothers' lounge to spread the news.

Laura looked sideways at Veda. "You were very impressive back there."

Veda gave her an arch look and then allowed herself to grin. "I'm sorry to complicate your opinion of me. But don't worry. You're still allowed to think of me as shallow."

Laura blushed, then laughed. "That might be harder than it used to be. . . . How are you feeling? You seemed a bit uncomfortable."

Veda answered by stopping and clutching Laura's arm. Laura froze. After a moment, Veda straightened up and stretched her back.

"After we tell the others, I wonder if you'd accompany me to the hospital wing. I rather think that things are getting started."

"You mean —"

Veda patted Laura's arm. "Don't fret, now. But I think the Project is really underway."

Chapter 9

* CONFIDENTIAL *
CLEARANCE CLASS 3 AND ABOVE

LEVI Status Report, 11-15-71
Executive Summary

<u>Parturition</u>

The first group of host mothers have undergone scheduled surgical deliveries, with the exception of one delivery precipitated by the onset of labor and completed surgically ahead of schedule. All outcomes were satisfactory. One unexpected complication, involving a human fetus holding one arm of the Tofa fetus, was resolved without injury to either.

The first set of babies were to be kept under observation in the main compound nursery for at least three weeks. Those delivered later could presumably be released in less time.

The Tofa nurses had attempted to provide some advance instruction in the care of newborn Tofa, but the usual communication difficulties had limited the information they could convey. Now they were holding nearly nonstop demonstrations on how to hold, feed, comfort, clean.

To the relief of their human caregivers, the Tofa infants did sleep. Most of their sleep behavior was unremarkable, but at intervals they would lie unresponsive with their eyes open and all six limbs moving lazily about. This motion did not seem to disturb the human twins; if bumped or brushed by an errant arm or leg, they would stir or murmur, and then fall back to sleep. They were similarly untroubled by the Tofa babies' sleep noises, a sort of ultrasonic snoring that could drive the more sensitive of the human adults out of the room.

The neurologists took their measurements and found nothing in either of the Tofa sleep stages approximating REM sleep. Their educated guess was that the Tofa did not dream.

Chief Nurse Harriet Gaho was the first to notice that the Tofa babies smelled different when they were sleeping. She summoned Mara to experience the difference for herself. First, she handed Mara an alert and squirming specimen. "Go ahead. Here — hold him between the upper and lower arms, like so. Put your nose up to his belly and take a good sniff." Mara obeyed, and narrowly escaped a punch from one of the flailing fists.

Harriet retrieved the baby and handed him off to a junior nurse. "Now come over here." She beckoned Mara toward to a crib where another Tofa baby lay fast asleep, back to back with his human sister. Harriet raised the basket of the crib up high enough that Mara could lean in and smell the Tofa up close. They retreated on tiptoe.

"I think I see what you mean. The first infant smelled rather like toast. The sleeping one is more like — it's a familiar smell, but I can't think what it is."

"It's something like the smell of vinegar, but not quite — naturally. I guess you don't do a lot of cooking."

Mara laughed. "That's an understatement. Anyway, I'll take your word for it."

"Maybe they smell different depending on what they're doing, or what physical state they're in. Could be useful for diagnostic purposes." Harriet made a note on her tablet, then looked back at Mara. "So, Dr. Cadell. Here they are. What do you make of them?"

Mara looked around at the sets of twins, some sleeping, some awake and signaling for one or another kind of attention; at the human and Tofa nurses bustling about. She found it difficult to speak: she was grinning too broadly.

* CONFIDENTIAL *
CLEARANCE CLASS 3 AND ABOVE

LEVI Status Report, 12-1-71
Executive Summary

<u>Housing for Subjects</u>

Where feasible, the infants are to be housed in dormitories, with frequent visits from the host mothers. This will allow uninterrupted access and greater environmental control. Those host mothers who have been accorded separate dwellings and who prefer to keep the infants in those accommodations are, for now, being allowed to do so. These situations will be periodically reexamined. . . .

Nikki glared at her father. "You can't make me stay here! My contract only held me until they were born! And it's *horrid* here. The exercise equipment is primitive. I need my personal trainer. There's only one masseur, and he's a clumsy, impertinent brute. And my friends won't believe my cover story much longer, and I'll be left out of everything. I'm coming home!"

Councilman Simpson glared back. He had been doing it longer, and was better at it. "Home, you say? If you mean the family residence, I decide who's welcome there, and if you leave here against my wishes, that will *not* include you."

Nikki put her head down and bawled. After a few moments, she took a quick peek up to gauge her effect, and found it disappointing. She sniffed loudly several times and sat up again. "Oh, Daddy, it's just so hard! I miss everyone so much! I don't have any friends here! I don't have anybody!"

"I suppose the children don't enter into your calculations?"

He was a fine one, she fumed, to talk about calculating. "You know I don't know anything about babies. And that nanny they gave me was so annoying! And I couldn't get any sleep with all the noise! But now that they're in the dormitory, I hardly see them, and I have nothing to do, and I'm *bored*."

"Can't you volunteer at something, at the compound? Where you can keep an eye on things?"

Nikki rolled her eyes. "If you'd really been planning ahead, you would have had me taught something technical, something they'd *need* at that place. They don't want me underfoot, any more than I want to be there."

"Nikki, you will just have to figure out some way to get the job done! I am not having you come home with nothing to show for all this. Now stop pouting and come look at what I brought you."

Time for a tactical retreat. Nikki sighed prettily, wiped her eyes and watched him pull the package out of his briefcase. "Oh, Daddy! It's *beautiful!*" As if she had anywhere to wear it. Which she would. Nikki had her allies. Including Mrs. Councilman. She'd get home sooner than he thought.

Tilda looked at her twins, cuddled close together in the crib. Mat-set had all four arms wrapped around Suzie. They seemed to cuddle any chance they got. Maybe they were glad to be free of separate amniotic sacs.

She looked down at Mat-set and remembered the rumors of Tofa with five arms instead of four. She had even seen pictures, but who knew whether they were authentic.

Certainly none of the Tofa Twin-Bred babies had been born with extra limbs.

Tilda glanced over at the big dormitory clock and then back down at the babies. She gasped and staggered a step back. Mat-set was still holding Suzie with four arms. So how was he scratching his head with another one?

Tilda looked around wildly for a chair, found one blessedly nearby, and sank down on it. She pinched herself. Nothing changed. Well, who said you couldn't pinch yourself in a dream and keep on dreaming?

She got up and walked, a bit unsteadily, to the intercom and buzzed for a nurse. Then she went back to the crib. Of course. Four arms, only four, and what was she going to do now?

She decided to be brave and sensible. If she had really seen it, the staff had to know. And if she hadn't, and she didn't wake up, then she was ill, and she should get the help she needed.

The chief nurse tucked Tilda in and watched her drift off to sleep, sedative patch in place. Then she went back to her station and called up the monitor footage on Tilda's twins.

Well, well.

* CONFIDENTIAL *
CLEARANCE CLASS 3 AND ABOVE

LEVI Status Report, 12-15-71
Executive Summary

<u>Anatomical Developments</u>

Observation of the Tofa infants has shed some light on the longstanding question of whether the number of Tofa

upper appendages is variable among the Tofa population.
The thickest of the four armlike appendages is apparently
capable of dividing when an additional upper appendage is
desired. . . .

Councilman Kimball bookmarked the spot in his agent's
report and opened his mail program. He owed an apology
to the young man who had claimed his poor showing
against a Tofa undesirable was due to the sudden
appearance of an extra appendage. Apparently the man had
been neither dishonest nor drunk.

After discharging that obligation, Kimball made a note
to seek further details as to the divided arms' placement,
reach, and muscular potential. His people needed adequate
information to prepare them for future confrontations.
After all, forewarned — he laughed out loud at the thought
— was forearmed.

Chapter 10

IN THEIR FIRST MONTHS as mothers, Laura and Veda had found several favorite spots in which to sit and chat with the babies in tow. Today, they sat side by side on a bench in the smaller garden, soaking up the sunshine. Both their sets of twins were amusing themselves in the asymmetrical strollers the Project engineers had devised. Judy and La-ren were exploring each other's fingers. Jimmy and Peer-tek were taking turns making funny noises. Every once in a while, one of the noises would make Judy and La-ren look up, before they returned their attention to each other.

Veda looked from Laura to Judy and back again. "She does take after you. There's the hair color, of course — how nice, that she has hair already! — but also something about her eyes." She sighed quietly.

Laura plucked a tree-seed out of Judy's hair. "I worry sometimes that I might pay her more attention because she's mine biologically, as well as being the human baby. I try to spend time with just La-ren as much as possible. Not that either of them is exactly vying for my company, if it means getting out of the other one's sight!"

"That's very tactful of you, dear. But I do sometimes wish I'd made the decision you did." Veda looked at Jimmy, who caught her glance, made a raspberry at her and then laughed. She turned back to Laura. "Well, I don't suppose I mean it, because that would be wishing Jimmy out of existence. He's really rather sweet."

The two women sat silently for a moment. A breeze brought them the scent of some nearby flower. Backlit yellow leaves glowed in the sunlight.

"Laura — about your spending time with only La-ren. Do you know, in all this time, I'm not sure I've spent more than a few minutes with only Peer-tek." She paused and took a deep sniff of the scented air. "What is it — *like*?"

Laura sat in thought for a moment. "It is different than being with Judy. I won't pretend it isn't. I flip back and forth between taking it for granted and being — amazed and surprised at this strange little creature. I notice the different smell more when it's just La-ren. And I keep somehow expecting facial expressions, and of course he doesn't have them. But I think I'm getting to know his body language." She laughed. "And all those hands! Now that he can grab things, I can't keep up!"

Veda smiled. "I think Jimmy gets frustrated that he can't reach as far as Peer-tek, or touch as many things at once." Her expression changed to what Laura called her "scientist at work" look. "I wonder when the human twins will start doing things the Tofa twins can't. And what they'll be."

Laura stood up. "Which reminds me. We've got to get these little guys back inside. It's Group Assessment time again."

Veda rolled her eyes, but followed Laura's lead. "I suppose it is. What was that old expression about stopping to smell the roses? I hope the children will get the chance, now and then, in between assessments and measurements and everything else that's planned for them."

* CONFIDENTIAL *
CLEARANCE CLASS 3 AND ABOVE

LEVI Status Report, 6-15-72
Executive Summary

Educational Methods

Our extensive access to the subjects and control over their environment allows for a comprehensive education strategy, from a point well before formal education customarily begins. The tentative plan for those twins raised in a home environment is to provide trained caregivers to assist the foster mother (and any additional parent figure) while providing age-appropriate educational support. The twins resident in dormitories will have numerous planned activities as well as many stimulating toys, games and other instrumentalities. The home-based twins will join the others for activities, and later for more formal schooling.

Language Proficiency

As a threshold matter, it is essential that both human and Tofa subjects become as fluent in Tofar as proves to be feasible. Toward that end, Tofa nurses will spend considerable time with each twin pair, except where the host mother is a Tofa who chooses to play a continuing active role.

Educational Objectives

Decisions will need to be made at the executive level as to what resources will be directed toward preparing the subjects for possible involvement in outside communities, as opposed to studying the subjects for their scientific value. There are also unsettled questions concerning the degree to which the subjects will be exposed to various details of Terran history. . . .

"*Possible* involvement? *What* unsettled questions? *What* details?"

Mara's assistant stood in the doorway, shoulders slightly hunched, flinching at each exclamation. Mara told herself to stop flogging the messenger. "Stan, I'm sorry. I know you're just trying to make sense of all the reports and messages from different departments. So tell me — what is this all about, and where is it coming from?"

Stan swallowed and shifted his feet. "I believe there have been some communications from the Council staff. Ah, some concerns have been raised about who might be held accountable if any, uh, interventions should lead to unpleasantness."

"As opposed to the peace and harmony we can expect without 'interventions.' The spineless — we need to push back on this, hard. For one thing, if the Council starts viewing us as primarily a research project, they won't maintain our funding long enough for us to become anything else. . . . And the 'details of Terran history'?"

"That didn't come from the Council. Some of our people have been asking whether it's such a good idea to inform Tofa — even our own Tofa — about our less admirable past episodes." Stan swallowed again and then looked Mara in the eye. "And Dr. Cadell, I have to say I see some basis for that concern."

Mara glared at him for a moment and then checked herself. Better to know what people were thinking. And he might even have a good reason for thinking it. "Please go on."

Stan appeared to consider relaxing, and to decide against it. "The Twin-Bred have to respect us. To look up to us. We're shaping their lives, determining their destinies. Especially the Tofa twins — they have to believe that we're benevolent and wise, that we know what's best for them and want what's best, alien as we are. If we tell them all about wars and atrocities and human folly . . ." Stan trailed off.

Mara hoped her expression was not too condescending. "Stan, think about it. Sooner or later, they'll have to know that we don't have it all figured out, that we don't really know what we're doing. Otherwise, why would we need their help?"

"Well . . . "

"And as for respect — how much will they respect us and our intentions, if they find out we've been keeping horrible secrets from them?" She sat for a moment, twiddling her stylus. "But I agree with some of what you're saying. We could overdo it. This isn't the time and place to expiate the guilt of our past with humble confession. We'll need to set the stage, very carefully."

"I've got an idea, sis."

"Now *there's* a surprise. What is it?"

"You've got how many thousands of novels and short stories in the data banks? Use 'em. Let the most gifted spokespersons humanity has produced explain humanity to these kids, in all its intermittent glory."

"Hmmm. That's worth considering. I could bring Laura Hanson in on it -- she's some kind of literature maven -- as well as the education staff."

"You're welcome."

<u>Educational Objectives (revised)</u>

The overall goal is to prepare the subjects for the various possible roles that their postulated abilities and characteristics would make possible. These range from mediation and arbitration to actual governance. Their education must therefore encompass social sciences including sociology, psychology, political science and cultural anthropology. It should also include as much as possible of the various scientific and technical disciplines that could arise in disputes concerning, e.g., city management, agriculture, power generation, infrastructure, atmosphere maintenance, and biological and chemical health and security. Training in public speaking and related skills will be desirable, although the complexities involved cannot yet be fully ascertained or prepared for. Materials will be tailored to the subject's ages and their individual capabilities.

Historical Terran conflicts, social inequities, etc., will be presented where necessary as examples of what can result from failures of communication and empathy.

Discussions continue concerning the use to be made of the extensive available library of Terran literature for children and adults. It has been suggested that the sociological and psychological curriculum may be appropriate for literary supplementation. . . .

Chapter 11

CHIEF NURSE Harriet Gaho had a rare interlude with nothing pressing to do, and was using it to walk in the garden near the infirmary. Now and then she would stop and bend over for a sniff of the large, pale yellow blossoms the humans called Lemon's Dream.

As she straightened up from a bush, Harriet caught movement out of the corner of her eye. A Tofa host mother had joined her.

"Hello," said the Tofa.

Harriet turned and looked up at the almost featureless face. Well, the Tofa host mothers all spoke some Terran, or so she'd heard. But there was something unsettling about the encounter, all the same.

Enough standing there looking foolish. She smiled, for whatever it might be worth. "And hello to you. I'm Harriet Gaho, Chief Nurse. And you would be?"

"If you are asking my name, it is Ra-tel-sen. If I may ask a question: what were you doing with the flower?"

Ignoring a sense of having fallen through the looking glass, Harriet replied, "I was smelling it. Smell is one of our senses. We take molecules of a substance in through our noses and analyze them." She always liked teaching, but this was a different sort of student.

"We have a similar sense. A different portal is involved. Your facial movements — am I correct that you enjoy this smell?"

"Yes, indeed. We had flowers back on Earth — Terra — that smelled nice to us, as a byproduct of smelling good to insects they needed to attract. Do your flowers attract any insects — very small animals — to help the flowers reproduce?"

The Tofa stood still for a moment, then blinked twice, slowly — a Tofa shrug. "At some point in the future, I may understand your questions better. Thank you for the conversation."

Ra-tel-sen turned and left, receding quickly with her long stride. Harriet stood looking after her, frowning in concentration.

Surely, even with its abrupt conclusion, this was a longer, more complex conversation than humans and Tofa could usually engage in. And what Tofa had ever said "thank you" before?

Or, for that matter, "hello"?

* CONFIDENTIAL *
CLEARANCE CLASS 3 AND ABOVE

LEVI Status Report, 7-1-72
Executive Summary

Status of Tofa Host Mothers

One development of interest is the apparent effect on Tofa host mothers of carrying human fetuses to term. (A team is developing hypotheses concerning other possible causes for the observed phenomenon. Its report is expected in approximately six weeks.)

One open question from the Project's inception was the nature of the bond to be expected between Tofa host mothers and the human fetuses, and later the human infants. Preparations were made for eventualities ranging from conduct endangering the human infants, to behavior approximating maternal in-species Tofa behavior (although, given the paucity of information concerning normal in-species behavior, this might be difficult to identify), to a complete absence of maternal behavior, to behavior reminiscent of human maternal behavior. The results have fallen on a spectrum between the latter two possibilities.

Of obvious interest was whether Tofa host mothers and the human infants they had carried would develop any mutual understanding comparable to what was potentially expected between Twin-Bred pairs. Until the human children develop more sophisticated linguistic and behavioral skills, this remains undetermined. However, the majority of the Tofa host mothers have displayed a significantly improved ability to interact harmoniously with, and to communicate with, adult human Project team members. The improvement was notable from a point commencing approximately 13 weeks before delivery, and has continued after delivery although the rate of improvement is declining.

Some involvement of the Tofa host mothers following parturition has been part of the Project plan, with the details and parameters left open for obvious reasons. However, senior staff are now exploring the possibility that any Tofa host mothers who are willing could become, not only continuing objects of Project study, but members of the Project staff. . . .

"Mara, I believe you're smiling. It becomes you. Do try it more often."

"And you're teasing, which you do quite often enough. But really, Levi, it's encouraging. The response of the Tofa host mothers is a very good sign. If carrying a human fetus has this sort of impact, sharing the womb with a fetus of the other species is even more likely to have some transformative effect —"

"Transformative. That is a word to give one pause. I don't recall you suggesting to the Council that you were out to transform humanity. Might've ruffled a few feathers, that."

"Whatever you want to call it, this change in Tofa host mother behavior certainly increases the odds that the Project wasn't a wild waste of time and resources."

"So now we have Tofa who understand humans better. Adult Tofa, whose bonding with individual humans is from a position of superiority, not the bond between peers. A pity we don't have an human analogue."

Mara stifled her irritation at having her good mood complicated. "Well, the human mothers are better at understanding their own Tofa babies than the Project staff are. But you're right, they don't seem any better at dealing with regular Tofa."

"Hmmm."

"Hmmm what?"

"You weren't at all sure about using Tofa host mothers. Some of the staff thought it would be a bridge too far, so to speak. That it would add too many variables, too much to keep track of, too many possibilities for trouble."

"Yes."

"Do you remember what ended the debate in favor of using them?"

"The Tofa showed up with all those extra Tofa embryos. After rejecting some of the human women we'd recruited."

"Yes. Those unrequested Tofa embryos — mysteriously perishable embryos, so the decision had to be made quickly. And most of them died in utero after all. Meaning that the principal result of those embryos' brief appearance —"

"Was the creation of Tofa host mothers. So this is all some sort of Tofa plot. Levi, I would like to call this paranoia."

"Call it what you like. Paranoia is part of my job description. Just keep an eye on those mothers."

Chapter 12

THE TOFA NURSE stood with lower arms extended as Til-sal staggered toward him. When Til-sal was close enough, the nurse scooped the toddler up with his lower arms and tossed him to his upper arms. The nurse rubbed his chin in a circle on the child's head, crooning congratulations in Tofar.

Chief nurse Gaho turned to the young human nurse beside her. "Know what we just saw?"

The young woman hesitated, then replied, "Could it be — like a kiss?"

"That's my guess." They watched as the tall Tofa tossed the small one in the air, caught him and plunked him down, then backed up and beckoned for him to walk again.

Soon the toddlers were everywhere, staggering around, two or four or occasionally five arms extended for balance — or reaching for the entrancing toys lying on newly accessible surfaces. Researchers learned to keep tablets, chemicals, and other paraphernalia hidden away in drawers — and then to requisition locks for the drawers.

Most of the staff tolerated the invasion with anything from resignation to good humor to sentimental fondness. There were, however, exceptions.

Annabelle Bloom, biogenetics specialist, shuddered as a year-old Tofa lurched by on thin stiff legs, arms splayed.

"Like a Frankenstein mated with a wagon wheel," she muttered.

Her department manager, passing by, corrected her. "Frankenstein's monster. Frankenstein was the scientist. People always get that wrong." He headed off to the dining hall for lunch.

"Yes, Dr. Frankenstein," Bloom whispered after he was safely out of hearing.

Now the Tofa child was gazing up at a microscope. He was not yet tall enough to see through the eyepiece, but he could reach the controls. He gave an experimental twist to a dial.

Bloom looked around for witnesses. She and the young Tofa were alone in the lab. She hissed at him. "Get away from that! Scat! Get out!"

The child jumped and turned around. Bloom looked into the alien eyes and swallowed sour saliva. "Out!"

The Tofa walked unsteadily out of the room, faster than he had entered, bumping into a cabinet as he went. Bloom waited until the child was some ways down the hall, then relaxed, breathed deeply, and found a towel to polish the dials on the microscope.

Walking Twin-Bred were a diversion, or a nuisance, but of scientific interest only to the staff studying Tofa physical and behavioral development. A great many members of the Project staff were eagerly awaiting the Twin-Bred's first words. Bets were laid as to the date, the language — Terran or Tofar? Some incomprehensible pidgin? — the subject, the individual and species — who and which would speak first?

Mara put a stop to the wagers in which the order of events was key, as these were likely to lead to disputes, inconsistent eyewitness testimony, and extensive review of security tapes. That done, she relished the excitement and suspense.

When the words came, among the first for both species was a word that some considered reassuring and others anticlimactic: "mama".

Then there was the Tofa word for hand. And "nu-nu" for nursing, of which Tilda confessed to being the origin. The Tofa word for "ball." And the Terran and Tofa words for sky.

The Tofa were first to learn verbs — including not only active verbs like "throw" and "run," but others like "look" and "wait."

                  * CONFIDENTIAL *
          CLEARANCE CLASS 3 AND ABOVE

Pronunciation Issues

One early result of the Project, now that the Twin-Bred have begun to develop language skills, has been resolution of a question concerning Tofa proper names. The sound between syllables of Tofa names, analogized to a human hiccup, has until now been impossible for humans to master fully. It appears that this limitation is not physiological in nature. To date, all but two of those human subjects who have begun speaking have proved able to produce it. . . .

There was no pidgin as such. There were Tofar words that humans found difficult, and Terran words that Tofa could not quite pronounce. Different twin pairs found different solutions. After a while, one of these would catch on and become part of the developing Twin-Bred dialect.

With not only host mothers, but dozens of other adults ready to echo and model and coax, the children progressed quickly from single words to short phrases. The Tofa advanced more quickly to full sentences. Harriet Gaho joked that their sentences had to match their arms.

Inevitably, there were surprises.

Mara closed her office door, retrieved a bar of chocolate from her stash of snacks, and sat in the chair near the window. She took a bite of the chocolate, breathed deeply in ecstasy, and sat back to relax for what felt like the first time in days.

"Oh, Levi, I don't know where to start. We're learning so much already, even while they're little children!"

"Details, woman, details!"

"One nice thing — something it turns out we have in common with the Tofa. They laugh. Lots of people had heard it — they just didn't know what they were hearing. It's a sort of whistle. They whistle rather a lot. People used to say that 'man is the animal that laughs.' Now we've found others."

"That's nice. Good to know the Council's investment is paying off."

"Stop that. We've also found out what they do instead of crying. They rock forward and back, and sometimes they hum. But there's something much more important. We think we know why none of us has been able to really master the Tofa language. Although there isn't much we can do about it, except to use the Twin-Bred as interpreters when they're old enough. It isn't a matter of anatomy, at least not as much as we thought. The membrane in front of their mouths vibrates in ways that aren't that different from vocal chords. Do you know — I mean, do you remember —"

"Let's not bother with metaphysical side issues like whether I remember things. Keep talking."

Mara took another bite of chocolate first. "Mandarin."

"An admirably concise explanation."

"Mandarin is a tonal language. Some people thought that if you were tone-deaf, you couldn't speak it properly. That the best you could do is stumble along, never knowing what you're getting wrong, either annoying or amusing the people who really speak it. It turns out that just about no one is tone-deaf enough to have that much trouble with it. But it's the idea I'm getting at."

"So the Tofa communicate with something we can't hear? Ultrasonic vibrations?"

"Mandarin is an analogy. We're still not sure — there may be something even stranger that we're missing — but we believe the extra level to the Tofa language is telepathic."

"And we know this how?"

"Well, of course we've exposed all the Twin-Bred to both languages as much as possible. It's a good thing the Tofa were so cooperative — supplying us with Tofa nurses. Which is something that still puzzles me. Why are they being this helpful? We don't know whether they even understand what we're trying to achieve, let alone approve of it."

"And after her tangent, she went on with her explanation."

"Shaddup. We've been recording twin-to-twin conversations in both Terran and Tofar. They're becoming fluent in both languages, or as fluent as they could be at their age. And of course we want to know what they're saying in Tofar! It would be utterly counterproductive to keep interrupting and asking questions, so we've been playing the human children audiovisual recordings of the Tofar conversations and making a game out of their giving us Terran translations. Except the children couldn't always translate the Tofar on the recordings.

"It took us a while to realize why. . . ."

Judy took a sip of juice. "Next one?"

"All right. Here we go. Just pause every few words, like you've been doing, and translate for us."

Judy started the playback. She let it run for a few moments and then paused, but didn't speak. Instead, she looked apologetic.

"Sorry. I don't remember."

The linguistic technician was confused. "Remember? We're not asking you to remember. Just listen and tell us what La-ren was saying."

"But I can't. I have to remember. The tape isn't — it isn't right."

The linguistic technician called in an audiovisual technician. They told Judy to run along — this would take a while.

"Can I bring the juice?"

"Huh? Oh, sure, sure."

They could find nothing wrong with the recorder or the playback. They decided to try the same tape with another translator. They tried Jimmy — Laura's and Veda's twins played together often, so if familiarity aided comprehension, he would be almost as good as Judy. But he could do no better. "The tape — it's missing something."

"What could it be missing?"

Jimmy shrugged.

The technicians consulted more senior staff. Mara led a brainstorming session. Could there be some other sense involved? More children were brought in, a few at a time, and questioned about whether they felt or smelled or saw anything special when they talked to their twins. Finally, Suzie said, "The head buzz. No head buzz with the tape."

Judy's face brightened. "That's it!"

The children all murmured agreement, while the adults looked at each other in silent bewilderment. All except one junior technician, who looked as if she was struggling with some guilty secret. After a moment, she cleared her throat. "Excuse me — I think I might know what they mean."

". . . The tech told us that she'd been getting an odd sort of mental blurring, like interference, when she heard Tofa speaking Tofar. Turns out she tests very high on PSI exams."

"So human children are participating in some sort of telepathic exchange. Have you tested the human Twin-Bred for PSI ability? And compared their results to human children who aren't Twin-Bred?"

"We're going to. We have to set it up, arrange for the control subjects. We may have to invent some new tests. This may be about receptivity to Tofa mental emanations, rather than something more general. If we do find that human Twin-Bred have some broader telepathic ability, we'll have to figure out how that might interfere with the experimental conditions.

"And there's something else . . . ."

Dar-tan stood in the kitchen. His sister Cindy looked over at him, wrinkled her brow, then ran over and gave him a hug. Their mother stifled a sigh — Dar-tan would always accept a hug from Cindy, not always from her. Then she looked again.

"Cindy, could you come here for a moment? Tell me — why did you go hug Dar-tan?"

"Face looked sad."

"But honey, Tofa don't exactly have faces. Not like ours. And not faces that show when they're sad."

"Dar-tan does! And the others. Other Twin-Bred. You see it?"

She looked back at Dar-tan as if he could have grown features without her noticing. "No, hon."

"Other Tofa — they see it. But they don't like it. They go all queasy. Dar-tan told me."

The host mother took a deep breath. "Sweetie, why don't you go stand next to Dar-tan until he feels better. I have to go write something down."

She went into the office and called up her New Observations file.

". . . So it seems both human Twin-Bred and the normal Tofa can detect something like facial expressions on Tofa

Twin-Bred. Which the Tofa find unsettling, while the human Twin-Bred take it for granted. It may be that just like the language, the facial expressions have a telepathic component. Unlike the language, though, this isn't something the Tofa normally use — it'd be an adaptation of the Tofa Twin-Bred to human influence."

"My, my. And just how far does this intriguing capability reach? Can the Tofa read our thoughts? And if they can, where can we hide from the shit hurricane when the Council finds out?"

Mara gazed out the window at a Tofa nurse walking slowly past, with several Twin-Bred of both species clustered around him. "We don't think it's quite that simple, or that drastic. We've seen no sign that the Tofa children can communicate with their twins — or with each other, for that matter — without any spoken language. Of course, there could be differences between the abilities of Tofa children and adults. We can keep observing the Tofa Twin-Bred as they mature — but of course, that isn't the same as observing normal Tofa adults. Though we do have the Tofa host mothers who have stayed with the Project."

"I don't think you can assume that Tofa who have carried human fetuses to term are normal."

"And the Tofa nurses and such. We've been reviewing recordings of them as well. We record everything and everyone. We haven't seen anything that looks like complete telepathic communication."

"Hmph. In your ostentatiously recorded setting, you haven't seen something the Tofa might want to conceal."

"And for what it's worth, we've also asked them whether they need words to communicate. They said yes. And some of our experts say the Tofa don't lie."

"Wouldn't it be pretty to think so."

The human Twin-Bred were tested for generalized telepathic ability with other humans. They fell within the normal variation for humans their age — except when the other human was a twin, as were several members of the staff. Results in those cases were slightly higher than otherwise. As expected, when human Twin-Bred were tested for telepathic communication with each other, their performance was substantially above general human norms.

As for Tofa norms, perhaps the Tofa Twin-Bred were normal for Tofa; perhaps they were above or below that baseline. There was no way to know.

Laura gathered her courage. One of the Tofa host mothers was right there, standing in the garden, looking across the nearest creek. She had no reason to wait.

"Excuse me. Good morning. Hello. . . . May I ask you something?'

The Tofa turned toward her, but said nothing. Laura looked up at the multicolored eyes and cleared her throat twice. "I hope I'm not disturbing you."

The Tofa made a wiggling gesture with her upper left hand. "I am not disturbed. You may ask your question."

Laura stood up as straight as she could. This must be how Veda felt — or had trained herself not to feel — when standing near all the humans taller than herself. . . . . She dragged her mind back to her purpose. "I was wondering something." She took her tablet out of her pocket and punched up a random page, then held it out toward the Tofa. "This is our language, Terran, in a form we can see instead of hear. We call it writing. You've probably seen it before."

The Tofa whistled very faintly. Laura blushed.

"Yes, I have seen it. Almost all the adult humans carry these tablets, and sometimes small packages of paper with similar markings. You were wondering whether we have something similar?"

Laura nodded vigorously. "I would have assumed that you do, because I'm so used to having things written down. But I couldn't quite see how it would work, for you. Because of how Tofar — how it works. The telepathic component. Do you understand what I'm talking about?"

The Tofa tilted her head slightly to the side. "Yes, I understand. Not everything we communicate can be written. We do not use writing as much as you seem to do."

"What about — do you ever write stories?"

The Tofa did not respond. The eyes had not changed, but somehow, Laura felt a stare.

Laura's report led to much speculation, and some heated discussions. Did Tofa have an oral storytelling tradition, or was the very idea of a story foreign to them? What conclusions could be drawn about Tofa culture and psychology from the possible absence of written literature? Did the reading of fiction spur the development of empathy, and were the Tofa inevitably lacking in that quality?

"Oh, nonsense!" huffed Wendy Jergensen, Literature Coordinator, when Henry Abuto from the Education Department suggested the latter. "Tell me that the many illiterates in Shakespeare's audience couldn't empathize with Romeo, or with Lear! Tell me that no one cried at Euripedes' *The Trojan Women* until they found a copy to read!"

"But is it likely that the Tofa have theater?" asked Carla Horn, psychologist. "Theater implies an audience. How far could the performers project the nonverbal elements of dialogue?"

Ms. Jergensen persevered. "What about storytellers, speaking to a handful of listeners around a campfire?

Mr. Abuto snorted. "Wishful thinking, Wendy! Anthropomorphizing!"

"Xenophobic jumping to conclusions!"

Carla Horn put her fingers to her lips and blew a shrill whistle, making everyone jump. "Round over! Fighters, to your corners!" The combatants and bystanders all relaxed; some laughed, some grumbled, but the subject was dropped for the moment, and everyone went back to work.

Chapter 13

KIMBALL TAPPED his fingers together, studying his diagram of confidential personnel. How best to use his operative on the Project's security staff?

The training the operative was receiving could prove useful in covering the tracks of other operatives. But that would mean knowing who the other operatives were. That sort of cross-involvement was against his own views of security. Better to have the operative give Kimball a detailed account of the Project's security procedures. And provide updates as needed.

Which would hardly keep the fellow busy. Nor was his nominal job likely to do so. Apparently, all the security staff were bored. There had been no mobs to repel, and the administrators were discreetly handling any malcontents within their borders.

Some of the human host mothers might be equally bored. The operative was a gregarious sort. It shouldn't be hard for him to make some friends. Friends who would gossip. One never knew what nuggets gossip might contain.

Laura had been sufficiently engrossed in her tablet that her soup had cooled. She took a spoonful and grimaced. The man at the next table saw her and chuckled. She looked over and smiled.

"I should know better than to bring a book to lunch. Or at least, to bring a book and then take a bowl of hot soup.

Chilled soup is one thing, but lukewarm soup isn't much fun."

The man picked up his own bowl and held it out to her. "Here — I don't really need this, with a big ol' sandwich in front of me. It's still nice and hot. And it'd end up in my beard anyway. Take it."

"Oh, no, I couldn't!" Laura waved away temptation.

"Yes, you could. And you can thank me by talking to me as you eat it." The man came over, planted the bowl firmly in front of her, and sat down. He smiled as if they were friends already.

"I'm Mannie. Well, Manuel, Manuel Jones, but people call me Mannie. You?"

"Laura Hanson. I guess I'm going to eat your soup, while it's hot." She took a spoonful. "Oh, that's nice. Thank you!"

"You're welcome. Glad to oblige. What's the book?"

Laura held her tablet out to show him. "*Last and First Men*, by Olaf Stapleton. It's early science fiction, about the human race changing in all sorts of ways, and leaving Terra."

Mannie stroked his beard, which was short and well groomed, not likely to end up catching soup. "So how much did he get right?"

"You could say he got things backwards. He has humans changing themselves pretty drastically before they ever leave Terra. We weren't so different from Stapleton's day, when we headed out. And where I am in the book, his humans are still in the Terran solar system. I don't know whether they end up leaving it."

"I guess you read a lot. Must have wasted a lot of soup since you got here." He shook a finger at her. Laura had to laugh.

"I think I've seen you around, with a pair of twins. Are you a host mother?"

Laura nodded. "My twins are Judy and La-ren. And you — is that a security uniform? What does security actually do, most of the time? If you're allowed to say."

Mannie shrugged. "Not a whole lot, to be honest. If any angry mobs show up, we'll clean their clocks. But that isn't too likely when no one knows about us. Which is part of what we do, making sure no one does know. We monitor the media outside for any signs of an information leak. We keep the security software up to date. And we keep our ears open, in case anyone's talking about sneaking off and spilling the beans."

Laura sat silent for a moment, taking this in. "So if any of us heard anything — suspicious, what would you want us to do about it?"

"Well, you could come and talk to any of us, I guess. But now that you know me, you could give me a call. We could meet over soup."

Laura exaggerated a frown. "Enough about the soup, already!"

"Seriously, though. One reason we were hired so early, years before the kids will be going anywhere, is so we could get to know the kids, and everyone here could get to know us. So you'd know you could rely on us. The more time I can spend with the mothers and the kids, the better." He pulled his face into mock sternness. "So it's your duty to the Project to have lunch with me. Often."

Laura tried and failed to keep a straight face. Laughing, she gathered her dishes and left without an answer.

Laura and Tilda sat drinking cocoa in Laura's kitchen. Tilda's twins, Mat-set and Suzie, were exploring the cottage. Judy and La-ren were acting as tour guides, pointing to games, naming toys.

Tilda sipped and sighed. "Oh, that's good. Cocoa feels so right on a cold day."

Laura gazed out the kitchen window at the lilac field and violet bushes, the raindrops from the latest shower sparkling in the sun. "My ancestors back on Terra wouldn't have called this cold. They lived where it snowed, for months, every year. I wonder what that was like. Of course, I've seen the pictures and films, but that isn't like living it. Now that would be cocoa weather!"

Tilda shuddered a bit. "I think it sounds kind of scary. Blizzards you could get lost in. And the water would freeze into ice on the ground. You could slip. I'd rather look at the pictures."

Laura sat, lost in her thoughts, for a moment longer, imagining snowflakes on a furry sleeve, breath frosting in front of her, footprints on a path. Then she shook herself and returned to the present. "I think this cocoa needs a muffin. Here, try one."

Now it was Tilda who seemed preoccupied. "I know I worry about things. I should learn to relax and enjoy life. Like my friend Mannie. He just laughs about things that would make me curl up and suck my thumb like Suzie."

Laura smiled. "La-ren was intrigued about that, the last time Suzie and Mat-set were here. For a while, he was trying one finger after another, seeing which one tasted best. It took a while —" Laura did a double-take. "Did you say Mannie? Would that be Mannie in security? Curly hair, beard, big smile?"

Tilda looked up, startled. Laura recalled a favorite picture book from her childhood, full of cute Terran animals: with her big eyes open wide, Tilda resembled the baby owl.

"Yes, that sounds just like him. How do you know him?"

"Oh, he rescued me from some lukewarm soup at lunchtime. Quite chivalrous of him. He seemed friendly."

"Yes, isn't he? And so easy to talk to." Tilda looked down at her cocoa.

"Tildie — did he say anything about his work?"

Tilda looked confused. "I don't know. I don't think so. He talks a lot about things he used to do — exciting things." Was she blushing?

First Laura, now Tilda. Or the other way round —- it rather sounded as if Mannie and Tilda had met more than once. And he'd made quite an impression. Under her breath, she recited: "She loved me for the dangers I had passed,/and I loved her that she did pity them."

"What was that?"

"Oh, nothing. Just a bit of *Othello* intruding."

Well, Mannie had said the security staff wanted the mothers and their twins to get to know them. But she was still uneasy, without knowing why.

She would talk to Veda. If there was a pattern to be seen, Veda was likely to see it. And she had a nose for secrets.

"Jealous?"

Laura waved away the question. "That's not the point. Oh, it'd be nice to think a good-looking fellow wanted my company especially — but I'd love to see Tilda have a romance. I just have a funny feeling about this."

Veda took a bite of muffin. "Mmmmm, these are good." She devoured the rest of the muffin and brushed the crumbs off her hands. "All right. Let's try to uncover what's behind your funny feeling. This good-looking security man told you that it was part of his job to get to know the host mothers."

"Yes. Well, not exactly. But he implied it, I think."

"And he doesn't seem to have said anything of the sort to Tilda."

"No. But maybe I seemed less — less easily spooked. He couldn't get to know Tilda if she knew it was part of his job."

"Are you afraid Tilda will get her hopes up? And end up getting hurt? She's a big girl, you know. A bit of a mouse, but she probably wouldn't want you trying to protect her."

Laura knitted her forehead. "It's not just that. I guess I'm not sure I buy Mannie's reasons for — for chatting with me, for getting so cozy with Tildie. I don't know enough about security to know what else it could be. I just have the feeling there's a missing piece somewhere."

Veda stood and carried their dishes to Laura's sink. She started washing them, speaking over the running water. "You could be right. And missing piece or no, it's somewhat offensive. I don't much fancy being examined under cover of friendship, or flirtation."

"Do you think we should say anything to Tildie? Or, for that matter, to any of the other mothers?"

Veda turned off the water and dried her hands on her skirt with a decisive gesture. "I do believe I'll have a word. It shouldn't take much to put them on their guard. Mannie will just have to protect the Project without our burbling all our girlish secrets in his ear."

Councilman Kimball ended the call and shook his head. After a promising beginning, his security operative seemed to be stymied. The host mothers were no longer interested in talking to him, let alone confiding in him. Ah, well. The man could still be of use. And the others might have better fortune.

Chapter 14

THE ALARM BELL broke into the various small noises of contented four-year-olds, human and Tofa, modeling electrical circuits out of colored clay. The teacher gathered his pupils together, checked the door for heat, poked his head out the door, and herded them down the approved escape route to the sunshine outside.

They milled around, mingling with other classes, chattering in their childish Terran and Tofar, while inside Project staff scurried around the corridors and checked monitors. When they found the malfunctioning alarm circuit, heads were shaken, shoulders were shrugged, a few curses were muttered or declaimed more wholeheartedly. The teachers separated out their classes and led the children back inside.

Thirty minutes later, a lab tech was startled to hear an abnormally quiet alarm bell coming solely from the classroom she was passing on her way to lunch. She ran to the door and opened it. La-ren and Judy were standing by the window, Judy's face lit with glee as their pitch-perfect imitation of the alarm bell sang forth. As the tech and the teacher watched in chagrin, the tone swelled louder: one by one, all the children joined in the chorus, interrupted by a few stray whistles.

The preschool teacher sat in his supervisor's office. The latter was clearly trying to fix on an appropriate attitude.

Her expression wavered between prim rebuke and self-important concern.

The supervisor cleared her throat in an elaborate rolling sequence. "I assume La-ren started it. The alarm bell is a good deal closer to a normal Tofa sound."

"Yes, and Judy picked it up, and then the rest. All the Twin-Bred are good at mimicking each other."

"What do you think they were trying to accomplish?"

The teacher suppressed the urge to snort; then the temptation to describe a dangerous conspiracy. "What were they up to? Nothing much. Kids that age like to mimic things, especially when there's something new. I doubt there was more than that, at least for La-ren. Judy did it because La-ren did. The others saw something fun starting and joined in. As it got louder, some of them may have thought they'd get to go outside again if they kept it up."

"And what have you done about it?"

"I told them that they'd had their fun, and now they shouldn't do it any more. That alarm bells were something to take seriously, because next time it might mean a real fire and we wouldn't want anyone to think it wasn't real and ignore it. That sobered them, or some of them. Judy almost cried."

"What about disciplinary action?"

This time he did snort, and turned it into a cough.

"Ma'am, I hope we can keep in mind that we are raising and training children who will, we hope, go out into potentially dangerous situations and to some extent take charge of them. They'll need creativity, spontaneity, and self-assurance. Nervous conformity to rules, or worse, fear of trying anything new that might be against some rule they haven't seen yet, is not what we need to foster."

The supervisor picked up her tablet and pecked out a reminder to see about the teacher's reassignment.

Mara opened the request forwarded by the Pre-Elementary Department. Another waste of time from that self-important bureaucrat! Fortunately she had heard about the incident from other channels. She keyed "Denied," and punched the send button with unnecessary vigor.

Today the twins had a different modeling assignment. They were making smaller copies of the large globe at the front of the classroom, showing the one massive continent and the scattered large and small islands in the single Tofarna sea.

"All right, children, put away your clay and form a circle for story time!"

The children hurried to comply. Story time would be special today: Jerry's host mother, Hit-ron-fa, had consented to read. A few of the adult Tofa had by now learned to read some Terran, but this was the first time that one of them would be reading aloud.

When the children were all in place, standing or sitting or leaning together as some of the Tofa liked to do, Hit-ron-fa held up the reading for the day. It was an actual book, printed large enough to be seen throughout the classroom. It was fortunate that Hit-ron-fa had an adequate number of hands for holding the book and turning its pages.

The teacher thanked Hit-ron-fa for coming, and by way of introduction asked, "Who can tell me what the title is?" He chose from the forest of hands, making the effort to find a human's; it was all too easy to call on the Tofa more often than fairness required, as their hands reached higher and obscured their human classmates'. Even if they refrained from raising several at a time.

Jamar studied the cover. "Blue-berries for Sal!"

"What's a blue-berry?" Suzie whispered to Mat-set.

"Hush. The story may explain. If not, you can ask later."

Wendy Jergensen, Literature Coordinator, stood in the corridor, just beyond the doorway, enjoying the scene. "Isn't it nice how interested the children are!" she commented to Andrew Smollen, Primary Education Supervisor, who stood beside her.

Mr. Smollen snorted, just audibly. "You arranged the reading, didn't you? I take it you consider this an appropriate fable."

"Indeed I do. Little Sal and Little Bear don't think the differences between them — or between their mothers, at least — are anything to be frightened of. They're just out there enjoying the blueberries."

"While their mothers find the confrontation frightening. Not so edifying."

Ms. Jergensen smiled. "Ask any parent, Robert. Children love stories where the children teach their parents a thing or two."

Mr. Smollen did not recall any such resolution in the book in question. But he had to admit the drawings were delightful.

Hit-ron-fa closed the book with a stately flourish. The children clapped and clapped. The teacher took the book, thanked the visitor and sent the children out to recess. Jerry did not join them. He lingered near his host mother. "Mama Fa?" He tipped his head back to look at her.

Hit-ron-fa scooped Jerry up and stood him on one of the desks. "This may be more comfortable. What is your question?"

"The book you read to us. Did you have books like that, when you were my age? What books did you like?"

Hit-ron-fa stood for a moment, buzzing almost inaudibly. Jerry wondered if she would simply turn and walk away, as she sometimes did. Instead, she picked up the book again and leafed through the pages. Then she laid it on the teacher's desk, picked Jerry up and set him on the floor. "Come and see."

Jerry followed Hit-ron-fa out the door. They crossed the playground and kept walking. Several of Jerry's classmates noticed them and stared or pointed. Would the teacher disapprove of this unscheduled expedition? Jerry put the matter out of his mind and hurried to keep up.

It had been years since Jerry had seen Hit-ron-fa's quarters. Little had changed. The windows in the prefabricated structure were still covered. On the floor was the light yellow mat, with color variations like the shadows of leaves. The scent from the lighted candle stung Jerry's nose slightly. There were no clothes, and thus no furniture meant to contain clothes. On one wall was a metal engraving of an unfamiliar creature peering out behind tall plants.

Hit-ron-fa paused in the doorway and looked up at a spot on the ceiling. Jerry could barely see the lens of a camera. Hit-ron-fa closed the door, dipped a finger in the melted wax of the candle, reached up and spread the wax over the lens. Then she took a box from the shelf and opened it, removing what at first looked like a pile of thin metal sheets. She pulled at one end and showed that it was one continuous sheet of metal folded like a thick square fan. Its surface was covered in symbols, all etched in thin lines.

"This is like your books. In some ways. It can be used to teach children about things that happened long ago, in case there is no adult available to explain them."

Jerry reached out a tentative finger to stroke the metal. "Can you read it to me?"

Hit-ron-fa put the book back in the box, the box back on the shelf. She opened the door and beckoned to Jerry. "I will take you back to your class."

Jerry followed Hit-ron-fa as slowly as he dared, dragging his feet on the mat as he headed for the door.

Mara stared at the screen, with its frozen image of the metal object in Hit-ron-fa's hands. Ron Keller from Tofa Relations and Sarah Cunningham from Linguistic Analysis waited for her reaction.

"Apparently the Tofa underestimate our cameras. Let's try to keep it that way. . . . So they do have writing. How do you transcribe telepathy?"

"Their written language must take a different approach." Sarah divided the screen into multiple parts and called up a series of images: a bull's head, a series of numbers, a black simplified silhouette of a walking human figure. "It's probably ideographic — using symbols for ideas, based on various conventions or associations. The symbols needn't have any connection to the sounds of spoken Tofar, or to whatever language components are conveyed telepathically."

Ron pounded his thigh with his fist. "Which means we could learn to read it. We have got to get our hands on that book!"

Mara massaged her forehead. "I gather you've ruled out simply asking any of them to teach us. Because of Hit-ron-fa's furtive behavior? Do we even know that's what it was?"

Ron bit his lip and released it again. "Dr. Cadell. If we assume otherwise, if we reveal what we've seen, then we could lose not just our chance at this artifact, but the chance of gathering other crucial information in the future. Please, let me set something up, some time when she'll be busy elsewhere . . . ."

"It had better be a time when all the Tofa are elsewhere. Which could be tricky. Let me know what you come up with — before you proceed. And have Security keep an eye on that camera feed until further notice."

Three days later, while Ron and his staff worked on their plans, Security informed Mara that Hit-ron-fa had removed a metal object from a box on the shelf and walked into the woods. She emerged a few minutes later without it. A guard was sent to investigate. He found a lump of fused metal in a puddle of acid.

Chapter 15

BRIAN STARED AT Veda in disbelief. He looked around the room as if searching for clues. It had changed since he first saw it, years before. Few of the expensive ornaments remained. One that did, given pride of place, was a broken vase, pieced back together with obvious though inexpert care.

"You want to get pregnant? Again??"

Veda laughed. "I know! I have to look in the mirror to be sure it's still me. But I really want this."

Brian walked over and hugged her, then stepped back. "I think I need a bit of convincing. Not about doing it, but about you wanting it. I'd hate to see you have regrets about something like this, later."

"I'll try to explain. . . . We both know I didn't get involved in the Project out of overflowing maternal instinct! We were hoping it'd help you, eventually, at the Bureau. And Daddy had his visions of breeding a ruling class. And you know I had my own — issues to work out, where the Tofa were concerned. But little by little, carrying the babies, being with them, I learned what it was to be a mother. I am a mother now. And I want to be more of one than I can be to Jimmy and Peer-tek. I want a child who's allowed to *be* a child, and doesn't have any great mission, and isn't being studied every minute." She looked self-conscious for a moment. "And I must admit, I'd rather like to have a child that looked like me a bit." She smiled archly. "*Even* more than Peer-tek does."

Brian declined to be diverted. "But what would it be like, for this child? None of the staff has young children, not yet anyway, and most of the other mothers don't have a man around. We'd be making a child who wouldn't have playmates."

"Maybe not playmates the same age — but lots and lots of older children. He —"

"Or she!"

"All right — he-or-she would get loads of attention. And there are all sorts of games and educational materials around — no one throws anything away if it was mentioned in any kind of report."

Brian pulled her close again. "Let's think about this just a little longer. And while we're at it, let's practice."

The offerings in the dining hall had expanded somewhat. In an attempt "to increase the opportunities for prandial bonding," the dieticians had been asked to find more foods that both human and Tofa Twin-Bred could consume. Some viral genetic manipulation of both species of twins had been necessary, and had required some fine-tuning. There was a close call when human Twin-Bred became unexpectedly and violently unable to tolerate oatmeal. The adjustment that solved that problem rendered a few of the children temporarily allergic to eggs. But in the end, it was all sorted out.

Dietician Julie Tran earned the undying gratitude of the Twin-Bred by inventing what everyone called Julie's Jelly. Made by boiling a Tofa-cultivated grain with pectin and combining it with chocolate and various seasonings, the jelly was so evidently satisfying a treat that many staff members took special catalysts in order to digest it.

Laura and Veda made their way through the lunch line, both eying the Julie's Jelly as the medical technician ahead of them took a large portion.

"Have you tried it yet?"

Laura reached for a dish of chocolate pudding. "I'm a bit timid about new foods, even when they're made entirely of traditional ingredients. I suppose I'll try it eventually. I assume you'll need to wait?"

Veda nodded. "No catalysts or alien grains for me these next few months! Not to mention that it looks seriously fattening. I am putting on as much weight as I'm told to, and *nothing* more."

They made their way to a table. Veda sat down with relief. "I'll be glad when I'm walking for one again. . . . I am rather enjoying the process, though, this time around. For one thing, I'm doing it entirely for my own satisfaction. Brian's all for it, after a bit of persuasion, but this little girl is *my* 'project'."

"Oh, it's a girl! You hadn't told me. How lovely. Do you have a name for her yet?"

Veda laughed. "You make it sound so simple! We've been debating for weeks. We've analyzed the character and fortunes of dozens of relatives. Brian was holding out for naming her after his Great-Aunt Betty, who supposedly never got a bad hand of cards. But I believe I've brought him around to my favorite." She smiled her most evil smile. "Actually, I like the name enough that I *invented* a relative. Dear Cousin Melanie — Melly for short — who never makes it to family gatherings, but I gave her *quite* the impressive resume."

Laura was swallowing a bite of sandwich and almost choked. "Veda, you are so good for me! I'm never going to take life too seriously with you around . . . like the way you helped me see the funny side of La-ren and Judy's little brush with the authorities."

Veda sniffed. "It was high time something reminded all these officious busybodies that the Twin-Bred are *children*. Of course they'll get into mischief now and then. They aren't going to spend every minute being test subjects and political solutions-in-training." She paused and looked down for a moment. "It took me a while to absorb that fact. But there's one thing motherhood will do for you." She smiled, a little ruefully. "It teaches you that even the best manipulators have their limits. Children have this irritating way of turning out to be themselves." She patted her prominent belly. "And now I get to learn it all over again. Please pass the salt."

The two technicians had been friends for years. Harry had helped Mike get the job at the Project. Now they were trading updates over beers.

"You hear about how one of the mamas is pregnant again? Not with twins or any such — just normal, like. Ms. Seeling."

Mike grinned. "Bit of a spitfire, isn't she? — for all she's so tiny. Pregant again, huh? I remember, before, with her twins, she got near as round as a balloon."

Harry laughed, then stopped and pointed at Mike. "Speaking of babies — that reminds me. The folks in Biogenetics finally got those Tofa host mothers to talk about something interesting. Namely sex. Except it isn't."

Mike took a swig of his beer. "Meaning?"

Harry wiped foam off his chin. "It's what a lot of people had been guessing. The Tofa don't have predetermined or differentiated genders. They aren't male or female, even when they do what we'd call female things. Like being pregnant."

"Do they care that we've been using female pronouns about them?"

"Hey, if you can tell what they care about. . . . But it gets weirder. Boy, does it get weirder. When they're not letting humans pop babies into them, you will never guess how they get pregnant."

"Ummmm..." Mike took another swig. "OK, nothing comes to mind. So give."

"Well, it isn't the birds and the bees. At least, not the birds. It's something like pollination."

"Say what??"

"They all walk around sending out these microscopic seed cells. And at any given time, some part of the adult population is in a receptive state. Which feels pretty good, apparently — sort of euphoric. When they're receptive, they can get pregnant just by *breathing*."

"Holy shit. It's like a baby plague!" Mike took a large gulp. "Ho-kay. I did not see that one coming. Would not have guessed that one. So — when our Tofa kids get older, how do we keep them from breathing in baby dust?"

"I'd say we can't. Even if we stop our Tofa from producing the stuff, they'll be going out into Tofa communities. It'll be everywhere. But that's only the first step. I'm sure we'll be able to inhibit one or more of the later stages."

"And what about the euphoria? Will they still have that?"

"No way to tell until we start tinkering."

Mike drained his mug. "Poor kids." He set it down. "Excuse me. I've got a date with some pictures. I feel like celebrating being human." He hustled toward the living quarters.

"YES!"

Siri O'Donnell looked toward the closed door of Kimball's office. Good news, obviously. She wondered if it had something to do with the latest report from one of their Project contacts. Someone in the biogenetics department.

Chapter 16

MARA THOUGHT once again of turning around. She visualized slapping herself in the face, and kept walking; told herself very sternly that she had protected herself long enough. After forwarding the reports about the singletons unread — a scientific and administrative sin — she would inflict upon herself a personal visit.

The Director of Special Programs for Unpaired Subjects, a young woman shorter than her title, came out to meet Mara, beaming. "We're so glad you're finally coming to see us! The children all know about you. They're likely to pester you for attention — but say the word and we'll shoo them away."

"Know about me?" For a moment Mara's chest went tight and she imagined some mysterious karmic force at work, betraying her via those she had betrayed.

"Know that you got the Project started, that you care so much about bringing human and Tofa together." As they entered the building, the woman pointed to a brightly painted mural of humans and Tofa holding hands and dancing around a circle. "Our kids are *big* on human-Tofa relationships. As you might expect."

Mara made a mental note to find out if any of the Tofa Twin-Bred actually danced. "I might expect some other things as well. All these children lost twins in utero. What sort of problems, and what sort of coping mechanisms have you seen?"

"Per the protocols — I understand you designed them? — they all know about their twins. We've filled in some of the details. They've learned that their mothers tried to carry human and Tofa babies together, but that something didn't work, and that one baby — usually the Tofa baby — was lost. We told them their mothers are happy that they survived and are doing so well. They don't see much of their mothers, but that's true for many of the intact twin pairs as well. Some of our chidren wish they had a mother 'like Judy's and La-ren's mother,' for example — but they don't consider themselves especially mother-deprived as a group."

"And twin-deprived?"

"We've told them that if they feel sad and miss their twin, that's natural. And that they can tell us — so we can try to cheer them up — or not tell us, just as they like. Some of them give their lost twin a name. Sinbad tried asking his mother what his twin's name would have been. She said they didn't give names before birth, so that was that. Of course, we don't really know whether that's the truth, but for our purposes it doesn't matter."

As they walked past a window, Mara could see a courtyard with a sandbox and several sets of playground equipment. It was a smaller version of the playground in the main compound. There were swings and see-saws and climbing towers, some sized for human and some for Tofa children, and some ingeniously constructed so that they could be used by either. As she watched, children spilled out of a doorway and ran to all corners of the yard.

"I'd like to go out there and observe the children in a recreational setting."

"Of course." The woman led Mara to another door. They emerged near a shaded bench, close to the playground but not so close as to attract much attention. They sat, and Mara pulled out her tablet to take notes.

She surveyed the scene. There were children who ran and shouted, and children who played quietly. A few were solitary, but most were in pairs, although one of the Tofa children had two human companions. She turned to ask how this had come about, but was distracted by a human boy and girl, approaching hand in hand. The girl, cheerful and grinning, was tugging the boy, who stumbled trying to keep up.

The girl announced herself. "Hi! I'm Rita! And this is my twin, Jerry! Hi! You're Dr. Cadell, aren't you?"

Mara nodded, bemused. Twin? "Hello, Rita. Hello, Jerry."

Rita pointed to Mara's tablet. "Are you writing about us? What are you writing?"

"Wait just a moment, and I'll show you." Mara quickly pulled out a stylus and sketched a quick cartoon of a little girl with a big grin, hand in hand with a boy with big round eyes.

Rita shrieked with delight, making Jerry jump. "It's me! It's Jerry and me! Jerry, look!" Jerry blushed and smiled.

"Can I have it? Can I have the picture?"

"If you'll go and play so we can continue our discussion, I'll send it when I get back to my office. It was nice to meet you."

"Okay! Thank you! Okay! Come on, Jerry!" Rita turned and pulled Jerry back toward the playground, stopping once to turn and wave vigorously. Jerry turned just as they reached the swings and gave a small wave of his own.

Mara turned toward her guide. "Did I hear the girl properly?"

The young woman looked confused for a moment, and then enlightened. "Oh, you mean about Jerry being her 'twin'. That's one of the adaptations we've seen. The children have rather blended the concept of 'friend' and 'twin.' They'll ask another child, 'Will you be my twin?' There are a couple of sets of what you could call 'friend triplets', but it's usually pairs. There's some shifting of friendships over time, but rather less than in most groups of children."

Mara swallowed hard. "Is it — enough?"

The woman gestured toward the playground. "On the whole, I'd say it is. We don't see children sitting and brooding very often. And none of them is clinically depressed, at least so far."

Mara watched the triad of one Tofa and two human children, who were using the swing set. The humans were on adjoining swings, while the Tofa pushed one with each of his upper hands. "Does the experience of having lost a twin seem any different for the Tofa singletons?"

"Well, the circumstances make it different. Since most of the lost twins were Tofa, the Tofa singletons are — rather in demand, you could say. They've usually been the first ones approached for the friendships I spoke of. So that's some compensation. But on the other hand, they have sometimes expressed some feelings of isolation. They know that if their twin had lived, there would be a human being that would understand them better than their human 'best friends' can."

Mara stared off across the playground until she was sure she could speak steadily. "I understand that the children's education is the same as the other Twin-Bred's."

"Oh, yes — with a few exceptions. They frequently have classes or do activities with the other Twin-Bred. Since we have so few Tofa here, we make a special effort to have those children spend time, both lesson time and recreation time, with the Tofa twins. Sometimes a few of the more independent Tofa come over here to play without their twins. We particularly encourage that, but we play host to individual human children, without their twins, as well."

Mara took a deep breath. It came easier than it had in a long time. "I'd like to see the rest of the facility. But I can already say — I'm impressed."

Chapter 17

"HENRY!"

Henry Abuto jumped. His supervisor, Mr. Fellows, stood beaming in the doorway.

"Remember back when you were a young sprout, and actually did some teaching? It's time to revisit your youth, my lad. Ms. Sinder has the galloping crud, and it's time for her class to learn about the fall of ancient Rome. Your very own lesson plan, I believe."

Henry saved his report and opened the lesson plan in question, more to give himself a moment to regroup than from any need to refresh his memory.

Of course, this was a stroke of luck. He had done his best to emphasize the ways in which inattention and complacency reduced any chance of preserving Roman civilization, to suggest the threat that could be posed by a numerically superior though technologically inferior enemy. But writing the lesson didn't guarantee an effective presentation. Now, thanks to one of the few Tofarna germs that still confounded human medicine, he could control that as well. His own feelings were another matter — but less important.

He did a double-take. "The fall of Rome? I wasn't aware that Ms. Sinder had progressed that far. And I should have been." He searched the departmental records. Ms. Sinder had apparently neglected to file the last several required updates. "While the lady recovers, she had better catch up on her paperwork. I would be better prepared to present the fall of Rome if I knew whether the — the students had

shown any appreciation or understanding of what there was
to lose."

Mr. Fellows patted him on the shoulder. "You'll find out
soon enough, my boy. But our ailing comrade is a better
teacher than she is a paper-pusher. The youngsters might
just surprise you."

Mr. Fellows got a faraway look in his eye. Henry,
suffering from stage fright and an uneasy stomach, was
unhappy to recognize the signs of imminent metaphysical
ramblings.

"Ah, Rome. So much to study, so many of the examples
of the best and worst of humanity at work — and yet, just
one thread in the vast tapestry of human history. We have
so much to teach these children! But Henry, just think of all
the history we're *failing* to teach them. No Tofa history,
Henry! What a gap, what a lack! It's such a pity Dr. Cadell
hasn't found a way...."

It was indeed ironic for Henry to be put in the position
of defending Dr. Cadell. "I gather the problem was circular.
The basic situation that led to this Project prevented the
staff from adequately communicating our need for the
teachers you describe." And a good thing too, Henry added
to himself. God only knows what sort of doctrines the
children would have been fed along with whatever passed
for Tofa history. History was a particularly fertile field for
planting political ideas. A possibility to which Henry
devoutly hoped Fellows remained oblivious.

"We could ask some of the Tofa host mothers to step in.
They may not be experts, but they have to know far more
than the rest of us. I'll write a memo." Henry had heard this
declaration of intent several times before. Fellows had
never followed through, but Henry reminded himself to
keep monitoring Fellows' output and intercept any memo
he might actually produce.

Fellows glanced at his tablet. "Great Scott, look at the
time! Off with you, lad. Gather your materials and your
wits, and get on over to Classroom D."

Henry looked around the room. Although he had known to expect it, it was still jarring to see human and Tofa, human and Tofa, one pair after another, sitting close together.

Henry cleared his throat. "I'm Mr. Abuto. I don't know if anyone has told you that your teacher is sick. I work in the Educational Planning and Analysis Department, usually, which is why you may not have seen me before — but I'm also a teacher, and I'm familiar with the subject you're studying. So I'm going to fill in until she feels better."

Up went a long thin arm. Henry pointed and the young Tofa stood up. At age six, he was already taller than a human child of eight or nine.

"Ms. Sinder would be sorry to miss our discussion. Could she join it from wherever she is?"

Henry folded his arms. "I'm afraid that won't be possible. But she can view it later, when she's able." Which meant he would need to be subtle.

Henry looked around the room. "Has everyone viewed the assigned lesson?" Human heads nodded up and down, Tofa heads to one side.

He looked the nearest human child in the eye. "We know what happened. So of course, we know that it could happen. But the Romans, or most of them — they didn't really believe it. They knew the barbarians were there; they knew there were more of them, many more than Romans; they knew there had been hostilities for generations. But they thought Rome would go on forever, that Rome could never be overcome."

He looked around the room again. "The fall of the Roman Empire had many causes, and many stages. But put in the simplest terms, Rome was overrun by Germanic tribes. By the barbarians, as they called these tribes."

Were they listening? He thought so. Henry continued.

"Now the Romans had been dealing with the barbarians for a very long time. Sometimes they fought them. Sometimes they made peace with them. Sometimes they more or less ignored them. Sometimes, in some cases, they assimilated them — let the most promising become part of their civilization." Was his language too advanced? He thought not; all the observations to date indicated that these children were precocious, well ahead of their peers outside the Project.

"All, in the end, temporary solutions." The word "incomplete" could have followed so easily; he held it back, thinking of the video record.

"Rome had considerable technological superiority. But naturally, over time, its enemies had the opportunity to observe Rome's technology in action, and to learn from it. And the emperors and elite of Rome did not concentrate on maintaining or increasing their technological edge. Eventually they lost that advantage.

"Now in the last centuries of its existence, what changed in the way that Rome dealt with these tribes? Anyone?"

The same Tofa raised his? its? hand. Henry nodded.

"In the 4th Century C.E., the Roman Army was having trouble recruiting Romans. So they started letting the Germanic tribesmen in. They would make a German warlord into a Roman citizen and put him in charge of a legion full of Germans."

Henry reminded himself to smile. "That's right. In fact, one whole tribe of Visigoths was let into the Roman army. They were supposed to fight off the Huns. Does anyone remember what happened?"

A human girl, looking tiny next to her Tofa twin, raised her hand. "They won. But the Romans didn't treat them well, and the Visigoths and the Romans ended up fighting. And the Visigoths won."

"Yes. And about ten years later, the Visigoths sacked Rome." Henry decided he'd gone as far as he could in that direction, and needed to muddy the waters somewhat. "What were some of the other problems with the Roman Empire in its latter days? They had some pretty wild characters for emperors, didn't they?" That won him a few faint chuckles and one quiet whistle. "Let's hear about a few. Anyone — who was your favorite bad Roman emperor?"

Henry remembered to call on both human and Tofa, and tried to look as if he were listening. But he was composing his next dispatch to Councilman Kimball.

Chapter 18

IF THE PROJECT had been conceived purely as a means of learning more about Tofa physiology, psychology and behavior, it would have been an avowed success well before the Twin-Bred left childhood.

Harriet looked out her window at the nearby playground. The children there were almost all human. Something had to be done to encourage the Tofa youngsters to play outside during the purple season. Unless something in the environment this time of year was actually bad for them, which would be hard to test for safely.

A knock on the infirmary door interrupted her thoughts. It must be a Tofa knocking. Their knuckles stuck up more and made a sharper sound. From the direction of the sound, it was no adult knocking. Harriet hurried over to open the door. Sure enough, it was one of the Tofa Twin-Bred. His leg was bleeding.

"Can you fix me?"

"Patch you right up. Then your body will fix itself. Come on in." The youngster followed her, limping. "How'd you do that? And what's your name?"

"I made a mistake running around the courtyard. I ran too fast around a corner. My name is Poo-lat. What is yours?"

"Harriet Gaho. Chief Nurse. You can call me Nurse Gaho, or just Nurse. When you grow up, you can call me Harriet. Up on that table, now."

The blood was a rich brown. She had seen soil that color. She wondered if other Tofarna animals had blood the same color, and whether it provided some camouflage when the animal was wounded. But surely a predator could smell the blood? She took a discreet sniff. Hard to say. The usual burnt-toast odor had an added hint of blackberry jam, but that was just how Tofa smelled when they hurt themselves, even something like a sprain with no blood showing. Of course, how it smelled to her didn't count for much.

Harriet cleaned the abrasion as gently as she could. A Tofa could not visibly wince, but he did flinch.

"So, Poo-lat. Why were you running around the courtyard?"

"We were taking turns, seeing whether the ones with long legs could get all the way around faster. We found out being taller makes the corners harder."

"Well, try and take your corners a little slower, at least until that heals up. The bandage will let air in and keep dirt and water out, so you can leave it on for a few days. It'll prevent infection as well. Have you learned about infections yet?"

"Not in school. My mother said something about them once. They make injuries worse?"

"Yes, and they can cause other problems. They used to make humans cough and sneeze, before we learned how to stop it. Have you seen a sneeze?"

"Yes. In an old movie my sister likes. It was like this." Poo-lat attempted to demonstrate a sneeze. It sounded like no sneeze she had ever heard or dreamt of, but she gave him points for trying.

"Off you go, now. Carefully!"

Poo-lat turned to go, then turned back. "Thank you for helping me fix myself." He turned again and left.

Harriet cleaned up after her patient and sat down at her desk, her mouth twitching now and again into a smile.

CLEARANCE CLASS 3 AND ABOVE

LEVI Status Report, 9-15-78
Executive Summary

. . . It has been verified that Tofa do have reactions to odors, or at least, reactions consistent with response to odor. The particulars have been, to date, somewhat unpredictable. . . .

Peggy came running up to Ren-tak, holding a handful of vanilla beans. "I'm going to help bake a cake! Don't these smell *good*?"

Ren-tak started back. "Good? *That*? I do not see you laughing. Seriously? Or are you teasing again?"

Peggy's mouth tightened, and she gave a warning sniff. Ren-tak hastily held up two of his hands. Once Peggy set to wailing, it could be the work of an afternoon to soothe her. "Please! I did not mean to hurt your feelings. Thank you for wanting to share with me . . . ."

Truth broke through diplomacy. "But really — that smells so *bad*!"

Peggy opened her mouth. Ren-tak covered his ears.

Mara ordered the dispensary to stock a wide range of aroma sticks. The dispensary chief found it hard to track down some of the varieties that appealed to Tofa senses. While both human and Tofa enjoyed cut apple, pepper, and cinnamon, and the smell of ground coffee created a passion in the Tofa Twin-Bred little short of addiction, the stick manufacturers produced only small, novelty amounts of skunk scent and methane emission.

Veda heard laughter and started to smile, then stopped when she realized there was no accompanying whistle. She went to investigate.

Jimmy was rocking back and forth on the floor, laughing too hard to speak. Peer-tek stood near him. He was wearing Veda's shower cap, Jimmy's overcoat, and Veda's bedroom slippers.

He turned as Veda came in. "You wear clothes. Jimmy wears clothes. Why does Jimmy laugh when I wear clothes?"

Veda kept her face sober with an effort. My turn to be a diplomat, she thought. "Peer-tek, honey, you don't need clothes. And you've never worn them before. Naturally Jimmy was — surprised." She gave Jimmy a furtive nudge with her foot.

"Are clothes about needing? Why does Jimmy need clothes? Why do you?"

"Well." This should be interesting. Maybe she'd end up a nudist. She could tell everyone her son talked her into it. "Humans get cold more easily than Tofa. I think. And besides — it's an old human custom, covering certain body parts. You know which. And Tofa don't have those. At least, not all the time."

Peer-tek's posture spoke of stubbornness. "I do not see why I should not wear clothes. Whether I need to or not. I see you trying on outfits. You enjoy the variety. You have fun. I want to do the same."

Veda shrugged. "Peer-tek, you may borrow my clothes, as long as you ask — which you did not do this time. And as long as you're careful with them. And Jimmy — you've laughed long enough. You're hurting your brother's feelings."

Jimmy stood up. "Aw, Peer, don't take it that way. Here — let's go find you a better hat."

They went off to ransack Jimmy's closet.

CLEARANCE CLASS 3 AND ABOVE

LEVI Status Report, 10-1-78
Executive Summary

<u>Conformity to Species Norms</u>

Some of the young Tofa have been found to be experimenting with copying human customs, including the use of clothing. It has been decided that this should be discouraged, as development of any such habit would add another dimension of difference between Tofa Twin-Bred and the Tofa with whom they will eventually be communicating. . . .

"STAN!"

Mara's assistant sighed and got up from his desk. That particular indignant bellow usually meant a problem with a status report. He brought his tablet with him, the latest draft on the screen.

"It has been decided??"

Stan called up the message. "The Tofa Relations Department —"

"The Tofa Relations Department apparently presumes that the children are idiots. Has it occurred to any of them that there can be a difference between a habit and an amusing novelty? Or that we could actually *explain* to the children that Tofa should not wear clothes outside the Project grounds? Is it for some reason essential that the twins should regard us as stuffy, overbearing killjoys?"

Stan backed out of Mara's office and started drafting a tactful memo.

<u>Conformity to Species Norms (revised)</u>

Some of the young Tofa have been found to be experimenting with copying human customs, including the use of clothing. They will be cautioned to confine this behavior to the Project environment. . . .

As the novelty faded, the Tofa Twin-Bred shed their borrowed garb, although Fin-gar retained some interest in the design of ensembles for the female humans. His fashions became quite the rage.

"Mama Laura? May I use some of your makeup?"

Laura was surprised. Judy had not shown much interest in "girly" activities. She had not realized that Judy even knew what makeup was.

"Sure, honey. Here — let me find you some that would be just right." She thought it prudent not to hand over anything too difficult to replace. "Don't get any of it on the furniture, all right? And show me once you're done!"

Judy nodded and hurried off to the bathroom with her hands full.

Laura went back to her knitting and her flute music broadcast. She had lost track of time when, half an hour later, Judy presented herself, beaming in triumph.

Laura dropped her knitting. Judy had blended every powder and liquid into a paste, somewhere between tan and khaki in color, and spread it over her face thickly enough to obscure almost every feature. Even her lips were covered.

"What in the *world*!?"

Judy was startled. "Don't you like it? I look like La-ren!" Laura thought she could detect some trembling of the coated lips.

"Oh, darling, it's just fine! It's very clever. I didn't know what you were planning, that's all. Here, let's take a picture. And then why don't you wash it off before it gets all over everything."

"I have to show La-ren first! La-ren! Look what I did!"
Off she ran to find her twin.

One thing became clear as the Twin-Bred grew. If there
was another species besides homo sapiens that made,
responded to and even required music, that species was not
the Tofa.

"Judy, why are you moving your foot up and down?"
Judy looked up, surprised. "Just listen! How can you
not?"
La-ren listened, but could find no clue to Judy's
behavior in the odd background noise the media box was
generating.
The situation grew that much more peculiar when
Laura came sweeping into the room with an unfamiliar
sideways motion, turning partly around and back again,
clapping her hands from side to side. As if things were not
strange enough, Judy went running up to Laura, and Laura
scooped her up and held her to her breast as they spun
round and round, Judy laughing with delight.
Could he somehow be dreaming? Was this what
dreaming felt like?

Mara worked on a cartoon of several human Twin-Bred
dancing ecstatically, while their Tofa twins stood nearby
holding all their hands over their sound receptors. "It's
fascinating. And no, Levi, I am *not* using that word
promiscuously these days! . . . We already see distinctly
human traits in the Tofa Twin-Bred and Tofa-like behavior
in the human Twin-Bred. But when it comes to music,
there's no crossover. The human Twin-Bred love music and

dancing as much as any children, and the Tofa Twin-Bred don't get it at all."

"Then we know not to try to win the Tofa over with campfire songs. . . . So, you'll be able to see how the twins respond to something they're unable to share."

It was Judy and La-ren's (and many other twins') seventh birthday. Laura had made their favorite cakes, and both children were pleasantly stuffed. Laura's father, Councilman Petter, had shown up for the occasion, and was watching benevolently from the one large armchair.

La-ren sat Judy down in the living room and told her to close her eyes. "Mama Laura and Grandpa Harold helped me find you a birthday present. Please wait here."

Judy sat, squirming in anticipation. Suddenly the room filled with the sound of drumming. Then a pulsing melody joined the percussion. Judy bounced up and down. She started drumming with her hands on her knees. She felt La-ren grab her hands for a moment, as something settled onto her lap.

As La-ren let go, Judy opened her eyes and saw a pair of drums on her lap, sized just right. Laura stood beside La-ren, beaming. Judy tentatively patted the drum on the left and felt its vibration on her leg. She started drumming harder and harder, laughing, jabbing her head up and down to the beat. La-ren stood over her, whistling. Grandpa Harold clapped in time. Laura tiptoed off to the kitchen to wipe her eyes.

* CONFIDENTIAL *
CLEARANCE CLASS 3 AND ABOVE

LEVI Status Report, 5-15-79
Executive Summary

. . . The behavior of the two species where visual artistic representation is concerned does not diverge to the extent of their appreciation of music. However, there are aspects of the artistic production of each species that cannot be perceived and/or appreciated by the other. These differences are greater as between Tofa Twin-Bred and the human Project staff, but exist to some extent between human and Tofa Twin-Bred. . . .

"Poo-lat, come look at my picture!"

Poo-lat obediently came and looked. He projected puzzlement. "Is that a farla tree? It is not the normal color. Are you imagining a different color?"

Sally was indignant. "It is the right color! Stevie, isn't it the right color?"

Stevie scratched his head. "Looks right to me."

Fel-lar joined the cluster of art critics. "No, Poo-lat is right. That is not the color of farla trees." He paused. "But you humans think it is. There must be a reason."

The craft room supervisor hustled over. "What's all the fuss about?"

Fel-lar explained. The man pursed his lips thoughtfully. "Well, I'm with Sally and Stevie, as far as how it looks to me. It must be because the paint is made by humans and formulated to fit their vision. Color isn't as simple as you'd think. The way we match pigments to reproduce the colors of light — we do it to fit the way our eyes process color. And apparently, your eyes and our eyes do that differently."

Sally nodded, a satisfied victor. "Then it *is* the right color." Poo-lat started to speak, then gave up and returned to his own painting.

Serena, host mother, poked her head into the rec room, attracted by the peals of laughter and accompanying whistles. "What's so funny?"

Ruthie ran over carrying the sketch pad. "Look what Jan-tel drew! See how it goes back and forth when you do *this*? First it's a chicken, and then it looks like Stevie! And then it looks like a chicken again! Stevie's a chicken, Stevie's a chicken. . . ."

Serena wrinkled her forehead. "It sounds like you're talking about an optical illusion. But I can't see it. Not the chicken part."

"Look *here*!"

Serena looked again. This time, as Ruthie pointed, she could see a tantalizing hint of a second image — but nothing clear or recognizable. "I guess it's one of your twin things. As long as you're having fun." She kissed Ruthie's forehead, blew a kiss to Jan-tel, and went back to her comfortable chair and her chat group.

Five minutes later, she was interrupted again. "Mo-om! Now he's making *me* a chicken! Make him *stop* it!" She sighed as she hauled herself back up. A mother's work was never done.

Mara was listening to music. She had done so more often of late, intrigued by the profound gulf between human and Tofa response to this stimulus. It might be worth exploring whether the Tofa would find the calm polyphonies of Bach, the atonal mathematics of Schoenberg, and the passionate romanticism of Rachmaninoff equally unappealing. She suspected there might be some negative correlation between music that humans found most emotionally stirring and music the Tofa found more tolerable.

Tonight she had chosen that most directly manipulative of genres, the soundtracks to old Terran movies. She had even left her office fairly early in the evening, so as to listen in the relative comfort and privacy of her quarters.

As the swelling choral waves of *The Mission* swept over her, it occurred to Mara that she was happy. It was a thought to be handled delicately, unlikely to survive attention, let alone examination. She left it to float somewhere just below consciousness, and sank back into the music.

Chapter 19

MELLY CAREENED around the corner and down the corridor, and plowed into long thin legs. Jak-rad plucked her up and juggled her from arm to arm to arm. She shrieked with delight. Veda ran up panting, apologetic. "I just can't keep up with her! I didn't know she'd be such a workout. Jimmy and Peer-tek weren't so *wild*!"

Jak-rad bowed to one side. "We Tofa have always been a good influence on our human siblings."

Melly wriggled to be put down. Then she held her plump body as tall as she could, stiffened, bent sideways and crowed, "We wurr uh good IN-fl-ins!"

Jak-rad whistled so loud that Melly clapped her hands over her ears.

Laura and Veda walked along the river near the woods. Veda set the pace, a brisk one suiting the still-chilly weather. Chief Nurse Gaho was spending her day off babysitting Melly: she had told Veda that she rather missed having three-year-olds running around, and wanted to take advantage of the only one currently available.

Laura, panting a bit, searched for a topic that would let Veda do the talking. "I noticed you sitting with one of the Tofa host mothers in the dining hall yesterday. Is that something you do often?"

Veda unconsciously slowed down, which suited Laura even better. "That was rather odd. I was just putting my tray down when she came up, introduced herself — Lo-ta-se, her name was — and asked if she could join me. In very good Terran. I was certainly surprised, but I didn't see why she shouldn't."

"Did you talk? What did you talk about?"

"At first, it was just chit-chat. The food, what the twins were up to, how Melly was doing. Then it was where I came from, my background. She rather led the conversation, asking questions. After a while, I decided it was time I took my turn. I asked her if she wouldn't mind telling me how she came to sign up."

"What did she say?"

"Well, she went Tofa on me, you could say. Up until then, she'd been somehow minimizing how — alien — she looked, her posture and movements and such. And she said it would be difficult to explain. Then she looked at me, quite directly, and said she was sure it would be the same for me. I wasn't sure what to make of that."

The two had slowed almost to a stop. Laura gestured toward a nearby bench, but Veda shook her head and sped up again. Laura grimaced and caught up to her.

"Then what happened?"

"Oh, we finished eating without saying much. She left first, thanking me for talking to her. Do you know, I think she — or maybe one of the others, I couldn't tell — did the same thing with Tilda the next day. I doubt they got much out of her."

"Got much? What do you think they're trying to get?"

Veda shrugged. "I imagine they want to know more about us. More than they can learn from living in this — unusual enclave of ours. They seem better equipped to understand us than the other Tofa, the ones outside — but they're *inside*, and can't observe the way we usually live. So they're doing what they can."

The two women rounded back toward the buildings. Veda sped up again; Laura, making a last effort, matched her and then pulled in front, and the two of them race-walked to the compound.

The day was warm as well as sunny, the first such day in months. Anyone who could be outside, was. In a courtyard outside the dining hall, Ra-ten-tis, Tofa nurse, stood surrounded by children. Most of the children were Tofa. The humans present were spectators: they were not equipped to participate.

Laura, passing by, recalled her childhood games of pat-a-cake. They had seemed intricate and challenging enough at the time. She had never imagined the marvelous complexity that could be achieved when each player had four hands to use. She wondered if the elusive fifth hand was ever brought into play.

As each young Tofa came forward for his turn, Ra-ten-tis would start slowly, with two hands moving at an easy speed to follow. Then the third, then the fourth hand would join the pattern, and faster and faster, while watching friends shouted encouragement, until finally the youngster would put a hand wrong and step back, whistling, to join the audience. And another would step forward, and the game would begin again, first slowly. . . .

When all the Tofa Twin-Bred had learned the first game, Ra-ten-tis demonstrated a game that a Tofa could play alone, using left hands against right. Now all the Tofa could play at once. They spread out to avoid striking each other or the human children.

Tired of standing and watching, Peggy turned to leave. Ren-tak caught her arm and said, "Wait! Watch Li-sen. Watch his left hands. You do those, and I will do the right, and we can play together."

With some false starts, and much giggling and whistling, the twins adapted the solitary game into a game for two. Seeing them, other pairs of twins dragged each other out of the circle and followed their lead.

Ra-ten-tis looked around at the excited pairs, and then at his remaining audience. He dropped his hands. "That is enough for today." Ignoring protests, he headed inside.

Passing one pair, he paused and waited for their attention. He spoke to Ren-tak.

"Why have you changed the game?"

Ren-tak looked at his twin, then back at Ra-ten-tis. "I do not understand. Naturally I wanted to share the game with my sister."

Ra-ten-tis stood a moment longer, then turned and strode into the compound.

Chapter 20

THE CHIEF OF the NivPourn police department was staring blearily at her desk. Her message device blinked frantically, telling her that it had reached its capacity.

Her deputy knocked on her open door. "Chief! And I thought I was here early. Some damn Tofa was blowing a whistle outside my house, and I couldn't sleep. Woke up half the neighborhood, I'd guess. Tried to get it to stop, but it wouldn't, and it had friends. Thought about calling in, but I decided I'd just come here in person. What brings you here two hours earlier than usual?"

The chief looked puzzled and annoyed. "That's strange. And not good strange. Something like that happened to me, too. Not a whistle — some sort of machinery. There was a group of Tofa carrying it around and cranking it. Made the damnedest racket. And look at this machine! What you want to bet that every call is from an angry citizen who couldn't sleep last night?"

The deputy put his face in his hands and groaned. "Great. Just great. This is going to get nasty in a hurry. And then what?"

The chief's prediction was correct. The reports poured in. Banging on metal. Antiphonal shouting back and forth. Attacks on chicken coops. Every odd and unwelcome kind of activity short of personal attacks, the common denominator being that they deprived the nearby humans of their sleep.

The chief rang up the mayor. He was not in his office, having tried to sleep in. The concealed recording of tearing metal, somewhere near his apartment, had shut off an hour after dawn. Chief MacDonald pulled on her coat and went to wake him up. She left her deputy to round up the borough chiefs.

The borough chiefs struggled to get their priorities, goals, ethos and tactics in order. Should they be planning reprisals? Armed conflict? Negotiation, despite the obstacles? None of these decisions, nor the decisions that would have to follow them, were made easier by lack of sleep.

B.C. Simmons plucked at the bandage where he had cut himself shaving. "Someone at the university has to be able to talk to these — people."

B.C. Nehru lifted her head out of her arms. "They've got two profs out there that claim to be experts. But the last I heard, no one had ever seen them actually *talk* to a Tofa — that is, get one to talk back."

"Then we've got to get the central government involved. What's the Council there for, if not to help out when a problem's too big for the local bodies?"

B.C. Skarsgaard looked skeptical. "Right. And we'll see how big they think our problems are. But by all means let's try it. Maureen, you're the best at talking to these types. Will you?"

B.C. Nehru nodded glumly.

"OK, then. Let's all go home and try to get some sleep."

The clangs, sirens, horns, whistles and gears started up again at noon.

The next morning, the Mayor left to confront the Council in person. He could not be expected to return that day. The others were far from sure that he would return at all until he could be sure of a good night's sleep in his own bed.

That day was the regional semi-final competition for high school marching bands. The local band's star Color Guard member suffered a concussion when she missed catching her rifle on a seven-count toss.

By Day Three, bands of enraged citizens were roaming the streets at night. Their night vision and coordination were substantially sub par. The groups of Tofa simply faded away from them and gathered again nearby. The exhausted police force had no better fortune.

During Day Four, some of the locals did catch up with a Tofa banging a metal pipe on a street lamp. The local hospital patched him up as best they could and sent him to the nearest Tofa enclave in a copter. The racket neither intensified nor diminished.

On Day Five, the Council Chairman put in a call to the Project.

Mara paced back and forth between desk and window. "It's so frustrating, Levi! They're coming to us, asking for our help, deferring to our expertise, and we've got nothing to give them. We've never seen anything like this among our own Tofa."

"And when you told the Chairman as much?"

"How could we be so unhelpful, what have they been paying for, and on and on."

"Did she have any more concrete suggestions?"

"She wants us to send the children. They're only eight! It simply isn't feasible to send them out into the world at their age, before they've been properly trained. If only this had happened a few years from now. . . ."

"Doubtless it will. Or something else equally troublesome. But back to the evils of the day. The Chairman found your response unsatisfactory?"

Mara kicked the wastebasket into the wall. "She threatened to close us down. The whole Project."

"Unpalatable choices. What will you choose?"

"To stall. Hope that whatever is happening stops happening, before we have to try. It's much too soon. But we don't have any choice, if it comes to that. We can't let them close us down. The children have nowhere else to go."

Day Six did not dawn peaceful, but the roving Tofa disappeared soon after daybreak. The exhausted humans lingered nervously for an hour or two, and then went to bed, sleeping lightly, starting at the slightest sound.

They braced themselves for the night-time cacophony. It did not come. The police made the rounds and found nothing.

Whatever had happened was over. For now.

* SECRET *
CLEARANCE CLASS 2 AND ABOVE

LEVI Status Report, 7-1-90
Executive Summary

<u>Consideration of Accelerative Techniques</u>

Due to the intermittently continuing incidents of interspecies friction, including the prolonged NivPourn incident from 5-10-90 through 5-15-90, Council staff gave consideration to, and discussed with Project staff, the possibility of applying experimental techniques to accelerate the maturation of the human and Tofa test subjects. Objections were raised on the scientific ground that accelerants would introduce a confounding variable, significantly reducing the validity and value of various data to be collected in the future, particularly where continuous data sets have been anticipated. Objections were also raised on the ground of prudence, given the relatively sparse data on the effects of the accelerative techniques. Those objecting on this ground included Project staff senior enough that the matter has been tabled for the time being.

Mara looked around the conference room. "I believe it's time to start — but we're missing a couple of staff."

The Meetings Secretary looked around. "I think everyone who's coming is here already."

"What about Ter Lo-ta-se?"

A commissary technician looked down with the embarrassment of a subordinate confronted with the failings of one of higher rank. "Ter Lo-ta-se left three weeks ago. Just packed up, thanked her assistant and walked out."

"With no explanation? Or stated destination?"

"Not that I've heard. No forwarding address, and her link is inactive."

"And of course we can't replace her. The host mothers aren't replaceable. Has anyone asked the others if they know what happened?"

The Technical Maintenance Coordinator cleared her throat. "The others are getting rather thin on the ground. It started months ago. Not all the sections had Tofa host mothers on staff, but four of the ones that did, don't. Same story — a pleasant and uninformative farewell. And most of the Tofa nurses and such have been leaving as well."

"How did I miss this? I should have known. . . . Did anyone try to stop them?"

"I gather they didn't seem interested in talking about it, and without knowing why they were leaving, no one had much chance of talking them out of it."

"And we could hardly hold them here against their will. Even if we could do it, it'd have a huge potential to blow up in our faces. Did we remind them about confidentiality?"

"I don't know. But Tofa don't seem to forget very much."

Mara felt the internal pressure that signaled Levi had something to contribute. She took a deep breath and let her mind go blank for a moment: some hint might drift in from his territory. The thought that surfaced had his flavor to it.

"Has anything changed lately in the Tofa political scene? Any shift in alliances, or any new tone in our relations with them, locally or otherwise?"

"I wouldn't have heard, unless it was something drastic — and I haven't heard about anything like that. The Tofa Relations folks might have some information."

"All right, let's get on with the meeting." Mara prepared herself to feign interest and hide her concern. She pushed the record button on her tablet, in case something was said to which she should have paid attention.

Mara sat at her desk, doodling a cartoon of a Tofa host mother striding away from a crowd of gesticulating humans. "Levi, I got your message and I'm meeting with our senior Tofa Relations man in a few minutes. What exactly are we looking for?"

"Mara, if there is ever a time when we know exactly what to look for from our Tofa neighbors, you and I will have retired on the ample pension of a grateful planet. But yes, I have a few thoughts. What makes Tofa host mothers different from all other Tofa?"

"Leaving aside the Tofa Twin-Bred for a moment — the host mothers understand humans better. Our speech, our expressions; maybe more fundamental things. They can work with us, to some extent. And the host mothers don't have the traces of human behavior that we see in our Tofa twins."

"So what might we be looking for, in Tofa relations, if the missing host mothers have returned home and insinuated themselves into Tofa governance?"

"We might be looking for — is it the dog that didn't bark? We might be looking for the absence of events, for fewer misunderstandings, even for helpful overtures. Not that it looks that way so far."

"Next question, sis: if any of this starts happening, should we be pleased?"

"Since it's your question, I assume a simple Yes is the wrong answer. . . . The host mothers didn't come to us and say, 'We can be of more use among our own kind, we can help humans and Tofa live together.' They just left, with minimal ripples. There has to be some reason for that."

"What gets harder to do if people know you're doing it?"

"Maneuvering. Manipulation. So — however smoothly things seem to be going —"

"They'll be going in directions you can't see, and didn't choose."

Mara took a moment to rest her head in her hands. Then she straightened up and opened the door to wait for her Chief of Tofa Relations.

Chapter 21

THE GRAY-HAIRED MAN with stooped shoulders was a regular at the Happy Hangout. His grumbling monologue was becoming regular as well.

"We shoulda wiped 'em all out when we first got here. The ship coulda done it. Planet woulda taken a beating, woulda been less hosp -- hospitable, but we coulda done it, and that woulda been it. Woulda been worth it."

He drained his mug and slammed it down. "Shoulda followed Hager's 3rd Law. You meet aliens and you got the edge, you take 'em out while you can. Just take 'em right out. No more problems."

The younger man at the next stool decided he'd had enough. "You're crazy, and Hager was crazy. A bloodthirsty crazy fella. They locked him up, didn't they?"

"Hager was no crazy. They railroaded the poor son of a bitch. He was smart as hell, and he told 'em the truth, so they railroaded him. He knew what he was talking about. We didn't get rid of the damn Tofa when we had the chance, and now they can spy on us and find out how to do what we can, and catch up. Then we'll all really be in the shit. And all you types will be looking around and whining and saying, "Hey, how'd we end up in this shit?' And I'm telling you how. We shoulda wiped 'em out."

"You wanta go outside and say yhat?"

"Gentlemen, gentlemen!" The bartender said a short and silent prayer to be forgiven the inaccuracy. "Let's bring it back down here. You bust each other up and you won't be able to sit straight and enjoy your beer. Now who's ready for a refill?"

Mara sat at her desk, writing and whistling.

" 'I whistle a happy tune...' That's a new one."

"Peggy wrote it. It's called Tofa Laughing."

"You could whistle almost anything and attach that description. But the name is particularly apt for this one. And it's pretty."

"I do get the occasional double-take when I whistle it. It's kind of funny."

"How refreshing, to see my serious sister messing with people's minds! Carry on. . . . By the way, we should discuss the upcoming elections."

"For Council seats? Is there anyone we can't afford to lose?"

"That depends on what our erstwhile allies might be willing to do to prevent losing. And you might want to take a look at who might be joining them."

On the news, Councilwoman Fuller pugnaciously assured the voters that she would singlehandedly put an end to the unspecified pseudo-scientific boondoggles that were all that stood between them and eternal prosperity. Evidently, she had not forgiven Mara's opposition to sending out eight-year-old Twin-Bred negotiators, or else force-maturing them into early adulthood. Mara changed the channel and found Council candidate Tunnet's ominous montage of backlit Tofa, in numbers greater than they were accustomed to assemble, followed by the brave declaration that next time, humans would not be intimidated, so long as they elected him.

Mara swore under her breath, grabbed her sketchbook and drew a quick cartoon of Fuller holding a tablet upside down and scratching her head, while Tunnet hid behind her shaking his fist. Then she closed her door, switched her phone to a secure channel, turned on her scramble field, and called the private investigator.

"Yes, good morning. I'm calling back as we agreed. I have your confidentiality agreement in hand, and I assure you I would be most unhappy if it were not strictly adhered to. I assume you received my initial retainer, and that it was satisfactory.

"Good. This job could be particularly easy, in the event that you are already doing it for other interested parties. I need everything you can find about a few Council members and candidates. I need to know information that could assist me in any future situation where persuasion is called for.

"Thank you, but I can't take full credit for what you're so kindly calling foresight. A — a consultant of mine thought it advisable. Given the ephemeral nature of political commitments, and the somewhat longer timeline necessary for certain scientific projects.

"Of course, I'll pay in full. Even if any of the subjects fails to win election or re-election. After all, there's always next time. Yes, I may have similar commissions in the future — if your performance proves satisfactory. I'll arrange a secure method of receiving your report."

She sat back in her chair. That should take care of the likely troublemakers. She wondered for a moment if she should expand the P.I.'s assignment to the rest of the current Council. But she had only so much room in her budget, and the larger the item, the harder it would be to bury it. She shrugged and went back to work.

Chapter 22

THE TWIN-BRED'S education naturally included an overview of human religions. The education department would have dearly loved to include Tofa religions, if there were any, but had been unable to extract any information on the subject from the Tofa host mothers or staff.

The human host mothers had been admonished not to complicate the planned course of the twins' instruction with religious education of their own. If any had violated the prohibition, she must have warned her twins not to give her away: none of the children mentioned any pre-existing notions as to deities or doctrine.

On the contrary, several of them seemed bewildered by the overall concept. Ms. Sinder did her best to explain.

"Human beings have an instinctive need for explanations. And beyond that, they look for ways to have some impact on the things that happen to them. Before humans developed the capacity to investigate the world scientifically, they made up stories to explain where the world came from, what fire was, what made crops grow, and so on. And if the stories included powerful beings — gods — they tried different ways to get those gods to treat them better."

Fal-lar raised a hand. "But did the gods respond favorably to these efforts? I see nothing in our reading to suggest it. If not, why did the humans keep believing the gods existed?"

"Well, sometimes, after someone prayed for rain, it would rain. That would make an impression. And if next time, the prayer didn't bring rain, the community could come up with some reason other than the god's nonexistence. Maybe the prayer wasn't good enough, or the person praying had evil hidden in his heart, or whatever. There was enough comfort in religious faith that people didn't easily abandon it."

Judy looked confused. "Why was it comforting to believe that a powerful god could keep it from raining when the community needed rain?"

Ms. Sinder sent up a half-serious prayer for guidance. "Religion isn't just about practical concerns. People — excuse me, humans — have always wanted answers to certain fundamental questions. Questions like: why am I here? What is the purpose of my life? Religions provide answers to those questions." She took a much-needed gulp from her water bottle.

Peer-tek and Jimmy looked at each other. "Ms. Sinder," said Jimmy, "We know why we are here and what our purpose is. We are here because Dr. Cadell brought us into being, in order to bring peace between the human and Tofa communities. Should we worship Dr. Cadell?"

Ms. Sinder gasped, choked, and sprayed water across her desk. La-ren jumped to his feet and ran toward her. "Are you ill? Shall I bring a nurse?"

Ms. Sinder collapsed into her chair. "No, no, La-ren, sweetheart, I'm fine. I was just — startled. Worship Dr. Cadell. Oh, no. Oh, my. We've gotten off topic here. Let's review the practices of the Terran religions you read about. Judy, can you tell me some of the ways that pre-scientific humans tried to please their gods?"

Jimmy and Peer-tek absorbed little of Judy's recitation or those that followed. As soon as class was over, they headed for one of their favorite retreats, a playroom that the Twin-Bred had outgrown and which had not yet been converted for other uses.

Peer-tek opened the discussion. "If Dr. Cadell intended us to worship her, would not the appropriate catechism and rituals be included in the curriculum?"

Jimmy picked up several long-abandoned plastic figures of Terran animals — a pig, a horse, a camel — and attempted to juggle them. "Is that really the point? Communities develop religions to satisfy their own needs. If we feel the need, it is our affair, not hers."

Peer-tek reached over and scooped the toy animals away from Jimmy, tossed them from hand to hand to hand. "Legend has it that gods can be dangerous if displeased. We should be discreet." He tossed the pig back to Jimmy and let the horse and camel fall to the floor.

"Anonymous worshippers, then." Jimmy picked up the horse and camel and tried again. "How shall we worship?"

"It would be more interesting to create dogma if we had more scope for creativity. We do, after all, know Dr. Cadell's basic nature and attributes."

"We could make offerings to our god. Some investigation may reveal what is likely to please her." Jimmy stopped juggling and looked at the animals. "Or we could experiment."

Mara's assistant stuck his head through the doorway. "It isn't your birthday soon, is it?"

"No. Not that I want people knowing when it is — but it's safe enough to say it isn't soon. Why?"

"Oh, one of the kids was asking me about things you like. I thought there might be some scheme in motion to get you a birthday present." He went back to his desk.

Mara forgot the conversation until two days later, when she entered her office in the morning to find several surprises atop the clutter on her desk. There was a stuffed animal of indeterminate species; a small vase of flowers; a cinnamon roll; and a ceramic object that might have been a portrait bust. Mara picked up the bust and examined it. It had no more facial features than a Tofa, but the shape of the head and some attempt to represent hair suggested that she might be its inspiration.

Mara cleared away a few print-outs and made room for the bust. She picked up the cinnamon roll and took a bite as she carried the vase of flowers to her assistant's desk.

Jimmy and Peer-tek sat by themselves at lunch to review the data. Peer-tek took a large spoonful of Julie's Jelly. "No more flowers. Pastry is acceptable. The success of the animal is unclear. Art is acceptable, but I am out of subjects. Our pantheon is rather limited."

Jimmy pulled out his tablet. "I found some interesting references. Many religions have rituals involving incense. Our aroma sticks could do as a substitute."

Peer-tek used his lower hands to cut up his vat-grown meat product. "And I have found a related custom that might be entertaining. Kindly go and get us seconds on the meat."

Jimmy returned empty-handed. "They said there were no more seconds. Lunchtime is almost over."

Peer-tek twiddled his lower thumbs and rubbed his cheek with an upper forefinger. "That is a setback. But service to a deity takes precedence over petty regulations. We will find a way."

The assistant cook opened the locker for some stew meat. Looking at the thick pink slabs, he wondered what real beef would look like. Then he noticed that something was amiss. He checked his inventory. Yes, he was right. There should be twice as much meat in the locker. Why was some of it missing?

Meanwhile, a security guard making his rounds near Dr. Cadell's quarters was alarmed to see flickering light outside her window. Arson? He pulled out his radio as he ran. Then he stood staring as his supervisor impatiently demanded to know what the fuss was about.

"Damned if I know, chief. But it's a mess, all right."

The mess was composed of a blazing pile of sticks, topped with charred hunks of meat, adorned with a circle of aroma sticks.

Catching movement in his peripheral vision, the guard whirled round to see a pair of Twin-Bred in the shadows, preparing to flee. "Stop right there, you! Did you do this? What the hell is going on?"

Peer-tek stood up straight with all the dignity he could muster. "Hell is not involved, officer. On the contrary. We are serving a god, not a devil. This is a burnt offering."

It was left to Ms. Sinder to explain to the twins that Dr. Cadell utterly disclaimed divine status. That she thanked them, but declined any further worship. And that they would be spending their afternoon recreation periods for the next two weeks tending the meat vats. And that this was discipline, not religious persecution.

Manuel Jones, security guard, reported the incident to Councilman Kimball in all its delicious detail. Kimball was pleased. When the time was ripe, it would be good material for propaganda. Always supposing that Dr. Bloom did not, in the meantime, make all such propaganda unnecessary. The twins would be reaching puberty soon. With luck, Bloom would be ready to take advantage of that transition.

Chapter 23

MELLY'S APPARENT normality as she grew from toddler to child, not to mention her potent charm, made an impression on several of the couples who had met during the Project, and on those few human host mothers and staff who had remained in pre-existing intimate relationships. An unspoken assumption against having "normal" children began to break down. More children were born. The pink dress and the green overalls that had been Melly's favorite clothes were passed down to the newcomers: at first, in a casual way, but then as a sort of ceremonial welcome.

The presence of younger children also provided the older ones with a financial opportunity: babysitting.

Melly jumped up and down. "They're here! Jimmy, Peer-tek, come see!"

Peer-tek scooped Melly up and planted her on his shoulders, holding her with his two upper arms. "The arrival of Judy and La-ren is hardly unusual. Or unexpected. In fact, they are several minutes late." He pulled open the door. "Welcome! Please come in and help me cope with my excitable sister."

La-ren plucked Melly from her perch and transferred her to Judy's waiting arms. "At your service."

Judy hugged Melly and set her down. "I'm sorry we're a bit late. We stopped off to pick up a few games. We weren't sure which ones you still had."

Veda came out of her bedroom, dressed to the nines. "Well, I'm off to pick up Laura. We'll see if either of us remembers how to dance. It may not be the sort of club I frequented in my misspent youth, but at least they've come up with some pale imitation of night life. . . . Good luck, you four. Buzz me if she brings you to your knees, or the equivalent."

Jimmy gave her a kiss on the cheek. "We'll take turns sitting on her. It'll be fine."

Melly charged at him. "I'll sit on *you*!" Jimmy squatted down so she could land on his knees. Veda picked up a jacket and escaped out the door, the sound of her heels receding rapidly.

La-ren put down the stack of games and spread them out on the table. "Here we are. We have checkers, Go, Junior Scrabble, Star Collector, Chutes and Ladders, Pachisi, and our Project version of Trivial Pursuit. What would you like to play, little one?"

Melly scrambled down from Jimmy's knees, ran to her room and returned with a dilapidated box. "*This* one!"

Jimmy and Peer-tek groaned in unison. Peer-tek put all his hands in front of his face. "Not another round of Candy Land. Of all the games to carry across the voids of space. I wish I knew which colonist to blame."

Judy pushed the other games aside, took the box and plopped it decidedly on the table. "I happen to like Candy Land. Melly, should we let them play, even though they're being so rude?"

Melly beckoned imperiously. "Come *on*, all of you. Play!" La-ren, radiating amusement, grabbed Jimmy and Peer-tek and towed them to the table. They played the game through three times before Melly started nodding over the board and finally let Judy and La-ren take turns carrying her off to bed.

"Mama Veda?"

Veda turned. Jimmy had an odd look on his face: somehow forlorn. "What is it, honey?"

"Mama Veda, please tell me about pets."

Veda sat on the sofa and patted the cushions. Jimmy came and sat beside her. She wished he would cuddle up against her, the way Melly still did.

"What do you want to know?"

Jimmy scooted toward her, just a little. "Some of the books you read to Melly — they talk about dogs. And cats. But dogs seem the most rewarding. Do they really play with you, and follow you around, and wait for you to come back from places?"

"Yes, honey, they do all that. And they kiss you — in their own way. They lick you with their tongues."

Jimmy wrinkled his forehead. "I don't know if I'd like that. It sounds — strange."

"Anything's strange when you're not used to it. You must have learned that."

"Did you ever have a pet?"

Veda sighed. "I was almost grown by the time people could have pets. There were other animals we needed more. Some people think we made them too soon." She smiled wryly. "I heard that someone on the Council really, really wanted a kitten. I don't know if it's true."

"But you've seen some. Dogs or cats."

"Yes. My father was on the Council. Pets were more common where we lived. . . . Cats are rather nice, too. At least, they're fun to watch. They seem to feel important, most of the time — except when they get excited and act like babies." Like the Council, she thought. On both points.

"Why don't we have any pets here?"

"I don't know, honey. The Tofa don't seem to keep pets. Not that we've seen, anyway. Maybe Dr. Cadell and the others didn't want to complicate things."

"One of the books I read — the boy's dog died. He was very, very sad. As if someone he loved had died."

"People do love their pets, honey. Pets are sort of like family."

Jimmy was silent for a moment. "So humans can love an animal that isn't human, and feel as if it's family. And we don't know whether Tofa do."

Was she being called upon to defend the Tofa? "That's right — we *don't* know. So let's not go jumping to conclusions."

Jimmy shrugged and got up. He headed for the door and then stopped. "Mama Veda, maybe when we're older, and we've changed some things — maybe we can get you a puppy. You'd like that."

The dear boy. Veda swallowed hard as Jimmy turned and left the room.

Chapter 24

THE SOCCER GAME was tied. Mahmoud O'Mara turned and smiled at Julie Tran, bouncing on her toes and pumping her fists. "Enjoying the game, are we?"

She tossed her head. "Go ahead, laugh! But I do love a close game! I was a pretty mean goalie back at school. In fact, as of this week, I'm one of the coaches."

"Good for you, then! Was adding soccer your idea?"

"I wish I could take the credit. It was actually Dr. Cadell. You wouldn't take her for a sports fan, and maybe she isn't. But she said it was just logic. When you've got players with different numbers of arms, you've got to find a sport where arms don't give you much advantage."

Mahmoud watched the Tofa racing up and down the field. "Still helps to have long legs. Look at 'em go!"

La-ren shouted in excitement. Judy had just scored a goal.

Julie pointed in La-ren's direction. "It's nice the way the twins cheer each other on. As a rule. Jimmy and Peer-tek can get pretty competitive with each other, when there's a game on. We're experimenting, putting them on opposite teams one day, and on the same team another day. It'll be interesting to see how it works out."

"I'd still like to see some basketball around here. Besides what the teachers play." Mahmoud shifted his feet back and forth as if dribbling the ball. "Maybe we can come up with a Tofa version. Two or three balls in play at one time. It won't hurt for the human kids to sit and watch once in a while."

"And the Tofa can watch when the human Twin-Bred learn to dive. None of the Tofa seem very keen on diving. Something about where to put their arms."

Peer-tek evaded three defenders and sent the ball flying toward the goal. Fel-lar leaped to block it, but the ball sailed in.

Mahmoud applauded. "And it's tied again. I hope you weren't betting on much of a point spread."

Julie wrinkled her nose at him. "Go on, you. I've got better things to do with my money."

Mahmoud's smile faded. "Here? Like what?"

Julie turned and watched the game.

The children stood, if their restless shuffling and leaning and whispering could be called standing. They were unused to separating into human and Tofa groups. Some sidled toward the other group as if the attraction between twins were too great to withstand.

Ms. Wilson clapped her hands for attention. "Now then! We're going to do a very important exercise. And it should also be a lot of fun. So listen up!

"You all know that when you're older, you'll be going out into the world, to try and help groups of humans and Tofa understand each other. Much of the time, you'll be coming into situations where Tofa are upset and humans don't know why, or vice versa. So that's what we're going to try today.

"Larry and Til-sal, you step out of your groups and stand together. You'll be the first to play the role of a mediation team. All the rest of you will get a turn another time."

Larry and Til-sal left their groups and stood holding hands. Larry looked relieved; Til-sal seemed more nervous about the task ahead.

"Now, this first time, we'll have the humans doing some activity together, and the Tofa will try to stop it. First, let's have the humans decide what you're going to do together.

When you've decided, go over to the empty part of the room and start acting it out." The children formed a huddle. There was much excited whispering, and some giggling. After a few minutes, the huddle broke and they streamed over to the other side of the room. With exaggerated movements and broad grins, they mimed the construction of a building. Some hammered; some sawed invisible wood; some laid imagined bricks one on top of another.

"Okay, now it's the Tofa's turn. Get together and decide what's wrong with what the humans are doing, why it's upsetting to you. Then go and make trouble!" She thought better of her phrasing. "Don't get too excited, you don't want anyone to get hurt. Just go and interfere enough that they can't work around you."

The Tofa children stood in a circle like a copse of trees, heads leaned toward each other. After a consultation notably quieter than their twins', they formed into ranks and advanced upon the builders. Poo-lat took firm hold of Stevie's hammer. Li-sen calmly began dismantling the wall of bricks.

"Okay, I'll be the sheriff." To a chorus of muffled giggles and whistles, Ms. Wilson stomped over and stood with her hands on her hips. She slapped her forehead dramatically, shook her finger at the Tofa, and then whipped out her belt phone and punched in a number.

"Larry, Til-sal — I've just called the Project, and they sent you out. Someone make a noise like a helicopter!" Poo-lat obliged, to the applause of his classmates.

"All right, team. Go to work!" She stepped back and yielded the stage with a flourish.

Larry and Til-sal looked at each other, clearly at a loss. Ms. Wilson suppressed a smile. "Would you like me to give you some hints?" Both of them nodded, in their different directions.

"Larry. Do you think you'd do better talking to the humans or the Tofa? Remember, these aren't Twin-Bred."

Larry shuffled his feet and said, "I guess I'd start with the humans."

"Right you are! And Til-sal, what about you? Would you go with him, or would you talk to the Tofa?"

Til-sal's posture suggested stubbornness. "I believe you want me to go talk to the Tofa. But I think we should go together and talk to everyone at once."

"Hmmm. Stand aside for a moment, over there. I'm going to talk to the two groups." Ms. Wilson beckoned the builders and protesters closer. She murmured to them for a few moments, then stepped back. "All right. Give it a try!"

Larry and Til-sal came back, once again hand in hand. As they approached, all the other children immediately started shouting, the humans in Terran, the Tofa in Tofar, pointing and shaking fists. Larry looked ruefully at Ms. Wilson. He held up his hands. Then he spoke as loud as he could without seeming to yell — in Tofar. "Silence, please!"

His choice of language caught the children by surprise, and the hubbub subsided. Before it could resume, Til-sal spoke in his most careful Terran. "Please let us be of service."

Ms. Wilson rubbed her chin. Almost inaudibly she said to herself, "Well, what do you know." She pulled up a chair and sat down to watch as the mediators calmed the humans and coaxed the Tofa into revealing their secret. Apparently all the construction had sloshed the water in the Tofa's giant bathtub.

The humans apologized. The Tofa were gracious. Then everybody went back to the bathtub and jumped in. Much imaginary splashing ensued.

They were reluctant to move on to their calculus lesson. But Ms. Wilson insisted.

The next lesson, it was Rose and Fel-lar's turn to mediate. Til-sal was allowed to decide the Tofa activity, which proved to be fishing in the river. Larry chose the reason for the humans to interfere. The interference got rather too enthusiastic, and Li-sen ended up with a sprained finger.

Acting on Ms. Wilson's instructions, the human crowd took no interest in a Tofa trying to speak Terran; and they refused to explain to Rose what they insisted should have been obvious to any right-thinking human. Rose and Fel-lar returned, crestfallen, to Ms. Wilson and asked for guidance.

"Not so easy, is it?" she said, in a tone of some sympathy. "You'll need to bring more in your bag of tricks. And we'll all be learning about it. But it'll take some time."

Now that Henry Abuto was teaching full-time, he was busier than ever, fine-tuning lesson plans, grading papers. He sometimes resented the way the work encroached on his evenings. But the biweekly discussion groups were different. Sharing his favorite historical fiction with eager youngsters was a joy, an indulgence.

He had not expected any Tofa to join. At first it was hard to lose himself in literary discussion with aliens present. But uneasy as it made him when he drew back and contemplated, he had gotten used to them. He could hardly help it, seeing so much of them. And some of them, he had to admit, were passionate and perceptive readers.

A knock on his office door scattered his thoughts. It was still his habit to keep the door closed, although he rarely seemed to work on confidential matters these days. "Come in!"

The visitor was a Tofa Twin-Bred. He was wearing the usual Tofa rain cape, leaving his arms free to move, and his tablet was in its waterproof case. H announced his identity, as Henry had asked the Tofa students to do. "La-ren."

Henry motioned him in and gestured toward a convenient corner where La-ren could lean. "Is that a suggestion for the group?"

"It is. I propose that we read this book. *Diary of a Young Girl*, by Anne Frank. It is an absorbing and moving tale. And I thought we could explore whether a girl in her circumstances would in fact retain the belief that 'people are really good at heart.'"

Henry was confused. "But La-ren — we read historical fiction. That is autobiography."

"Autobiography? You mean — the Anne in the book —"

"Anne Frank who wrote the book is the Anne Frank who lived it. It started as her diary. When she thought the war would be over soon, she edited the earlier portions, in the hope it would be published someday. As it was, though she did not live to see it."

"I thought — I thought the name — was a rhetorical device."

La-ren was no longer leaning in the corner. He stood very straight, and then started to rock, swaying forward and back, humming softly. Henry had heard of this before and discounted it, but now he believed: the alien child was crying.

Henry sat and waited for La-ren to gain control of himself. An idea struck him, and he pulled his tablet to him and called up a file.

"La-ren — you might be interested in this. It's Anne's original diary, before she rewrote it. It's quite interesting. In a way, it's more impressive than the diary as published. You can see how she grew, in those two years, from a thoughtless and carefree little girl to the young woman whose voice has captivated so many."

La-ren had stopped swaying. Silently he held out his tablet. Henry touched the tablets together to transfer the file.

"And La-ren — you have your answer. It was possible for her to believe in goodness, even with all the evil she saw around her."

La-ren tilted his head in the sideways Tofa nod. It no longer troubled Henry as it once had. "I will remember that. When we are older and go out into the world, we may see much disturbing behavior. I will try to keep in mind the possibility that Anne was correct. Thank you, professor."

La-ren turned and left. Henry sat staring at his desk for a long time.

Chapter 25

SIRI O'DONNELL was accustomed to calibrating her curiosity. She might be Kimball's confidential assistant, but it was his prerogative to set the limits of that confidence.

It was, nevertheless, unusual for him to exclude her from the details of a long-running operation. She had assumed that sooner or later, Kimball would choose to tell her what he was trying to achieve by inserting moles in the LEVI Project. It was certainly later. Kimball had been re-elected twice. One of those campaigns had been a close one. He might have wondered if his opponent would dig up any of his covert activities, or what would become of those projects if he lost. He might have talked to her about such things, some late night as they sat running poll numbers and calculating tactics. He had not.

It was becoming difficult not to speculate about just what was going on.

Siri heard the buzz of the secure phone line. She shook her head as if to dispel inappropriate thoughts, and took the call. It was Dr. Annabelle Bloom, Kimball's contact in the Project's biogenetics department. No visual, but Siri could hear her excitement as she asked to speak to Kimball immediately.

"The Councilman is out of the office, Dr. Bloom. He is due back in approximately three hours, and should be here for another two hours after that. Can you call during that time, or should we set a time later in the week?"

"I can't call back today. And believe me, Kimball is going to want to hear about this as soon as possible. And not just on the phone. He's going to want a written report this time. I have one ready, and I'm going to send it."

Siri frowned. "I'm not sure —"

"Damn it, this can't wait! It's fully encrypted, of course. And I have the secure address to send to. Tell him to get all his questions ready for my next call. This time next week. Believe me, he'll be there, if he has to blow off a stadium full of voters to do it."

Dr. Bloom ended the call before Siri could respond. Moments later, she heard the ping as the file arrived.

Sighing, Siri called up the appropriate phone log. She was about to enter the time and caller when she paused. This might be her only opportunity, after years of waiting. Could she really ignore it and wait for who knows how much longer?

Siri had never found it necessary to inform Kimball of her own expertise with decryption software. Or with using software and hiding all traces of its use. Even a confidential assistant had a right to a few secrets of her own.

Siri closed the office door, set the scramble field, and got to work.

Kimball called out cheerily to Siri as he came through the door. It took her a beat longer than usual to respond. She didn't seem quite her usual imperturbable self.

"Siri? Is something wrong? Family troubles?" She had a large extended family from whom she normally kept her distance, but occasionally some domestic storm would grow large enough to engulf her.

Siri's smile seemed forced. "Yes, sir, I'm afraid so. It's nothing important. I'll be sure not to let it affect my work. I'm sorry."

Kimball waved away her apology. "To work, then. Any calls? I expect Dr. Bloom checked in?"

Siri nodded, looking down at her tablet. "Yes, per usual. Nothing special to report. She'll call at the same time next week, if she can."

Kimball picked a leaf off a plant on Siri's desk and twirled it. "I'm rather hoping for more from her. It should be soon. Well, we've both been at this game long enough to learn patience, haven't we?"

Siri hesitated a moment. "Yes, sir. You would think so, sir. Councilman, I believe I've gotten everything done for tomorrow. Would it be all right if I left a bit early? I am a little distracted just now."

"Certainly, my dear. I'll see you tomorrow morning. Tell the uncles and cousins to work things out. I can't do without my Siri — at full capacity. Until tomorrow, then." Kimball went on into his inner office and closed the door.

Siri wandered through the large park in the center of the city. It was called Central Park, a name she found unoriginal, though she understood it to be a historical reference of some kind. It was unusual in containing both benches for sitting and stands for leaning, and picnic tables both low and high. A river cut diagonally through the park; the bridges spanning it had elaborate metal handrails with three alternating heights.

It was good weather for walking, for lingering, for playing, for an early outdoor supper. The slanting sunlight turned the yellow bushes lining the walkways into glowing gold. Siri climbed a hill commanding a view of a larger river. A single Tofa sailboat was just visible, the sun catching its multiple small sails.

Siri descended and walked onto one of the bridges. She stood and watched as three Tofa children played a game of tossing pebbles. It looked like the old game of Tic-Tac-Toe, but more complex. She moved on, then stopped again near a group of adult Tofa using one of the tall picnic tables. The Tofa nearest to her was telling a story, gesturing with three hands and holding some sort of vegetable stalk with the fourth. The others were whistling in appreciation.

Which of them would die, when Dr. Bloom's — when Kimball's — plan came to fruition? And which would survive, for a time, but irretrievably sterile?

It was such an ironic scheme. Use the Tofa Twin-Bred, born to bring peace, as bringers of death. Use their spores, the seeds of new life, to put an end to life present and future.

Siri had been party to extreme measures before. She had, not long since, helped Kimball procure substances lethal to humans, substances that would not be detected in any normal autopsy. She knew he had found other ways to deal with Tofa who posed — he believed — some particular threat. And of course, she had known for years that he disagreed with that long-ago decision to settle an inhabited world without removing its inhabitants. She had not considered it necessary to judge that view. It was a matter of history. She need not agree with her employer on whether history was regrettable.

History. She remembered lessons about cultural clashes that had ended in the near obliteration of one culture and its people. As she recalled, it had been accident as much as intention, or more so.

And now she had one week, at most, to decide whether her inaction, her obedience, her competent job performance, would kill or sterilize every Tofa on the planet.

Kimball was relieved to hear Siri tapping away on her tablet as he entered the office. She had been absent the day before, for perhaps the second time in all the years he had employed her. He hoped the annoying family fracas was at an end; he had become almost dependent on her efficiency and intelligent anticipation of his needs.

"Good morning, sir. I'm so sorry about yesterday. I found your notes, and I'm getting everything updated. I've made tea — shall I bring some in to you? Oh, and I stopped on my way in for some pastry. Orange and cinnamon rolls. If you'd like one."

Kimball was in no great need of tea, but he did not want to reject her gesture. And it would go well with the pastry. "Yes, thank you, Siri. You spoil me. It's good to have you back."

Siri said nothing, but rose to pour the tea and fetch a plate for the pastry. She placed them on his desk as he hung up his hat. She left and closed his door, considerate as always.

Henry Abuto had not been watching the news. He was confused, at first, by Siri's reception of his monthly call. She had not had to explain before: the others had known already.

"Yes, Mr. Abuto. A great shock. It was just three days ago. He came into the office, sat down at his desk, and had a stroke. There was nothing anyone could do — too much of his brain was irretrievably damaged. I've been here almost nonstop, ever since, getting his affairs in order, handling loose ends — but you don't want to hear about me.

"Yes, of course I know that you've been reporting to him in a confidential capacity. I hope you won't mind my saying — the Councilman had the impression, lately, that you'd rather lost your enthusiasm for the job. Yes, he was a very perceptive man.

"It's really quite simple, Mr. Abuto. Mr. Kimball never involved anyone else on the Council, or on its staff, in his, ah, side projects. They're over, Mr. Abuto. All of them. You will receive a proper severance amount — in fact, it's already been deposited in your account. And I wish you, and your students, the very best."

Siri hung up. That made all of them except for Dr. Bloom. Could she afford to wait? If Dr. Bloom was as oblivious to news coverage as her colleague, it might be dangerous to delay. She turned on the news. The story was playing again, complete with the expected ponderous tributes from the dead man's political allies and enemies.

Siri was relieved to see the call coming in, only moments after the broadcast moved on to other matters.

"Dr. Bloom. Yes, it's terrible. We're all devastated. I was thinking of calling you, to make sure you'd heard the news.

"Yes, I believe Mr. Kimball did read your report, the day you sent it. In fact, he was working on a response. Yes, in writing. It would be encrypted, of course, and it might not be complete, but under the circumstances, I'll send it at once. Yes, he did give me some general idea of what was in it. It seems he'd changed his mind about something. He was telling you to stop work on some special project. Yes, to stop altogether. And to destroy all notes and materials.

"What was that? Doctor, I really don't believe he'd go to the trouble of writing a reply contrary to his actual intentions. It's not as if anyone else would be in a position to read it. I believe he didn't want to wait for the next opportunity to speak on the phone. He had me standing by to send what he'd written as soon as he finished.

"Oh, Dr. Bloom, I hope you aren't thinking of carrying on, in spite of his decision. That would be — I have to say, that would be disrespectful of his memory. And, if I may speak pragmatically — you know, don't you, that he had other, ah, operatives on the premises? I believe there was one whose standing orders were to ensure that all the others adhered strictly to his instructions. And yes, that operative called just a little while ago. He or she — I'm sorry, I can't be more specific — is aware of the Councilman's last request where your work is concerned. I really wouldn't take the chance of ignoring it.

"Yes, of course. Given how close you were, it's only fair that your final payment should reflect your status. It's already in your account. Do keep in touch, Dr. Bloom. Especially if you decide to leave the Project. Mr. Kimball would want me to make sure that you were well provided for. In fact, he left a fund for just such purposes. Until then, Dr. Bloom. Take care."

Siri hung up, reflecting that it was just as well that Kimball had not been quite so thorough as she had suggested. She would do her best to keep tabs on the good doctor. And if Bloom left the protection of the Project, Siri would find her and bring her a housewarming present. Including tea.

Part Two

Chapter 26

CHIEF NURSE Harriet Gaho looked around at the adolescent Twin-Bred crowding into the room. They were more or less evenly mixed, human and Tofa. Many were there with their twins, but some had come separately, or were singletons.

"All right, everyone, let's get organized. If you've come from outside, hang up your slicker or your cape over there, and try not to sprinkle everyone else." She waited for the chaos to subside. "Now, then, let's get started. First, I want to hear from you what you hope to get out of this class. What good is first aid training? Oh, and say your name first."

Poo-lat was the first to raise a hand. "Poo-lat. I have never forgotten my first visit to this infirmary. I found it fascinating. I wish to learn as much as I can about medical science."

Harriet's mouth twitched. "Well, this will be a pretty humble beginning, but talk to me later about what else you can study. Next?"

A human hand this time. "Jimmy. If I can do something for myself, I don't have to find someone else to do it for me. So why not learn?"

"Peer-tek. I am here to prevent Jimmy from gluing his hands together." A brief scuffle, quelled by a stern glance.

"Anna. If we're out on a mission and one of us gets hurt, it would be best if we could help each other, without depending on others."

"Peggy. I wasn't going to come, but I cut my finger a few minutes ago in art class, so I was heading here anyway." A murmur of laughter and whistling.

"All right, then. Peggy, come up here and show everybody your finger. Let's get started."

Ms. Wilson's Diplomacy class was ready for a more advanced lesson. At least, she hoped so.

"We've had many lessons and practice sessions about coming into a conflict situation and finding out the cause of the trouble. Now it's time to start solving the problem once you've identified it. What's the one thing that defines the right solution? Who's done the reading?"

A forest of hands rose up. Well, after all, they were a motivated bunch. She pointed to La-ren.

"The right solution is the one that everyone can live with. That addresses everyone's underlying concerns to an acceptable degree. Otherwise, there is only the illusion of a solution. Because it won't last."

If only the text had summed up the matter so neatly! "That's right. A 'solution' that unravels a week or a month after you leave is no solution at all. Jimmy — is La-ren saying that everyone has to be happy with your solution? No, don't look at Peer-tek."

Jimmy chewed his lip, then grinned. "Can I look at La-ren, then?"

Ms. Wilson let the children laugh for a moment. "All right, then, back to you, La-ren. Is that what you were saying?"

"Not exactly. We may not be able to make everyone happy. The goal is not to leave anyone too unhappy."

"Just so. And now I want all of you to get your tablets out. Assume that your proposed compromise involves a change in the times that humans and Tofa will fish in the town's biggest river. Whom do you need to convince, and how might you go about doing it? Write for fifteen minutes, and then we'll compare ideas. I'll be right back."

Ms. Wilson felt the need for a moment's privacy. She walked rapidly down the hall to the lavatory and leaned on the sink, looking at her reflection. It was smiling. It looked, perhaps, a bit intoxicated.

Ms. Wilson and her reflection pumped fists in the air. After years of preparation and preliminaries, they were finally getting somewhere.

Ms. Jergensen, Literature Coordinator, and Mr. Smollen, now elevated to Secondary Education Supervisor, were having another discussion.

"I noticed that your latest list included the novel *Adam Bede* by George Eliot. Please explain."

Ms. Jergensen tried to look neither annoyed nor guilty. "Well, it's one of a number of possibilities I reviewed to give the youngsters practice at inferring the mores of an unfamiliar culture. Much of the plot turns on a prohibition against premarital sex, but nowhere is that rule explicitly stated. There's also some useful discussion of class distinctions, which isn't something the Twin-Bred are familiar with first-hand."

Mr. Smollen peered at something on his tablet. "One of a number of possibilities. It certainly is. And why did you choose *Adam Bede* in particular?"

Ms. Jergensen had hoped she would not need to offer this explanation. She thought she knew how it would be received, but she soldiered on.

"*Adam Bede* presents a theme I thought the children needed to consider: that in the end, good intentions matter less than actions. That actions can be irrevocable."

"Or to amplify somewhat: that one misguided act can doom the actor as well as innocent parties. You needn't look surprised that I actually know the work in question. I do not owe my present position entirely to political skills."

Ms. Jergensen was glad she was not given to blushing.

"Ms. Jergensen, we are sending our young people out to meddle in others' affairs, with what is — despite our best efforts — a necessarily inadequate preparation. They will do their best, and sometimes they will be wrong. That is already a sufficiently daunting prospect. Do you wish to terrify them into utter paralysis?"

Ms. Jergensen forced a laugh. "I think you're overestimating their susceptibility."

Mr. Smollen stood and ushered her out of his office. "It is my assessment that governs. Find another book. You might try *Pride and Prejudice*. In which errors may be corrected and sinners may be somewhat protected from the consequences of their sins."

Chapter 27

MARA WALKED THROUGH the dormitory on her way back from lunch. She passed a Tofa standing at a desk in one of the study nooks, reading a textbook about chemical compounds and their uses. She could not always identify the Tofa Twin-Bred when their human siblings were absent, but she thought it was Sel-ran, Lao-tse's brother.

Sel-ran looked up, saw Mara; stared in her direction; then smiled broadly, despite the lack of lips or cheeks.

"Mara mia!"

Mara stopped breathing and for a moment of panic could not start again. When the air came back she gasped for it, then looked around wildly for some stable support. Finding a pillar, she stumbled to it and clung to it as an anchor. The young Tofa was looking at her; despite his minimal features, he bore an expression both concerned and sardonic, a familiar expression though she had never seen it.

After two tries, she was able to speak. "Is there the remotest chance that I'm neither asleep nor insane?"

Sel-ran shrugged — her father's shrug. Then another moment of staring. His face resumed its expected absence of expression.

"I do not understand your question. When my human brother sleeps, he does not walk and talk. I have heard that some humans walk and talk while sleeping. I do not know whether you walk and talk when you sleep. I do not know what insane means."

"I saw a human expression. You spoke to me the way —
in a way you couldn't have known about. You moved your
body in a human gesture."

Sel-ran blinked slowly twice — this time, the Tofa
equivalent of a shrug. "There was contact; it ended."

"There was contact!? How was there contact? Did you
make it happen?"

"An interesting question. I have no answer. Is it a
matter of concern?"

Mara ran to her office, ignoring curious glances and
stares. She slammed the door and leaned against the
window sill, panting. "So talk to me. What in hell, what
amazing thing just happened? Levi! Are you there? TALK
TO ME!"

"Sorry, sis. I think I'm speechless. Hey, take it easy.
Don't cry. You haven't cried in years. I'm not used to it any
more."

"And I'm not used to — I'm not used to seeing YOU! In
an alien child! And I said they couldn't read minds! But
nothing like this — I mean, nobody's talked about the Tofa
spilling their secrets. And even if they wouldn't, because
after all, it's about secrets — with all the monitoring, we'd
have seen it by now. We'd have seen evidence that the
children were poking about in people's heads."

"Mara, isn't it obvious?"

"I'm not the only twin. We have several staffers who are
twins. We looked for them, gave them hiring preference —
as long as we had a place for both of them."

"Which makes it highly likely you're the only one here
who has lost a twin. It may be the combination — the
twinship bond, and the void that should have been filled."

"What will I do if Sel-ran tells someone? Or if someone
checks that monitor feed?"

"If anyone asks questions, you can say that Sel-ran
somehow tapped into a dream you had. That'll keep them
busy, and it isn't far from the truth."

"Far enough to waste people's time. And corrupt the scientific process."

"We're borrowing trouble, Mara mia. But if it comes down to it, you'll have to decide whether your credibility and possibly your position here are more important, scientifically and every other way, than any distortion of the data. Besides, it's possible that the researchers would actually learn something from following it up. You can pull rank and plead schedule to stay out of it yourself."

"I'll still worry."

"Naturally. You're addicted to worry. It may as well be about something this interesting."

For the next two weeks, Mara attempted to bury herself in her work. There was certainly plenty of it. She caught up on administrative tasks, and then invented new ones. She dropped in on various departments, heard progress reports, solicited complaints.

One morning, she found herself gazing out the window with no memory of how long she had sat or what she had seen. She looked at her desk and saw the drawing she had made, in the sketchbook she did not remember opening: a young Tofa, with human facial features where blankness should be, and a sardonic expression.

She tore the drawing out, crumpled it into a tight ball and stuffed it deep in her wastebasket.

"Mara? Isn't it time for your call with Dr. Tanner?"

"I canceled it. I just sent a message — I didn't talk to him. I don't know what to do, Levi. It's been hard enough, carrying on when I can't give him details of what happens in my life. This — even if I could talk more about the Project, even if he knew about the Twin-Bred, I'm not sure I could tell him what happened. With Sel-ran."

"Yes, you could. You trust him. Deservedly."

"But anyway, I can't. There's no way to tell him anything meaningful without the details, this time. And if I can't talk about something this big, there isn't much point any more. But I have to figure out what to say to him. I owe him a decent explanation. I don't want him to think I've stopped respecting him as a doctor."

"I think Dr. Tanner is tougher than that. What you do owe him is a decent goodbye. He cares about you — being one of the few for whom you've made that possible."

"Got any suggestions?"

"Truth, when feasible, is sometimes less complicated than spinning a tale. Tell him that something important happened, and that you can't tell him enough about it. That you're OK, and you'll be fine, even though you wish you could go on working with him. And that I'm here as his man in the field, to pick up the pieces when necessary."

"I may do just that."

She took a deep breath, another, and another, and then reached to connect the call.

Chapter 28

MARA PAUSED on her way into her office to talk to her assistant. "Well, we lost our last Tofa host mother. Hit-ron-fa."

"She stayed quite a bit longer than any of the others."

"Yes. She seemed content here. And she spent a fair amount of time with the children. She even seemed to take an interest in the child she carried — the surviving human, of course."

"How is the child taking it?"

"He's sad. His best friend — his 'twin' — is doing her best to cheer him up, and the other children are trying to help."

"What do we know about why she left? Or why she stayed until now?"

"What do you think? Not much, naturally. But she apparently made a cryptic comment or two. Something about wishing she had choices."

"Dr. Cadell? We've got a Tofa delegation outside the administration building. A big one."

The tech looked sick to his stomach. Mara switched her monitor to the security feed and selected the entrance to the administration building. "Big by their standards, but not by ours. Hmmm. I wonder if the size of a typical Tofa crowd is related to the physical limit of their telepathic projection of speech elements."

"Dr. Cadell!"

"Sorry. Now take a deep breath. Yes, literally! Have they said anything?"

"They want the children. I'd say, they're demanding the children. We're not sure if they want all of the Twin-Bred, or only the Tofa ones."

"Which twins are up this week for Tofa community contact?"

The tech fidgeted. "I'm sorry — I haven't checked."

"All right, you keep breathing. I'll look it up. OK — this week it's Judy and La-ren. Get them over here, and I'll talk to them. And put together a security team — as tall as possible."

Waiting for the twins, Mara reviewed their files, and the accounts of the last three unscheduled Tofa contacts. She mentally rapped her knuckles — she could have seen this coming. There had been a request to review status reports, granted in part, with selected and redacted samples. Then had come a request to watch twins interact — referred to the parents of some of the twins being raised in home environments.

Judy and La-ren had never handled a contact before. Mara buzzed the contact supervisor. "Judy and La-ren are on Tofa contact rotation, and it's show time. It looks like a ticklish one. There's may well be some governmental involvement. Are they up to it, or should I substitute a more experienced pair?"

"I assume you need an answer immediately. I hate immediately."

"Sorry. So answer."

"Shit. I think they can handle it — and I think they'll let you know if they can't. You can have another pair ready as backup. They're on the tall side, which may help. One way we're in luck — Judy's especially fluent in Tofar. As much as any of them."

"Thanks. Get on the security feed and stand by, in case I have questions or you have suggestions."

The tech ushered in Judy and La-ren. Mara stood up.

"Judy, La-ren — please look at this security feed. We've got a delegation here, and we have an initial idea of what they want. Would you like to hear it, or would you rather start from scratch?"

La-ren buzzed for a moment. "Tell Judy, but not me. I will speak first to the delegation, and compare my understanding to what Judy has been told."

"Judy, I'd rather they didn't know at first how well you speak Tofar. It may not matter, but I'm playing a hunch here. We're sending you out there with some human adults. We'll have additional security standing by. If either of you feels you need their assistance, turn toward the security camera and touch your chin twice."

The twins looked at each other. Judy appeared amused at this touch of melodrama.

"Are you nervous?"

Judy looked at La-ren, then back at Mara. "We're excited that it's our turn. We're curious. If necessary, we can worry later."

Mara beckoned to Judy. She whispered in her ear, then sent her back to La-ren's side. She pointed to the door, where the rest of the contact team had assembled. "Off you go."

"You're shaking, sis. Tell me what happened."

"It's just low blood sugar. I forgot to eat. . . . They seemed surprised to see the twins. They weren't sure whether to talk to them or to the human adults. La-ren pre-empted. He's a cool customer, that one. He welcomed them in the name of all the Twin-Bred. He asked whether they were just paying their respects, or whether they had a request of some kind."

"In Tofar, I presume. Grab a snack and keep talking."

Mara obeyed. "His initial greeting was first in Tofar and then in Terran. That got them buzzing a bit. The rest was all Tofar. The tallest one did most of the talking. You know, even the Tofa Twin-Bred have trouble sometimes in understanding the normal Tofa. But they're certainly better at it than we are."

"I should hope so. Cut to the chase already."

"They did demand the Tofa twins. They didn't say why. La-ren asked them. They just stood there. La-ren said something to the effect that the Twin-Bred were children and children did not decide where to go, or with whom. He told them the Twin-Bred were important to the humans, and important humans would have to decide what happened to them. That's based on La-ren's report. Judy says he also told them the Tofa Twin-Bred would not want to leave their twins behind."

"How did she seem to feel about all this?"

"Well, you know the human Twin-Bred are harder to read than other children. I wouldn't say she was very upset. I think she has confidence in us, that we'll keep the Twin-Bred together and keep them from harm."

"Dear innocent babe. Do we know if the Tofa have made this demand through governmental channels as well?"

"It appears not. I got both the Science and Tofa Relations Sub-Chairs on the line and told them, and I'd say they were surprised. To put it mildly."

"And if you were putting it less mildly, they were apoplectic, panicky, ineffectual, and sure it was all your fault."

"Indeed. They called in the new Chairman. He was gloating. His moment had come. He thought. I asked to speak to him privately."

"Oh frabjous day! Are we glad that you kept up on your opposition research?"

"I am very grateful to my wise and ruthless consultant. The gentleman is now awaiting our recommendations. The Science Sub-Chair is waiting for fresh underwear."

"What will you be kind enough to recommend?"

"We're not going to self-destruct. If that's even what the Tofa intended. We're trying to come up with a way to give them something. Of course, since we don't know why they wanted the children, we don't know what a compromise should look like. The tricky thing is being sure we get them back."

"So don't send them. Make the Tofa come to you. You can set aside facilities for them to use. If they don't want you watching, you can tell them you won't."

* CONFIDENTIAL *
CLEARANCE CLASS 3 AND ABOVE

LEVI Status Report, 3-1-86
Executive Summary

<u>Tofa Examinations of Subjects</u>

The Tofa have completed their series of tests on Tofa twin subjects. Efforts to limit the Tofa subjects made available were abandoned as overly problematic.

The Tofa did not express interest in testing the human twins. There appeared to be some attempt to exclude the human twins from testing sessions, but the Tofa twins' refusal to proceed under such circumstances ultimately led to human twins being given the option of observing. Their presence has provided cover for the undisclosed recording of the test sessions.

Testing took place in a temporary structure on Project grounds, built and furnished by Tofa workers under Project staff supervision. The Tofa appeared to be testing for various scientific and technical abilities.

Project staff devised comparable tests to administer to the human twin subjects after the Tofa tests were concluded and the Tofa personnel made their final departure. The test results for Tofa and human twin subjects were within the same general range. . . .

"So the Tofa want to know if Tofa Twin-Bred would make good scientists. Scientists and engineers. Is that what they've hoped to gain from all this? There's little doubt that we have the more advanced technology. Are they looking for a boost?"

"That would be rational. If their thought processes are too different from ours for them to just copy what they see, they may be looking for technical translators. Have the politicos figured this out yet?"

"The idea is percolating through the governmental machinery — "

"Watch your metaphors, sis."

"Then don't make me talk shop before I've had my coffee. You may get some whole elaborate caffeinated-beverage conceit. Except I couldn't come up with it without coffee. Where was I?"

"You were going to tell me whether the Project was in danger of being shut down by politicians intent on maintaining technological superiority."

"The short answer is, not now. Through psychology, persuasion, and just a bit of blackmail, I think I've preserved the status quo — with some additional security, and the promise that we won't be releasing any new-and-improved Tofa into the wild just yet."

"Mara, you're talking about dozens of adolescents. They will be getting more curious, more restless, more rebellious. The Tofa Twin-Bred will be increasingly aware of their isolation from their own kind. Their human twins will be sympathetic, and will view any attempt to overcome restrictions as exciting and romantic."

"I know, I know, and we'll just have to face those problems as they come. Along with whatever other problems turn up. . . ."

Joey paced back and forth across the back yard, scowling and muttering. When he progressed to kicking the lawn furniture, his mother Sarah planted herself in his path, folded her arms and waited.

"You've been upset for weeks. I know you're getting older, and you need your privacy, but I think you need to talk to someone. I'm not used to offering — you always talk to your brother, and that's what I expect, I understand that. But is there something that you can't talk to him about?"

Joey twisted back and forth, grabbed his hair and let go; hands in fists, he punched his thighs.

"I don't understand it! I don't know what's happening! I keep feeling so strange! I'll be walking around and watching people, and suddenly I feel — I don't know what! I don't like it! I don't like not understanding! How can I not understand myself!"

Time to confirm her hunch. "You say you'd be watching people. What people?"

Joey pondered for a moment. "Uh . . . Cindy. And Anna. I forget who else."

Sarah gingerly reached out, waited for signs of refusal, then pulled him into a gentle hug. "Honey, I think I know what's going on. You're growing up. You're a young man, and you're noticing girls the way a young man does."

Joey stared. "You mean — am I getting ready to reproduce?" Now he stood very still. "But why would I have all these feelings? Are they — are they like side effects? What are they for?"

Sarah felt herself blush. She wondered whether Joey knew what blushing meant. She wondered more whether Phillip could handle this discussion if she punted. Wasn't it better for fathers to have "the talk" with sons? But if the son was different, this different from other boys — would Phillip really be a better choice?

"Joey, sweetheart, I'm not sure how to explain it to you. But it's all right. Everything's all right. You'll get used to it. It'll turn out to be fun. And — you should talk to one of the doctors about, uh, reproducing. They'll tell you it isn't really time yet."

Sam and Ze-ten walked beside the river in the field behind the compound. The slow-moving river reflected the gold and ivory foliage on its banks. Ze-ten bent over and scooped up the water in his two largest hands, sealing his fingers to keep it from spilling. Sam licked his lips. "Scoop some for me?"

"Have you taken your catalyst supplement?"

"I may be absent-minded lately, but I'm not that bad."

"Your mind is not exactly absent. It is fairly close at hand. Hovering in Gina's vicinity."

Sam kicked a rock in Ze-ten's direction. "It's not funny. I don't know what to do! I guess it's even worse for other humans — I don't know how they stand it. You don't know what it's like, and that's none of your doing, so don't look so superior."

Ze-ten finished his drink and stood silent.

"Zee? How about that water? Or do I have to use my own sloppy methods?

"Ze-ten?"

The Tofa turned to face his twin. "The difficulty is that I do know. Or rather, I do not know what it is like for you. And I know I should not. But there is something I am feeling that makes no sense."

He projected bafflement and embarrassment. "When I am in the presence of some of my fellow Tofa here, I feel drawn to notice them more closely. I feel a certain pull in their direction. It does not seem to correlate with shared interests or compatible personality or efficient division of duties. It reminds me of your budding biological imperative. Which is very different from ours, or so I understood."

Sam squatted, scooped up water, drank it, and stood with dripping fingers. "Brother. Or should I say, oh, brother. I'm sorry. We've got some cross-species empathetic contamination here. I wonder if it's happening to the others."

"I am reluctant to inquire. Or to self-report. But I will do so. Withholding information is inconsistent with our purpose. If we are to be such strange concatenations of human and Tofa ingredients, there should at least be some societal benefit."

"Zee, we humans call that feeling sorry for yourself. Quit it. You and I, we are benefit enough — for ourselves and for each other. The rest will come, if all goes well. And if it doesn't — we'll find lives for ourselves, lives that work for us. Power to the lab rats!"

Ze-ten projected the equivalent of a smile. "Rat solidarity, then. Let us scurry back and have lunch."

Dr. Sanders heard the modulating tea-kettle whistle and decided to investigate. She followed the sound down the nearest residential corridor and into the third room on the right. Ginny and Se-too were sitting and standing, respectively, on the soft carpet. Ginny was making faces at Se-too, and Se-too was flapping all five arms, and laughing his whistling laugh louder than Dr. Sanders had heard any Tofa laugh before.

Curiouser and curiouser. While the Tofa Twin-Bred could read some human expressions, they usually showed a rather superior attitude toward the variety of same. And something else was different. The doctor did a double-take.

"Ginny, what are you wearing!"

Ginny started and turned away, then apparently realized it was pointless. "It's just something I found. I think a delivery driver left it. It was outside on the fence."

"But it's blue! You know we don't allow blue here. The Tofa — well, some of them dislike it for some reason, and because we don't know why —"

Ginny assumed the familiar expression of adolescents compelled to explain to the clueless. "It's not that they don't like it. They like it a lot! Look how much fun Se-too's having! It just shouldn't be *abused*. I wouldn't wear this in school, or none of the Tofa could pay any attention to the lesson. But here in our room, what's wrong with a little fun?"

"Blue is fun for the Tofa??"

"Well, a kind of fun. Like the beer the staff like to drink when they watch sports. They get pretty loud and silly, but it doesn't do any harm."

"So blue is an intoxicant. And you wouldn't want it around when there's anything serious going on."

"Yes, anything like school."

"Or elections," murmured Dr. Sanders.

"So they weren't being arbitrary. They were being puritanical."

"That's not fair, Levi. There are good reasons not to want people voting drunk. Alcohol service laws were common on Earth, partly to keep politicians from buying drinks for voters and taking them to the polls afterwards. The Tofa probably assumed the color would affect the human voters the way it affects them."

"I assume you forwarded this information to the various municipal authorities?"

"Naturally. On 'I told you so' letterhead. Concrete results, Levi!"

"Concrete. Yes. One could even call it the beginning of a foundation."

Chapter 29

FINDING HIS TWIN reading,Cra-set loomed over her and looked down at the text.

"*Babe, The Gallant Pig*. I remember that story. You have read it four times."

Anna shrugged. "Why should I stop with the first reading? Nobody says, 'That was a fine piece of music. I'll never listen to *that* again.' But some people treat books that way. Not I!"

Cra-set blinked twice. "I would just as soon omit the first hearing, if it is music. . . . Let me recall. Babe is the pig who wants to tell sheep what to do. A task normally reserved for sheep dogs."

"Yes. And the sheep listen to him. Most of the time."

"And you intend to emulate him. Out you will go, to where the city dwellers await, and you will tell them to walk here or circle there."

"Go ahead, laugh. It's inspirational reading. Morale-building."

Cra-set blinked again. "It would, however, be useful if there were sheep dogs to emulate. We will have considerably less guidance than your young hero." He left Anna to his reading.

Executive Summary

<u>Core Mission Readiness</u>

A recent assessment by Education Department personnel, particularly those associated with the planning and delivery of lessons in diplomacy, negotiation, psychology, sociology and history, indicates that deployment of Twin-Bred in at least some conflict situations may well be feasible in less than a year. Mission protocols are being developed. . . .

Stan heard the crash of Mara's chair against the wall and cringed. He had thought he was safe: the draft status report had gone out three days before. He sighed and headed for her office.

He knocked, and jumped back as the door was thrown open a fraction of a second later. Mara stood in the doorway, panting with rage. Stan tried not to recoil visibly, and then noticed with relief that her baleful glare was not directed at him, or at anything in particular. Relief quickly gave way to concern. "Mara, what's wrong?"

She grabbed her tablet and thrust it toward him. He recognized a passage from the status report. Was he the target after all? Then he saw that the document was a response to the report, rather than the report itself. He had no time to see more before she pulled the tablet away again and shook it at him. "Those scum-sucking cretins. Those moribund, dysfunctional imbeciles. Years ago, when the twins were only children, we were supposed to throw them into the fray. And now that they're older, and trained, and nearly ready — those hypocritical, pusillanimous bottom-feeders. . . ."

Stan gently grasped Mara's hand, pried her fingers off the tablet one by one and extracted it. "Development of the described mission protocols may be a nonoptimal utilization of staff resources. Further deliberation and study is required before consideration of authorization of any potentially destabilizing . . . " He had to stop as Mara grabbed for the tablet. It seemed prudent to keep it out of her reach a while longer.

"Further study," she spat. "Study by whom? Apparently not by the scientists whose entire job, whose entire life it has been for all these years — oh, those myopic, misbegotten . . ."

She paused for breath, and looked up at Stan with just a hint of self-deprecating humor. "Yes, she's on the rampage again, isn't she, Stan? I'm sorry. You just back on out and let me breathe fire a little longer, and then I'll put together a meeting. We'll get things moving again. Somehow." Her expression belied the optimistic words: as her fury ebbed, what remained looked like sullen discouragement.

Stan laid the tablet on Mara's desk and walked out, resisting the impulse to tiptoe. He closed the door behind him and returned to his desk. As he roused his computer from its slumber, he thought he heard Mara murmuring in her office, as though she had found someone whose conversation brought more comfort.

"Levi, I don't know what to think. Is it just more fall-out from the Tofa testing incident? Or are we up against some more fundamental obstacle?"

"There, now. You have two alternative hypotheses to test. That's familiar territory."

"I don't know why I thought they'd actually let this project have a chance to succeed. That's not how my life goes, ever."

"I do hope you're not adding self-pity to your emotional repertoire. It's neither productive nor entertaining. Of course the politicians are dragging their feet. That's the principal use they make of those appendages. We'll find ways to goose them along."

"Daddy! Come in."

Councilman Stewart Channing stepped inside and gave Veda a quick kiss on the cheek. "Where's my granddaughter?"

"She's over at the compound. 'Helping' the dieticians. She loves to cook, and they let her hang around the kitchen once in a while. She's always so proud when she gets to help make something. She'll be home in a couple of hours, bearing leftovers. If you can't wait, we'll go over there and see her. But Jimmy and Peer-tek are here. Here's Jimmy now. Jimmy, your grandpa's here!"

Stewart shook Jimmy's hand with an assumed heartiness. Veda ground her teeth. Her father was not one to ignore the absence of biological connection. She had given up remonstrating. Besides, there was something of more immediate interest to talk about.

"Daddy, what *is* in that box?" Though she thought she knew.

Jimmy leaned toward the box. "You told me about cats once, and I have viewed about them. I believe there is a cat in that box. The sounds are right."

Stewart beamed. "Happy Birthday, pumpkin!"

Peer-tek came into the room. "Pumpkin? We harvested pumpkins several months ago. They were significantly rounder than Mama Veda, even if she is rounder than in my earlier memories."

Stewart and Veda burst out laughing, to Jimmy's and Peer-tek's bewilderment.

Veda patted Peer-tek's nearest hand. "It's just an expression, honey. Like 'honey.' It's his way of saying he loves me. Like I love you." She glanced at her father; he looked away.

Peer-tek leaned over the box. "You didn't tell us that today was your birthday. I hope you are having a happy birthday, Mama Veda. I am glad your father has brought you a present. What is the present?"

"Ask your brother."

Jimmy smiled smugly. "It's a cat. I recognized it. Without even seeing it!"

"I remembered you liked cats. And it's become — difficult to keep cats in areas where the Tofa may be visiting. Did I tell you that our home has been chosen as a model for the Tofa to see? It's an outreach program." He sat in the nearest armchair; Veda sat on the couch.

"Congratulations, Daddy! So why can't a model home include a cat?"

Stewart shifted in his chair. "Well, the Tofa don't seem to take to cats. Or so some people think. So we're erring on the side of caution. I hope it won't be a problem, here — with, um, Peer-tek or the others . . . ." He trailed off.

Veda patted his hand. "Daddy, thank you. It'll be lovely to have a cat." She hoped so, in any event. She opened the box and lifted out a sinuous Siamese. It gave a soft yowl. She placed it carefully in her lap.

Peer-tek blinked twice. "The cat does not disturb me." He examined it closely; the cat ignored him. "It is very interesting. I have no idea what it is thinking. Do cats think?"

Veda laughed. "Well, they certainly know what they like. And don't like. How they decide, I don't know." She paused and looked around. She saw nothing that looked like cat food. "What does it eat?"

"I left a few bags of its food outside. Couldn't carry everything at once. I'll send you more when you need it. Or bring it, of course. When I can manage. You know how busy they keep me."

Veda suppressed a smile. "Of course, Daddy. We all know how important your work is. But you're welcome, any time."

Jimmy reached out hesitantly. "Will it mind if I touch it?"

"Only one way to find out, sweetie. Just move slowly and be gentle. But if it seems to object, move your hand away faster, or you could get scratched."

Jimmy hesitated, but seemed to feel he could not honorably withdraw from the attempt. He laid a careful hand on the soft fur. The fur evidently felt good; he moved his hand to follow the curve of the cat's body. Then he jumped a little. "It's vibrating!"

Veda had to laugh again. "It's called purring, honey. That means it likes what you're doing."

"Peer-tek, you try!"

Peer-tek blinked twice. "Perhaps later. I do not wish to introduce a complication."

"Well, I've got to go, if I'm stopping by the compound. Happy Birthday, baby." He stood up and donned his overcoat with not entirely concealed relief.

"I'll walk you over." Veda lifted the cat gently and placed it on the couch, making a mental note to improvise a litter box. As they left, Peer-tek was standing over the cat, extending one finger and considering.

They walked in silence until the compound was close ahead. Stewart kept darting quick glances at Veda and clearing his throat. Finally he stopped and turned toward her.

"You know, Sabrina moved back last month. She's living near us."

He waited for a reaction. Veda gave him none.

"Every time, I hope it'll be you coming next."

Veda stood in silence.

"Veda, haven't you stayed here long enough? You know how awkward it is for Brian to commute, when this place doesn't officially exist. And I miss you! And Melly. I'm not getting any younger, Veda."

"Daddy, you're hardly old and doddering! And you do get to see me. Us. It's official business for you to come here."

"It's not like having you at home. Or near home, with other — in a normal neighborhood. Living a normal life."

"You didn't care so much about my living a normal life when you saw a use for me. Before the political winds shifted. You were quite insistent."

"So now you're punishing me? By isolating yourself out here with all these —"

"Don't say it!" She started walking, and he scurried after her. "No, Daddy. I'm not angry, not really. I had my own reasons — not that you noticed. . . . And this is my life now. I don't want it to be different. What we're doing out here — it's important. I may not have had quite the right experience to join the scientific or technical staff, but I'm part of the effort. I'm raising my boys to be good and decent, and to use their skills to help others. And if things work out — they could do great things, I know it."

"And Melly? What's her place in this grand plan?"

"Daddy, she's the happiest child! She has dozens and dozens of what amount to big brothers and sisters. And she's learning most of what the older children are learning. They're getting a fantastic education, Daddy. Better than any children get back home, I'd wager. Whether Melly wants to be a scientist, or a historian — or a politician! — she'll be well prepared."

Stewart shook his head. "I don't know what to say to you. Aren't you even thinking about it? About coming home?"

They were almost to the entrance. Veda stopped again and put a hand on his arm. "We can't really see what's coming. Everything we're here for — none of us really knows if it'll come to pass. You know the saying, 'Be careful what you wish for.' Please don't wish too hard for me to come home, Daddy. Please — please wish for us, for the Twin-Bred, to do what this world needs so badly."

Stewart smiled a little painfully. "By gum, I've raised an idealist. What would my colleagues say?. . . Very well, my dear. I wish you the best. And I'll come when I can."

Veda leaned over and kissed his cheek. "Please do. And don't forget the cat food."

Veda plunked the cat on the empty chair in Mara's office. Mara stared. "Good Lord. I've only seen a few, and so long ago! It's like seeing an alien." She laughed a little. "So to speak."

"My father brought it. There's some concern the Tofa may not like having them around, and he's the Tofa's tame Councilman of the moment. . . . What do you think? Can we keep it here?"

"Has Peer-tek seen it? What was his reaction?"

"Curious. Cautious. Not hostile. Yet another way the Tofa Twin-Bred are different from other Tofa?"

"Let's not over-generalize. Not all humans are fond of cats. But it's an interesting data point." Mara gazed over Veda's head, thinking hard. "If it were a dog, I'd wonder if this was yet another case of human trait crossover. Humans and dogs co-evolved, after all. Human reaction to dogs may be instinctive. Cats are a different story, at least to some extent. Cats tolerate people, for their own purposes, and some people find that independence endearing. And cats have their dignity. They don't like disrespect. For cat lovers, that's quite all right. Cat lovers are the sort of people who can take another species on its own terms."

"Well, I rather hope that most of our Twin-Bred — human and Tofa — are that sort of people. . . . So what shall I do with it?"

"Keep it, by all means, if you don't object to it. In fact, I have a plan for your new arrival."

The memo went around the next day to the teachers of Diplomacy. Each of them was to work a visit from Veda and her cat into his or her curriculum.

Veda sat at the front of the room with the cat — now named Mia — in her lap. The twins in their pairs came up and squatted down beside her, one on each side. Ms. Wilson had told them they could take turns looking at the cat and stroking it, and should then write down their thoughts about it, to be shared when all had had a turn. Mia was of a fairly unflappable disposition and took it all quietly, honoring the occasional pilgrim with a purr.

When all had filed past, Veda put Mia in her box and slipped away. Ms. Wilson called for her students' attention.

"All right. Before you read your notes to each other, let's get a few preliminary reactions. How many of you liked being near the cat?"

Most of the humans and about half of the Tofa raised one hand apiece.

"How many of you didn't like being near it?"

Five Tofa raised a hand, more hesitantly.

"It's all right. Ka-teer, why didn't you like it?"

Ka-teer swiveled slightly back and forth and blinked. Ka-teer's twin Mario patted Ka-teer's nearest hand in reassurance. Ka-teer spoke with some hesitation. "It was different. I had never seen one before. I could not predict how it might react to me, or what it might do."

"Yes, cats can be rather inscrutable. . . . You didn't know enough about it, and so you didn't — what, didn't trust it?"

"Yes! That is just how I felt."

"That's very interesting, Ka-teer. Thank you. I want all of you to think about what Ka-teer has just said.

"Russell, you see Tofa every day, and all our Tofa see you humans. Do you know how often most humans out there see a Tofa? And vice-versa?"

Russell cleared his throat. "Not very often. Maybe once a week?"

Ms. Wilson looked around the room, from human to Tofa to human. "I know how strange this will seem to you twins, but many humans see a Tofa two or three times a year, and usually from a distance. And many Tofa see humans even less often. There are members of both species who have never seen the other."

Ms. Wilson looked around sharply to hush the murmurs that spread round the classroom. "Ka-teer, if you saw a cat once or twice a year, briefly and with minimal contact, do you think you would learn much about it? Enough to become more comfortable with it?"

"No, Ms. Wilson. I probably would not."

"Just so." The classroom was completely quiet now. "When you go out into the world, you will be meeting with humans and Tofa who do not understand or trust each other. Your job will not be simply to talk to your own species and convey the results. You will need to show them, by example and by your leadership, that they can learn about each other, and learn to trust. It will be a challenge. But I and all your teachers will keep preparing you to meet it.

"We'll all read our notes now. Peggy, you go first."

As Peggy lifted her tablet, Crel-tan leaned over to Simon and whispered in his ear. "And let us hope that when we meet our own people, they do not regard us as cats."

Chapter 30

MELLY SAT entranced in front of the viewer. Brian came in and kissed Veda on the neck. "She's viewing it again?"

"For the *fourth* time this week. . . . I was afraid it'd make her sad, but it doesn't seem to have that effect on her."

Melly paused the viewer and ran up to be kissed. "Daddy, I have an idea, and I want you to talk Mommy into it."

Veda laughed. "At least you're up front about it!"

Brian dropped into a chair. "Let's hear it."

"I want to put on a play. With Twin-Bred actors."

"Hon, you don't mean —"

"Yes. *Romeo and Juliet.*"

Mara ushered Veda and Melly into her office. "Mother Veda, how good to see you. Melly, you keep growing! Are you trying to catch up with Peer-tek?" Melly started to roll her eyes, then politely refrained.

They sat down. Veda plunged in. "My enterprising daughter has an interesting idea."

Melly leaned forward. "I want to put on a play. For everyone here. With Twin-Bred actors. I've been watching this play lately, and I think it'd be just perfect. With a few changes, maybe."

Mara tried to remember if she had ever anticipated adding anything like theater producer to her job description. "And the play is?"

Melly squirmed a bit in her chair. "It's maybe not what you'd expect. But it's all about warring clans, and trying to make peace between them, and how people don't have to take sides just because their families did."

Mara turned to Veda. "Mother Veda, is she suggesting what I think she's suggesting?"

Veda smiled, a bit sheepishly. "If you're guessing *Romeo and Juliet*, you're right. I've explained that the idea of a human and a Tofa falling in love is rather — impractical."

"*Mom*, I *know* that humans and Tofa can't — you know. I *said* we could change it." She turned back toward Mara. "They could just be really, really good friends. Almost like brother and sister."

"But Melly — the characters wouldn't be Twin-Bred, would they? And normal humans and Tofa — they don't usually understand each other very well. Or become friends easily." Veda stirred as if to speak, then sat back as if thinking better of it. Melly did not notice.

"But *some* of them might. Like when two people see each other and fall in love, right away. If there's love at first sight, why can't there be best friends at first sight, too?"

Mara stroked her chin, and batted aside the stray thought that a beard could be useful on some occasions. "Hmmm. It is intriguing. There is the obvious connection to our efforts here. Have you any actors in mind?"

Melly beamed. "I think Peer-tek would make a *terrific* Romeo. And Becca looks a lot like the Juliet in the play I saw. And they both like to talk a lot."

"Well . . . let me consult a few of the other staff. But I think we might give it a try, if you can find actors who are interested, and people to do set decoration and the like. Think about making your sets portable. We might just want to take this show on the road."

Melly's eyes were wide. "You mean — show it to other people? Outside?"

"Maybe. Later on. After all, who needs to hear the play's message more than the Capulets and the Montagues?"

"Mom!"

Veda looked over her shoulder to where Melly was hunched over her tablet, concentrating with all her might. She put down the carrot she was peeling and joined her. "Do you need some help, hon?"

"Do Tofa have 'loins'?"

Time to call for reinforcements. Veda turned and shouted, "Brian!"

"Seriously, Brian! It's not just the awkward questions, it's the unanswerable ones. We know that the Tofa don't have our male/female gender set-up, but we know so little about what they *do* have. We don't know how their friendships work. We don't know what their parent-child relationships are like. We don't know if young Tofa can keep secrets from their parents. We don't even know for sure if young Tofa *live* with their parents!"

"Can't she just cut out everything where we aren't sure of a Tofa equivalent?"

"And leave what? There'd be darned little left. Not enough to make for a satisfying play. I hate to say it, but I think she'd better wait until we know enough about the Tofa to fill in at least *some* of the gaps."

Brian sighed. "She could be a grown woman by then. OK, I'll talk to her."

Melly cried; but she had to agree. "I don't want to waste everybody's time on a play that isn't even good. Then they wouldn't want to help with the next one."

"That's the spirit! Why don't you find something you can stage in the meantime? And sooner or later, we'll know enough to come back to *Romeo and Juliet*, if you still want to."

Nine weeks later, Melly triumphantly directed a production of *Little Red Riding Hood* with a small Twin-Bred cast and elaborately painted sets. It was a hit.

Chapter 31

CINDY THREW down her tablet. It clattered against the desk; Dar-tan hastily checked it for damage. Cindy scowled. "I don't want to *do* this any more!"

Dar-tan projected puzzlement. "What exactly do you want to stop doing?"

Cindy gestured wildly. "All of this. Studying all the stupid things people have done before, and all the stupid things they're going to keep doing. Practicing how to talk people into being less stupid. And once we get started — being in public all the time. Being around angry people, and who-knows-what Tofa. But that's what I'm supposed to do, and for how long? Forever? And *no one* has ever asked us if that's what we want to do with our lives!"

Dar-tan reached toward Cindy's hand and then pulled back. "Are you sorry that you were born here? That we are twins?'

Cindy grabbed his nearest hand and kissed it. "Oh, no, Darrie, of course not! I love you! I would never want to be a singleton. I would always want to see you and spend time with you. And I would hate not knowing any more about Tofa than the people out there. But — I don't care if I was created as a test-tube ambassador. It's not *me*."

Dar-tan stood silently for a moment, then asked: "And what is?"

"I'll bet you can guess that."

Cindy felt his smile. "You want to hole up in a lab somewhere and tell a computer how to make animals. Cows. Horses. Zebras. Bunnies."

"What's so funny about rabbits? I read about people keeping them as pets. And of course you can eat them too."

Dar-tan opened his communication program. "There is no reason to wait. We can collaborate on a message to the Biological Sciences Supervisor. We will tell him together."

"And if he says no?"

"We will use the skills you despise to negotiate the bureaucracy, and to negotiate with it. If necessary, we will simply insist. It would be foolhardy in the extreme for the Project to rely on a mediation team that might have its own agenda — particularly if the agenda was to show that its members should have been left at home."

"My, my. So some of your Twin-Bred are so audacious as to act like real people, with their own preferences. Even their own ambitions."

"I guess we had some dim notion that this might happen, because we've been trying to prevent it — we've been, I guess you could say indoctrinating them since they were young children. But that only goes so far, obviously."

"How nasty did things get with Cindy and Dar-tan, before anyone brought you into the loop?"

Mara finished her drawing of Cindy, Dar-tan and a host of farm animals surrounding two human adults. "Not very. They went to O'Mara in Biological Sciences first, who didn't know what to think, so he talked to Barrows in Training, and Barrows talked to me."

"And the upshot is?"

"Cindy is now the animal biogenetics unit's first student-apprentice. She's thrilled."

"And the scientists in that division will get some practice dealing with human Twin-Bred peculiarities. And Dar-tan? What happens to him?"

"We're going to do some role-playing exercises involving uneven-numbered teams. And he's very good at mathematical modeling. We can involve him in some of the nitty-gritty research work."

"So all's well that ends well. For that pair at least."

"It's going to be a good deal tougher to deal with the others. . . ."

Randy and Jak-rad stood side by side, as tall as they could stand. Mr. Barrows thought of the expression "shoulder to shoulder": if their respective anatomies had permitted, that would have been their posture.

"We both want the same thing, in our different ways. We want to go back to our people."

Mr. Barrows concentrated on appearing patient and calm. "What do you believe you could do, in your communities of origin?"

"I want to be a farmer." Randy spread his arms wide, almost knocking into Jak-rad. "Not like here, with our little gardens and sheds. I want to run a really large hydroponics set-up, and a whole lot of soil-space, and see which is better for which kinds of crops. I want to feed lots and lots of people, and design and improve and maintain industrial-size equipment."

Mr. Barrows nodded. "And you, Jak-rad? What is your dream? I mean, your idea of a different future?"

Randy, if not Mr. Barrows, could sense Jak-rad's frustration. "I do not know. How could I know? I know nothing of what Tofa do. I do not know how they work, when they work, why they work, what they work at. I do not know how they live with each other. Since the Tofa host mothers and nurses left, the only Tofa in this place are Tofa who do not know any of those things either."

Mr. Barrows turned to Randy. "Randy, we could try to find a way for you to join a human community. We could look for a sponsor, someone to keep an eye on your welfare, and a farming unit that would like some enthusiastic young labor. But first, we would have to — to retrain you. You and the other human Twin-Bred don't look and act just like typical humans your age. Or any age. It could take months before you'd have a good chance of living in, say, the agricultural sector of Campbell City, and having people just think you're strange. Which isn't the best way to live, anywhere."

Randy looked mulish. "I'll take that chance."

"And you, Jak-rad." Jak-rad waited. "You must see that it's that much more difficult for us to help you achieve your goals — just because of the situation you've described. We don't have Tofa contacts that we can trust even as much as our human ones. And we can't possibly train you to fit in. But some years from now — I know that sounds impossible, at your age, but if you can wait, there's a good chance we'll be in a much better position, more knowledgeable, more connected, in a few years' time."

Jak-rad shook his head in what Mr. Barrows despairingly noted as an all-too-human gesture. "I will find a way. I will take my chances."

Months later, Randy and Jak-rad waited at the helipad. Randy's ride would arrive in minutes. Unofficially, it was Jak-rad's ride as well. Randy was heading for a job and a rented room. Jak-rad had Tofa currency estimated to suffice for two weeks' subsistence.

Randy squeezed Jak-rad's near hand. "I can't believe we're doing this." Training had much reduced the Tofar traces in his speech, but when he spoke to Jak-rad they reappeared.

Jak-rad squeezed back carefully. "It is frightening. But I would rather be afraid than trapped. Or bored. It may be some time before my life is boring. By which time it may be a relief."

"You smell different." Jak-rad had stopped taking the chemical suppressant that kept Tofa Twin-Bred from processing Tofa seed cells. "Do you feel different?"

"That is difficult to say. I may be imagining some changes. At this time, with my wishes being gratified in a manner I had thought unlikely, and with the consequences so uncertain, I would be experiencing varying emotions in any event."

Randy sighed. "I've hardly seen you for weeks." Jak-rad had spent as much time as possible immersed in recordings of normal Tofa, and the rest around the Tofa Twin-Bred, while Randy had assiduously avoided both.

"And here we wait to be parted for what may be the rest of our lives."

Randy grabbed Jak-rad's arm. "Don't you believe it! All our friends here — it won't be long before everyone knows about the Project, and they'll all be out there helping humans and Tofa understand each other and get along. Once that's happened, no one will mind about us. We'll be able to visit. The Project will know where I am. You just find a way to tell them where you are!"

Jak-rad twitched one shoulder in what he hoped was typical Tofa fashion. "I hope they do not find out from some lurid account of my premature demise. But I will do what I can."

They heard the copter's approach at the same moment. Jak-rad spoke quickly. "We are not to talk in front of the pilot. Goodbye, twin. Grow giant beets and carrots, wonders to behold. And be safe."

Randy nodded and wiped his eyes on his sleeve as the copter touched down.

But most of the Twin-Bred remained eager to fill their predestined role. Eager, and impatient.

Chapter 32

JUDY STOPPED and flattened herself against the wall, listening around the corner to the voices expressing varying amounts of agitation.

"I thought our missing host mothers were out there stopping this kind of thing."

"Maybe they are, some of the time — but obviously, not enough."

"So what's the current status in Campbell City?"

"Most of the humans are holed up in their units, and a few are going around looking for something to break. Of course, the Tofa don't care for big glass windows, so guess who's taking the property damage."

"And the Tofa?"

"They've restored power to the orchard barns, but not to the poultry barns. . . ."

Judy ran quietly on her toes back to the room she shared with La-ren. They had moved into the compound when they became teenagers and cared more for the society of their peers.

"Something's happening! They're fighting in Campbell City, and no one knows what's going on, no one understands it!"

La-ren showed frustration. "How did you find out?"

"They were too upset to look for eavesdroppers. It's a good thing I can hear nearly as well as you. La-ren, I want to do something!"

"Agreed. We have a purpose. Collecting data and fine-tuning approaches has become a comfortable habit. Inertia has set in. We cannot depend on others to realize the appropriate moment for intervention."

"Who else is ready? I wish Jimmy and Peer-tek could come, but Melly might find out and say something. Or try to tag along! "

"Steven and Bon-tok will be willing. They are tall, like us. That will be useful. Rose and Fel-lar will want to come. Who else?"

"Maybe Anna and Cra-set. Why don't you go and sound them out. I'll hack into the news feed and find out more about Campbell City."

The Campbell Crier story went planetary overnight.

Secret Government Race-Mixing
Experiment Revealed:
Test Subjects Escape, Stunning Local
Population

Campbell City residents thought things
were bad enough, after Tofa from the city's
north side appeared in the human section
and cut power to several agricultural
buildings. Small groups of angry human
residents roamed the streets, and efforts to
resolve this latest crisis proceeded slowly.
That was before things took a turn for the
truly bizarre.

Thursday evening brought the sudden
arrival of eight beings appearing to be
human adolescents and Tofa of
indeterminate age, but startlingly different
from either. The apparent humans'
movements, facial expressions and accents

were variously described as "alien,"
"abnormal," and "Tofa Lite." The apparent
Tofa displayed some movements
reminiscent of human body language. Tofa
officials arriving on the scene appeared to
find these beings unsettling, although they
did not display any reaction identifiable as
surprise. All eight of these unexpected
visitors spoke in both Terran and Tofar to
the rapidly growing crowd.

Human law enforcement officials dispersed
the crowd and took the intruders into
custody. After repeated demands for
information from local authorities, and
several requests for interviews from this
paper and other news outlets, the Planetary
Council issued a press release disclosing
the existence, for more than
fifteen years, of a secret research program .

. . .

Mara paced back and forth across her office. Some
small detached part of herself wondered how long it would
take to wear a trench in the floor. "Adolescents. You warned
me. Restless, rebellious and romantic. This is our fault. The
Project's. Mine. We should have been talking to them more
about the future, including them in the planning process —
and damn it, we should have been further along! We've
been studying and monitoring and report-writing, and
politician-stroking, and just when were we going to get
started on the mission the Project was created for?"

"When the politicians would let you. Although given the
recent obstruction from those quarters, we should have

been working on some more devious alternative. That's my failure, Mara mia. Devious is my department."

"Your failure, my failure. It's no time to fool ourselves, Levi. To fool myself."

"It's no time to make things harder on yourself, either. Leaning on me does you no harm, and it does the twins no harm. Whatever helps you go forward, that's what you'll do."

"Forward, then. We've got to go on the offensive. We've got to use the public's interest, try to redirect it, to intrigue them and make them want to see more, instead of wanting to crush the scary new thing crawling around. We'll give interviews, leak tantalizing details to friendly sources, find pilot projects for the kids to work on. We've got to see whether things can go any better than they did this time. Whether the Project is actually going to help this planet, or prove to be an academic exercise that ate up the lives of a lot of good people."

"Boldly she rode and well. Charge!"

"But first I have to get our twins back."

"Let's think about that for a second. You need a demonstration project. The kids are on site — and it may be very hard to arrange that a second time. You've already got attention. They probably can't make things too much worse — did I really say that?"

"Yes, but go on."

"And if they do any good at all, and if you do have any friendly press to help you, you can spin it big time. And that, sister mine, is as optimistic as I get."

"Campbell City, then."

Chapter 33

JUDY, ROSE, AND Anna took turns sitting or lying on the two cots at ground level. None of them felt like perching on the upper cots. Steven was in the next cell, with a sleeping drunk and a talkative pickpocket. The guards had taken care not to put these strange new prisoners in cells with any of the townspeople arrested for rioting. The girls were cold: while they had dressed for the cooler weather, the guards had confiscated their jackets.

Anna got up and leaned against the bars to listen to the pickpocket's tales of lifting the mayor's phone and a beauty queen's diary, the narrative frequently drowned out by the drunk's snoring.

Rose paced the short width of the cell and back again. "Where are the others? How do we know they're safe?"

Judy turned away. "They have to be safe. I won't think about anything else." She covered her ears as if it would stop her thoughts.

Anna turned back toward them. "As they were bringing us here, I saw another corridor with tall ceilings. They're probably down that way. I imagine human prisoners would be difficult about being locked up with Tofa."

Judy let her hands drop and tried to smile. "Maybe, when we've changed things, human and Tofa can sit happily together in the same cells."

Rose sat down and pounded her fists on her thighs. "Why did we just rush off like that? Why didn't we find out more about how people dressed and talked and wore their hair in the city? Why didn't we try to be less — different?"

Judy sighed. "I don't know if looking like the local residents on the outside would have made us blend in more, or just seem that much stranger."

Anna came over and massaged Rose's neck. "We acted quickly because events were moving quickly. If we had waited, we might be sitting back at the compound, wishing we had intervened while there was still time."

Rose started to cry. Judy tried not to join in. "But at least, our twins would be there with us."

They all heard the footsteps approaching. A guard jingled keys in the hallway. "All right, you four! I don't get it, but you and those Tofa buddies of yours have a meeting with the mayor."

La-ren and Fel-lar stood in the visitor's room of the Campbell City jail. The rioters and petty criminals who should have had visiting hours were loudly protesting the way the room had been taken over by assorted aliens and freaks. Across the room stood a single Tofa.

They had agreed that Fel-lar would speak first. "Do you know that the humans in this city are angry?"

"Yes. We understand that the destruction of human property is the result of this anger. We did not anticipate that. We had taken precautions against any violence against ourselves."

"You disconnected the power to several agricultural facilities?"

"Yes. We have also removed the contents of certain agricultural storage sites. We have not been informed whether that action has been discovered."

In the observation room, Rose spoke softly to Judy in Tofar. "Do we inform the authorities immediately, or await an explanation?"

"We wait. Without an explanation, we make things worse. With one, we may make things worse, or we may not."

Back in the visitor's room, La-ren asked, "Are all these actions related?"

"Yes. We have been waiting until the unrest had ended to discuss the matter with the human authorities."

La-ren repressed the urge to whistle. "There is a temporal problem with your intentions. The unrest is unlikely to end until the explanation is delivered."

"We had assumed that the unrest was inevitable and would end as fatigue disabled its participants."

"If the humans are able to understand the explanation, further unrest may be avoided."

Four sets of twins sat at the conference table, across from the mayor, the police chief, and the city attorney. Judy and Anna, in particular, had urged the Tofa twins to sit. "When we can do something they see as normal, we should take that opportunity."

Judy smiled at the officials. The stiffening in the police chief's posture suggested that her smile was somehow disturbing. She forged ahead. "We have learned the Tofa's intentions, and we believe you will find them reassuring."

"Isn't that great. They had good intentions!" snarled the mayor. "And can they make the trees grow new fruit? Do the Tofa have a few hundred chickens to spare? Are they going to return the supplies they stole? Or maybe they have a few more intentions to go before they're done?"

"Would you like us to explain their intentions?"

The city attorney nodded.

"You realize that the Tofa do not fully understand the scope of human technologies. They underestimated your ability to deal with biological threats. The Tofa became aware of an infectious agent affecting this region. The Tofa specialists in charge of containing damaging biological agents are largely autonomous. They are not accustomed to providing prior notice of their actions. They moved to isolate and destroy —"

"The grain, the root vegetables — they're all *destroyed?!?*"

"Fortunately, the process had barely begun. It has been arrested and the material will be returned to you as soon as the appropriate Tofa are assured that your biofilters have eliminated the infectious agent."

The police chief snorted. "I don't care a whole hell of a lot whether they're assured or not. We're talking grand theft here."

Judy looked at Anna. Anna's voice was the most soothing and well modulated among the human twins present. Anna turned to the city attorney, as the only official who had made no impatient outbursts. "The need to take prompt action against biological infestations is understood in both human and Tofa society. The lost resources are an unfortunate casualty of the existing communication difficulties. We believe the Tofa are willing to explore procedures for reducing such difficulties. We would be concerned about how such efforts might be undermined by treating recent events as a law enforcement matter."

The city attorney looked thoughtful, while the police chief let out a harsh burst of laughter. "Are we supposed to care whether a bunch of teenage science projects are 'concerned'? Who do you think you are, anyway?"

La-ren wished he could answer that question. They had agreed that discussing their greater purpose would be impolitic at present. He would not say that they were there to save the world.

"All right, people. This joint meeting of the Planning and Tofa Relations committees will come to order. Let's sum up how our impromptu trial run went."

The head of the Planning Committee pulled up a file. "Summing up may be premature. The kids are home, but they may be going back if the loose ends keep dangling."

Mara glanced down at her tablet. "I gather the kids were about to start learning how to set up some kind of communication and problem-solving system that'd keep working after they left. If they go back to Campbell City, that's what they should go back to do. Next time -- assuming we're heading for next times -- we'll have to make it clear up front that the twins are there to start a process, not to handle it indefinitely."

That got a laugh from psychologist Carla Horn, whom Mara had dragooned into attending. "If you're expecting to get around the basic human tendency to blame any remaining problems on the ones who tried to help, good luck to us. Maybe it'll work on the Tofa."

"Speaking of which." Mara turned to the contingent from Tofa Relations. "We've heard about the initial human response. What about the Tofa's?"

One of the younger members spoke up, drawing a disapproving glance from his superior. "We've finished our initial debriefing, and so far it seems the Tofa took at most a mild interest in the twins' involvement."

Mara scrolled through a list on her tablet. "Overall, things are looking a lot less apocalyptic than they did a few days ago. I think it's worth starting to plan what we'll do next if the Campbell City situation is resolved. Do we actively seek out situations for the kids to tackle, or just wait for them to pop up?"

Carla motioned to speak. "If we sit and wait, we have no opportunity to control the timing and make it work for us. Let's troll for opportunities. We'll need to tread delicately — we don't want our inquiries to stir up dissatisfactions that haven't really surfaced. But I'm sure we can find a few situations that people have been grumbling about."

Mara looked around the table. "We started out with a team of four twins, simply because that's how many turned out to be sufficiently hot-headed and full of themselves. . . . What is the optimal size and composition of a mediation team?"

The second-in-command of the Planning Committee hesitated as if waiting for someone else to speak, then weighed in. "The minimum will be one twin pair, always.

We can't tell in advance where the explanation lies. And it'd be best to have most of the contact be same-species."

"Are we sure of that?" asked Carla. "After all, neither human nor Tofa Twin-Bred are exactly species-normal. Their mannerisms and speech habits — we've yet to see how much of an obstacle they'll be, in dealing with their own kind."

Mara cleared her throat to draw their attention. "We'll play it by ear. Whether it's best for contact to be human-human and Tofa-Tofa, or otherwise, we'll need at least one of each. We can compare the reactions and results when we send one pair and when we send two. What about security?"

The head of the Tofa Relations committee drummed his fingers on the table. "This will tend to be delicate. All our security is human. That means dominance games with the human officials and who knows what with the Tofa. And the security people aren't trained mediators. We'll have to start some crash courses in how not to muck things up further. I doubt we'll be able to send them with much in the way of weapons — probably nothing lethal to either species. It'll depend on what kind of invitation we can extract, but I'm guessing one security man per twin is the most we can manage. If the twins divide up, at least one member of the security team should stay with each one."

Mara pushed back her chair. "Carla, please work with the Tofa Relations team on sending the feelers out. Then show Planning what you've come up with. Please, everyone, keep the bureaucratic dancing about to a minimum. And keep me posted. Thoroughly."

Randy contacted the Project right after the events in Campbell City, asking for news of Jak-rad. He called every week, still asking. But from Jak-rad, they heard nothing.

Chapter 34

THE RUMORS ON the cybernet were various and inventive.

The Twin-Bred were the result of genetic experiments. Of cut-and-stitch surgery. Of some unimaginable old-fashioned breeding experiment.

The Twin-Bred were child prostitutes. The Project compound was a luxurious whorehouse. The rich and sybaritic were entertained there by any desired combination of human and Tofa young people. The Twin-Bred who had been seen in town were the oldest, but the available selections included children as young as five or six.

The Twin-Bred were only a front for what was Really Going On. The Project was actually building a superweapon. Producing illegal and unprecedently potent drugs in massive quantities. Communicating with other aliens, kinds that no one else had ever seen. Communicating with Terra, after all these years. Preparing for an invasion from the aliens or the Terrans or both.

There were no Twin-Bred. It was all a hoax, done with crude costuming and swallowed by the gullible. It was a vast money-laundering scheme. The Council had used the money for gambling. For bribery. They had lost it in ill-advised investments. It had been spent on invisible clothing for the Council Chairman. It had been spent on the Chairman's divorces from six different secret wives.

The Twin-Bred existed, and were grievously oppressed. They were laboring in sweatshop conditions, producing everything from small electronics to clothing to medical supplies to foodstuffs. The conditions were so bad that they were constantly dying off, replaced with new victims.

The Twin-Bred were pets. The procedures used to produce them had backfired and eliminated all intelligence. They were being used for medical experiments. They were being butchered for meat.

The Twin-Bred had slaughtered all the human scientists at the compound and were plotting the overthrow of all human governments. Of all Tofa governments. The population would become their slaves. Their sex slaves. Their food.

Mara slammed her tablet on the desk. It broke. It was the third she had had that month.

The Public Relations Coordinator quietly swept up the pieces and threw them in the trash. "Mara. We simply must try something. The results of this sort of publicity are — unpredictable."

"Do you really think that anything we say, any stories we distribute, will make any difference? 'A lie races around the world while the truth is putting on its boots.' We can't possibly catch up, let alone keep up, with all the nonsense out there."

"Eyewitnesses may be more convincing than all these amateur fictioneers. We're sending out our teams when requested, but it'll take quite a while for those reports to accumulate. In the meantime, we can invite some relatively fair-minded and credible local citizens to visit us. See what we're really all about."

Mara looked around for something else to break. "Come see the exotic creatures. Careful, don't feed them. They might bite."

"Mara, that attitude isn't helpful. I must insist that you consider this idea. Consider it seriously."

The staff's consensus was that it should be attempted. Mara capitulated. Contacts were employed; criteria were established; invitations were issued. The visitors would be coming.

Judy and La-ren, Steven and Bon-tok, were present to greet the visitors, along with Mara, Carla Horn, and the Public Relations Coordinator.

The Coordinator made the introductions and gave a short speech in welcome. The party then made its way toward the auditorium, where a short film had been quickly pieced together. Their path took them through a classroom wing.

Ms. Flitters, society matron, suddenly stopped and stared. The rest of the party turned to see what had attracted her notice.

"I thought — I heard something rather strange. From in there."

The visitors surged toward the nearest classroom. There were indeed strange sounds coming from within.

They crowded into the doorway. Ms. Flitters staggered and clutched the gentleman to her left, who ran a taxi service and knew everyone in town. Carla Horn let out a stream of quiet profanity. The Public Relations Coordinator simply groaned.

Poo-lat was holding Anna on a leash with one hand, cracking a whip — when had they manufactured it? — with another, and holding a hoop with a third. "Jump, human creature! Jump!" he roared. Around the classroom, twins were sitting in their best approximation of lascivious poses. Several were drinking from tall glasses filled with luminescent liquids.

Mara laughed, and laughed, and laughed.

"Mr. Chairman, I do, of course, apologize for what took place. But please, consider the circumstances. These young people have been trained from infancy to perform what they and we have always treated as crucially important work. They have at least the normal amount of self-respect. And they are young, with every young thing's portion of mischief.

"First, they are subjected — and not by us, I might add — to the most ridiculous and insulting collection of slanders imaginable. And then, we put them on display, to be gaped at. Well, they gave us something to see."

Annabelle Bloom ate her sandwich and listened to the gleeful retellings of the Tour Group Incident. The consensus seemed to be that the Twin-Bred had defended their honor, and a good thing too. Annabelle said nothing: her sympathies lay with the traumatized visitors. Bad enough, for the inexperienced, to subject oneself to dozens of Tofa at once, and an unknown and artificial breed of them at that. To have the frightening rumors equaled or exceeded before one's eyes — she hoped Ms. Flitters' nightmares were not as upsetting as her own had been, when she first arrived.

The incident left its mark. Supporters on the Council grew fewer. But the requests still came in, and the missions went on.

Chapter 35

"I WANT TO see Sel-ran again."

"Be frank, Mara mia. You want to see me again."

"Of course I do! I'm not sure why I haven't tried it again, in all this time. Of course it was disorienting, and somewhat frightening. And I was waiting to see if anyone would find out."

"Which it doesn't appear anyone did. Did you perhaps feel a bit deflated about that?"

"And then I have this other fear, that somehow it might make you go away for good. . . ."

"I'm not Eurydice, and you are not Orpheus, and you never promised not to look back at me. Or in any other direction."

"It does feel like breaking the terms of some fairy-tale bargain."

"Mara, if you've kept me around this long, despite every emotional and practical reason to cut me loose, then I don't think I'm going to vanish in a puff of neurons because some Tofa equivalent of a psychic manages to channel me.

"Mara? Lost for a comeback?"

"What if I saw him more than once? What if it's possible to see you in him, on a regular basis? Would I lose you the rest of the time?"

"If you did, Mara, it'd be because you were satisfied with the new arrangement. And if you're satisfied, and I still exist in some manifestation, then I don't see the problem. And if it were a problem for you, you'd solve it. I have faith in your internal self-discipline."

"So when do we go find him?"

"After breakfast."

Sel-ran was not in his room. Mara headed toward the dining hall, hoping to find him on his way from breakfast. She was not sure she would recognize him; if she didn't see a Tofa she was certain was Sel-ran, she would have to find some apparently casual way to ask after him.

There came a Tofa she did recognize: La-ren, with Judy close behind him. Here was an opportunity to ask about Sel-ran's whereabouts. She hesitated, searching for the words.

"Never mind, Mara. It seems we don't have to wait."

It was La-ren speaking — and on his face, that same impossible smile.

Judy stopped dead. Her face went as blank as a Tofa's.

Mara gripped her arms to hide her shaking. She went through her checklist: the surroundings looked as they should. She was the right age and gender. She was dressed appropriately. Judy and La-ren looked as they always had, with the one stunning exception.

"I'm awake. And it's happening again. And not with Sel-ran."

"Correct on all counts. Well, this is an interesting development. I suppose we shouldn't be surprised. We had no reason to think Sel-ran was exceptional. You had a few discreet tests run on him, I believe."

"What the hell, what the hell is going on here!"

Judy was the one trembling now, her teeth clenched, her eyes furious, her fingers stiffened almost into claws.

Mara moved toward Judy, who backed away.

"Judy. Please believe me — La-ren is all right. This is a temporary thing that's happening." She hoped she was speaking the truth. She would not think about whether she might hope otherwise. "It's happened before. And I'll explain it all to you, in a few minutes. La-ren is — I don't know if he's doing me a great favor on purpose, or if it just happened."

"If it's temporary, then make it stop! NOW!"

Mara looked at La-ren and blinked back tears.

"I think Judy has every right to demand the status quo ante. And it appears likely that we will have further opportunities. You and Judy need to have that discussion as soon as possible. Before anyone else becomes involved.

"I'll see you soon, Mara."

La-ren went blank and stayed blank, at least to Mara's eyes. He turned to Judy, who ran up to him and squeezed him in a fierce hug.

"La-ren, what happened to you! Did she do something to you?"

"That is not how I would describe it. But I would like to be present when Dr. Cadell explains things to you."

Mara led the twins into a nearby vacant office, closed and locked the door.

"I need you both to promise to keep this to yourselves, unless and until I tell you otherwise. For all our sakes. . . ."

La-ren and Judy hurried in silence to their room and closed the door. La-ren leaned against the corner walls while Judy paced back and forth.

"I don't like this. It's — it's creepy."

"Judy, my dear human sister, are any of the Twin-Bred in a position to call someone creepy? If I understand creepy, it means unnatural, something frightening because it is unexpected and not fully predictable. We are all creepy."

"What was it like?"

"It was like answering a knock on the door, and then stepping aside and letting someone enter. Someone who, due to unusual circumstances, asked to use the telephone."

"So it happened to Sel-ran, and now it happened to you. Could it be any of you?"

"That would be a reasonable hypothesis. There are reasons not to test it."

"Do you mean we shouldn't let it happen again? Or are you saying it should be just you, whenever she wants to use the damn telephone?"

"This is interesting. You do not ordinarily cuss, and you have done so twice this morning. That usage is rare among human Twin-Bred, is it not? Our influence has damped your vocal range to some extent. . . . There is no need to be so angry."

"I'm as much afraid as angry, or more so. I'm afraid of losing you, or having you change. We're part of each other, just as we are."

"As Levi was part of Dr. Cadell. They did not mature together, but they shared the prenatal environment, almost to its conclusion, and they are the same species. The bond is known to be strong, even at that stage. Levi's existence, if we call it that, is evidence. And if Dr. Cadell had not lost and loved Levi, she would not have thought of the Project, and we would not exist. For that, we owe her more than understanding and sympathy."

"If we owe her something, so do all of us, all the twins. Why should it be you, every time from now on?"

"There is the issue of security. The issue of creepy. Dr. Cadell has kept her Levi — past and present — a secret from everyone connected with the Project, and for good reason. Her purposes, her mental stability, her objectivity, would all be questioned if this secret were revealed. Our own security and our ability to pursue our purpose are tied to her continued position and prestige. The circle of those who know this secret should not be expanded unless absolutely necessary. For the same reason, Mara will understand the need for restraint in taking advantage of this latent connection."

"Will she?"

"If not she, then Levi. I have, after all, become acquainted with Levi, and he is a canny and cautious fellow."

Chapter 36

* CONFIDENTIAL *
CLEARANCE CLASS 3 AND ABOVE

LEVI Status Report, 10-15-87
Executive Summary

<u>Mission Assignment Issues</u>

Some issues have arisen concerning the criteria to be used in the deployment sequence for mission teams, now that deployments are actually taking place. . . .

Mara kept her face fixed in what she privately called her ignoring-bureaucratic-bullshit smile. "Councilman, I had hoped we would not need to revisit these matters. It was agreed years ago that the Project staff would come up with criteria and assess the readiness of particular teams in relation to those criteria. Sometimes a particular problem will require particular skills, and that need will override the list order. But you cannot expect us to base assignments on — other considerations."

The councilman smiled back. It looked like his telling-underlings-where-they-could-stick-it smile. "Dr. Cadell. Your Project has enjoyed an unprecedented level of funding all these years, with remarkably little interference from this Council. Those of us with relatives among your population have complied with your restrictions on the length of visits, and your reluctance to allow members of your community to travel —"

"That was a matter of security. Of maintaining the secrecy about which the Council has been very insistent."

The councilman rumbled on. "We could talk all afternoon about the scientific reasons why my grandson and his Tofa partner are not your first choice for whatever the next mission turns out to be. I have no intention of jousting with you on your preferred turf." He tapped something on his tablet. "There -- I've sent you the details of a mission I've arranged, one well suited to Nathan's talents. And which you *will* assign to him. Call terminated."

Mara muttered to herself as she made a quick sketch of her adversary in an unlikely and undignified position. Then she called the head of the assignment criteria team.

"It appears we have no choice but to accept some interference in our assignment procedures. Nathan and Li-sen are going out of turn. I'll forward you the details as soon as they've been forced down my throat."

The man gave a quick snort of laughter. "Thanks for the heads-up. So -- this is some kind of a political set-up?"

"That's a good guess. The councilman in question certainly doesn't seem to harbor any doubts as to how well things will go."

"Are we going to tell the twins that they may not be dealing with a genuine conflict?"

Mara hesitated. "Damn. Not yet. Tell them — tell them there are aspects of this mission that we can't discuss until afterwards. For scientific reasons, to avoid contaminating the results. We'll tell them when they come back. We've got that long to think of some way of salvaging their pride."

Nathan and Li-sen sat in the copter, rain streaking past the windows. Each had Mayor Bronson's report on his tablet. A Tofa delegation had appeared in his office, carrying an extracted portion of some Tofa mechanical equipment. Apparently, it had suddenly broken, and they believed human sabotage to be responsible.

"Well, Lisa, what do you think?"

"We were sent out of rotation. The file refers to possible human sabotage of Tofa machinery in a grain production facility. You are good at engineering, which would presumably be useful in determining whether this occurred. The question is whether engineering is in fact the central issue."

"You think someone's analysis of what is troubling the Tofa is incorrect? Or do you mean that if there is sabotage, the reason for it is the real problem?"

"Either. Or both. I believe we should be open to multiple possibilities. And not too ready to be told how to do our job."

"Come in, come in!" Mayor Bronson's greeting was notably hearty. A problem serious enough to require their assistance did not seem to have dampened his spirits.

"You've seen the file. I know you're eager to get out there and see what's going on. But do you have any questions first?"

Li-sen tipped a hand toward Nathan, who would be their spokesman — in that office. Nathan asked, "Was the factory accessible to humans?"

"Well, we're not really sure whether it's guarded, or how well. Maybe you can find that out."

"Is there any possibility that there was sabotage, but that Tofa performed it?"

The mayor seemed startled at the idea. "Now that's one worth checking. Hmmm. You do that! But I'm doubtful about the whole sabotage idea. They're not that mechanically sophisticated, you know. They're probably being paranoid about something with another cause altogether. Our local Tofa are the suspicious type."

Nathan nodded to Li-sen. "I guess we're ready to see the site, and meet the Tofa who need our help. How are we to get there?"

"I'll have someone show you the way. Then we'll stay out of your hair. Yours, that is, young gentleman! No offense. Yes, we don't want to get in your way. You're the experts."

He summoned an underling and ushered them from his office.

As they left the building, following the underling's directions toward the Tofa quarter, Nathan asked Li-sen, "Did the mayor's behavior seem just a little — off — to you?"

"That is hard to say. Now that you have planted the suggestion, I cannot trust myself to answer objectively. We could both do with some additional training in interpreting normal human expressions."

"Remind me to talk to the Coordinator, when we get back."

The mayor and his assistant watched from his window as the twins headed off. The assistant turned from the window and clapped briefly. The mayor bowed.

The assistant pursed his lips. "You really think this will come off?"

"Sure it will. My brother-in-law says there's no way a reasonably competent engineer, even a young one, will miss that metal fatigue. Which would cause the breakage in the part the Tofa were waving around. It's the sort of thing that can result from defective design."

"Except when it doesn't. What if the kid is too good?"

The mayor waved him off. "Like you said — he's just a kid! And you know they come here to solve problems. You think he's going to go for the conclusion that'd cause them? No, we gave them the idea, and they'll go for it. Another species conflict averted; swelling music, roll credits."

Nathan and the Tofa engineer — Ser-nal-sim by name — examined the machine. Li-sen had made the introductions and stood by in case anyone wished him to take part, but Nathan's Tofar was adequate to the purpose. Li-sen reflected that engineers had their own language, spoken or not; there seemed to be no communication difficulties. He retreated to a comfortable wall and leaned there to wait.

The two were examining several different parts of several different machines. Li-sen noted with interest that both Nathan and the Tofa were using occasional Terran words. He recalled historical instances of the same phenomenon when a technologically dominant culture interacted with those less advanced.

After a few minutes, the colloquy broke up, and Nathan came over to report. "I've found something that could explain the failure of that coupling. Metal fatigue. There was an uneven stress load, and — well, the short version is, culprit identified."

"And the reason for the metal fatigue?"

"It's usually a design defect, a failure to understand certain properties of the metal or of the likely stresses thereon. Fatigue happens. It's the special case of the more general principle. You know the one. . . . But that's actually a good question. I'm not entirely satisfied. I want to check some of the other components made of the same material, exposed to other stressful conditions."

A movement caught Li-sen's eye. He looked up to see the Tofa engineer using some sort of scanner or recording device on one of the machines. He turned back to Nathan. "You would expect to see incipient failure of these other components as well."

"Yes — in which case, they've got other trouble brewing, and had better do some preemptive maintenance and design review. But if I don't find it — well, then things will get interesting."

Nathan went back over to Ser-nal-sim, and the two started surveying the surrounding equipment.

Fifteen minutes later, Nathan was back, looking perturbed, and Ser-nal-sim was standing tall and stiff near the machine where the failure had occurred.

"We did find similar trouble — and it's good that we found it — but not everywhere that you'd expect. It's only showing up in parts of the machinery run by a particular control system."

"Have you inspected the software for that control system?"

Nathan lifted an eyebrow. "Of course. It's based on the same program as the software that is not malfunctioning, but there are differences that shouldn't be there."

"Can you think of any non-intentional cause?"

"In a word, no. And there hasn't been any recent attempt to tweak the code for any purpose -- so it isn't just incompetent software engineering. I think we've got sabotage, after all. Plus an attempt to conceal it. There's historical precedent, you may remember — using malicious software to emulate poor design. Though I'd guess someone reinvented that wheel."

Li-sen webbed and unwebbed the fingers of his lower left hand. "For some purpose. That may be the end of the problem to consider first."

"Let's attack it from both ends at once. I'll talk to Ser-nal-sim about the grain market and whether anyone would want to interfere with it. You talk to the plant manager about who could have gotten in here unobserved."

Li-sen and an unfamiliar Tofa walked up to where Nathan and the Tofa engineer were conferring. Nathan spoke as they approached. "Li-sen, we haven't come up with anything compelling. The plant is one of several that processes grain, and there's no single person or entity that would profit that much from its being out of commission. Have you come up with something?"

"I fear we have. The plant manager suggested I speak to Hal-net-dat." Li-sen gestured with a lower hand toward the newcomer. "Hal-net-dat was with the delegation that visited Mayor Bronson. He was in the waiting area outside the mayor's interior office for some time before the mayor admitted them. The waiting area is decorated with pictures of the mayor's personal and political acquaintance. In one such picture, the mayor was standing in close proximity to several other human adults. One of them, a woman, had hair the color of the mayor's, and a similar shape of head and body. Next to her was a man.

"Hal-net-dat was working later than usual one night, three days before the broken part was discovered. He believes he saw that man — the man in the picture — walking away from the factory. It is not an area where humans customarily walk, even in the daytime."

"Did anyone in the delegation confront the mayor with this information?"

"No. It was considered premature. Hal-net-dat was not sure of the human's identity. He is not sure even now. Of course Tofa do not distinguish between human individuals as readily as humans do. Or as I do. I have seen security footage of the area from the night in question. It is necessary, now, that I return to the mayor's office and see the picture there."

"And if it is the same man? Do we just tell the mayor that yes, we've solved your problem, and it's close enough to bite you?"

"I think not. If the evidence supports the likelihood that the mayor is familiar with the saboteur, we will temporize and retreat to discuss alternative courses of action."

"Lisa, this could be bad. If we confirm human sabotage, and by a local political leader — this could explode. It'll be worse than if we hadn't come at all."

"Then we had best draw upon our diplomatic creativity. We can begin considering contingency plans while we travel."

The two Tofa helped them summon a copter to return to the municipal center.

"Well, boys? What did you find? Everything all worked out?"

Nathan followed the mayor into his office. Li-sen remained in the anteroom.

"We found metal fatigue that could have caused the problem. It would explain what happened. We've informed the plant manager. We're going to go back there before we leave, to check the rest of the facility for similar problems. Just to be helpful."

Mayor Bronson beamed. "That's great, son! Good work! I'm sure your people back at the Project will be proud."

"Is there a room we could use to begin composing our report?"

"Sure, sure. Down that corridor, the empty office on the left, at the end. No one's using it just now, and the people in the offices nearby are in a meeting downstairs. Just pop in again before you leave. See you then!"

Nathan walked back into the anteroom and beckoned to Li-sen. The two walked quickly down the hallway to the empty office. They went in and closed the door.

As they had agreed in the copter, they spoke in the Twin-Bred dialect of Tofar. Nathan spoke first. "Well?"

"It is the man. I have no doubt."

Nathan relapsed into Terran for a moment. "Crap."

"Agreed. Do you have any hypothesis as to why someone close to the mayor would have sabotaged the equipment? Or whether the mayor is complicit?"

"No, and I don't see how we can form one. We don't have nearly enough information, or any way to get it. We need allies. Human ones."

Li-sen wove the fingers of his upper left and lower right hands together. "I believe I have a possibility in mind. There is a journalistic establishment in this town. We should be able to track down its location. Someone in that organization would have the background information that might assist us. As well as a certain occupational curiosity."

"Don't forget the occupational tendency to spread the word far and wide."

"To humans, yes. We have been told that Tofa rarely follow the human news media. But in case that is incorrect, we will have to negotiate a period of discretion."

The editor of the Hubbard Herald rubbed his hands. "My goodness, this is a juicy little cherry bomb. Well, I'm afraid I can't come up with some instant explanation. I will tell you that our esteemed mayor is given to scheming, and to tripping himself up. Not half as clever as he fancies himself, that man."

Nathan stared at the scrap of metal in his hand. "We have to have something to tell the Tofa. They may not take this — meekly. Not if we just tell them that yes, the humans sabotaged your plant, and aren't you happy you know the truth?. . . I have to admit — we're in over our heads." It was not an admission he had imagined making.

"I gather it's too late to fudge on the issue of whether sabotage occurred?"

Li-sen gave his approximation of a nod. "We identified the sabotage before we identified the likely culprit. It was the Tofa who completed the puzzle."

"So you need something to tell them, to keep the lid on. And fast. . . . How's this? You tell the Tofa that you have ensured that a thorough inquiry will be made into the reasons for these shenanigans. That you have brought into your confidence a party who has every reason to investigate, and no reason to hush the matter up. And you assure them that the results of the investigation will be made available to them."

Nathan was close to tears. "We don't really know what will happen. If that will be enough. There must be something else we can do!"

Li-sen touched his hand. "Brother. We have uncovered something beyond our capacity to negotiate. Or our authority. We have done our best. This man's suggestion is a sensible one."

"And what do we do? Do we stay here and ride it out?"

"To what purpose? I do not think the mayor will be asking for Project assistance. We can ask the Tofa whether they wish us to linger. We will make clear that we are available. If they do not want us, then it is time to go home."

Mara showed Carla Horn the article on her screen. The Hubbard Herald had used one of its largest headline fonts. "'Mayor Bronson Resigns Amidst Unanswered Questions; New Mayor Deplores Provocative and Destabilizing Political Operations'! Somehow I doubt that's what our friend the councilman had in mind. I could enjoy all this, if I didn't have the feeling we're going to be blamed for it, somehow, sooner or later. I don't suppose the councilman would help deflect any adverse publicity."

Carla shook her head in exaggerated pity at Mara's naivete. "Surely you're joking. The councilman and Mayor Bronson were political buddies. . . . What do young Nathan and Li-sen make of it all?"

"I hear they're a bit shaken up by the magnitude of what they stumbled into. But they're proud of themselves, nonetheless. As they should be. And I was worried about how to salvage their pride. Let that be a lesson, Carla. Be careful what you wish for."

Chapter 37

*** CONFIDENTIAL ***
CLEARANCE CLASS 3 AND ABOVE

LEVI Status Report, 1-1-88
Executive Summary

<u>Team Reception Among Local Populations</u>

The teams sent out under controlled conditions since the initial Campbell City incident have encountered significantly less local hostility. Following the successful completion of their missions, several have been shown substantial hospitality. . . .

Max waved his fork in enthusiasm. "They showed us a good time, all right! It was all humans except for Tas-tan here, but they were in a mood to celebrate, and no one gave Tas-tan any trouble. Well, there was this one character that kept asking to count his arms, but we ignored him." Tas-tan noted with interest that his twin's diction had picked up characteristics of the McAffrey locals'.

Artemisia's expression would have been worshipful if it had been less envious. "So what did you get to do?"

"Well, first we went to a show. There were a lot of sparkly costumes, and costume changes, and bouncy music, and the costumes got scantier as it went along. . . . Then we went to what they called a bar. It was mainly a place to drink and dance. They kept giving Tas-tan drinks. I guess they wanted to see what would happen when he got drunk. Which, by the way, is not something I'd ever want to see! But of course alcohol doesn't have that effect on Tofa."

"And on you? Didn't they want to see you drunk?"

Max grinned. "I'd say so! They were very generous with the drinks, all right. I did take one of those pills that are supposed to keep us sober. But the standard dose is two. I thought I may as well not let all those drinks go to waste completely. I'm glad Tas-tan and our security folks were there to steer me back to the copter afterwards."

Tas-tan tapped his twin's shoulder. "You are forgetting the card game."

"Right! After we'd been drinking for a while, one of the locals suggested we play a game of four-in-the-hand. They seemed to think we wouldn't know how to play, so I didn't want to embarrass them by saying we've been playing it here for years. I guess they just play it for fun — they wouldn't be using it to develop nonverbal communication between twins, the way we do. At least, they didn't play as if they had that kind of experience. . . ."

Tas-tan noticed that there was less in the way of boisterous good humor and laughter among their hosts than had been evident earlier. He suspected they had not expected to lose money to their guests, at least not in quantity. Could the nonverbal cues he and Max had been exchanging be contrary to the local variant of the game?

As he grew more uneasy, he remembered a very old video entertainment he had viewed a year or so before, from a genre known as the "western." The westerners had taken card play very seriously. So seriously, in fact, that someone had been shot with a projectile weapon when the other players believed him to be cheating.

Tas-tan put down his cards and gave Max the signal that meant a change of plans. "Excuse me. We will have to be departing soon. We seem to have accumulated a certain amount of currency. Could we convince you to let us spend it by purchasing a final round of drinks for the establishment?"

The expressions around him changed in what seemed to be a salutary direction. The cards were quickly put aside, and the waiter summoned with loud shouts.

Max shrugged sheepishly. "I guess that might have gone wrong. Good thing Tas-tan was thinking."

"Instead of drinking."

"That's right, rub it in. . . ."

Artemisia thought it all sounded thrilling. She couldn't wait for her turn. Which should be soon — she'd gotten a look at the assignment list. She finished her lunch, said her farewells, and went off to review the standard mission protocols one more time.

Artemisia and Hal-tet stood proudly side by side as the sheriff of Benford finished her phone call. "Yes, sir. We seem to have things under control now. Yes, you can have the militia stand down. We've got it straightened out, pretty much. I'll send you a report in the morning." She disconnected. "Good job, you two. I think we would have got there, in the end, but I'm sure you speeded things up a little bit."

Artemisia reminded herself not to frown. Of course the local authorities would want to minimize the Twin-Bred's contribution; the important thing was to have made it. "Well, we're happy to have done our — bit. I guess we'll be on our way." She hoped that despite her comments, the sheriff was grateful enough to offer them some entertainment, but she wasn't going to angle for it.

Hal-tet signaled her that something was not as expected. "I seem to have lost sight of our security escort. I did see them following us back to this location. Where are they now?"

"Oh, they'll be along. I hope you'll let us show you the sights a little bit before you go. Some of our deputies would like to stand you a drink or two, and the local Tofa would like a chance to get to know young — Hal-tet, is it? — a little better. It's just down the street."

That was more like it. And she could see the security team entering the building the sheriff had indicated, along with several adult Tofa. She and Hal-tet followed the sheriff out the door.

An hour later, Artemisia was not sure that socializing with the locals was all she had expected. The bar was noisy, and almost everyone was taller than she, so it was difficult to keep eye contact with Hal-tet (absorbed in conversation with the other Tofa) or with the security team. There seemed to be more men than women in their party, and the men were getting rather more attentive than she was used to.

"Here, pretty lady. Have another drink." The glint in the man's eyes was probably complimentary, but she was not sure how to respond to it. The easiest thing was to accept the glass and take a sip. She was glad that she had taken both her pills.

It was warm in the bar, and she had dressed for outdoors. She excused herself from her companion and went to the back door. She'd seen a small patio there. It would be quieter, and she could get some air. She did not see the two men nod to each other and follow her.

Hal-tet had not realized that he had the habit of locating his twin every few minutes, until he found himself in an environment that made it more difficult. The dense crowd, and Artemisia's small stature, complicated matters. He told his Tofa companions that he would return to them shortly. One appeared ready to protest, but he headed off to survey the area.

Artemisia was nowhere to be found. Well, if she was not inside, she must be outside. He scanned the room for exits and saw a back door. He headed toward it. As he approached, he heard some sort of commotion, and a sound that could have been a muffled scream.

Hal-tet broke into a run, shoving startled bar patrons out of his way. He slammed the door open, hearing it crack loudly against the wall. An adult human male was holding Artemisia against a wall, with one hand over her face. Another was unfastening his lower garments.

Hal-tet froze for a moment, then let out a shout he had never heard from himself or any other, human or Tofa. The men jumped. The one holding Artemisia hesitated, then released her. The other backed away, fumbling with his clothing.

Hal-tet strode forward and pulled Artemisia toward him. With a lower arm around her waist and an upper arm around her shoulders, he walked as fast as Artemisia could manage, ignoring the defiant shout from behind him: "At least we tried to show her about a real man!"

Hal-tet and Artemisia stood at the helipad, waiting for the copter. The security team, faces stiff with embarrassment, had followed them out of the bar and now stood some distance away, ostentatiously scanning the surroundings for any sign of trouble.

"Hal." Artemisia could not force herself to speak above a whisper. Hal-tet leaned closer to hear her. "Was that — was that —"

"It would have been. Rape."

"I thought so." They stood in silence for a moment.

"Are you hurt?"

"My arms are sore. They'll be bruised. And my shoulder — I might have pulled something."

Hal-tet laid a long finger on her shoulder and then pulled it away. "Is it feasible to kill them?"

Artemisia looked at him and shuddered. What she was seeing was not like human fury: it was colder. The odor that rolled from him was like chlorine gas.

"Let's just get out of here as soon as we can. Please."

* CONFIDENTIAL *
CLEARANCE CLASS 3 AND ABOVE

LEVI Status Report, 2-1-88
Executive Summary

. . . The team has been debriefed, and analysis of the events is continuing. Recruitment of additional security personnel is being discussed, given that the need for confidentiality, while still present, no longer offers as serious an obstacle to terminating current employees or recruiting replacements.

Until further notice, mediation teams have been instructed to decline offers of entertainment and to leave immediately after their efforts have been concluded. . . .

Chapter 38

IT WAS CHANGE Day once again. Almost all the staff had gathered to watch the transformation at dawn, along with those human Twin-Bred who were willing to attend without their twins. Mara's assistant caught her heading for her office and dragged her to join the others.

Many of the staff lingered at breakfast afterward. Mara sat long enough to wolf down a muffin, took her coffee and headed for her office at last.

"You know, sis, you could start talking to Dr. Tanner again. The Project is no longer secret, to put it mildly."

Mara threw her jacket over her extra chair and sat down at her desk. "There's still the matter of your — appearances? Either I tell him, or I hide it from him. I don't like either alternative."

"You never really explained why you don't want to tell him."

"He might think this was carrying things a little far. Involving others, risking my career. He might say you'd gone from a basically healthy coping mechanism to an obsession."

"You've already come up with a nice scary diagnosis without him — doesn't seem like you have much to lose by seeing if he agrees."

"Do you? Agree?"

"Not really. It's not as if you were neglecting your work or doing it less well. Or neglecting your acquaintances any more than you always have. Seeing me may be a temptation, but not an obsession. Any other bogeymen I can dispatch?"

"The same one as before. I'm afraid that anything I change could be the one change too many. The one that makes me lose you."

"Silly Mara. We've already survived how many therapeutic discussions with our little family household intact?"

Mara opened her mail program. "I'll think about it. Maybe after the next time."

"Which is when?"

"Judy and La-ren have a mission coming up. I should speak to La-ren anyway. I can ask him to stop by. Levi — There's something I want to do, when I see him. Something we've never been able to do."

"I was wondering when that would occur to you."

"But if I do this, I'm sure to cry."

"If you must."

La-ren's tablet buzzed an incoming call. "La-ren, it's Dr. Cadell. When are you and Judy leaving for Anson Center?"

"Tomorrow, at approximately noon."

"Please stop by my office sometime today, then. When would be convenient?"

"That would depend on the amount of time necessary. And on whether you wish Judy to accompany me."

"That's — that's up to the two of you, La-ren. I know your memory is excellent. You can pass on to her anything I say about your mission. She may have a preference one way or the other — based upon the last time we met."

"Understood."

Mara heard the distinctive knock of Tofa knuckles on her door and hurried to open it. "La-ren. Thank you for coming. Judy preferred not to come with you?"

"Yes. She finds it easier to contemplate our arrangement than to witness it."

Mara gestured toward what she understood to be the most comfortable bit of wall in her office, and closed the door behind La-ren. "I didn't ask you here just — just for that favor. Although I would greatly appreciate it, after we talk about the Anson Center situation. Actually, about the way all the missions have been going lately."

La-ren leaned against the wall and appeared to gather his thoughts. His attitude, as best she could read it, was simultaneously serious and relaxed. "Per protocol, Judy and I have reviewed the recent mission reports. There has been a disturbing new element. From the beginning, we have encountered distrust and sometimes hostility from the humans involved, at least upon first arrival. Until recently the Tofa have reacted with anything from mild interest, to disinterest, to amusement. That has begun to change. In several recent missions, the Tofa have appeared impatient, uncomfortable, with our Tofa team members. Revulsion is too strong a term for what they have displayed, but it is on the same continuum."

"Can you think of anything that would account for this change in Tofa attitudes?"

"We have not changed in any obviously material way. We are of course growing older. If our role is somehow less appropriate for fully mature Tofa than for younger ones, I am not aware of it. But such could be the case."

Mara picked up the pot of hot chocolate her assistant kept full for her. She poured a mug for herself and looked inquiringly at La-ren. He nodded his sideways nod; she poured more chocolate into a mug shaped for Tofa convenience and handed it to him. As he held it under his chin and took a sip, his body odor shifted in the direction that indicated intense pleasure. It mingled pleasingly with the smell of the chocolate itself. How lovely that chocolate, one of her few indulgences, had turned out to be so appealing to Tofa.

She dragged her mind back to the discussion. "You've cut to the heart of the matter. Don't be alarmed — it's a human expression meaning that you've identified the most important issue. Our efforts are hampered by our very limited knowledge of Tofa psychology and culture. What we've been able to learn from you and the others is much better than nothing, but it falls far short of the way we understand human community dynamics. We'd hoped that the Tofa host mothers and nurses would fill in at least some of those gaps, once we could communicate with them better. But you know how that turned out."

La-ren slurped up the last of his chocolate. "It has been years since the last adult Tofa left the Project. Perhaps the time is ripe for some attempt to renew contact — an attempt in which the Tofa Twin-Bred could participate."

Mara took the mug from him and put it on her desk. "That's an excellent idea. I'll put together a brainstorming session. I'd like you to be there -- I'll schedule it for after you and Judy return."

There was a moment of silence. Mara finished her own chocolate, draining every drop and licking the rim of the mug before putting it down. She was gathering her nerve to address more personal matters when La-ren spoke again. "Concerning the recent change in Tofa attitudes: Judy has a hunch."

Mara, nervous, suppressed a giggle at his choice of words. "A hunch. Yes?"

"Something about the timing of these and other events, and their occurrence in varied locations and situations, leads her to intuit that this change is in some manner orchestrated. That it is being deliberately fostered."

"By whom?"

"Her hunch has not led that far. We will continue observing. If circumstances permit, we may ask that question."

Mara sighed. "I guess that's as far as we can go with this, for now."

"Which allows us to turn to other concerns. To the favor you mentioned. Which I am happy to grant."

"I still feel that it's asking too much. But — if you don't feel that way, then whenever you're ready. And thank you. Oh — could I ask you for one thing more? Could you turn around and then turn back? It might make this transition feel — well, a little more natural."

La-ren nodded; turned his back, then faced her again, wriggling his arms and shoulders as if getting comfortable in a new suit.

"It's good to see you, Mara. You don't look in the mirror often enough. Though when you do, after these sessions, it's a bit strange to see you left-right reversed. . . . You didn't ask him."

Mara's chest was tight. She forced herself to breathe evenly. "I couldn't. I'm passing the buck to you. You'd know, wouldn't you, if — if he'd object?"

"I believe I would. And I don't believe he does. It's not as if he's never done anything like it with Judy. You may recall that you saw it once."

"That's right, I did. I like to think of them — having that."

"So quit stalling, sis, and get over here."

La-ren opened his two lower arms and folded the others aside. Mara was, indeed, crying as she walked over to him, and put her arms around him. And hugged her brother tight.

Chapter 39

THE HOVERCAR dropped off the mediators and security team, then flew off to find itself a parking spot and await their recall. The craft was one of a small fleet recently designed and built by the Twin-Bred as a class project. It could accommodate human or Tofa drivers or passengers; its dual controls could be deployed or stowed depending on the driver. Such craft had obvious utility for blended communities; the mission teams now made a point of arriving in them.

They were met by four humans and two Tofa, who returned their greeting with silent nods and short buzzes, respectively, and led them to a nearby building, down its entrance corridor and into a small room. The Tofa beckoned to La-ren and pointed down the corridor. When one member of the security team moved in that direction, the Tofa held out a rigid upper arm in obvious refusal. This was against protocol, but not unprecedented. The Tofa had been increasingly reluctant to allow ordinary humans, other than those involved in the dispute, to be present during mediation.

La-ren turned to Judy. "I will contact you if I wish to consult during the session. Otherwise, we will meet back here and share our experiences."

"Good luck, La-ren. Whatever luck is."

"Remind me to inquire further on that subject when we return." La-ren gave Judy a reassuring tap on the cheek and followed his Tofa escort out of the room.

Judy sighed as she watched her brother leave. Separation was one of the unpleasant aspects of these missions.

She caught motion in her peripheral vision, turned around and gasped. The four humans had abruptly grabbed the security guards and were tugging them toward the door. Two more humans came in and performed a quick and rough search for any weapons they might be carrying. They found the guards' stun guns and tossed them aside. The others pulled and shoved the guards across the corridor to another room, thrust them in, slammed and locked the door. As she drew her breath to scream, someone slapped a hand tight across her mouth. Others held her arms behind her back.

The rest of the men filed back into the room. One of them looked at her and ostentatiously shook his head.

"You really one of those twin freaks? You look almost normal. Pretty, too. You get yourself out of that place, you could find a man, start living a proper life."

Judy tried unsuccessfully to bite the hand at her mouth. She struggled violently enough to break free of the hold on her left arm, but not her right, and she was soon secured again.

"This is getting old," muttered a voice from behind her. "Get a chair and some tape. We don't know how long things will take, and she just kicked me."

Judy fought harder than she had ever imagined fighting, and asked herself hopelessly why fighting skills had not been part of her or La-ren's education. She thought she slowed them down a minute or two before they succeeded in gagging her and tying her to a heavy wooden chair.

The two Tofa who joined La-ren in the empty room did not seem eager to discuss the problem facing the community. La-ren waited a while, then asked, "Please tell me more about the purpose for which my sister and I have been invited."

The thinner of the Tofa turned slightly away. "That invitation was not unanimous."

More silence.

La-ren tried again. "We were told that a dispute has arisen concerning the methods and locations for adding chemical supplements to the water supply."

The other Tofa responded this time. "There are more important problems. Which we will solve."

"That is interesting. Have you developed new methods of resolving community disputes without outside mediation?"

"That is a question not easily answered without extensive discussion. Which will not take place today, with you. There are some humans who wish to meet with you."

This was unusual so early in a mission. It might be promising. Perhaps there were human members of this community who wished to improve their cross-species communication skills. "I am ready to meet with them. Will you be taking me to them?"

"You will wait here. They will be coming."

The Tofa turned and left, closing the door behind them. La-ren had little time to run through various opening overtures before it opened again and eight humans filed through. They were all average or above average adult human height. They seemed to have come from some manual labor, for they were carrying various implements — a hoe, a shovel, a metal rake, and others he could not immediately identify. From some of the tools came a familiar and soothing smell, the smell of disturbed soil.

La-ren wished Judy were present to help him assess the humans' demeanors. Several of the men were shifting their weight back and forth between their feet, and others were exchanging glances in a somewhat jerky fashion. He thought he smelled something like the beer consumed by some of the human Project staff.

One of the men stepped forward and said abruptly, "Got some questions for you. You come here to talk, don't you?"

La-ren began to doubt his original hypothesis. These did not seem like humans eager to improve their communication skills. Unless they had been instructed to do so because those skills were particularly deficient.

"How did they make you lot, anyway? Genes in a blender, was it?"

La-ren reviewed his briefings as to what could be disclosed. "Twin pairs like Judy and myself were carried together by a human host mother, seventeen years ago. Since then, we have been raised together, so that the connections formed by our shared uterine experience have been intensified."

"That's it?"

"If I understand you, yes."

His interrogator seemed satisfied. "So when you're gone, that's it? No baby half-and-half's on the way, no production line, none in the tank waiting to come out?"

The men were surrounding him now. One of them said, "That's all right, then." And raised the shovel.

* SECRET *
CLEARANCE CLASS 2 AND ABOVE*

LEVI Status Report, 5-1-88
Executive Summary

<u>Lethality Incident</u>

. . . The hovercar returned with the surviving human and the body of the Tofa twin. Debriefing indicated that the human, Judy Hanson, had been carried to the car in restraints and made to instruct her abductors as to how to set the controls for the Project compound. The security detail remains missing. A factor in the current moratorium is the unwillingness of security personnel to accompany future mission teams without lethal armament, and the difficulty of negotiating acceptance of teams carrying weapons adequate for self-defense against large groups.

According to inspection and subsequent autopsy, the Tofa, La-ren, died of numerous blunt force injuries. . . .

The staff on duty were gathered in the common room. There had been no announcements or meetings; the news was traveling by less formal methods.

"Did the Tofa know what the humans had planned?"
"Who the hell knows?"

"Why did they let Judy get away?"
"Nobody's sure. Judy isn't talking much, but from what I hear, she doesn't really know. Maybe humans didn't want to kill a human — and she's got fewer Tofa quirks than some of them — or maybe something else was going on."

"Do they know who did it?"
"They've got some suspects in custody. At least, they were in custody. We're not sure what's going on. The authorities ID'd them because one of the killers made his rounds of the bars and was boasting about it, and another one sobered up and had some qualms after the fact, told his mother all about it and his sister-in-law turned him in."

"Has Dr. Cadell come out of her quarters at all?"
"Not since we heard. Not for a moment."

The Deputy Administrator for the Long-Term Emissary Viviparous Initiative was accustomed to having politically difficult situations land in his lap — but none as challenging as this. He shifted uneasily in the witness chair. The Council had insisted that he appear in person: their need to posture and expostulate could not, apparently, be satisfied via any long-distance communication.

"Dr. Serkin, tell us if we are missing something. Wasn't the Project instituted — and repeatedly funded — in order to reduce the likelihood of interspecies violence? Hasn't that hope proved disastrously misplaced? Haven't your 'missions' of interference produced exactly what they were supposed to avoid?"

Dr. Serkin tried to appear calm and unintimidated. "First, we have had one setback. Tragic as it is, there is no ground for over-interpreting it into an indication of overall failure. There have been several notable successes, instances where mediation teams have resolved disputes which could otherwise have escalated —"

The Council's sub-chair for Tofa Relations looked at him with some sympathy. "Doctor, when was the last time you achieved such a result?"

Dr. Serkin scrolled through his tablet, more to buy time than to find the answer he already knew. The last three teams sent out before Judy and La-ren's trip to Anson Center had reported little progress. There had been plans to send the teams back for further attempts, but now. . . .

Time to change the subject. "There is another indication that things may not be entirely as they seem. We have, of course, been in communication with Tofa authorities. Communications assisted, by the way, by our Tofa twin subjects. We would have expected the Tofa to be even more upset than this body about the murder of an innocent Tofa youth. But we have not met with anger or denunciations." Although even the Tofa Twin-Bred were somewhat at a loss about how the Tofa were taking the news. There was something cryptic about the Tofa response. Dr. Serkin wished that Dr. Cadell would come out of her room and help figure things out.

Mara could feel Levi waiting. She would not let him speak. She was curled up on her bed, in a position too tightly clenched to be called fetal. She would think only of the tightness of her muscles, the feel of the bedspread on her cheek, the rhythm of her breaths, the hum of the environmental unit, anything that that was sensory and immediate, nothing that could dislodge her and send her down a vortex of despair.

A new sensory input. A knock, repeated. Then a sound. Mara shuddered. The sound meant something. It was her name.

"Dr. Cadell! Mara! Please answer. It's Carla. Even if you don't need to talk — and I think you do — please, just say something."

Levi took advantage of the break in her concentration. "Mara. I know what you're thinking. Of course I do. And you know it isn't true."

"Do I? It feels true. There are more things in heaven and earth — to say nothing of this damned planet. . . . It could be true."

"Mara, you are not a jinx! Your touch is not fatal! And neither is your love."

"I can never take the chance again. I can never touch you."

"Mara mia — sufficient unto the day is the evil thereof. We have enough to grieve over, without forecasting future griefs. . . . This time I won't tell you not to cry. One of us must."

She did, for a long time.

"Levi! What about Judy? Where is she? Is anyone with her?"

"I don't know. Which isn't good enough. We have to find out, now."

"She won't want to see me. I'm the last person she'll want to see."

"If she's with friends, or under observation, we can vanish. On your feet, Mara! And bring your master key."

She was already reaching for it.

Mara pushed past a startled Carla Horn, still standing in the hallway, and ran. She burst through the infirmary doorway. "Is Judy still here?"

"No, we released her this morning."

Mara turned and ran on, ignoring the stares of Twin-Bred and staff. She rounded the corner. There, Judy and La-ren's room, now Judy's alone. Mara skidded to a halt, tried to stop panting, and put her ear to the door. There were no voices; she heard no movements. She knocked once, waited, knocked again.

No answer. She pounded on the door. Finally, she called. "Judy! Please! I won't take a moment — please answer!"

Nothing. She fumbled for the master key, unlocked the door and shoved it open. Judy was on the longer bed — La-ren's bed. She lay still, sprawled, her left arm hanging loose, a row of patches on it. Mara ran inside and pressed the emergency call button on the wall. Then she ran to the door and screamed.

Mara looked around her quarters. They seemed somehow unfamiliar, as if she had been away for years. She stumbled to the bed and collapsed on it, shoes dangling off the edge.

"She's all right, then."

"Yes. At least, she's alive, and medically recovered. They got to her in time."

"What now?"

"If Laura's father were still alive — but there's no use wishing. Judy and Laura are staying with Veda and Melly. Having Melly around will be a helpful distraction. We hope. Jimmy and Peer-tek have a room in the main compound now, so she won't be constantly around a — a complete pair of twins. And she'll have some time away from places where all her memories have La-ren in them. As if that will make a difference. Levi — what if I did this? What if she looked at me and saw — saw how twisted she could become, how crippled and desperate —"

"That is quite enough of that, Mara. You're going to call Dr. Tanner as soon as I finish lecturing you. When Judy looked at you, she saw someone who has suffered, yes, but she saw someone who has survived! And turned that suffering into world-changing achievement."

"World-changing. I think we've seen just how much I changed the world."

Chapter 40

THE CROWD gathered in a grove of trees near the river behind the compound. The never-born twins, lost so many years before, had been studied, then cremated. This was the first time they would bury their dead.

The long narrow coffin rested beside the long narrow hole. Mara, Laura, and Judy stood closest to it. Judy stepped forward.

She stood in silence for a moment, looking slowly around the crowd of humans and Tofa.

"I don't understand.

"I don't understand why we're here. I don't understand why we've lost my brother, our La-ren. I don't understand death. And I don't understand hate and murder.

"I don't understand killing someone who came to help you. I don't understand a crowd of grown men killing a boy.

"I don't understand why this happened now, and not the first time or the other times we tried to help.

"I don't understand. But I still hope.

"I still hope that we can help humans and Tofa understand each other.

"I don't see why La-ren had to die for it. But I still hope we can do what we were born for. I'm still willing to try.

"And I'm still willing to live. Thank you, Dr. Cadell, for giving me a second chance to make that choice.

"I know — I know very well — that I will never be the same without La-ren." Many of the human Twin-Bred and staff were crying now. The Tofa rocked back and forth. "But

I know that you will all be with me. That you will help me when you can. I know that I am not alone.

"I know that you will all miss La-ren. That you loved him. That we still love him.

"My sweet brother. Our brave spirit. Goodbye."

She stood a moment longer, then walked back to Mara and Laura and took their hands. They stood together as the hole was filled with sweet-smelling clay.

Judy, Laura and Mara walked back with Veda and Melly. Judy stopped outside the cottage. "You three can go on in. I just need to talk with Dr. Cadell about something. I'll see you soon."

Melly opened her arms for a hug. Judy knelt down and squeezed her tight, kissed her forehead, and then gave her a gentle shove toward the cottage. Laura hesitated for a moment, gave Judy another hug, broke away and stumbled inside.

Judy turned to Mara. "Let's walk some more. Along that river."

No one had lingered near the grave site. They followed the nearest river on into the sparse purple woods. Judy stopped and put her hand on a tree.

"This was the La-ren tree. Is. I always told him it looks like him. Its branches remind me of how he used to hold his arms. And it's taller than the others."

She kissed the nearest branch, then turned to Mara.

"Dr. Cadell, there's something you should let me do. I want you to let me tell the others — or at least some of them. About your brother. About what La-ren did for you."

"Judy, why? Are you thinking that I — that it harmed him somehow? That it distracted him, made him less careful, less alert to trouble? I've asked myself that, and it kills me that I'll never know —"

"No! It's nothing like that. Helping you, bringing Levi to you — it didn't trouble him. And as strange as it seemed to you, it didn't seem so strange to him. I'm sure he wasn't thinking about it at the wrong time. No — I want to find someone else. Another Twin-Bred who can help you the way La-ren did."

Mara's jaw dropped. She turned and found another tree, leaned against it. "But — you didn't like it. It felt wrong to you. Why would you want it to happen again? How would the next twin feel?"

"I was so stupid. I thought it was drawing La-ren away from me. When he was right there. When I could see him every day." Judy fought back tears. "Now I know. I know what's it's like to lose him. To be incomplete. La-ren didn't want you to feel like that. He was proud of helping you. He wouldn't want those — those murdering bastards to put a stop to that, too. I could explain. I could explain it all to some of the others. I know whom to trust. And I can find a pair where one wants to help and the other doesn't mind."

Mara stood up, walked back to Judy's "La-ren tree," and put a hand against it. "Judy, I don't know what to say. I'm grateful for your kindness. I'll have to think about it. What I've lost — it doesn't compare, not at all. But when we lost La-ren . . . it was La-ren, the only time I ever held my brother. It hurts that much more. I'm not sure how I feel about — opening myself up again."

"If it was hard to lose, isn't it worth having? Would you rather live without it, always?"

"Judy — if the other Tofa twins can do this for me, as Sel-ran and La-ren did . . . have you thought about — Judy, what could they do for you?"

Judy stared off into the trees. "It's not the same. Levi lives in you. You kept him alive. You made him what he is. I'm sorry — I don't mean to hurt you."

Mara smiled ruefully. "It's all right, Judy. I know he doesn't have his own reality as La-ren did. Although I wonder, sometimes, whether there's more to him than just my wishes or inventions or wild guesses. There we were, together, those first months. Maybe, just maybe, there was a person there already, someone to know — someone I knew."

"I didn't have La-ren inside me that way. I didn't need to. I don't know if he's there now, enough for someone else to reach him."

Mara motioned toward the compound. They started back, walking in silence. When they reached the cottage, Mara stopped and held out her hands. Judy held out hers, and Mara grasped them. "When you're ready, we can find out."

Part Three

Chapter 41

THE HUMAN mayor of Varley stood to greet his visitor. He expected to remain standing. He had worn his arch supports. But the Tofa surprised him. "We may sit, if you like. I wish you to be comfortable." Her — for some reason he was thinking of the visitor as female — her Terran was remarkably good. She folded herself into the largest chair in a manner he had not seen before; it looked uncomfortable, but he didn't see how he could suggest anything different.

"Thank you. I listen better sitting down — and I'm eager to hear what you have to say. I gather there have been some changes in your community that I should know about?"

"There have. And in several other communities. Others like myself are meeting with leaders like yourself, to explain these changes."

"May I record our meeting? If there's anything you don't want mentioned outside this room, you have only to tell me. Whatever isn't confidential, I may release for broadcast, after my staff has reviewed it."

The Tofa nodded. He had never seen a Tofa nod, at least not in that direction. "That is perfectly acceptable. I am quite accustomed to being recorded." He had the fleeting sensation that she would have smiled, if that were possible.

Zachary Flint, the Chairman's confidential assistant, insisted on speaking to Mara immediately, and never mind her weekly staff meeting. Mara closed the door to her office and pressed the "receive and record" button.

"Mara? It took you long enough. What the hell have you people sent out into the world?"

"Are you saying there have been more attempted missions since the moratorium? I don't see how there could be. Since the last time, we've kept a very close watch —"

"No, dammit! Not your half-baked would-be ambassadors. The Tofa! This new kind of Tofa, who speak Terran better than my son-in-law, and seem to have every local Tofa official wrapped around their rotary-jointed fingers! The Tofa who are calmly suggesting that really, the time has come for joint human-Tofa local councils. The Tofa who just want the chance to keep the peace, who reassure us that their greater understanding of how humans tick can lead us all into the promised land of peace, prosperity, and not having to worry our little human heads. The Tofa!"

"Zack? Before I try to answer your questions, I need to check on something. I want to give you accurate information. Just hold on." Without waiting for permission, she put him on hold-and-hide, shoved back from her screen, and put her head in her hands.

"Levi. Is this what I think it is?"

"Well, now we have confirmation of what happened to our vanished host mothers. And it may well be that this is why they left us. The question is: is this why they came to us in the first place?"

"You mean, the whole business with the extra Tofa embryos? Do you think they were planning, that far back — what? To try to form a connection with us, or learn about us, through the host mother process?"

"While we're feeling out-played, Mara mia: maybe this explains why they cooperated at all. With the Project. Was there one Project, or were there two?"

"If they were planning from the beginning, running their own experiment, we have to ask ourselves: did the two Projects pursue the same goal? Ours hasn't done what we hoped. Should we be grateful that they had another plan?"

"Our Project hasn't gone so well, you say. But it started out with some success. Why has it foundered? And just before the Tofa host mothers reappear as the new Tofa power elite?"

Mara jumped out of her chair and walked to the window. She stared out at the host mother cottages. "No. I will not believe this. Why should we conclude that the Tofa mothers sabotaged the Twin-Bred? What evidence is there?"

"It may be there, if we look for it. And there is the absence of other hypotheses."

"We should look for those too. And not just us."

"Much as I esteem my own discernment, I agree. This is too big. We need to get everyone involved."

"Oh, Lord — Flint's still on hold."

"It's a good thing we talk fast. . . . Get rid of him. Tell him we're checking out some answers. In motion, sis! We've got things to do."

The auditorium was packed. Every security measure they could devise was in place. Every senior staff member and many of those more junior, every Twin-Bred, and every host mother considered sufficiently trustworthy was there and waiting.

Mara stepped forward.

"We have never met like this before. We have never had such need of each other's insight and counsel. We have never had such decisions to make.

"I hope you have all reviewed the briefing I've prepared. If so, you know what we suspect.

"We must decide whether we believe that the Tofa authorities — starting before this Project began, before many of you were born — manipulated the Project to create Tofa who could understand, interact with, and even govern human communities. If there are other explanations, we must assess them.

"If we decide that the evidence supports this hypothesis, then we must decide what predictions to make, and what actions to take, in response.

"If the Tofa did all this, then we could view their scheme as an alternative to what we all have worked for and planned. We must ask ourselves whether this alternative is likely to succeed, as we hoped to succeed. Whether it will bring peace and a stable future to this planet we share — or whether it will trigger worse conflicts than this Project, and possibly the Tofa, have worked to prevent.

"If we have been manipulated, we must decide whether to expose and oppose the manipulators — or whether to swallow our pride, and potentially our own dreams, and work to make a success of the plan that has supplemented or even superseded ours. Or are there other alternatives to explore?"

Mara looked around the room. She took a slow, deep breath.

"And now, I will start this discussion by speaking for myself only. There is one thing I must say. One fact that must not be forgotten — although there are other facts that may mitigate it. If the Tofa created an alternative to the Twin-Bred, and then used their influence to cripple this Project — then they are responsible for every casualty in the conflicts we have been unable to prevent. And. They. Killed. La-ren."

"Sit down. Someplace soft. Lean back. And tell me all about it."

Mara plopped down on the shabby armchair she had brought from her old apartment. The touch of the worn fabric was like visiting a distant and innocent past. "You'd think I'd be all talked out. But after my initial — outburst? — I didn't do much of the talking. And it went on, round and round, for hours.

"We ended up agreeing on one simple fact: we have to try to work with them. To negotiate ways for the Twin-Bred to keep going out there and trying to help. Even if the Tofa host mothers are better with humans than normal Tofa, there aren't that many of them. And we have no reason to assume their skills can be transmitted or delegated."

"We have no reason to assume we know what they can do. But go on."

"So we'll offer to help. We'll ask them which problems they'd like to bring us in on —"

"Which bones they'd like to throw."

"We have to try something! If the Twin-Bred do a good job on what the Tofa host mothers consider less important or less interesting or in any way less desirable problems, that's a start."

"That doesn't sound like hours of discussion. Did you talk about what would happen if all these ideas get nowhere?"

"Yes, of course. Dar-tan asked if we would keep the Project going in any event, for scientific purposes. I had to say the odds of continued funding were not good. I wasn't sure if I should, but I decided I had to tell them about my conversation with the Council Treasurer. . . ."

Mara held on tight to the side of her desk, to keep as tight a grip on her temper. "Mr. Treasurer, you know the Project was in large part, even primarily, established for scientific purposes. Certainly we all hoped the Twin-Bred would have the capacity to take part in public affairs, but that was only speculation. What we knew was that there would be great and ongoing scientific returns on our investment."

The Treasurer smirked. "Yes, I seem to recall the Council emphasizing the scientific aspects of your mission, some years back — only to meet with an intemperate response. . . . Dr. Cadell, with respect, you have had sixteen years of studying these Twin-Bred. I'm sure it will take years for scientists — yours and others — to absorb and analyze everything you've learned already. There is, among some on the Council, a sense that you have reached the point of diminishing returns."

"And what is the alternative? That all our Twin-Bred move into the local human and Tofa communities and start over? With what transition period, what resources?"

"As for the Tofa youngsters, that would be up to the Tofa authorities. The humans — I'm not at all sure the nearby towns are ready for an influx of immigrants with such, ah, disturbing characteristics. And with no local support systems, no usable job training. . . ."

"Where the hell does that leave them?" Don't shout, she told herself, a little late. "I'm sorry, Mr. Treasurer. But I don't see what you're suggesting."

"Of course, nothing has been decided. But at least on an interim basis, they could remain at your facility, with some supervisory personnel. You have some small agricultural programs already in place, I believe — they could be expanded. We could find some other productive tasks for your young people to perform, to pay for their continued maintenance."

Mara held onto her composure long enough to invent an incoming call and get off the phone before she ran to the toilet and threw up.

"Shall we call it a reservation? A concentration camp? A productive ghetto?"

"Whatever you like. It means we're running out of time."

"I doubt the entire Council has already embraced the treasurer's particular brand of pragmatism."

"No, we still have a few members who will give us the benefit of the doubt, at least for a while longer. Some of them would like to see us succeed. And we'll make sure they hear immediately about any good news."

"I believe you have more to tell me."

"Yes. I've been sneaking up on it. I don't know quite how to talk about it.

"If we can't turn it around — if they can't find a way to work with the new Tofa leadership and get back out into the communities — Artemisia was the one who suggested it...."

Artemisia raised her hand to speak. "We keep talking about having no future here. That's here! Why are humans here in the first place? Because they didn't like the future they had, back on Terra. So they went looking for one somewhere else! If nobody wants us here, except as slave labor, then let's move on and find our own place! We have the skills. We may not have all the know-how, but we'll find a way, if we have to. Let's leave this planet to tear itself apart, or live under the Tofa host mothers, or whatever it's going to do. Let's leave!"

"So the backup plan is an exodus."

"Yes. But first, we do our damnedest to reach the Tofa host mothers. To get them to listen."

Chapter 42

BON-TOK AND Tas-tan were reading together from the same screen: *Stranger in a Strange Land*. They finished at the same time. Bon-tok turned to Tas-tan. "How will we summarize this book for the group?"

"We could say that it chronicles the journey of Valentine Michael Smith, a human raised on the planet Mars by that planet's indigenous sentient species. He returns to Earth as a young man and must try to learn the ways of his own people, while the humans who help him also learn from him about Martian beliefs and abilities. There is an informational site that describes the novel as exploring Mr. Smith's interaction with and eventual transformation of Earth culture."

"That is not necessarily accurate. At the book's conclusion, it is unclear whether Earth culture will be transformed, or even affected in any significant way."

Tas-tan buzzed softly. "And it might be as well to remember what befell Mr. Smith."

They sat contemplating his fate in silence.

Mara and the rest of the senior Project staff had gathered in a large conference room with representatives from the human and Tofa twins and from the humans carried by Tofa host mothers. Mara spoke first.

"We've tried to open a discussion with the Tofa host mothers, or with someone who admits to being able to contact them. We haven't found anyone — cooperative. But we do have contacts in several cities who were sympathetic to our efforts in general. We could get some limited assistance from them in trying again. I'd like to hear ideas from any of you about how to do that."

Carla Horn gestured toward Ron Keller from the Tofa Relations department. "Ron and I have been talking about whether to send another team out, on some credible assignment, to one of the towns that's had a visit from a host mother. Some opportunity for contact might arise. Of course, this would be on a strictly volunteer basis."

Peer-tek turned toward her. "And have all previous missions been compulsory? An interesting implication."

After an awkward silence, Bernie, one of the singletons, raised his hand to be recognized. "We've discussed the matter. This should be our job. They're our mothers. Do we know which host mothers have shown up where?"

Mara consulted her tablet. "The local council for Bovatown had a visit from a Tofa who may have been Ter Ra-tel-sen. Your host mother, Bernie. And Samantha — the first visitor, in Varley, was Ter Fen-sin-ta, who carried you."

"I wouldn't count on any help from Varley," said Carla. "The mayor's fussed and bothered enough that he wouldn't want to complicate his life any further. But the mayor of Bovatown might be interested. Before — earlier, we were talking about sending a team there. There have been some complaints from the Tofa community about the landscaping in the parks."

Bernie turned toward Nedra. "Your Tofar is better than most of our group's."

Nedra looked embarrassed. "Maybe. And I've worked with Bernie on quite a few school projects. We don't need much explanation to know what the other is thinking. We'd make a good team. I volunteer."

Mara looked at Bernie. "Are we jumping the gun here? Are you volunteering?"

"Well, yes."

"Anyone else?" Mara looked around the room.

"I don't think anyone else should come." Nedra spoke very quietly. "We don't know how dangerous this will be, but we've seen what can happen. We don't know if our mothers can protect us. We don't even know if they'll know we're there." She stopped and bit her lip, then went on. "And we don't know how they feel about us now — or how they ever did . . . ."

There were no answers to those questions when the hovercar returned from Bovatown, empty except for the two bodies, both bearing neat projectile wounds to the head.

At the next meeting, the vote was not unanimous, but there were very few in the minority. Those few would not be compelled to take part, but they as well as the majority thought it likely that when the time came, they would all be on board. Literally and figuratively.

The Twin-Bred were leaving.

Chapter 43

MARA STARED levelly across the desk at Councilman Hanley. "You know this is the best way out for you and your colleagues. You've been handed a hot potato. We propose to take it off your hands, permanently. No unpleasant news stories about maintaining a compound of freaks at public expense. No scares about invasions of half-alien monsters. No political hay made out of keeping a lot of innocent young people locked up and used for forced labor. One major commitment of resources, and then no more, ever again. We aren't asking for any sort of pensions or retirement bonuses for the Project staff."

"But you are asking for access to top secret archived material about, and artifacts from, the spacecraft that brought us here. Information your Twin-Bred will be using, for purposes we have to take on faith."

"We can accept remote monitoring of the areas where the ship and its components are being assembled."

Councilman Hanley studied his fingers. "This will take some thought, and some discussion. I see the advantages. As well as some political land mines." He stood up. "I'll get back to you."

Councilwoman Fuller took the call on her secured line. "Of course I'm glad to discuss this again, Mara, but do you really think we have anything new to say on the subject?"

"Don't think of this as lobbying, Councilwoman. Think of it as constituent service. You have quite a few voters out here."

Fuller raised her eyebrows. "Are you sure? I'm not certain all your busy scientists took the time to update their records last year, when the law required it. And even before then — I really don't recall seeing any votes come in from your Project during the last election. Must be all that security you have in place — guess it blocked the transmission. A shame."

Mara took a deep breath, then another. She could feel Levi telling her to stay focused. "Thea. Apparently I need to clarify certain points. I am aware that you have succeeded in covering up the misadventure we discussed some years ago."

"You mean, I managed to frustrate your attempts at blackmail."

"If you will. But I don't know why you seem to have expected me to — to abandon my interest in your activities since then. I'm sending you a scrambled file, and the key to decode it. You may be able to guess at some of its contents. The information is in safekeeping elsewhere. I believe you would find it difficult to find and eliminate all copies."

Fuller's face was red. Mara recalled the saying "if looks could kill."

"If you insist on preventing our Twin-Bred from escaping the trap they're in, then I suggest you look up the term 'Pyrrhic victory.' Councilwoman, if we're going down, you will go before us."

The copter descended through the rain and touched down; the hum of its motors fell quiet. The men and women who emerged came cautiously, looking around, staying close together.

Mara came forward, with a smile she had practiced in the mirror. "Welcome! Please, come this way. Thank you so much. I know you'll find it exciting — and illuminating — to work with our budding young scientists and engineers. We are all so grateful for your help."

One gray-haired woman cleared her throat. "Well, it isn't every day we get the chance to work on a spacecraft! And who knows when such a chance would come again." She blushed. "And of course, we're looking forward to meeting your — young people."

"This way, then."

Human Twin-Bred Gina sat absorbed in her tablet. Her boyfriend Tom came up behind her and tickled her neck. She shuddered. "Not now, Tommy."

"Sorry, love. What are you reading?"

She showed him the text. "*Rebirth*. It's an old book about some young people with telepathic abilities. They live among people who don't understand, and think they're — an abomination. Some of them are injured. The rest are running away, into the wilderness. But then they get a message from people far away, people like them. Right now, those telepaths are coming to take them away from the others."

Tom put a firm hand, this time, on her neck and massaged the tense muscles. He spoke gently. "Lucky them. It's harder when nobody's coming, isn't it? When you have to rescue yourself."

She grabbed his hand and kissed it.

Judy and Mara walked down the corridor to one of the empty classrooms. It was used for small seminars, rather than lectures or labs. There were writing desks with padded chairs, and tall standing desks, but these had been pushed aside.

The four young Tofa turned toward them as they entered. Judy put an arm around Mara, who was trembling.

"I don't know what to say." Mara looked from one tall figure to the other. "I'm not used to coming to people and — hoping for something from them. I don't want any of you to feel that you have to do this. That you owe it to me, or anything of the sort. You don't."

Li-sen came forward and took her hand. "What we owe is for us to say. And none of us is here unwillingly."

"I'm not looking for — for full contact, today. I was hoping you could tell me — if you could sense whether it would be possible, without actually doing it."

"Let us find out."

Li-sen let go her hand and returned to his fellows. They all stood in silence. Mara closed her eyes and leaned against Judy.

Fel-lar was the first to speak. "Yes."

"Yes?? You mean — you think you could?"

"He is, you would say, ready and waiting."

Peer-tek spoke next. "At your service."

Then, Li-sen. "Awaiting your pleasure."

Slow tears ran from Mara's closed eyes. "Thank you. All of you. I just — I just wanted to know."

They did not speak of how little difference it would make, once the Twin-Bred were gone.

"It may be hardest on the singletons. At least the twins will have each other, as they always have."

"Are they invited?"

"Of course. The children have spent so much of their time together, twins and singletons. There are some solid friendships between the two. And now both groups have had casualties. No, the doubts aren't on the twins' end of things."

Melinda sat disconsolate in the empty classroom. Sinbad came in and sat down beside her; the two pressed close together as singletons often did.

"A penny for your thoughts?"

Melinda tried to smile. "How much was a penny, anyway?"

"I doubt you were sitting here thinking about economics. What is it?"

"What else could it be? I don't know what to do."

Sinbad picked up a stylus and tossed it back and forth. "You don't have to know yet. Not quite."

Melinda sighed, a deep, slow sigh. "We're almost out of time. The final drawings for the ship will be made soon, and they have to know how big to make it! And besides — I have to *know*. Not knowing is worse than all the rest of it."

"What would you do, if you went back?" Toss, toss.

"Dr. Horn says we should try to imagine it, both ways. Going along in the ship, or moving to some human town and starting over." Melinda's hands clenched into fists. "But they're both so — unimaginable."

Sinbad dropped the stylus and took her hands. "Let me help. Close your eyes." She obeyed. "Now think of yourself in a mess hall. Instead of the field outside, or buildings, there's the black sky, and stars. And in the mess hall — there's Bon-tok, juggling the cutlery again."

Melinda giggled, just a bit. "And Ruthie is tickling Jantel. And then he picks her up and dangles her upside down."

"Oh, no, not in the middle of lunch!"

"All right. I see where this is heading. Home is where your friends are. But we can make new friends."

"Can we?"

In the end, none chose to stay behind. Singleton or twin, they were all Twin-Bred, and they would seek their future together.

Chapter 44

THE TWIN-BRED, twins and singletons, had gathered in the smaller common room. Scramblers were on full, and staff and parents had been respectfully asked to avoid interruption.

Nathan began, without preamble. "You all know what we need to decide. We may not all agree, but we need to come as close to a consensus as possible. We are leaving. If anyone else — staff, parents — wants to leave with us, will we take them?"

Judy spoke next. "I think it depends. There are some people that we'll want to take, if they want to come — because we love them. There are people who should be allowed to come, because we owe it to them. And because they've given up so much, for the Project, that they'll have nothing when we go."

Ren-tak stirred in the corner where he stood. "We must be careful of sentimentality. Humans who changed their lives to accommodate the Project can change their lives again when it is dissolved. Humans are fairly adaptable — and indeed, it is only the most adaptable of the older humans that we should contemplate including. While the most adaptable are the least likely to desire it. I do not say that none of them should accompany us. I do, however, caution against bringing with us the seeds of the dissension we were unable to end on this planet."

Nathan nodded. "Anyone who isn't a Twin-Bred and comes along on a ship full of Twin-Bred is going to feel isolated much of the time. That doesn't sound like a good idea to me."

"Unless," noted Peer-tek, "that person is isolated already, and accustomed to it. If anyone wishes to join us whose interactions with human staff and parents are no more than superficial, the risk of that person destabilizing the community in the future would be less."

Judy shook her head impatiently. "We're all talking about the same thing. The same person. Maybe more than one, but we're all talking, at least, about Dr. Cadell."

"Does anyone know whether she would want to come with us?"

"She may not know herself. The issue is whether that choice should lie with her."

"And parents? Some of us are still very close to them." Peer-tek pointed an upper hand at Suzie, who joined her mother Tilda every day for breakfast.

"Some of our parents will miss us a great deal. But parents — at least human parents — have never been guaranteed continued connection with their children. Emigrants throughout human history, at least, have left families behind."

By the time they were weary of talking, they had only made one decision.

"They asked me. Invited me to join them."

"Don't tell me you're surprised."

"I thought they might want to be shut of all of us — all the planners and schemers of both races who set them on this strange and pointless path."

"You made them better than that — you planners and schemers. You should be proud."

"Of course I am. Proud of what they've wanted to do, and tried to do, and what they accomplished in that brief window allowed to them. Proud of their courage and their good hearts. God, what courage! To set off away from everything they've known. . . ."

"As you point out, everything they've known has proved somewhat disappointing. What they have left is each other, and they are becoming realistic enough to know how poor their chances would be if they didn't bug out."

"I hope they have enough time. It'll take many months before they're ready. And God knows how many times we'll have to re-fight the same battles, to hold off hostile forces."

"Let's assume they finish the ship, Mara. And figure out where to take it. There isn't much point in assuming otherwise."

"Right."

"Would you have any plain-old-human company?"

"They haven't decided. Which of course means that anyone else they'd invite hasn't decided."

"You would, we may hope, have me. One way or another."

"And don't think you weren't invited along! They like you, it seems. . . . Levi, do you think I had — ulterior motives? When I supported this plan, when I didn't try to talk them out of it? Of course I wanted them to save themselves, if we weren't sure we could save them! But I did hope they'd offer me a space. And if they'd stayed, and the Project was dissolved —"

"It would have been just you and me again, the old way, with none of the nice audio-visual-tactile upgrades. Sis, relax. You were taking a chance on losing them all forever, when you might've been able to stay near a pair or two at least, somewhere on this planet. So let's just assume you did try to do what was best for them. As you always have."

Mara let the matter drop. She curled up in the shabby old armchair and turned on her music player, closing her eyes and letting the music flow through her. Sadness and hope, blended together: *West Side Story*'s "Somewhere."

After Mara told the Twin-Bred her decision, there were more meetings. All but a few of the Tofa Twin-Bred could make the Levi connection.

Mara rarely indulged herself by allowing the contact to proceed. But every now and then, when she was more discouraged than usual, or had lost sleep from anxiety-driven dreams, the Tofa would see her need.

"Hey, sis. Try a nightcap tonight. Or a mellow-dream capsule. This place needs you wide awake and ready to kick ass as necessary."

Or another time: "I'm going to make a bet with Fel-lar. I'm betting the next planet has fungi we can eat. You want in?"

Or simply: "Mara mia. Be brave. It's going to be splendid."

The astronomy professor held long consultations with her best pupils, who then headed meetings with the others. Computing resources were taxed to their limits. There was data to gather and difficult choices to make, and only so much time.

The group as a whole had to decide whether to aim for the planet or comparable body most likely to sustain them, or for the most likely place to refuel. Most of the available data was in the archives, preserved from the time when their planet had been only a possible destination. Since that time, astronomy had been less important, at least to those who allocated resources, than subjects of more immediate practical utility.

The old data was updated with new observations, enhanced with few but tantalizing refinements in analytical technique. There was enough to make the question easier to answer. Sites suitable for refueling were within (by interstellar standards) easy reach, and plentiful enough that if one proved unsatisfactory, they would not have made a disastrous gamble. Destinations likely to provide a home were less accommodating. The only planet they could reach without refueling, and that might have served their needs, was in a different direction than any refueling stop, and the gaps in their knowledge of it were enough to daunt even the most impatient.

It was necessary, then, for the travelers to retain the ability to analyze spectral emissions and any other data that might help them make their crucial choice in mid-journey. Whatever trade-offs, sacrifices, deprivations that might involve, there was no choice. Lists were written and re-written, items added and deleted. Twin-Bred came triumphantly forward with ingenious work-arounds scribbled down at bedside tables in the middle of the night. Meanwhile, there were other decisions to be made, or at least contemplated, on the assumption that all their planning and labor would be successful.

It was Artemisia who first raised the subject. She and Hal-tet, Nathan and Li-sen were stress-testing metal samples. Li-sen was first to notice that she was staring blankly in the direction of the shielded transparent chamber, even though her sample had finished cooling. "What has diverted your attention?"

Artemisia started, then turned to face him. "I was just thinking. About all of us, the colony we're going to be. Almost all twins — to start with. But what about later on? What will it become?"

Li-sen whistled softly. "I am not sure whether this is borrowing trouble, or some more optimistic version. If we survive to form this colony, will we suddenly be unable to make decisions about its future?"

Artemisia frowned. "We need to know what our goals are. Are we just hoping to survive somewhere long enough to grow old and die naturally, working for our own subsistence instead of doing whatever the Council would force on us? Is that worth all this work, and risking all our lives, maybe more than staying would do? Me, I want something more inspiring to think of when we're stuck in a tin can for however many months or years."

Hal-tet joined the conversation, prudently turning off the motors doing their best to deform his sample. "I would like to hear your ideas. I have wondered how we could preserve the special character of our community."

Artemisia looked a little shy, then visibly pushed herself to continue. "Well, we're going to stay as high-tech as we can. Information is the most important cargo, and the easiest to fit in — as long as we find ways to keep it safe. That includes medical and biological know-how. And the equipment we need to use it — that's another reason I've been thinking about this. With all the prioritizing and list-making, we need to make sure we have the means to — to keep the Project going. The most important part of it. Us."

Nathan looked puzzled. "Are you talking about longevity tech? We're already taking what we need for that, and Fal-nat's team is trying to refine the techniques as much as he can before we leave."

"No, that's not what I mean. I don't mean extending us, individually. I mean continuing the idea of us. Making sure that we are not the first and last and only generation of Twin-Bred."

Artemisia looked from one to the next. "Many of the humans have already formed pair bonds, but none of us — that I know of — has faced the question of what happens next. Well, it's time. The Project made us. We know how to do it. When we have children, will Nathan's be humans who don't really understand Li-sen's children? And the other way round? Or should we have children like us? Aren't we glad about what we are? Aren't we *proud* of what we are?"

Hal-tet projected uncertainty. "There is a great deal to think about. To begin with, all we know of Tofa carrying human and Tofa twins is how those pregnancies ended. We may think we know why it happened, but we cannot know for certain. If Tofa cannot carry a pair of Twin-Bred to term, what then? Will only our human members be allowed to have children? Or will Tofa produce Tofa, with an eventual imbalance in our population?"

Artemisia walked over to him, reached up and held his nearest hand between her own. "Dear Hal-tet. Now I think you're the one borrowing some trouble. Of course we'll have to be flexible. We'll have plans, and we'll learn, and we'll make new plans. But I have this feeling — I think it's right. I think it can happen. I think it's *meant* to happen."

Nathan turned on the torch in his hand and watched the flame, then turned it off again. "I don't believe in things happening for a reason. No fate, just the way things fall. But whatever and why-ever — are you saying that anyone who wants to reproduce has to have twins, one of each? What if someone gets sentimental in a different direction and wants to do everything the natural way? What about Rebecca — she's so tiny, I don't know if she could carry twins and still stand on her feet. What if some of the Tofa want to find out more about real Tofa, normal Tofa, the only way they can, after we've left Tofarn far behind?"

Artemisia started packing up her station. "Well, isn't it better to start asking these questions now, and asking each other? Better than finding out the hard way that we're heading off to who knows where, utterly relying on each other, but hanging onto different ideas of what we're doing it for. I'm going to start talking to the others about all this. And then we'll see."

Hal-tet turned back to his control board and switched the motor back on. Then he switched it off, turned to his twin and gently laid a hand on her head. "Artemisia. My brave sister. Thank you for looking so boldly into our future. I look forward to joining you in it. And to watching your twins grow." He turned again and went back to work.

Chapter 45

MARA TRIED TO rub away her headache. After years of practice, her administrative skills had improved somewhat, but she still loathed the work. She glared at her chart of staff member departure dates and severance payments. Not everyone was patient about fleeing the sinking ship. She wondered if she should continue to insist that all research be fully written up and reviewed before its author could move on. Did it really matter if all the scientists' reports were finished and filed? Who would be reading them?

She jumped as the alert sounded for a secured call coming in. It could hardly be good news. And the call was from an unfamiliar line, although it bore a Council extension.

Mara closed her door and turned on her scramble field. She forced herself to press the receive button. "Cadell."

"Doctor. I am so glad to reach you." The caller was a woman, well groomed in an unobtrusive way. Her voice was pleasantly modulated, almost lilting. "I have something extremely important to discuss with you. I cannot overstate how important. And extremely confidential. And probably urgent. Would I be correct that you are not currently leaving the Project grounds for any reason?"

Mara nodded. She had not thought about leaving, had had no reason to leave, but the suggestion felt dangerous.

"I will come to you, then. If there is somewhere where we cannot be overheard or recorded. Do you have such a place?"

Mara nodded again. She tried to think of some way to appear less passive, to seize the initiative, but before anything occurred to her, the woman was speaking again.

"My name is Siri O'Donnell. I would rather explain my business in person, but there is always the possibility that I will fail to reach you. There is also the possibility that delay will prove catastrophic. So please, as soon as we end this call, there are steps you must take."

This had gone far enough. "Ms. O'Donnell, you call from I don't know where, and expect —"

The caller held up her hand to stop her. "I realize I appear impertinent. Please give me the benefit of the doubt, until we meet, at least so far as to take certain precautions. Your scientific staff includes a Dr. Annabelle Bloom. She has not left the premises?"

"No, she's still here. Though she's due to leave soon. After her final debriefing."

A disturbing expression, a momentary contortion, flitted across the caller's face. "Her final debriefing. I believe I have information that will materially affect the nature of that meeting. In the meantime, it is imperative that you prevent her from transmitting any information to the outside. Or even to others in the Project, if possible. Particularly any encrypted files. You must find any such files to which Dr. Bloom has access."

Mara's temper was rising. "You seem to be insinuating some sort of unethical conduct by a member of my staff. Am I supposed to take these actions without giving her an opportunity to defend herself?"

The caller looked alarmed. "Please, it is very important that you do not alert Dr. Bloom. After our discussion, if you still believe I have maligned your employee, I will not protest any action you wish to take. But please wait until then."

Mara shook her head in frustration. "And what if you, as you put it, 'fail to reach' me? What do you suggest I do then?"

The caller's face was grave. "In that event, Dr. Cadell, I would ask you to pray for my soul, should you be religiously inclined. And I would urge you to find someone — someone you trust absolutely — who is able to decrypt files. And after that person reveals what Dr. Bloom has kept hidden, I am confident you will know how to proceed."

Annabelle Bloom looked around her quarters and considered her options. Her credentials were impressive, and her recent work — even omitting her most groundbreaking research — should make it easy to find new employment. Except that when one's most recent employer was unpopular, one's own merits might be overlooked.

One advantage she might glean from the Project's dissolution was distance from the unknown watchdog with whom Siri had threatened her. Always supposing that the watchdog even existed. It was unlikely that an agent of a dead politician would consider it worthwhile to keep track of her activities, after all this time, and without the advantages of propinquity.

Kimball could hardly be the only one interested in her work. With careful inquiry, she should be able to find others. They might be impressed by its scientific value. Or, like Kimball, they might wish to pursue its practical applications. Either would do.

Veda, panting a bit after a brisk and satisfying walk, was surprised to see a copter sitting on the riverbank. She was more surprised to see Mara approach the copter with a woman whom Veda thought she recognized, but who had no connection — had she? — to the Project. She paused and watched as Mara escorted the visitor to the copter. The copter rose and flew off toward the city. Mara stood looking after it. Veda could not see Mara's face, but her posture was odd, excessively rigid.

Veda emerged from the forest and approached with some caution, coming up behind Mara and pausing a few paces away. She made a point of treading heavily, not wanting to take Mara by surprise. But Mara did not seem to hear.

Veda cleared her throat. There was no response.

"Mara?"

Finally Mara turned. Veda saw her face and stepped back. "My God, Mara, what is it?"

Mara stood staring at Veda, or past her, or through her, as if staring at a field of bodies. Then she turned and beckoned for Veda to follow her. They set off along the river to a point where the land rose slightly and there was a clear view in all directions. Mara stopped abruptly and whipped her head from side to side.

"Here. We can see if anyone's coming. And I've got a scrambler on me. I don't think anyone can hear us."

Veda decided to start with the one thing she understood. "That woman — didn't she work for someone on the Council? I remember seeing her at my father's office, and at official functions."

Mara shivered despite the warmth of the day. "Yes. Oh, yes. Someone on the Council. But he's dead now. Kimball. Councilman Kimball. I never saw it. I worried about some of the others. I investigated some of the others. And all the while, there he was."

"There he was. But what was he doing? And what does it matter now?"

Mara seemed lost for words. Veda stepped close to her and put a hand on her arm. "Mara. Whatever is going on, you've got to handle it. And I can help you. Now tell me."

Mara told her.

Veda rarely cried. She had cried at La-ren's funeral, surrounded by many others also in tears. It was awkward to be one of only two people crying. By good fortune, she happened to have a handkerchief in her skirt. Veda wiped her face, blew her nose, frowned at the handkerchief, and tucked it back into her pocket. She told herself sternly to stop shaking.

Mara wiped her eyes on her sleeve, sniffed, and muttered something under her breath.

"What was that? He didn't warn you? Who — Kimball? Why ever would he?"

Mara looked startled. "No, not Kimball. Someone who usually sees things coming. It doesn't matter. . . . Veda, I have to deal with Bloom. There's no time to lose. Will you help me?"

Veda raised her eyebrows. "Of course! What are we going to do?"

"I'd like to burn her in the center of the compound like the witch she is. But we'll need to be rather more discreet." Mara reached into her pants pocket and took out a small bottle. "Siri gave me this. It's more or less a truth drug. God knows what else that woman knows about. . . . We'll give it to Bloom somehow, and find out where her files are and whether anyone else has seen them or knows about them."

"And then what? The files will be encrypted, surely?"

"We'll have to find someone who's good at decryption. But whom can we trust? Siri gave me a list of the other moles — oh, yes, there are others, but none of them sound very dangerous — but if Bloom has told someone, then that person could have talked to someone else, and — oh, my God. . . ." She buried her head in her hands.

Veda gripped Mara's shoulder. "Hang on. One thing at a time. Maybe Bloom hasn't told anyone. And as for decryption — if I do say so, my Peer-tek is *very* good at it. It's a hobby of his."

Mara's head jerked up. "Tell one of the twins? How can I — what would that do to them? I can't imagine what they'd feel. It might even — will the Tofa Twin-Bred even feel the same about their twins, after hearing what humans are capable of?"

"Mara, they've learned enough history to know what humans are capable of. Yes, it'll be different when it's here and now, and about them. But really, they have to know. They're heading off to who knows where, and who knows what sort of people they'll find there. They have to be ready for the worst. And it isn't as if — well, let's hope Bloom isn't part of some substantial movement. We'd best get moving on finding out. . . . But what do we do with Bloom after we've squeezed her dry?"

Mara's smile would have terrified Annabelle Bloom. It was frightening enough to Veda. "This truth drug — it's rather toxic. Fortunately."

Veda shuddered. Then, practical as always, she started considering which Twin-Bred would be best suited to deal with disposal of the body. She could consult Mara about it later, when Mara had had more time to calm down.

Word soon got around that Dr. Bloom had fallen ill, shortly after dinner. As no one else was sick, the food was exonerated. It turned out that her illness was a rare one, and highly contagious. Presumably one of the visitors from the city had brought it, though it must have had a long incubation period to manifest itself now, and it was curious that no one else showed symptoms. Dr. Bloom was being kept in isolation while research continued on an effective treatment. Her condition did not even allow her to take calls or return messages.

"Annabelle!"

Annabelle Bloom opened her eyes. She felt tired and disoriented. She was in a bed in a room. A woman was sitting beside the bed.

"Hello, Annabelle. My name is Veda. I'm going to ask you some questions. You'd like that, wouldn't you?"

There was something odd about the woman's tone, but Annabelle was too tired to care.

"You're very good at your job, aren't you, Annabelle? Better than anyone knows. You've done something special, something secret. Tell me about it, Annabelle."

Somehow, tired as she was, she wanted to answer. "I found out how to do something with the spores. The Tofa Twin-Bred's spores."

"Yes, I know. What a clever girl. You were going to use the spores to kill the Tofa, weren't you?"

"Yes. But that was years ago. I had to stop."

"Was anyone else helping you? Did anyone else know about it?"

Annabelle tried to think. "Well, there was Councilman Kimball. And his assistant, Siri. And she said there was someone else. She said I had to stop my work, or the other person would — would make me."

"What did you do with your work? You must have wanted to keep it."

"Yes. I was proud of it." Annabelle heard a strange sound. It might have been the woman grinding her teeth. "I thought I might be able to show someone, someday. And now that we're all leaving, I might find someone who's interested. I should be recognized. It was groundbreaking work. People should know about it."

"But now the Twin-Bred are leaving. Won't that put an end to your work?"

Annabelle had just enough energy to laugh. "That's all you know. Tofa spores are in the air, all over. We can isolate them from air samples. We don't need the Twin-Bred, now that we know how."

The woman looked upset. "You keep saying 'we.' Have you shown anyone or told anyone yet? Anyone at all?"

"Not yet." The woman heaved a huge sigh and slumped down. Annabelle wondered why. "But I'm going to, soon."

The woman laughed. It was a strange, ragged sort of laugh. "Well, Annabelle, I wouldn't count on that."

Veda and Mara sat in Mara's office, door closed, scrambler on. Even so, their exchange was terse, enigmatic.

"Well? Did she tell anyone?"

"No. We were in time."

"You know where to find her files?"

"Yes. I'm going to tell Peer-tek this afternoon."

They sat quiet for a moment.

"Veda — whomever else Peer-tek tells, you should tell Jimmy. Separately. So he'll understand if Peer-tek — needs a little time, afterward."

Veda was having none of that. "I refuse to act as if Jimmy were somehow implicated. As if Bloom and Kimball are the real face of humanity. Maybe you can't understand how twins feel about each other, even after living around them — but I think I do. It'll be all right."

Mara looked startled, then let out a quick snort of laughter. Veda had no idea why, but she was just as glad to end the discussion. She stood up.

"Do you want to see the report?"

Mara turned pale. She looked as if she might vomit. "Not one word of it. Not one evil, stinking word."

Veda nodded in understanding, turned and left.

Jimmy sat, and Peer-tek stood, with Veda in her living room. She had borrowed Mara's scrambler. She was holding a tablet. Her expression suggested that she was holding something both disgusting and radioactive.

"Boys." She seemed at a loss for words. Neither twin could remember a time when Veda had not known exactly what she wanted to say.

Veda lifted the tablet. "This tablet contains an encrypted file. The contents of this file are — terrible and dangerous. No one here — no one who's *still* here has read it, but Dr. Cadell and I have a general idea of what it says. I should tell you. But I can't stand to say it. I'm sorry. You'll have to read it yourselves. Peer-tek, I'm sure you can decrypt it. You have to. Keep the decrypted text on the same tablet, and don't let that tablet out of your sight. Eat with it. Sleep with it. And don't let anyone handle it. If anyone asks about it, make up some excuse.

"Once you've read the file, we'll want to hear your thoughts about what to do. Should we destroy it without a trace? Is there any reason to preserve it? And should we let anyone outside the Project know about it? And do we dare?

"But any discussions *must* be secret. This is Dr. Cadell's scrambler. Use it any time you talk about this matter at *all*. Do you understand?"

Jimmy and Peer-tek looked at each other. Peer-tek turned back to Veda. "We understand enough."

Veda clenched her jaw to hold back the tears. "My dear boys. Off you go now." Jimmy rose, and the two of them left the room. Veda waited until they were out of sight, then lay down on the couch and curled up in a ball. She closed her eyes tight and tried to steady her breathing, and to think of nothing.

It had not taken long, after all. Peer-tek was as skilled as his mother believed. Reading the decrypted file took longer. It was detailed — so detailed that it was hard, at first, to grasp the essentials. Without Veda's warning, they would have believed they were misreading it.

When both had finished reading, there was a long silence. The tablet lay on the reading stand in the twins' room. Jimmy was afraid to look at his brother. Instead, he looked down at his hands, clenched together on his lap. He had to say something, and had nothing to say. "Petey?"

Peer-tek looked up. "This restores a certain balance."

"What??"

"Until now, it has appeared that the Tofa community posed the greatest threat. By sabotaging our mission, they threatened the peace, the very future of Tofarn. By their methods, they threatened the Twin-Bred. Now we have a human threat. Balance."

Jimmy stared at Peer-tek. "Is that all you have to say? Aren't you afraid?"

Peer-tek let out a very faint whistle. "I am petrified. But I would rather not think about it. I prefer to solve the problem, so I will not need to be afraid."

"The biggest, scariest, nastiest question is whether to tell the Tofa. The Tofa community, outside. Don't they have a right to know? So they can figure out a defense? If Bloom could dream this up, someone else could do it too. Any time."

Peer-tek tapped his fingers together in an apparently random sequence. "Until the Tofa host mothers revealed it, humans did not know how the Tofa reproduce. If the Tofa had realized how the process could be turned against them, they would not have shared that information. We would be informing them of an unsuspected vulnerability."

"They already know — they were told, that first mission — that the human community has more advanced biological science."

"Then we would be confirming the fact, and pointing out a dangerous corollary. And we would be validating any suspicions that the most pessimistic Tofa might harbor as to how humans would use that superiority." Tap, tap-tap, tap. "And we have no reason to assume that the Tofa have the expertise to counter the threat."

"If they have any chance of doing that, they'd probably need Bloom's research as a starting point."

Tap-tap-tap. "Which would mean multiple copies, or at least multiple access points to that information. Increasing the chances of a security breach."

"If they found out — there are so many more Tofa than humans. Could this be the last straw? Would they just overwhelm the humans with numbers? To save all the Tofa, would the Tofa try to kill all the humans?"

Peer-tek's hands fell still. "Possibly. Don't you think that humans, in a comparable position, might do the same?"

Jimmy gulped and nodded. "And the humans may use their technological superiority in self-defense if the Tofa go on the attack."

"So. If we share this information to reduce the chance of future catastrophe, there is a significant likelihood of triggering it in the present. I believe our decision is made."

Jimmy looked up, startled. "Our decision? Aren't we going to talk to Mama Veda? Or Dr. Cadell?"

"To what purpose? Are you prepared to be overruled? I am not." Peer-tek picked up the tablet, keyed a sequence. "This should not take long. There. The data has been deleted and overwritten." He lifted the tablet and threw it to the floor with all the strength of his strongest arm. The casing cracked. Jimmy looked around, picked up the reading stand, and smashed it down on the tablet. He handed it to Peer-tek, who smashed it down again. They took turns until all that was left were fragments, scattered, twisted and crushed.

"I'm sorry, Mara. I didn't see this coming. It appears my imagination has its limits."

"Levi — for one moment, one short instant, when she told me, I thought of the way the Tofa have used the Project, and what they did to La-ren, and I thought: serves you right."

"Hush, Mara mia. Don't cry. It doesn't matter what you thought. It matters what you did. You protected your twins. All of them. And the rest of the Tofa."

"Yes, I'm a real hero. I'm a killer. And it makes me sick. But not sorry."

"Damn straight."

The staff was sorry to hear that Dr. Bloom had died of her illness. The body was cremated immediately for fear of contagion. Her friends and coworkers held a memorial service. They invited Dr. Cadell, but she sent her regrets.

Chapter 46

JIMMY AND NATHAN managed to meet for lunch, a formerly trivial matter now harder to arrange. With all the work to be done on the ship, its equipment, its furnishings, few of the Twin-Bred had flexible schedules or any spare time.

Mumbling around his sandwich, Jimmy asked, "Does anyone know whether Cindy and Dar-tan are coming with us?"

Nathan looked surprised. "Of course. They've never lived out there, and they wouldn't be any safer than the rest of us. And Cindy'll be our best hope of making animals that can live where we end up."

"We'll have a job keeping her in check. She won't want to wait for planetfall — she'll want us to have pets running around the ship to keep life interesting."

"I might just go for that. I'd like a de-scented skunk for a pillow, myself. . . . I wish we could see Randy and Jak-rad again."

"Randy's afraid that if he came here, he wouldn't be let back out again. He's keeping a very low profile these days. And no one knows where Jak-rad is."

Nathan left his last bite of sandwich on his plate. "Where. Or if."

The smaller game lounge had become the place for bull sessions about what the Twin-Bred's planet would be like, and what they would call it when they found it.

"I think we should call it Tweeling. That's 'twin' in some old language. Or Futago. That's another." Changying checked the coffee pot, found it empty, put it down again.

Sinbad stretched muscles sore from hours at the tooling station. "That's rather — expected. We should pick something more random. Like, I don't know, Elbows. Maybe in Tofar, since you folks have so many."

Dar-tan did his best imitation of a snort. Many of the Tofa Twin-Bred admired the sound, but they had varying degrees of success in producing it. "Possibly we should wait and see what we are naming. It might have tall spiky forests, like the one near Campbell City, but all over. Then we can name it Porcupine. An animal I am glad you humans did not import, by the way."

"Don't give Cindy ideas. She might make one from scratch."

Changying pulled a caffeine patch from his pocket and applied it. "What do all of you most want to find, on our new world?"

Sinbad grinned. "Porcupines, for sure." Sel-ran threw a patch dispenser at him. He caught it neatly and put it in his pocket.

Elspeth gazed off into the distance. "I'd like to see desert. Long vistas, rolling sand, dunes." She shook herself and chuckled. "As long as I don't have to live there all the time!"

Sandy brandished her pocket mirror. "I'd like the light to be more flattering. Pinker. Like the proverbial rose-colored glasses." She laughed cheerfully.

Ramses put in a vote for finding marble. "I'd like a material that's really good for sculpture, without having to make it ourselves. It feels silly to *make* a big block of something when most of it will just get chipped away."

Dar-tan put down his cup of chocolate. "It might be as well to ensure that we get there. Back to work, all of you!" He led the way, and one by one, they followed.

Meanwhile, the Tofa Twin-Bred sought to predict the extent to which they would be transformed when they eventually became fertile. Fel-lar and Peer-tek questioned Mariko about how she felt when she saw an attractive male. "We are trying to imagine how it will feel to go through a receptive period once we stop taking the chemical suppressant. Your birth control patch does not suppress your response to sexual stimuli. Perhaps the feelings are comparable."

"You'll have to let me know. . . . Let's see. When I see Ahmed walking up — or better yet, when I see him walking away — I feel . . . well, some of it is a localized sensation. That may not be what you're after."

"No. For us, that comes at a later stage, and we can extrapolate adequately."

"Right-o. Well, I breathe a little harder. I feel something like hungry, but not. And a little squirmy. Damn, this is heating me up, just talking about it. Especially that localized sensation you aren't interested in."

Another day, the talk was more serious.

Rose broached the subject that many of them had talked about only to their twins. "What do we do if we find a planet and it already has people on it? A sentient population?"

No one wanted to be the first to answer. Finally Peggy spoke. "The easy answer is to say, let's not. Let's wait for a planet that's just for us. But we may not have that luxury."

Ren-tak touched his sister's hand. "We are living witness to both the difficulties and the rewards of taking the chance."

Peggy patted him back. "What worked for us might not work again — if anyone's thinking along those lines. And would we try different pairings of twins? Or triplets?"

"Always presuming," Fel-lar put in, "that the species were sufficiently similar to make the attempt. And that we could obtain cooperation from the indigenous population. Cooperation which might not have been forthcoming here, if the Tofa had not had their own reasons."

That day's consensus, with no strong objections, was to search for a world that showed no signs of civilized or pre-civilized inhabitants. And if no such world was forthcoming — "We'll play it by ear," Peggy announced. "So to speak," Ren-tak added.

A member of the Project's agricultural research group had a request for the team from Campbell City. Could they find someone willing to work with them on biogenetic reconstruction? Someone who had been involved in the bovine project?

The Campbell City group's gravitational stress consultant knew someone who might be willing and available. "And she'd be thrilled to get back into the bovine area. They've pretty much given up on it. I don't remember how the Tofa first found out about it, but ever since, they've put up one obstacle after another. Don't know what they have against cows."

"That's a real shame, since it seems that cow's milk is good for pretty near anything that ails a Tofa. With milk in their diets, they fight off illness better, they have fewer growing pains — they even seem to see in the dark better. But of course we don't have it fresh, and if something goes wrong with the powdered stuff we've been replicating — or with the replicators — well, that'd be it."

The visitor pulled his beard thoughtfully. "I wouldn't think they could know that, the ones who've been getting in the way. It's a damn shame how little we've been able to communicate. Your lot had the right idea, trying to do something about it."

The agricultural researcher turned away.

Greg Ganges, an avionics engineer from Campbell City turned off his welding torch. "You know, I just don't get it. Sure, you folks are a little strange, but we got used to you quick enough. Why do you have to up and leave the planet, without even knowing what's out there? Couldn't you give us more of a chance?"

Nathan kept his eyes on his diagram. "We always thought we could go into human communities and function productively. That they'd let us prove our worth, at least. It seemed to be working that way, for a while. And then we ended up with three dead Twin-Bred. And the people who don't want us dead are willing to let us stay, so long as we turn this place into something useful like a manure refinery."

Greg shrugged. "Seems like something stirred folks up. The news feeds, and the rumors that come out of nowhere, and all that. Well, it's a shame, that's all."

He turned on his torch again.

Judy paced back and forth. "Maybe we gave up too quickly. If we did, it's my fault. I haven't tried hard enough to look past — we always knew there would be dangers, that there could be setbacks. . . ."

Suzie drummed her fingers on one of the tall writing desks. Her brother Mat-set put a hand over hers to quiet her. She shook it off. "The team from Campbell City doesn't seem to mind being around us any more. If we could find more ways to work together on projects — not just come in and act like we know it all — maybe? . . ."

Peer-tek looked up from his calculations. It was odd to see him without Jimmy nearby, but Jimmy was acting as test subject for the latest control cabin furniture calibrations.

"Perhaps we can suggest some collaborative projects. We should discuss them with Dr. Cadell and others. The time has passed for impulsive adventures." Judy and Suzie nodded.

"However." Peer-tek's tone was harsh enough to draw their startled attention. "We must not slow our preparations or reveal to our collaborators that any doubts have emerged. Even if we find that other possibilities exist, the question remains whether it is worth the cost of pursuing them.

"One thing is clear. If we do not complete our preparations, if we do not build the ship and board it and leave this planet now, we are here for the rest of our lives, be they short or long. There will be no second chance."

Greg Ganges called Mara on the day the Campbell City team was next scheduled to appear.

"Dr. Cadell — I hate to say this, but we won't be coming out today. Unless something changes, we won't be back, period."

"What's happened? Was there some — incident, when you were here last? Is there anything I might be able to do?"

"Nothing happened, at your place. Everything's been going great. We've really enjoyed working with your kids, once we got accustomed to them. They're a bright bunch, and easy to work with. And that's what our reports said. So we were pretty surprised when the word came down. Some higher-up somewhere pulled the plug."

Mara waited a moment until she could talk without cursing. "I'm very sorry to hear it. I guess there's nothing more for me to say, except how much I and everyone here appreciated all your help, and your willingness to help."

"Say goodbye to the kids for us. Tell them — like people used to say, tell them 'bon voyage.' It means 'good journey', or something like that."

"I know."

Mara tore an unfinished cartoon out of her sketchbook, crumpled it and threw it across her office. "Someone is doing everything they can to make sure our kids don't change their minds. They start working well with the locals — the locals stop coming."

"There are several candidates for the Someone. The human authorities may want to be sure that hot potato gets tossed out into space. Or the Tofa might want whatever they've gone to all this trouble to get."

"Whatever? Don't we already know? Don't they want to be the ones in charge, the only ones the rest can turn to?"

"Probably. But the Tofa seem to be good at what used to be charmingly called killing two birds with one stone. I believe I see something we might have guessed earlier."

Mara jumped as someone knocked on the office door. "Not now!" she called out sharply. There was a moment of silence and then footsteps moving away.

"Out with it, Levi!"

"Patience, Mara mia. Think with me. What is the main thing the Tofa host mothers would be accomplishing by cutting short a program that could reduce tensions between the Twin-Bred and the rest of the population? By ensuring that they see no future here?"

Mara looked at the corner of her office. Atop a low filing cabinet stood a globe of Tofarn. Before humans came, there had been no such globes. No Tofa had ever seen Tofarn from space.

"Oh my God."

Ter Ra-tel-sen sat in her spacious new office. As Tofa Eminence of the Western Region, she merited large and well-appointed quarters. There were intricate drawings on the walls. The leaning posts were of burnished metal, sculpted for maximum comfort.

The crudely sculpted clay globe on the standing desk might have looked out of place, if not for its significance. It had been a gift from the human child Ter Ra-tel-sen had carried, copied from a globe of polished stone. It showed the planet Tofarn — Tofarn as seen from afar.

Someday, someday soon, Tofa eyes would see the reality represented by this ball of clay. Finally, there would be Tofa in space. Tofa would do as the humans had done. Tofa would move on to other stars.

"Well, Mara mia, I believe you're catching on. It took us long enough."

Mara stared out her open office window. The morning sun lit up the Lemon's Dream flowers on a nearby bush; the breeze bore their creamy scent. Tree-seeds drifted across the river.

"It's space. The Tofa want the Twin-Bred to go into space — at least, the Tofa Twin-Bred. To be the first space-going Tofa. They're driving them off the planet. First they helped us make Tofa who would be better at science and engineering. Then they stayed out of the way, or were helpful, as we gave our Tofa the best training we could in those areas. And now they're sending them running for their lives."

"Carrying the Tofa genome, if not exactly Tofa culture. A modest beginning for imperial ambitions, but better than none, it seems."

Mara turned away from the window and collapsed into her chair. "And whether we like it or not, we can't oppose it. Because it *is* their only chance."

"So it seems. But don't despair, my sweet sister. Remember, it won't be the schemers out there, on those new planets. It won't be the ones who used you. It'll be your Twin-Bred. Your children. Don't you think they'll do you proud?"

Chapter 47

THE IRONY MADE Mara feel sick. Now, months after the Project had tried so hard to make contact with the Tofa host mothers, one of them was initiating such contact. Was summoning a representative of the Tofa Twin-Bred, for purposes unspecified. An escort would be provided.

Mara sent the message on to all the Twin-Bred, along with a note asking that they choose a representative for the meeting, and that the representative come and see her before the escort arrived. She had a hypothesis to impart. Perhaps this meeting would confirm it. Or perhaps, if she dared hope for so much, they would learn that she and Levi had it all wrong.

Fel-lar stood and waited for the older Tofa's attention. Pen-tol-pa was chief assistant to Ton-lal-set, who had been a host mother, and was now Eminence of the Southern Region. After what he apparently considered a suitable interval, Pen-tol-pa turned and inclined his head to the side in greeting.

"Ton-lal-set has read the reports of the team from Campbell City who were assisting in construction of the ship. She and others of her caste found much of interest. They are gratified at the skill with which you and your fellows have met the challenges of the task. Your education has done what it was meant to do."

Fel-lar turned away. "Our education, like our existence, was intended to fit us for tasks which we have not been allowed to perform."

Pen-tol-pa let out the faintest of whistles. "As multiple intentions were at work, there is truth in both our statements.

"There is one aspect of your preparations, however, that is not entirely consistent with the original plan."

Rose heard Fel-lar's step and spoke without turning away from her screen. "Fel-lar, please come and look at this design for the medication regenerators. I think I've found a way to improve their efficiency." Fel-lar had stopped and did not come over to look. She turned and flinched at the anger radiating from him. "What's happened?"

Fel-lar spoke in Terran. "Is Judy nearby?"

"No, she's taking a walk with Dr. Cadell. What happened?"

"Nothing, because I did not allow it to happen. Nor will the others. But the attempt is enough."

"This is about the summons from Ton-lal-set?"

"I did not see Ton-lal-set. The message came from an assistant. Apparently we are not being sufficiently predictable puppets. They did indeed design us to be the first space-going Tofa, to establish Tofa colonies. But they did not intend for us to complicate the picture by bringing human companions."

Rose, never speechless, found herself almost without words. "What — what in — they knew from the beginning what Dr. Cadell and the others expected! They knew about human twins, the bonds between them!"

"Once again, our assumptions overlook the obvious. We were created because humans did not understand Tofa, and Tofa did not understand humans. And yet over and over, we have expected understanding. The Tofa apprehended and capitalized on some aspects of the possible influence of humans on Tofa, given intense uterine and postnatal exposure. But they apparently did not understand the likely emotional consequences, despite whatever efforts may have been made to explain such. It is possible that this point was not emphasized. Or it may not be in the nature of — unaltered Tofa to accept the possibility of a familial bond with another species."

"And what do they expect us to do, on this world that they've helped to hate us!"

"I believe your formulation would be that they could not care less."

Rose was pacing back and forth. Fel-lar caught her as she swung by and curled one strong arm around her.

"I left without giving a definite answer, so as to ensure I did not disappear without conveying this information. Before I came to report to you, I sent a message to Pen-tol-pa, the assistant, and to Ton-lal-set. And to every other former host mother whose location we have ascertained."

Rose started to smile, then to grin. "I think I'm going to like this."

"I was blunt. I told them all that if they were to interfere in any way with our joint expedition, that there would be no other. And that we would use the ingenuity of both our species to ensure that the remainder of their grand plan ceased to progress in a satisfactory manner."

Rose's smile faded. "Will they accept that answer? What else will they think of, and what will it cost us?"

"We will increase security at the construction site, and at the design facilities. And we will accelerate our preparations. We will, in fact, get the hell off of this planet as soon as possible."

Chapter 48

THE TOFA leadership's attitude tipped the balance: the Twin-Bred decided that Mara need not be the only human invited to join them. The decision did not make things easier. The closer a Twin-Bred was to parent or sibling or staff mentor, the more painful the possibilities for all concerned.

Laura and Judy sat in the family cottage, looking at the untidy stacks and rows of books on the shelves.

"I would miss books," Laura sighed. "Tablets aren't the same. And they don't smell right."

"I think I heard of an Old Book aroma stick. We could find some before we leave."

Laura's eyes filled with tears. " 'Before we leave.' I can't absorb that. But it's all or nothing. Either you and I are part of 'we,' and 'we' leave, or there's no 'we' anymore, not for the two of us. . . ."

Judy put an arm around her and hugged hard. "I want you with us, so much. But it has to be right for you, or we'll both end up miserable, and I'll feel guilty for the rest of my life, and you'll start wishing — that I'd never been born — if you don't already. . . ." Judy struggled for control.

Laura extracted her arm so that she could do the hugging. She pulled Judy to her and laid Judy's head on her shoulder. "Hush, love, hush, hush. . . ." She rocked Judy gently back and forth, and started to croon a favorite lullaby. "Under baby's cradle in the night. . . ."

Judy tried to laugh. "La-ren used to do arithmetic problems in his head when you sang lullabies, so he wouldn't be so impatient for you to finish."

Laura kept rocking and singing, hoping to answer the question Judy had not quite asked.

Peer-tek looked up from his diagrams of the safety circuits in the fuel controllers as Jimmy threw open the door. "You have bad news."

Jimmy stomped to the window and stared out. "Veda came to see me. She didn't bring Melly. She said Melly was too upset."

"They have decided to stay. I thought they would. Veda is no adventurer. Brian has his work outside the Project. And they would be frightened of the uncertainties, for Melly's sake as well as their own."

Jimmy turned around, tears running down his face. "How can we leave Melly here, with all of us gone? She's spent her whole life being everyone's pet, everyone's little sister. She's had all that love and attention and excitement. It's like the air around her — she's never been without it. And now she's going to lose all that, and have to start over in what might just as well be a new planet! — as far as the people are concerned, anyway. And everyone she meets will think that almost everyone she ever loved was some sort of disgusting creature, and maybe that she's tainted by having grown up with us. And with all that, she loses me too? And I never see her again, never, no matter how long I live, no matter how long she lives. . . ." He sank down onto the couch and sobbed.

Peer-tek came and stood over the couch. He reached down with a lower hand and caressed Jimmy's head. "Twin. What choice is there? We cannot take her without her parents. Or make them see things differently, even if their choice was not a reasonable one."

Jimmy spoke without looking up. "We could stay."

Peer-tek let out the warbling burst of sound that meant he was startled. "Stay? The only Twin-Bred on Tofarn, except Randy and possibly Jak-rad? Even if we could stay in safety — and how could we? And how could Veda and Brian and Melly be safe, if we did?"

"They could get a place somewhere outside the city, somewhere isolated. Or no, we could. They could visit us there. Brian's job pays well. He could bring us what we'd need, whatever we couldn't grow or raise for ourselves."

Peer-tek stood in silence for several minutes. Then he spoke quietly.

"Once, several years ago, I spoke with Veda about her childhood. It was very interesting. She showed me some of the stories she had read. One of them was about children — brothers, I think — who ran away from an evil stepmother, and lived in the forest. They covered themselves with leaves in the fall, and with flowers in the spring. You remember about fall and spring, on Terra?" Jimmy nodded. "And I believe they drank the dew on the grass, and fairies brought them berries and nuts to eat, and told them what mushrooms to pick.

"Jimmy, you are dreaming a story like her story. But you set the fairies too hard a task. And the brothers would find their lives empty and meaningless, for all the fairies could do. And the evil stepmother cannot be trusted to stay out of the forest."

Chapter 49

FEL-LAR MET the visitor in the wood farthest from the central buildings, as the message had instructed.

"I would say you are welcome, but recent experience is not encouraging as to your leadership's intentions."

The visitor blinked twice. "If, as we are informed, you have received some education in the sciences of group behavior, you will not be surprised that factions may exist who oppose the leadership on certain issues. Some in our community believe we could have found better uses for you, and even your foster siblings, than driving you off the planet. A somewhat larger group believes the currently ascendant faction was short-sighted in failing to ensure that when you carry our species into space, you carry as well a more thorough knowledge of our history and achievements and of your own nature. I am here to discuss how to address this deficiency, so far as is practical in the time remaining."

"Many of us have wondered why, before their departure, our Tofa host mothers and nurses did not share more of such information."

"Share is the key concept. You and your twins, not to mention the omnipresent human staff and monitoring equipment, share incessantly. There was insufficient consensus about the advantages and disadvantages of enlightening the human community about the Tofa to such an extent."

Fel-lar turned away and rocked back and forth. When he felt able, he turned and spoke with a hum distorting his words. "If there had been a consensus in favor of understanding between human and Tofa, our mission would have been allowed to continue. And I would not be standing here, waiting for scraps of my informational birthright to be doled out to me, before I leave the world that should have been mine."

The first hurdle was how this information was to be conveyed. Neither the number of Tofa interested in enlightening Twin-Bred nor the time remaining before their departure would allow for all instruction to be done in person. Audiovisual recording was not feasible, given the telepathic elements of Tofar. The Twin-Bred would have to learn to read.

To this end, the visitor brought two books, sheets of metal accordion-folded and etched with writing. One was a specially prepared Tofar-Terran dictionary, with Tofar ideographs and the corresponding Terran words. The other was a primer a Tofa child might use.

The Twin-Bred formed a team, headed by Nathan, to search the software archives for translation programs and adapt them as necessary. Meanwhile, the books were shared and copied. When Jerry first held one of the books in his hands, he put it down again, went to his room and cried for half an hour.

The emissary returned several weeks later. He brought a tablet, loaded with files written in the same symbols the Twin-Bred had been studying. The files appeared to be instructional materials from Tofa elementary schools. Twin-Bred who had fewer technical tasks to perform, or had largely completed those they had, studied the files if so inclined. Many human Twin-Bred were sufficiently intrigued to invest the time; many Tofa were angry enough to resist the temptation. They would have the opportunity to reconsider on the voyage.

Subsequent visits, still apparently clandestine, brought more advanced lessons. Soon the Tofa Twin-Bred were requesting more files on subjects in which someone had a special interest. Often the interested party was human, a fact the Tofa Twin-Bred did not disclose.

The pattern changed when visitors began arriving in twos and threes, and expressed willingness to answer questions. At least, some questions.

Fel-lar and Peer-tek stood around the communal writing table with the three adult Tofa. It was Fel-lar's turn to ask a question.

"Change Day. The humans wonder why you do nothing to mark the occasion, or at least, nothing that seems enjoyable. Before our time, they questioned whether Tofa could see colors, although other incidents suggested that we could. Now they know that we see colors but differentiate between them somewhat differently than they do. I and my fellows have somewhat mixed feelings about the color change, but we do not know why."

The thinnest of the visiting Tofa buzzed for a moment. "Indeed, color is not always something to celebrate. Please look at your screens."

The young Tofa both stared at the succession of images. First, a predator: they recoiled in near unison, recognition quicker and deeper than any conscious knowledge. Next, the same creature standing out against pale yellow and beige vegetation. Last, the same setting — but the predator faded to near invisibility against the backdrop of violet and lilac, mulberry and mauve.

"For our ancestors, the transformation the humans so enjoy was a time of great danger. We have long since eliminated these creatures, but not the reactions we evolved to escape them. Many prehistoric communities migrated seasonally to areas that the color transformation did not affect."

Fel-lar seemed lost in thought. After a moment, he began whistling softly.

"Humans see blue and purple as spectrum-adjacent."

The older Tofa whistled back, more loudly. "No wonder they expect us to celebrate a world of purple! Except, you tell me, they did not formerly understand the effect of blue."

"And the Terran sky is blue. . . . If there is, as some humans believe, a sentient power that created the universe," responded Fel-lar, "its enjoyment of irony must be considerable."

The next time, perhaps inspired by the discussion of color, the visitors brought images of artwork. The younger Tofa were entranced. Here was art that spoke to their color sense, to their sense of light and shadow. Here were optical illusions, visual puns, every kind of play and subtlety.

Fel-lar did not like feeling grateful to these envoys from a culture that was rejecting him. But he knew he would never be the same, that he would carry these images with him into space, and that all the new and wondrous sights he would be seeing would flow through him and emerge as art. At least the visitors would never get to see it.

During another lesson, Li-sen asked: "When we were younger, there was an unfortunate incident that could have had grave consequences. In NivPourn. For six days, the Tofa engaged in activities whose common factor was that they made it almost impossible for the local human community to sleep. What was the explanation for these activities? Did the Tofa realize their effect?"

The visitors buzzed for a moment. One of them turned slightly away to indicate refusal. "Not every subject is appropriate for discussion. Ask another question."

So there would be no answer — unless they could learn it for themselves, some day.

Finally, the visitors were ready to discuss Tofa reproduction and family life.

"When a Tofa has received a seed cell, its implantation and development can be made more likely by joint activity of several Tofa. The process also has recreational aspects. Are you aware of this process?"

Sel-ran projected what a sufficiently sensitive human would have seen as a smile, a somewhat unpleasant sensation for the visitors. "We have some basic information. We would appreciate some elaboration on the subject. Which reminds me: there is some concern about what effect the atmosphere of a different world might have on the viability of the airborne seed cells. Would it be feasible for you to supply some reasonable quantity of samples, for use in tests when we have located a possibly viable planet? It would be a serious setback were we to settle, and reach a point of no return, on a planet where we could not procreate naturally."

"I will investigate, but it is a reasonable request. We wish for your colony to flourish. To continue: gestation normally takes nine satorbs. What humans would call 8.25 months. This is an approximation. Toward the end of gestation, the mother instructs the fetus more precisely as to when it should emerge. I use the singular, although there are sometimes twins —" (he nodded toward his audience) "— or rarely, triplets."

Peer-tek stiffened. "The mother is able to give the fetus instructions?"

"Yes. This ability becomes stronger as the pregnancy advances, and continues to strengthen for some time after birth. It then wanes as the young Tofa becomes more capable of independent action."

Peer-tek and Sel-ran exchanged the signal for a topic needing urgent discussion after the visitors' departure. Sel-ran returned his attention to the speaker. "Please tell us more about Tofa families. And then, we hope you will return to the process you mentioned. We do not wish our colony to be ignorant of the possible refinements and variations."

Although, he thought, we might just manage to invent our own. Maybe our humans can give us some ideas. Species cross-pollination, as it were. Yet another way the Project had advanced the cause of science.

Sel-ran and Peer-tek stood at the convergence of two creeks. A light drizzle was falling; they ignored it.

"So. Did the Tofa host mothers expect that they could dominate the human fetuses they carried? And continue to direct them after birth?"

"Why not? They might recognize that there was some uncertainty, but they had every reason to hope so."

"The actual result — their own greater understanding of, and ability to interact with, humans — may have been a surprise to them. A compensatory benefit, allowing their plans to proceed, if not quite as they had anticipated."

Peer-tek whistled very faintly and said in Terran, "Not quite as they had conceived them."

Sel-ran flicked a pebble at him and continued in Tofar. "There is the question whether understanding, and interaction based on that understanding, are all that is now at work. Whether having carried human fetuses, they have some ability to manipulate humans, even if it was not strong enough to subvert the Project."

Peer-tek whistled again. The smile Jimmy would have seen, had he been there, would have had some bitterness. "A perfect question for scientific study. I can visualize the protocols. Unfortunately the Project staff will not be in a position to proceed with it."

"There is also the matter of our lost Tofa companions. Those carried by the Tofa host mothers. It has already seemed likely that their deaths were not accidental. Did the mothers simply expel them? Or did they order them to die?"

Peer-tek shivered and started walking back to the compound. Sel-ran caught up and walked beside him. It was not a question they would ask their visitors. There would be no answer, and it made little difference.

Chapter 50

"JUDY?" LAURA stood in the doorway of Judy's room, where Judy was scrolling through a checklist of medical supplies. "May I interrupt you for a bit? There's something I want to tell you."

Judy looked up and stretched. "Please interrupt me! But I think I know what you'll tell me." She was smiling now. "You and Sabir?"

Laura's attempt at a poker face dissolved into a wide grin. "Yes! Yes yes yes!"

"You mean you said Yes, or he did?"

"Impudent child!" They were both laughing now. "Actually, he did. And then he asked me, and I said Yes."

Gradually they grew quiet. Laura looked down at her hands.

"Mom, it's all right. It's as it should be."

"Old folks staying put and decently gathering dust while the young people go forth?" Laura's smile was shaky.

"Finding love the easiest, most natural way you can. Staying where you have roots instead of taking crazy risks, holding on to what you have — that's *right*, if you can have it. I'm so glad you can."

"Before you leave — if you can make time, I want us to talk and talk and talk. About your childhoods, about all the things you and La-ren did together that I never found out about, about all the things you like and love and hate, about what kind of world you dream of finding. . . . I want all of you that I can have. Before you go."

"Only if you'll hold up your end. I want to hear all about your childhood. And about your parents' childhoods! And what this world was like then. Before I leave it, I want to know more about what I'm leaving. . . ."

They looked at each other with streaming eyes and then embraced.

Laura heard a knock on the cottage door and went to answer. She was somewhat surprised to see who stood at her doorstep. "Dr. Cadell!"

"Laura — please call me Mara. A request I should have made a very long time ago."

Laura was startled, but quickly reached out and grasped Mara's hand. "Mara. Thank you. Would you like to come in? Or would you rather go for a walk?"

"A walk sounds good. I have something I want to tell you, and I think it'll come easier if I'm walking. But first, I have something for you." Still standing on the threshold, she held out a large envelope. Laura took it and pulled out a drawing. In spare, strong lines, it showed Judy and La-ren, standing on two sides of a familiar tree.

"Judy showed me — after the funeral." Mara cleared her throat. "It's the tree she called the La-ren tree."

Laura fumbled for the sofa and sat down with the drawing in her hand. She fought back the need to cry. When she felt she could speak, she looked up at Mara and said, "Thank you. It's beautiful. I'll treasure it. But I don't quite understand."

"You will. Please walk with me."

Laura laid the drawing on a side table, stepped out and closed the door behind her. Soon she would be returning to the land of locked doors. It had been many years since she had locked a door. But then, it had been as many since she had lived without the constant scrutiny of recording devices. What might she want to do once she was unobserved again?

As they started off, Laura glanced sideways at Mara. She was staring straight ahead and did not seem inclined to begin the promised revelation. Laura decided on a delicate nudge. "I still feel as if I took advantage, back before the twins were born. You didn't want to talk about how the Project came about, and I lay there on my sickbed and asked you. I'm sorry."

"Please don't apologize. It was a perfectly reasonable request. I owed you an answer. The problem was that the answer was all mixed up with something I felt I couldn't talk about. There was really no reason I couldn't separate the two. I suppose the real problem, for me, was that I wanted to confide in you — all the way. And I didn't have the courage."

"Why should you have trusted me? If this was something you needed to keep secret, how could you know whether I would talk about it?" She chuckled a little. "Without knowing what it is, I don't know whether you could have trusted me. Maybe I would have thought the other mothers were entitled to know it."

"Maybe they were. But I don't think the Project would have happened, if they had."

They walked toward the woods and took a narrow path between two creeks. Laura noted that this was a path that intersected no other paths, through a part of the wood where the trees were not so closely set as to provide any good hiding places. Even now, with the Project on the verge of dissolution, Mara was taking no chances.

Mara took a deep breath. "My twin. The twin I lost. His name was Levi."

Laura stopped in her tracks. She turned and faced Mara. "Levi? L-E-V-I? As in —"

"Long-Term Emissary Viviparous Initiative. Yes. It was our little joke. Levi's and mine."

Laura and Mara were headed back out of the woods. Laura was quiet. She knew now about Levi. She understood why Mara had withdrawn from friendship, all those years ago. Mara had told her secret — hadn't she? — and yet Mara did not yet seem relieved. There must be another secret, another layer.

"Mara? Is there anything else? Because — if there is, I hope you'll tell me. I promise to keep it to myself. And I don't see how I could hurt you with it. It's not that I need to know. But I can see you need to tell me."

Mara stopped walking. She did not turn toward Laura. "There is something else. And it's even harder to talk about. I don't know how you'll feel about it. You may be upset or angry. But I do need to tell you. You have a right to know. And I want to thank you." She swallowed and blinked her eyes. "Laura, do you know Sel-ran?"

"Sel-ran? Well, yes, I've seen him now and then. We see a lot of Veda's twins, Jimmy and Peer-tek, and Peer-tek and Sel-ran are good friends. Why?"

"Something happened a few years ago. Something I had never dreamed could happen, ever." Mara told the tale in as few words as possible. Laura listened, wondering if it was possible that Mara had imagined the incident. Could Mara really be somewhat — unbalanced? And what did this have to do with her?

Mara must have read the questions on Laura's face. "Just wait a minute. You'll see why I'm telling you this. And you'll see that I didn't imagine it. Judy can tell you that."

"*Judy*? I don't understand."

"Just listen."

Laura and Mara sat on a bench near the river. Both of them needed some time to regain their composure before returning to the compound. Mara had had the foresight to bring handkerchiefs.

Laura blew her nose. "No, I'm not angry. It was for La-ren to decide. I am sorry that Judy felt — excluded. I'm glad she feels differently now. . . . But why did you want to thank me?"

"For them. Both of them. La-ren was — so kind. And Judy too, in the end. As you are. You carried them, and you raised them, as much as we let you. . . . You deserve a great deal of credit for what they became."

Laura shook her head and put away the handkerchief. "I could argue the point, but it doesn't matter. I did my best, and they do us both credit. I'll always be proud —" She fumbled for the handkerchief again.

The two women sat in silence, listening to the river. Neither knew the other's thoughts, but each guessed them to be much the same as her own. Finally, Mara stood and nodded toward the compound. Laura rose, and the two walked back to the place they could still, for a short time, call home.

The departure date was dictated by the ship's construction schedule and the positions of the planetary bodies involved. Fortunately, the schedule had allowed a final Landing Day observance.

A few late tree-seeds floated past on the warm breeze. Raindrops from a recent shower glittered on the pale yellow ground cover and the tawny trees. The human and the Tofa Twin-Bred stood in separate groups, facing each other near the river closest to the compound. Mara stood between them, off to one side. It was so quiet they could hear the water-beetles landing on the surface of the river.

Mara gestured for their attention — unnecessary, as she already had it. She spoke softly at first, then louder.

"We are here to celebrate a holiday whose meaning we have never truly known. We will leave this world, still not knowing everything that it means. We may suspect that its observance in years past has done little to bridge the gaps between the species that came, and the species that may or may not have welcomed them.

"But for all of us here, more than for any of those we will leave behind, this is a day to celebrate. This is the day that human and Tofa found each other. This is the day that led to all of you. This is the day that brought us to a brotherhood never conceived of, let alone brought to fruition, anywhere before, in all of time and space.

"So all of you — join me in celebrating. Happy Landing Day to us all."

She gestured again. In twin waves, the groups of humans and Tofa came together, twin joining twin, singletons in a circle, until all except Mara stood hand in hand. Mara listened to the soft chatter of Terran and Tofar. Mine, she thought. I made this.

Lost in reverie, it took her a moment to see that Fel-lar had left Rose's side and come to stand beside her. She turned to him with a questioning look. He looked gravely back at her. "May I?"

The tears came as Fel-lar took Mara's hand. "Happy Landing Day, Mara mia. Nicely done."

He leaned over and laid his face against her cheek. Somehow, she felt a kiss. Then Fel-lar stepped back, bowed slightly, and went back to Rose. Mara stood gazing across the water, holding her cheek.

Chapter 51

OF THOSE few members of the Project staff invited to accompany the Twin-Bred, there were three (besides Mara) who chose to do so: Emily Wilson, teacher of Diplomacy, an art which would be needed aboard ship and perhaps beyond; Seth Baruti, teacher of Statistics, the oldest staff member, who apparently nursed a passion for astronomy; and Chief Nurse Harriet Gaho. Harriet explained: "I'd be bored silly with nothing but humans to look at. And none of these kids have learned enough to nurse a shipful of other kids. Not even Poo-lat — I'm not through with him yet." But true as all that might be, everyone knew that Harriet had loved and cared for her charges for too long to let them go.

Mara had somehow expected that no others would cast their lot with the voyagers. She scolded herself for her surprise. How self-centered of her to assume that of all the staff, hers was the only drama reaching its denouement.

The four older humans decided to meet twice a week, whatever their schedules and obligations. They would be something like family; they had better learn how to be a harmonious rather than a dysfunctional one, and to establish that pattern while they could still get some relief from each other's presence as necessary. Carla Horn found time to give advice and help resolve the occasional friction. As the date of departure grew near, they gained confidence in their ability to live together at close quarters.

There was little more to be done.

Mara sat in her office, indulging and tormenting herself by looking through reports and videos from the Project's early days. She lingered over the video of an early Diplomacy class. The children had been so happy, so unaffected by the implications of their task, the difficulties and dangers ahead. . . . The whistling of the Tofa Twin-Bred in the video mingled with a sound from here and now, her assistant whistling his favorite tune. The bouncy popular number fit oddly with his frequently anxious demeanor.

What would Stan find to do, after all these years at the desk outside her office? She jumped to her feet and went to the door. "Stan? Could you come in here for a minute? You won't need your tablet."

Stan tilted his head. "That sounds ominous. I'd think you were firing me, if that wouldn't be redundant." He waited for her to head back into her office and followed behind her.

Mara offered him hot chocolate. How seldom she had thought to make the offer. He accepted, looking amused, as if he were thinking along similar lines.

Mara sat in her chair and beckoned him toward the one he had so often occupied. "Stan, what comes next for you? This Project has sucked up your life like a sponge, and I don't know what it's given you in return. What are your prospects? I wish I could be of more help, but I'm stunningly lacking in influence these days."

Stan slurped his chocolate. "I don't know about that. It's not as if *every* scientist on Tofarn is part of the Project. There are others, and some of them will figure that anyone who kept up with you might be worth a second look." His mouth twitched. "And then there's the other part of your reputation. It's no secret that you don't suffer fools gladly. Or that you can be a bit — temperamental." He paused and tensed a bit, waiting for signs of temperament. When none came, he relaxed and went on. "I expect that bosses who've had a few people quit on them will see me as a good bet."

Mara gave a brief snort of laughter. "I'll certainly do everything I can to praise your competence as well as your enduring patience. . . . Have you actually been in touch with anyone?"

"As a matter of fact, someone's just been in touch with me. Someone on the Council staff." Stan drained the last drop of chocolate from his cup and licked his lips, then set the mug carefully down on Mara's desk. "The gentleman was rather vague. Someone wants to talk to me, about something, and there are benefits in store. I'm not sure if he was talking about future employment, or something more along the lines of debriefing. We'd better make some time, before the final diaspora, for you to go over what nuggets of information I can trade for any available goodies, and what I should be sure to forget."

Mara tried to swallow the lump in her throat. "Stan, you've been so loyal. To me, to the Project — even now. I don't know how to thank you — for that, for everything."

Stan stood up, his expression an unfamiliar mixture of warmth and indignation. "I'll tell you how. You go out there, and have a good life, and do great things. More great things. You show them just how puny and unimportant they are. You make everything they did into the best thing that ever happened to you -- and to the kids. You do that, Mara." He stopped, panting a bit, and stood a moment as if irresolute. Then he darted toward her, gave her a quick and awkward hug, and walked quickly out of her office.

* CONFIDENTIAL *
CLEARANCE CLASS 3 AND ABOVE

LEVI Status Report, 4-1-89
Executive Summary

<u>Future Communications</u>

Work continues on perfecting means of communication between the departing spacecraft and Tofarna scientists. There was a proposal that a reduced Project team should remain intact in order to conduct such communication, but there was insufficient support for this alternative. . . .

"Well, sis, they seem determined to kill the Project off entirely. No half-hearted measures for these folks."

Mara worked on a cartoon of a clown with gloved hand to his ear, listening to a broadcast from a distant ship. "Which further reduces the chance that any messages we send will be used for scientific purposes as well as political ones. But I suppose there's always some chance. We're trying to set up an avenue for separate direct transmission to human and Tofa scientists."

"You can request, oh so sweetly, some confirmation that anything that should get scientific attention has done so. And that anything that should be published to the public at large, gets published."

Mara finished drawing the clown's bemused expression. "And if they don't feel like complying with our requests?"

"My, my, it's so hard to predict what radiation and other space conditions will do to communications equipment."

Mara contemplated her cartoon and then put it aside. "We might not need to manufacture difficulties. Those yahoos are likely to muck up the frequencies, or neglect proper maintenance of the equipment."

"Do you want them to tell you what's happening here? Whether the Tofa elite manage to keep the lid on things, or outright take over, or whether it all goes to hell without you? If you don't get updates, you could miss your chance to say you told them so."

"I don't know. There are times when I just want to shake the dust of this planet off my shoes and never look back. Which might be just what we need. We can't live always looking backward."

"Is it better to live with a silence where all your past has been?"

Mara sat unmoving for a moment as though listening to the silence. "I don't know."

Sam Chambers, senior Project deputy for science, poked her head in Mara's office door. ""Mara? Got a minute?"

"Of course. There are so few left. I'm going to miss you terribly."

"Don't get me started. . . but on a happier note, there just might be something useful for me to do after all of you depart."

Mara motioned for her to sit, then got up to fetch hot chocolate for them both. "That sounds like welcome news, if it doesn't fall out from under us. I'm sorry. I've taken to shooting gift horses in case they bite me. Oh, Lord, stop me before I metaphor again! You were saying?"

"You sound different. As if your plans have loosened you up somehow."

Mara brought the mugs back, handed one to Sam and sat down. "There's nothing like an utterly unknown future to relax one. What's your good news?"

"You know the Tofa who've been slipping out here to fill in the gaps in our Tofa twins' education."

"Yes. It's a somewhat ironic version of 'better late than never.' There's some new angle?"

"One of them asked to speak to 'any human Project staff member who might be open to unusual suggestions.' I gather I was nominated. Peer-tek acted as interpreter, but I know enough Tofa to follow along somewhat. Anyway, their little group wants to maintain some contact with us after the Twin-Bred leave."

Mara set her mug down with a thunk. "Did he explain what they're looking for?"

"There was some interpreter-interpretee back-and-forth about that. It remains a little vague. I got some generalities about supplementing the knowledge gained some years back by the host mothers, and providing a conduit for information in return. Not that there were any promises of the latter."

Mara rubbed her thumbs together thoughtfully. "Sam — all these machinations. All this intricate and ruthless maneuvering. Why didn't they just ask us for the technology they wanted? Or offer to trade for it somehow, knowledge for knowledge?"

Sam raised an eyebrow. "Saying what you want makes you vulnerable. Human psychology, maybe, but it could be a universal principle. We don't know their lifespans. It's conceivable that some of them may remember first-hand what our ship looked like coming in. They don't know the extent of our current offensive capacity. If we had known they wanted to leave their planet — well, imagine yourself in their position. Would you want a space-going race with intimidating technology to know that you were thinking of providing competition? They might wipe you out while you were still all handy in one place. Not that we would have."

Mara did not answer. Sam noticed that Mara's mood had changed; she had gone pale and looked somehow drained. Sam excused herself and left to write up her report.

Judy, Rose, Fel-lar, Steven and Bon-tok stood by a creek near the compound and tossed pebbles across. The Tofa's greater accuracy allowed them to create little structures: Fel-lar and Bon-tok were collaborating on a pebble pyramid.

"This information we are receiving. Our belated education in all things Tofa." Bon-tok tossed another pebble, just missing its intended niche. "What shall we do with it?"

"Do with it?" Fel-lar tilted his head. "Aside from bearing it with us as we found the great interstellar Tofa empire?"

Rose stroked his nearest arm. "Twin, don't be bitter. What am I saying? Go ahead and be bitter, but that doesn't answer the question."

Bon-tok tired of his pebbles and let them fall. "This heterodox faction of Tofa has provided us with information that no human on this planet possesses. That the Tofa do not particularly wish humans to possess, especially those humans who will remain on Tofarn. What should become of this material when we depart?"

Judy tossed her pebbles into the creek one by one, gazing at the spreading ripples. "We have one more chance, it seems, to do what we were meant to do. To help humans and Tofa understand each other." She scooped up a larger rock and threw it hard into the water. The splash made Rose jump. "And if we dismay certain Tofa who have had things their own way lately, that's a bonus."

Sam Chambers looked at the message on her screen in some puzzlement. The list of senders seemed to include all the Twin-Bred. The heading read, "TO BE OPENED AFTER THE SHIP DEPARTS." To enforce this restriction, the huge file attached had an ingenious time lock: it could not be opened until the day and time the ship was expected to escape the planetary gravity well.

Sam set her station to remind her when that time came. Everyone would need some distraction around then. It would be good to have something to look forward to.

Jimmy and Peer-tek provided a few key tidbits of information about Tofa history and customs to Melly and Veda, so that they could revive the *Romeo and Juliet* production. While the Twin-Bred completed work on the ship and its contents, mother and daughter worked feverishly to finish the script. Melly's best friends among the Twin-Bred managed to make some time for rehearsals and construction of a few sparse sets. They scheduled a single performance for the entire Project, three days before the departure date.

The activity was a welcome distraction for Melly, and therefore even better news for Veda. Melly had been threatening to stow away on the ship and go off with the Twin-Bred, and Veda had a healthy respect for Melly's ingenuity and strength of will.

Chapter 52

DR. TANNER TOOK the call with pleasure. It had been a long time.

"Mara. How good to hear from you. I know how busy you must have been, helping your twins prepare for their journey."

"Not just the twins, Doctor. I don't suppose you've heard — it isn't common knowledge." Mara hesitated. Dr. Tanner could think of only one revelation that might be coming. Could he be right?

"I'm going with them. On the ship."

Yes, he had read her correctly. He supposed he should not be so surprised, let alone shocked.

He chose his words carefully. "That is as big a decision as I have ever seen a patient make. Or a friend. Have you had anyone with whom to examine all the ramifications? And your own motivations?"

Mara visibly suppressed a smile. Had she caught the hint of wounded professional pride behind the question? "Doctor, I know you would have helped me a great deal, if I could have spoken to you about it. But there was much I still could not discuss. And there are other matters — things I could have told you, but I was afraid."

"Afraid, Mara? Let us pause there a moment. When you fear to reveal something to me, what is it that you ultimately fear?"

Mara let herself smile this time. "Doctor, we talked a long time ago about the ways in which you're a father substitute. I've been walking on a bit of the wild side, although not in any way you're likely to have imagined. I wasn't sure you'd approve. . . ." Then, more soberly: "I was afraid you would think I'd crossed a line. Or lost control."

Dr. Tanner shook his head. "Mara, I think you know that I have wished for you a somewhat greater capacity for letting go, for relaxing. Your fear of losing control has held you back from enriching your experience. If you've overcome that fear, I am unlikely to disapprove."

"Doctor — before I leave, I want you to know what I've been keeping secret. You will be the only person to know it, outside the Project — in fact, the only person besides the Twin-Bred. And I'm going to ask a friend to help me tell it." She beckoned to someone outside his view.

"Mara, could you set your screen for a broader view, so I can see your friend?"

He saw and heard Mara chuckle. "I think that's a good idea. He's on the tall side."

The image shifted. Dr. Tanner was considerably startled — though he chided himself for it a moment afterward — to see a Tofa standing at Mara's side.

"Dr. Tanner, is your line set for maximum security?"

"Mara, you know I always set it so, whenever you call."

"Thank you, Doctor. Here we go."

He unwrapped an aroma stick and waited. Something for which he had no words was changing as he watched the Tofa. When the Tofa spoke, he actually jumped at the human intonation.

"Greetings, Doctor. It's so good to finally meet you. I have a great deal to thank you for."

Dr. Tanner grabbed his chair as if it could anchor him to reality. "Is this — could it be — I would rather hear it from you. Young man, would you introduce yourself?"

Was it the Tofa's body language that somehow suggested a smile?

"I believe you've recognized me without an introduction, Doctor. But yes, it's Levi. In the flesh, for a moment, if not the usual variety. And please don't be concerned — it's a thoroughly consensual arrangement, and not one that we abuse."

Dr. Tanner blinked rapidly. "No, I'm sure you do not. After all, I have known Mara for a long time. And you, through her accounts. While you seem to have the sense of mischief that Mara has denied herself, I am confident that you share her moral character. And her good heart."

"Oh, Mara's catching up on the mischief a bit. I have high hopes for her. . . . Doctor, we don't want to keep young Peer-tek here, and Mara has a good deal of work to do. I'll sign off, and let the two of you say your goodbyes."

"Goodbye, Levi. It has been a rare privilege indeed."

The Tofa was pure Tofa again. He nodded his head slightly to one side, turned, and walked out of view.

"Mara." He saw that she was crying. "Mara, what is it?"

"I'm just so glad you know." She wiped her eyes. "And it's still — it's still a highly emotional experience, every time. It isn't something we do very often. It doesn't seem wise, somehow."

He nodded. "This is hardly a situation with precedent. But I have faith in your intuition. . . . How great a factor was this — phenomenon, in your decision to accompany the Twin-Bred?"

Mara sighed. "How can I know? It weighed in the balance. I had little enough to stay behind for — and what you just saw, it meant I had that much more to lose if I did stay. . . . There were other reasons. And I'm tired of looking backward. Whether I'm sensible or crazy or something entirely other, I'll make the most of what's ahead."

Dr. Tanner beamed. "A better statement of health I could not ask for. Mara, thank you for calling. Thank you for your trust, now and for so long. And if I may use a somewhat old-fashioned formula — God bless you."

"Goodbye, Doctor. Thank you for everything. We'll be thinking of you. In fact, if we find mountains, we'll name one after you, someday, somewhere."

He laughed. "Make it a lake. I love to swim. Ah, there's so much we've never managed to talk about! But I won't keep you. On your way, my dear. On your way."

The auditorium was packed. Not since the meeting after the Tofa host mothers reappeared had Mara seen it so full. They had all learned so much since then, for good and ill.

The center of the room had rows of seats, for those inclined to sitting. Standing areas flanked the seats. On the stage was a backdrop created by Fel-lar and Sally, human and Tofa artistic styles interwoven. At stage right stood a structure that would serve as balcony.

Mara, Melly and Veda sat together in the front row of seats. Mara turned to the proud director and her mother. "I'm so glad you were able to do this. I wish we could do what we talked about, and take the show on the road, to the humans and Tofa who needed to see it."

Veda and Melly exchanged knowing glances. Veda asked Melly, "Shall I?" Melly nodded, a little smugly.

"Hal-tet is taking a holo of the performance. See him up there? Later on, after the ship leaves" (beside her, Melly stifled a sob) "we're going to travel around with the recording. The kids have already written ideographic Tofar subtitles. We'll show it in human and Tofa and blended towns and cities. To anyone who'll come."

Melly leaned over. "If they let us, that is."

Veda nodded. "If they let us."

Someone had dimmed the lights. The crowd gradually ceased its rustling and murmuring, and settled down into expectant silence. A spotlight hit the stage, and Judy stepped forth.

> *Two households, both alike in dignity,*
> *In fair Verona, where we lay our scene,*
> *From ancient grudge break to new mutiny,*
> *Where civil blood makes civil hands unclean.*

Mara closed her eyes. "Yes, Levi? You had a comment already?"

"I was just thinking about that dignity. I've always thought the Tofa had it over us in that department. In spite of the whistling."

"Shut up and listen."

From forth the separate homes of these two foes
A pair of star-cross'd friends will take their life;
Whose misadventured piteous overthrows
Do with their death bury their parents' strife.

Mara thought of the Tofa babies carried by the Tofa host mothers. Babies never born, sacrificed — deliberately? — so that the mothers would learn enough about humans to move among them, to work with them, possibly to control them. No need for fiction, she thought; we have had our deaths. The babies, La-ren, Bernie, Nedra. Will their deaths end the strife, or just postpone it? She was suddenly glad she would not be there to see.

Chapter 53

THE GRAY-HAIRED man with the stoop had added a new verse to his familiar song. "Damn Tofa gonna be running things from now on. Hell, they're already running things. Ain't natural for humans to let some damn aliens tell 'em what to do."

The younger man at the next stool spluttered in mid-swallow. "We're working together. The Tofa who spent time at that Project learned enough about us to work *with* us. And they can work with the Tofa too, 'cause they're not freaks. No one's been killed lately, nothing burned up, everything's settling down, all over. But you wouldn't know good news if it crawled out of your mug and bit you."

The gray-haired man snorted. "Who knows what happened at that place? Who knows whether these new Tofa are the old kind or something they cooked up in there? I don't trust 'em, and you're a young damn fool to trust 'em, and we're all going to end up in the soup. Heh. Yeah, maybe we'll really end up as soup. Maybe that's what they've been wanting."

"Last call, gentlemen!" The bartender turned to hide his sigh of relief. He was ready to go home, and to hell with all this worrying about tomorrow. They were probably both wrong, somehow or other.

"Cottage rose. Pipe tobacco. Chocolate? We're taking the real thing, but it won't always be handy for smelling. Chocolate. Vanilla? Yes, vanilla."

"Mara? Are those what I think they are?"

"We won't be back, Levi. And whatever we may find, it won't be what we're leaving. It's time to stop playing games with myself about what I like, what I need, what I deny myself and why."

"Now that is a very interesting statement. Long overdue. And I trust — in fact, I insist — that you apply it to something more than aroma sticks."

"If I understand you — Levi, I was a grown woman before they were born."

"And they've grown up, more or less. And you'll be together for a long, long time, during which they'll mature further, and eventually the age difference will be a technicality. We already know the human Twin-Bred don't let having twins keep them from forming bonds with other humans. You'll have the medical tech to stay in your prime for many years yet. I'm not telling you to start trawling the waters tomorrow. Just let things happen. You'll have a lover by five subjective years out, maximum."

"Levi? What scents do you think you would have liked? I want to take those too."

"Leather. Well, you like that one too. Don't deny it. . . . Whiskey. Terran wood smoke. Baby powder. Don't make faces. Why not? Apples. Fresh-cut grass. Terran ocean. Maybe where you're going, there'll be something like grass, or ocean. . . ."

"Where we're going."

"Oh, and definitely rotten fish. I'm so glad someone preserved that one."

"Consider yourself kicked."

"I see you're taking the latest."

"Yes. I hardly need to — so many of the others will be carrying it — but I wanted some of my own."

The new aroma stick was a present from the Chemistry Department. A parting gift to the travelers: the scent of Tofarna soil.

* CONFIDENTIAL *
COUNCIL MEMBERS AND TOFA EMINENCES ONLY

LEVI Status Report — Final
Executive Summary

<u>Transitional Logistics</u>

The staff have been given a definite schedule for completing all work on site and for relocating all equipment, files and other Project items. HR is assisting those Project team members who have not completed their arrangements for professional transition. Discussions continue concerning the disposition, security and levels of confidentiality of the data and analyses gathered during the Project. Host mothers still living on site have been provided with relocation allowances.

<u>Resolutions</u>

The text of the a resolution thanking the Project staff and subjects for their contribution to scientific advancement and human-Tofa relations has been submitted to the Council's Resolution Committee for approval. The final text will be engraved and placed on a memorial to be erected at the site of the former compound, along with the Council's resolution recently approved, expressing the Council's hopes for continued cooperation and open dealings between the Council and the Association of Tofa Eminences . . . .

The Twin-Bred and the few older humans filed into the ship. Most of the twins were in pairs, but a few had gone back for something, or stayed behind for some last-minute task or private moment, so that each straggled in separately. Fa-teer and Mario were among these: Fa-teer had gone to say another goodbye to the cat.

Mara carried a fresh sketchbook. She started whistling as she approached the doorway: "Tofa Laughing." As she grew closer, she heard others within the craft pick up the tune. She entered the ship to the sound of music, or laughter, or both.

The End

APPENDIX

<u>Characters (Partial List)</u>

Mara Cadell: scientist, originator of the Project
Levi Thomas: Mara's lost fraternal twin
Dr. Tanner: Mara's psychologist
Stan: Mara's Project assistant

Laura Hanson: a host mother
Judy and La-ren: Laura's Twin-Bred
Councilman Harold Petter: Laura Hanson's father

Veda Seeling: a host mother
Brian: Veda's husband
Jimmy and Peer-tek: Veda's Twin-Bred
Melly: Veda's and Brian's daughter (younger than
Jimmy and Peer-tek)
Councilman Stewart Channing: Veda Seeling's father

Tilda: a host mother

Councilman Alan Kimball: member of the Council
Siri O'Donnell: Alan Kimball's confidential assistant
Henry Abuto: member of Project educational staff and
agent of Councilman Kimball
Dr. Annabelle Bloom: member of Project scientific staff
and agent of Councilman Kimball
Manuel (Mannie) Jones: member of Project security
staff and agent of Councilman Kimball

Sam Chambers: senior Project deputy for science
Harriet Gaho: Chief Nurse at Project
Carla Horn: Project psychologist
Wendy Jergensen: Project Literature Coordinator

Ms. Sinder: Project history teacher
Andrew Smollen: Project Primary and later Secondary
Education Coordinator
Emily Wilson: Project teacher of Diplomacy

Artemesia and Hal-tet: Twin-Bred pair
Cindy and Dar-tan: Twin-Bred pair
Jerry: human Twin-Bred singleton
Nathan and Li-sen: Twin-Bred pair
Poo-lat: Tofa Twin-Bred
Randy and Jak-rad: Twin-Bred pair
Rose and Fel-lar: Twin-Bred pair
Sel-ran: Tofa Twin-Bred

Hit-ron-fa: Tofa host mother
Lo-ta-se: Tofa host mother
Ra-tel-sen: Tofa host mother
Ton-lal-set: Tofa host mother

Read on for a taste of
the sequel to *Twin-Bred* --

Chapter 1

AND SO THEY were underway. The good ship *Star Seed* left Tofarn behind at a speed that no human — to their knowledge — had traveled in generations, and no Tofa had ever approached.

Or it might be the good ship *Destiny*, or *New Frontiers*, or *Newer Frontiers*, or *Enterprise*, or *Hatikvah*, or *Beagle*. There were some who still held out for their unchosen favorite. Many of the Tofa Twin-Bred, and a few of the human twins, preferred the Tofar word for "spore," which the adult humans were unable to pronounce. A few flippant passengers persisted in calling the ship the *Skedaddle*. It hardly mattered. There was, after all, only one ship, and they were aboard her.

Some did not want to watch the planet recede — those most bitter, and those already fearing homesickness. The rest crowded around the window-like transparent panels and the multiple viewscreens.

A girl whispered to the boy beside her, "It's just like the globe. You remember — the big shining one. The one we copied in clay."

The boy put his arm around her. "No, it isn't," he whispered back. "This is like nothing else, nothing at all."

Mara took a deep breath, savoring the previously unknown odor of new spaceship: various metals and plastics, with an overlay of circulated air freshener. If she were staying awake, she knew she would soon cease to notice it. But she was not planning to be awake for long.

She checked that her belongings were stowed efficiently in the designated storage cupboard. She did not want anyone rearranging them while she was sleeping because she had taken too much space. The thought lingered, annoying her with its lack of scientific rigor: she would not be asleep. The team that had rediscovered and refined the suspended animation techniques used by the Tofarna colonists would be justified in taking umbrage at the idea. But the term had caught on, inaccuracy notwithstanding, and apparently even she had acquired the habit.

"I don't believe it, sis. You're actually going into SA with the first group? No hanging about to supervise, to second-guess, to kibitz?"

Mara was absurdly relieved. She had not heard Levi since boarding the ship. She had been fighting back fears that her twin's spirit was somehow tied to the planet where he had almost been born; that by casting her lot with the Tofa Twin-Bred who could channel Levi, reaching greedily for a more complete experience of him, she had inadvertently left him behind. "Levi, I've been in charge for almost twenty years, since before the Twin-Bred were born. You should know how desperately I need a rest. And as you imply, if I'm awake — or whatever you want to call it — I'll feel as if I should be taking charge, even though it isn't my job any more."

"That's going to be interesting. Rotating captains? Flying by consensus? I give it a week. Don't you want to weigh in on who should really run things, once they figure out somebody has to?"

"As a matter of fact, I've left some notes. Files labeled according to various contingencies that might arise, available if the others want to see them — and easy to ignore if no one feels the need to consult me. One of those files has my thoughts, as an experienced if reluctant administrator, on what sort of leadership team might be most successful. And I am delighted that I'll be in no position to hear how *that* one is received."

She rearranged two bundles, then put them back as

they had been. "Time to go."

"Sleep tight, Mara mia. I'll see you in your dreams."

She had spent enough time poring over plans, and then prowling through the unfinished craft, to know her way around. Some of the human and Tofa youngsters she passed on the way to the clinic seemed less certain of their path, but she left them to their own devises. They may as well learn.

Passing one of the transparent panels, she yielded to temptation and paused to look out. This particular panel did not face Tofarn, which was just as well. She felt the expression of awe and delight spread over her face as she gazed at the stars. It had been worth the haggling, and the extra work on filters for high-intensity photons and such, to have these windows — which some, in an imprecise nod to tradition, were calling "portholes" — instead of merely arrays of microscopic cameras. When she came out of SA, she would not have to face a constant battle with latent claustrophobia; she would have a way to look Outside. Thankfully Harriet Gaho, now Chief Medical Officer, had been willing to make the claustrophobia argument without inquiring too closely as to who on board might be affected.

She took one last long look at the expanse of stars, and headed down the corridor to the clinic.

As she stood in the long line at the clinic door, Mara made a point of eavesdropping on the murmured conversations all around her, so as not to dwell on the prospect of suspension: drastically slowed bodily functions, utter helplessness, dependence on the ship's technology and on the alertness of those remaining awake. Listening, it did not take long for her to notice something peculiar. She had expected to be surrounded by waiting pairs of twins, and so she was. But the twins were not discussing the SA process, or chatting casually to dispel nerves. Almost every pair she could overhear was, in one manner or another, saying goodbye.

She maneuvered through the crowd until she could see inside the clinic. A diminutive girl was lying in the nearest SA capsule. Her Tofa twin bent over her, holding her hand in his lower left hand, his upper right hand stroking her hair. "I will be here when you are revived. Then it will be your turn to hover over me. I may even let you sing to me, on that single occasion." The girl was almost unconscious; her mouth twitched in an attempt at a smile.

Mara turned to look at the twins behind her. "Just what is going on here? Are you all splitting up, one going into SA and one staying awake? For God's sake, *why*?"

Averted eyes, shuffled feet, a general air of embarrassment.

"I said why! Someone is going to explain this -- or this line is going nowhere, slowly!"

Anna, standing close next to her twin Cra-set, cleared her throat. "Well — there are different risks for those in SA and those who aren't. The SA modules are more heavily shielded against radiation than the ship as a whole. If something happened so quickly that people couldn't get to the more sheltered areas, the ones in SA would have a better chance of surviving. And on the other hand, if we had to evacuate in a hurry, we don't really know if the automatic lifeboat functions on the SA modules are going to work as they're designed to work. So quite a few of us have decided to split the risk."

Mara tried to process what she was hearing. "I don't understand. You're deliberately increasing the chances of being left without your twin? Of surviving *alone*?" She had known all her life that she had a hot temper, and there had been much to trigger it, but the volcanic intensity of this anger was new. She tried to hold it back enough to speak coherently. "Did your teachers, did I, somehow fail to impress upon you the fundamental isolation in which most of us stumble through life? Did we neglect to make clear that you have been blessed with an exceptional gift of companionship?" Her anger was winning the battle. "Are you all CRAZY!?"

Anna reached for Mara's hand. Mara snatched it away so violently that her nails scratched Anna's wrist. Cra-set looked at her, somehow projecting an intimidating coldness despite the lack of such expressive elements as nose, mouth or eyebrows. Mara fought back remorse and glared at him, at Anna, at them all.

Anna patted Cra-set's nearest arm and turned back toward Mara. "If Cra-set and I were to die together, then neither of us would be left to grieve, but nothing would be left of either of us. If one of us survives, then something of the other may, also. We all know about Levi. . . ."

Mara was shaking. She must have appeared dangerous: Cra-set stepped protectively in front of Anna and spread all his arms, even dividing his upper left arm to form a more effective barricade.

"LEVI IS NOT REAL! LEVI IS A FANTASY!!" Mara threw herself against Cra-set's arms as if pounding the walls of a padded room. "He's a symptom, a mental illness! And you're all asking to go *insane*?"

Fel-lar appeared from somewhere. Had he been in line? Mara did not see his twin Rose. He motioned for Cra-set to step aside, and stood in front of Mara, his large marbled eyes looking down into hers. "I must differ with your analysis — or rather, your statement, as I do not think you are accurately summarizing your usual opinion. I believe your own Dr. Tanner has opined that Levi, even if a fantasy, is a benign and beneficial coping mechanism — not a sign of instability, let alone psychosis. Or so Levi has informed me, on one of the occasions when I provided a receptacle for his consciousness."

Anna added, "As for Levi's reality: a wise man on Terra once said, the question should be 'A real what?' Whatever we call him, you know, as we know, that he has a distinct personality, wherever it comes from. If you had known him as a living twin, the way we Twin-Bred know each other, and for as long, how much more would he be?"

Mara looked wildly around. "Where's Judy! Ask her what it's like! Ask her if you should all be setting yourselves up to lose a twin and go on alone. Ask her!"

Judy tugged with all her strength, gritting her teeth

behind the gag as the ropes cut into her wrists. Her sobbing breaths filled her ears. She started to rock back and forth, trying to tip the heavy chair onto its side.

La-ren leaned against the wall nearby, watching her efforts. As the chair legs lifted in the air and thudded back to the floor, he commented, "I do not think this is a useful tactic. You will not gain any mobility from being restrained in a horizontal position."

Judy paused in her efforts, panting. "I have to try something! I have to come and rescue you! Why didn't they teach us what to do, how to defend ourselves? WHY?"

La-ren wove the fingers of his left hands together and unwound them again. "Defending ourselves, we might injure those who sent for us. The political consequences could be severe, affecting the Project as a whole. We were created to resolve interspecies conflicts, not to complicate or aggravate them. I would say that given the alternatives, any one team, any one team member, is considered expendable."

"*You are not expendable!*"

La-ren did not answer.

"*I am not expendable!*"

"Subjectively, I share your viewpoint. I'm sorry, little twin."

"Please, tell me what I can do! There must be something I can do!" Judy began rocking the chair again.

From the corner of her eye, she saw La-ren shake his head, as Tofa Twin-Bred did, and no other Tofa would. "We are out of time, Judy. I died ten minutes ago."

Judy screamed herself awake. Awake, she looked around for a moment, disoriented; then inhaled deeply. She would keep on screaming, scream herself raw. . . . But something was distracting her, trying for her attention. Was it a sound? A voice? Or another, far more beguiling dream?

"I am sorry your sleep did not refresh you."

Judy looked around her cabin. Of course, it was empty. The extra bed taunted her. Even the singletons preferred to share quarters with their special friends, their "twins," and the ship had been built for double occupancy throughout. She had reflexively rejected the offer of a single cabin built especially for her, a decision she had later and often wished she could retract.

She held her breath, waiting, afraid to hope.

There it was again.

"Seeing me is not part of the arrangement. At least, not without the assistance of our friends. They were willing to assist Dr. Cadell, so I am optimistic."

"LA-REN! . . . La-ren??"

"Yes. After a fashion. I'm sorry it has taken this long. It may be that you needed time for your first grief to subside —"

"It hasn't. It won't. I need you, and you aren't here, and that will never be all right!"

"No, it never will. It is a wrong done to both of us, and I am very sorry for us both."

Judy got up and walked shakily into the tiny bathroom. The wild-eyed face in the mirror frightened her. "And I know I should be grateful. I am! It's like breathing again, hearing you . . . but it's also like waking up from a dream of dying, and seeing that your arm is gone, or your leg."

She felt his smile, the smile that had never been something to be seen. "In my case, I would prefer an arm." And then, a flood of sympathy.

Judy tottered back to the bed and sat down with a thump. "I don't know what I can say to you. What I can ask you. It's all so crazy. What I want to ask, you can't possibly know. But it's haunted me, imagining it, over and over. . . . Was it terrible? Were you frightened? You must have been so frightened." She broke down into enormous gasping sobs.

The storm subsided; she listened for his voice, and heard nothing. What if that was all, one brief visit, a few delusional moments, and then silence again? She could not endure it, not after that glimpse of renewed companionship. She would try again with the medical patches, when everyone was busy with shipboard business. No one would blame her, or if they did, it wouldn't matter.

"Judy!" La-ren's voice again, but she had never heard La-ren so stern. "You are finding it difficult to live through my last moments, even in your imagination. Do you intend to require me to live through yours?"

She caught her breath. "It's not like that. It isn't. Is it?"

"You had best behave as if it is. I have no intention of reducing any influence I may have by helping you assume otherwise."

She went back into the bathroom and splashed her face. The water felt wonderful. She could use a shower — to put it mildly. She had not been conscientious about hygiene, or concerned about appearance, over these last months.

She turned to lock the door to her cabin, then remembered that the lock had been disabled. She was not yet trusted with such a guarantee of solitude. She ground her teeth for a moment. It was humiliating. Then she undressed and put on her robe for the trip down to the communal shower facilities.

"That's a good girl. Your hair is greasy. Human hair has always fascinated me, and I am particularly fond of yours."

Judy snorted, for the first time in months. "So fond of it that you used to pull it regularly, until we were ten at least."

"I concede that it was an immature form of appreciation. Now get in that shower, and tell me about everything that I have missed."

Mara stood at an otherwise unoccupied window, staring out at the stars without seeing them. On the tablet in her hand was a drawing of a line of Twin-Bred pairs, waiting patiently; the twins at the front were plunging daggers into each other's chests.

"What, sweeting, all amort? And awake? What happened to putting aside all responsibility in favor of carefree suspension?"

"You know what happened. The damned fools. The blithe young idiots."

"I assume you're referring to that little scene where you gave me a few unflattering labels. I forgive you. But how will staying awake improve matters?"

"If they're all determined to set themselves up for disaster, I'm going to do what I can to prevent it. Whatever that turns out to be. I certainly can't do it from SA."

"It's probably a mistake. But I'll admit I'm just as glad you'll be where the action is. This is my first time on a starship, and I want to see every part of it. Let's be here, there and everywhere, and make thorough nuisances of ourselves."

Mara felt a reluctant smile tug at her mouth, and saw it reflected dimly in the window. "All right, then. Let's start with the galley. I need some medicinal chocolate. Dark."

Connect with Karen A. Wyle Online

Learn more about Karen A. Wyle by looking her up on:

her author website, www.KarenAWyle.net
Twitter (@WordsmithWyle)
Facebook, at www.facebook.com/KarenAWyle
Goodreads, at www.goodreads.com/kawyle
or her blog, Looking Around, at
http://looking-around.blogspot.com

Like the book? Please tell readers!
Online book reviews are enormously helpful --
and old-fashioned word of mouth is terrific as well!